Revolution

Hailing from Sioux Falls, South Dakota, Megan DeVos is twenty-six years old and works as a Registered Nurse in the operating room. Her debut *Anarchy* series amassed over 30 million reads on Wattpad, winning the Watty Award in 2014.

THE ANARCHY SERIES

Anarchy
Loyalty
Revolution
Annihilation

Revolution

MEGAN DEVOS

ORION

First published in Great Britain in 2018 by Orion Books,
an imprint of The Orion Publishing Group Ltd
Carmelite House, 50 Victoria Embankment
London EC4Y 0DZ

An Hachette UK Company

1 3 5 7 9 10 8 6 4 2

A CIP catalogue record for this book is
available from the British Library.

ISBN 978 1 4091 8388 4

Typeset by Input Data Services Ltd, Somerset

Printed and bound in Great Britain by Clays Ltd, Elcograf S.p.A.

www.orionbooks.co.uk

For my dear friends and family,
who have loved me from the start.

One: Genesis

Grace

The dark night was filled with the gruesome soundtrack of war as the chaos unfolded around me. Gunfire, explosions, and bone-shattering screams of terror and agony ripped through the air. Mesmerising tongues of fire engulfed a building next to me, the heat of the flames searing into my skin and melting my thoughts. War cascaded through the camp, tearing apart buildings and people alike as I tried to figure out my next move.

A mixture of terror, adrenaline, and gut-twisting anxiety coursed through me as a sudden shadow streaking towards me caught my attention. I'd barely turned my head to look before I recognised who it was, and the despair hardly had a chance to sink in before his body collided roughly with my own. The wind was knocked from my lungs. I hadn't seen him for days, and I was certainty not excited to see him now as he wrestled against me on the ground.

My last remaining family member.

My brother.

Jonah.

'You filthy traitor!' he spat angrily as he struggled to pin me down.

His arms fought to secure mine as I shoved at his chest to try and throw him off me. I was at a significant disadvantage beneath his weight, but I never stopped moving for a second. My legs thrashed as I tried to kick him off, but it didn't work.

'Get off me!' I hissed angrily. Frustration ripped through me as he gripped my shoulders and pulled me off the ground only to slam me back into the dirt. Air rushed past my lips as again my breath was knocked from me. I managed to free one of my fists long enough to swing it upward, connecting my knuckles to his jaw. The hit was strong enough only to cause him to pause his attack.

'You betrayed us,' he seethed, glaring down at me with bulging eyes. His actions were strong and urgent, giving no thought to potentially hurting me; on the contrary, that was his goal.

'No, I didn't!' I yelled back.

But that was a lie.

I had betrayed them.

All this flashed through my head in less than a second as I struggled against him. He gripped my wrists tightly, wrenching them to the side as he tried to pin them down. I twisted beneath him, making it difficult for him to control me.

Panic flashed through me as I saw him pull back and rip a knife from his belt. The long, sharp blade glinted in the light of the fire burning next to us as he hovered over me. Heavy pants escaped both of our bodies as I pushed up against his chest, trying to create more space between us, but he was too strong.

'Jonah, don't—'

'You chose your side, Grace. Now you can die with the rest of them.'

'No—'

I huffed out in frustration as I exerted all my strength.

2

My arms shook with the effort of pushing him off, as his blade inched closer and closer by the second. Sweat dripped from his brow to land on my skin, his teeth gritted in determination just as mine were.

This was it.

My own brother was going to kill me.

I could feel the point of the knife on my chest now, directly over my heart. The sharp edge had just started to break the skin when I remembered being in such a position before, only under much different circumstances. Hayden's face flashed through my mind as he hovered over me, pinning me down in the soft brush of the forest as he taunted me. I remembered the way he'd thrown me off him with his hips. I was in a similarly vulnerable position as now.

Without further hesitation, I summoned every ounce of strength I possessed to use my legs as leverage. Jonah had been so focused on guiding his knife that he momentarily forgot about the lower halves of our bodies. In a split second, his body rolled to the side into the dirt, freeing me from his weight long enough to roll away.

'You little—' he seethed, scrambling on the ground.

I jumped to my feet. Without thinking, I took a deep breath and cocked my leg back before swinging it forward with all my strength. The heavy part of my boot collided with his jaw, jerking his entire head to the side before his body followed, going slack in the dirt – clearly unconscious from the blow to the face. His chest rose and fell still, telling me he was alive.

'Arsehole,' I muttered. I couldn't resist aiming one more kick at his side, swinging my foot just as hard at his ribs.

I should have taken his knife and plunged it into his chest as he'd tried to do to me, but I couldn't. I couldn't kill my own brother.

I did, however, duck to take the knife from his hand as well as the two guns he had stowed in his belt. Air ripped through my lungs as I panted heavily, exhausted but determined to find Hayden. My hands moved quickly to make sure both guns were loaded, slamming the magazines back into the chamber of each. Soft metallic clicks told me they were both ready to use. I kept one in my hand before storing the other behind my waist, keeping the knife in my other hand.

With that, I cast one last derisive look at my brother's prone body before sprinting into the chaos. More than one building was fully engulfed in flames, and more than a few bodies had already fallen to litter the pathway. I didn't pause long enough to see who they were, terrified I'd recognise someone I cared about.

It seemed that everywhere I looked, shadows darted through the night. Friends, foes, it was impossible to tell. Gunshots rang out so frequently that it was hard to determine which direction they came from, much less who was shooting at whom.

My feet carried me on, searching for one face amongst the pandemonium: Hayden. Out of the corner of my eye, two shadows collided before fists started to fly. A few punches were struck before a sickening wet *thunk* sounded – the sound of a knife finding its target. One shadow stilled on the ground as the other stood, rising from their position before darting off again.

'Hayden!' I shouted, unable to resist any longer. I needed to find him before my heart hammered its way out of my chest.

'Hayden!'

Panic ripped through me as I moved towards the largest fire I could see. If Hayden was anywhere, he'd be in the thick of it all to defend those he cared about. I was about to round the last corner that would lead me into the fray when I saw two more shadows emerge from between some huts.

One was much smaller than most others, and it darted hastily from the gap in the buildings. The reason for the haste became clear as a much larger, more menacing shadow emerged immediately after. The larger shadow gained on the smaller one, closing the distance quickly. The larger person was just about to jump on the smaller one when the fire illuminated their faces, sending a wave of horror through me.

Jett.

The second face was someone I recognised from Greystone but didn't know by name. He was in his early thirties, bloodlust clear in his eyes as he chased after Jett.

The man launched himself into the air, about to tackle Jett to the ground, at the same time I aimed my gun in his direction. Without pausing even a second, I fired, sending my bullet rocketing their way. As if attached to a rope, the man's body jerked to the side as the bullet sank into his skull. As he fell, his body had enough momentum to allow it to crash into Jett and trip him.

A shrill scream of panic left Jett's lips as he fell to the ground, beneath the corpse. Jett twisted jerkily beneath him, confusion and terror clear in his eyes as he took in the wide, blank stare that met his.

'Jett!' I shouted, rushing forward. He squirmed fearfully, unable to free himself. As soon as I reached them, I squatted down to shove the man off enough for him to wiggle out from beneath. The man's body toppled into the dirt as Jett stood shakily, tears pouring down his cheeks. I hardly had time to straighten up before he launched himself into my chest, hugging me tightly as he sobbed uncontrollably.

5

'You shouldn't be here,' I managed to say. I had never been in such a frenzied situation before and it was so unsettling. I didn't want to know what effect it would have on naïve, innocent Jett.

He didn't respond as he hugged me tightly. As much as I wanted to be able to comfort him, I couldn't. I could feel time slipping away, every second I wasn't with Hayden adding to my alarm. My eyes scanned the area around us, searching for enemies or allies in need, but for the moment, we were alone.

'Come on, Jett, come with me,' I said quickly. Impatience and anxiety had taken over, hastening my actions. I separated myself from him and stuffed the knife into my pocket before gripping his hand in my own. With one final hasty look around, I turned back from the madness to lead him away.

My eyes landed on a small hut, bordered on either side by a few others of similar size. I practically dragged a still sobbing Jett behind me. My gaze never stopped scanning for danger as we approached, but I still saw nothing as we reached the door. Without hesitating, I threw my shoulder into it to force it open.

A terrified squeak greeted me as I burst through the door, though it was too dark to see anyone.

'Please don't kill us,' a small voice said, from the corner of the room. I squinted into the darkness, my eyes finally adjusting to make out two little girls pressed into the corner. I had never seen them before, but it was easy to assume they were members of Blackwing just trying to stay out of the fray.

'I'm not going to kill you,' I said as calmly as I could. 'I'm on your side.'

The smaller of the two, who looked to be around four or

five, peered up at me with wide eyes. The older one, maybe nine or ten, looked up in fear before I saw her gaze shift to Jett in surprise. He'd managed to stop crying now but still had tears streaked down his face as he stood next to me.

'Jett?' the older girl asked.

'Hi, Rainey,' he murmured quietly, as if embarrassed all of a sudden.

'Jett, you know these girls?' I asked hurriedly, desperate to get back outside and find Hayden.

'Yes,' he answered.

I hunched down so our eyes were level, locking my gaze on his.

'You're brave, right, Jett?'

'Yes, I – I'm brave,' he stammered.

'I know you are,' I told him. 'Listen to me closely, okay?'

He nodded in determination, his features hardening as he did so.

'I need you to protect them, all right? You stay here with them until this is over and shoot anyone who comes through that door that you don't know.'

His eyes widened as he gulped harshly. I felt jittery and anxious as I wasted time here with Jett.

'Can you do that?'

'Yes,' he said tightly. He took a deep breath and nodded before speaking again. 'Yes, Grace, I can do that.'

'Good, I know you can,' I said, shooting him a quick, tense smile.

'Here, take this gun. Remember what I said about shooting? Two eyes for moving, one for still?'

'I remember.'

'I have to go, but you can do this. Someone will come and find you when this is over. Keep them safe, Jett.'

'I will, Grace, I will!' he said firmly. He puffed his thin

chest out as he tried to appear brave. A small sense of pride washed over me as I nodded encouragingly at him. With that, I turned back towards the door. I had just reached it when I heard him speak again.

'Grace, you're going to find Hayden, right?'

'Yes, Jett. I'll find him,' I promised. I'd just slipped outside, the door nearly closed, when I heard Jett speaking softly to the two girls inside.

'Don't worry, I'll protect you.'

My stomach clenched tightly at his words, desperately hoping they were true. I closed the door behind me and started running again. I had a knife and a gun with a single round. I sprinted back towards the centre of things, kicking the dirt with each step.

All around me, fights had broken out. Fists flew, knives slashed, guns fired, and bodies fell. So many bodies – more than I could count – were piling up as I darted through camp. I ignored the wave of nausea that rolled through me and tried not to think about how many lives were being lost at this exact moment.

Finally I rounded the last corner, and no amount of mental preparation could have prepared me for what I saw. Amongst the brawling people, raging fires, lifeless bodies, and endless carnage stood a horrifically shocking centrepiece. The eight-storey tower, the pride of Blackwing, was burning from the ground up.

Fear gripped my heart as I remembered exactly where Hayden had gone before he left me: the tower. It was nearly impossible to see through the thick, choking smoke that smothered the night air. Keeping my gun and knife in hand, I darted forward again, both terrified and hopeful that I would find Hayden.

A sudden flash of movement to my left appeared as

someone jabbed a knife at me while I ran by, but the blow was stilled as another body tackled the first to the ground.

'Oh no you don't!' shouted a familiar voice. My eyes darted towards the wrestling pair, sending a shock of recognition through me as I saw Kit on top of a man from Greystone. I hardly had time to be afraid for him before he landed two powerful blows across the man's face, followed quickly by a flash of his knife across his throat. Instantly, bright red blood flooded from his neck.

Just like that, Kit had killed him.

'What are you waiting for, help him!' Kit shouted, as I realised I was gaping at him. He threw his hand towards the tower. As quickly as he'd arrived, however, he was gone, leaving the lifeless corpse to sprint off towards another enemy.

From this new position, I could just make out a shadow a few stories up, hunched over as he lugged something behind him. He was about halfway down the tower, above at least two stories of flames. The curve of his back and the small halo of hair was all it took for me to identify him: Hayden.

It was difficult to see what he was doing, but there was no ignoring the fact that the closer he got to the ground, the closer he got to the inferno.

'Hayden!' I shouted. He didn't seem to hear me, however, as he continued to drag whatever he had behind him down the stairs. My heart thumped painfully hard against my ribs. A scream of agony cut through the air, accenting my fear. This wasn't fear for myself, however: this was fear for him. How was he supposed to get down?

'Hayden!' I shouted again. His head jerked towards me as he caught the sound, and he leaned over the rail to squint down at me. It was then that I saw he had his shirt tugged up over his nose in an attempt to block the choking smoke.

'Grace!' he called back in surprise. 'Get out of here!'

'No!' I yelled back. Every second he wasted was a second the flames grew fiercer. 'You have to jump, now before it gets too high!'

Why hadn't he jumped in the first place?

Much to my horror, he retreated over the railing, cutting himself completely from my view.

'I can't,' he grunted. It was difficult to hear him over the roar of the flames and the sounds of war raging on around me. While most of the gunfire seemed to have transitioned to hand-to-hand combat, yells, screams, and the occasional burst of flames continued.

'*Why not?!*' I demanded, actually stamping my foot in the ground in frustration.

He didn't answer, sending a wave of fear washing over me.

'Hayden!'

My eyes scanned the ground, searching for something to act as a cushion. All I could see was dirt, a few patches of grass, and most horrifically, the occasional body. A heavy grunt and a loud thud jerked my attention back up the tower, where I breathed a sigh of relief as I saw Hayden once again.

The reason for his slow descent was suddenly clear as I saw him drag two heavy bundles along after him.

No, not bundles.

Bodies.

I couldn't identify who they were, but I had a strong suspicion about one. But if Hayden was risking his own life to lug that worthless piece of trash down the tower, I was going to be furious. Barrow did not deserve to live.

'Hayden, leave them! You have to jump now or none of you will make it!'

I sounded cold, heartless, but I didn't care. All that mattered was getting Hayden out alive.

'*No*,' he hissed angrily, as if frustrated by the whole situation. He was only one storey above the flames now, three above the ground. I huffed out in angry exasperation as he leaned over the side again to inspect the ground. His skin was streaked with black from the rising smoke all around him, and his T-shirt had fallen away, leaving him exposed. A deep cough rumbled from his chest as he squinted through the smoke.

'Grace, see that hay bale over there?' he called, pointing between two of the nearest huts.

I jerked around and squinted through the darkness to see what he was indicating.

'Yes, got it,' I said, reading his mind as I sprinted away. I leaped over a fallen body, without looking. The bale was nearly as tall as I was and incredibly heavy. Luckily, it was round, and I positioned myself behind it and threw my shoulder into it to try and roll it.

My feet dug into the ground as I shoved again, letting out a yell of frustration before I finally managed to dislodge it from where it had settled. Once I got it moving, it was much easier, and I continued to throw my shoulder into it as I rolled it towards the base of the tower.

I met resistance when the bale collided with a lump. I cringed as I realised it was probably a body and tried to wipe the thought from my mind. Sure enough, when the bale finally moved, a body was revealed beneath it. Making sure to avoid stepping on it, I manoeuvred around it before finally reaching the base of the tower.

Burning flames heated the air as I stood mere feet away, whipping my knife from my pocket to slash the ties that held the bale together. Instantly, the hay lost its form and collapsed into a pile of twigs, aided by my fervent pushing and shoving. As soon as I had it spread, I jumped back and looked up at Hayden.

I was relieved to see him watching me, though he disappeared quickly as he ducked down once again. Every second that ticked by seemed like an ice pick hammering at my heart despite the overwhelming heat. Finally, a limp arm emerged over the railing as I heard a loud grunt from Hayden. The arm was followed by a leg and a torso. Hayden leaned over, barely managing to lift them over the railing.

'Okay, Grace, move her as soon as she's down,' he called.

'Got it!'

He didn't hesitate any longer before shoving the unconscious body over the side, careful to ensure she cleared the flames below. I watched in awe as her body soared through the air, blonde hair fanning out around her as if she were in slow motion. In a split second, she landed with a thud in the pile of hay. I cringed before rushing forward.

After reaching down to grab her arms and pull, I saw who it was. Her eyes were closed and her skin was covered in black smudges, but her chest rose and fell slowly as she drew life-sustaining breath: Maisie.

Without hesitation, I dragged her away from the fire, leaving her to settle in the grass before returning to my position.

'Hayden, hurry,' I urged, bouncing on my feet. A quick glance around told me that everyone thankfully was too busy fighting to notice my work at the base of the tower.

There was no warning as a second body fell, the thud much louder this time. My face contorted in disgust: as I suspected, Barrow lay in the hay, very much alive and very much unworthy of Hayden saving his life. Despite my reluctance, I gripped his ankles and tugged as hard as I could, grunting loudly as I yanked his heavy body out of the way. I managed to set him next to Maisie before I carelessly dropped his legs and darted back to the tower.

'Hayden, come on,' I muttered anxiously under my breath. My hands shook by my sides as he climbed carefully over the railing. Deep coughs ripped from his throat as he spluttered against the choking smoke. I let out a shout of panic as his body swooped forward, his eyes flickering closed for half a second before he snapped out of it, jerking his body back upright.

It looked like he was seconds away from passing out as the smoke closed in around him.

'Jump, Hayden! Jump!'

But his eyes drifted shut again, the feeble cough he gave causing his chest to cave in as his body leaned dangerously far over the side.

'Hayden!'

My shrill attempt to snap him out of it didn't work. I watched in frozen horror as gravity took over, pulling his body down over the edge. His limbs flew out limply and the breeze pushed his hair back, his body twisting uncontrollably. The space between him and the ground disappeared as he landed with a heavy thud, his back taking most of the fall when he landed in the thinning pile of hay.

'Hayden,' I breathed as I jerked forward, nearly tripping myself as I flung my body down into the hay next to him.

His arms were thrown out by his sides, and his legs were bent somewhat awkwardly. I collapsed beside him and took his face desperately in my hands. A thin line of blood trickled from his lips and trailed down his neck.

'Hayden, wake up, please wake up,' I begged. Tears pricked at the back of my eyes, but I fought to fight them off. I felt like I was going to throw up. 'Come on, please . . .'

He didn't respond. I hovered over him, unsure of what to do. The skin on his throat was dirty and hot as I pressed the pads of two fingers to it, feeling for a pulse. Panic ripped through me as I felt nothing, but was calmed when I shifted them and felt a faint thudding beneath my touch.

He was alive.

It was only then that I noticed the faint, weak breaths between his lips. A gasp of relief so loud ripped through me that I nearly collapsed. He was alive. Hayden was alive.

It was as if that realisation brought everything back at once: the blistering heat of the fire, the raging sound of it as it consumed everything in its path. Sound, too, as I heard the endless onslaught of bullets, the dull thuds of bodies beating on others, the agonising shouts as people died around me. It all closed in on me as I clung to Hayden's limp body.

Everywhere I looked, I saw people falling. One shadow killed another, sending him sprawling into the dirt. A mysterious bullet connected with a target, wiping the tension and life as fast as the bullet itself. A few yards away, a body burned before me, fermenting the air with the sick smell of singed flesh.

War was everywhere, invading my senses and taking over my every thought. There was nothing I could do except protect Hayden. Darkness overtook me as I closed my eyes. My arms roped around his neck as I leaned over him, shielding him from the desolation of man and his twisted capabilities.

Suddenly, the loudest sound rocked me to my very bones. There was a flash of light so bright that it burned through my closed eyelids, followed quickly by a bang so loud I thought my eardrums had been shredded. Next came a burst of scalding heat.

That was it.

Light.
Fire.
Heat.
Darkness.

Two: Carnage

Grace

A dull buzzing invaded my senses, and heat from all directions seemed to assault my skin – behind me, on each side, and beneath me. *Beneath me?* My eyes finally managed to flicker open as I forced myself to sit up. The heat was explained immediately as I took in the still-burning fires all around me.

Then I saw Hayden. He lay on his back in a pile of hay exactly where he'd landed after falling, eyes closed and lips parted as soft puffs of air escaped. Just as before, I felt panic start to rise as I brushed his hair back off his face. My hands felt jerky and uncoordinated as I let my thumbs trace lightly over his cheeks.

'Hayden,' I said softly, trying to wake him gently.

I was vaguely aware of the lack of sound, though I didn't give it a second thought as I tried to wake him. When before there had been shouting, gunshots, raging fires, now there was only the crackling of flames as they continued to burn. Not even the marked change in atmosphere could draw my attention from him.

'Hayden, please . . .' I begged quietly. The fact that he was breathing was the only thing keeping me sane. My heart was beating so hard that it felt like it was about to break in half.

He coughed once, causing my stomach to twist anxiously. I ducked closer.

'Yes, that's it, come on,' I murmured urgently.

A deeper cough rumbled from his chest this time. His striking green irises were finally revealed to me as his eyes flittered open.

'Grace.'

His voice was even deeper and raspier than normal thanks to the damage inflicted on it by the copious amounts of smoke he'd inhaled – but it was enough to make me collapse with relief against his chest. Over and over again, I let his name fall from my lips as I finally let myself believe he was all right.

'Hayden, you're okay?'

He groaned lightly in confirmation but didn't resist my hug. I felt his hand rise weakly to land on my side, where his fingers brushed feathery light over the slightly singed fabric of my clothes. It was only then that I noticed my skin was stinging too.

'First step's a doozy,' he muttered flatly.

A half gasp, half laugh choked from my throat as yet another wave of relief washed over me. When I finally managed to release him, he shifted to prop himself up on his elbows with a grimace. Surely he was in pain, as he'd just free-fallen from two stories into a meagre pile of hay.

'You're an idiot,' I told him. He was probably the only person I knew who would risk his life to save someone so undeserving as Barrow. I would have had a hard time leaving Maisie behind, but I wouldn't have given Barrow another thought. It seemed I was constantly being bombarded with proof at how much better Hayden truly was than the rest of us.

'Yeah, probably,' he agreed, pursing his lips tightly together.

'You should have left him.'

'Yeah, probably,' he repeated.

My hand reached out to push a matted lock of hair out of his face before my fingertips traced lightly over the cut on his lip that had already started to dry. His gaze burned into mine, matching the intensity of the fires still roaring around me. In the absence of fighting all around us, we fell into the bubble that often encased Hayden and me.

'Are you sure you're okay?' I questioned, studying him closely. He blew out a deep breath as he heaved himself up into a sitting position, levelling his face with mine.

'I'm just fine, Grace,' he lulled. His voice still sounded like it was weighted down with smoke. I wondered how long before it would go back to its naturally deep tone.

I wanted to confront him to see if he was being truthful, but his gaze fell on the other two people who'd been throw haphazardly from the tower: Maisie and Barrow. Yet another deep cough rumbled from his chest as he moved to stand up, his actions slow and stiff thanks to the damage his body had surely suffered.

'Hayden—'

He ignored me as he started in their direction, rolling his shoulder around its socket once as he moved. I rose immediately to follow him, jogging to catch up just as he arrived at the first, smaller body. Maisie was just starting to stir as he stooped down and brushed his hand lightly over hers.

'Maisie,' I heard him murmur. She let out a groan before her eyes opened. She blinked a few times before she sat up, clearly less affected by the smoke than Hayden had been, thanks to succumbing to it sooner. In his efforts to drag both

18

Maisie and Barrow down the stairs, Hayden had worked much harder and inhaled more of the smoke.

'Hey,' she responded. Her hands rubbed at her eyes where soot from the smoke had started to gather in the fine wrinkles, smudging the streaks along her skin.

While Hayden made sure she was okay, I glanced around. Although the tower still burned along with a few of the buildings nearby, there was no more fighting, though I couldn't figure out what had stopped it. People moved around, shadows in the flickering light, as they examined those other shadows that lay stilled on the ground. My momentary sense of relief began to be smothered by dread as I realised what the next few hours would bring – evidence of the carnage of war.

A gruff cough tore my eyes from where I'd been watching someone stoop to assess a fallen body to see Barrow sitting up a few feet over. Anger seared through me at the sight of him, and I had to hold myself back from going over and kicking him in the nose. He looked a bit thinner than he had the last time I saw him, as if his time of inactivity at the top of the tower had caused his once firm muscles to start atrophying.

'You're still here,' he muttered as his eyes landed on me.

'Yep and I'm not going anywhere,' I spat back reproachfully. I had several reasons to hate him – his obvious mistrust of me, his attempts to overthrow Hayden, and, of course, the way he'd taken me and assaulted me when I'd tried to return to Blackwing – all of them driving my desire to push him into the flames burning a few yards away.

'Grace,' Hayden muttered warningly. He shot me a disapproving look before intercepting the glare I shared with Barrow. Then he turned his back to me. 'Come on, get up.'

My arms crossed bitterly over my chest as I watched

Barrow rise, the anger only slightly settled by the relief that Maisie had risen along with him. A man who happened to walk by jumped as Hayden called out to him.

'Frank,' Hayden said sharply. The man looked vaguely familiar and I remembered seeing him on various guard duties throughout Blackwing. 'I need you to take these two to see Docc, then I need you to put Barrow in a hut where you can guard him. Got it?'

Now that the tower was gone, it appeared he'd have to figure out a new plan to keep Barrow under control. Frank nodded immediately, hitching the large gun slung over his shoulder menacingly as he shot a glance at Barrow.

'Thank you, Hayden. For what you did,' Maisie said, stepping forward with a gentle smile.

'Sure thing,' Hayden rasped. Another cough came as he nodded, silently signalling them to be on their way. Barrow, I noticed, said nothing at all to Hayden to thank him for saving his life. I scowled at him as he stalked away.

'Stop it, Grace,' Hayden said, jerking my gaze back to him. He frowned at me as he clearly noticed my attitude.

'He didn't deserve that,' I told him.

'He helped raise me. I couldn't just let him die.'

I couldn't find enough compassion to agree with him. 'People's pasts have nothing to do with their present,' I muttered. Surely my own brother could attest to that; the evidence of it was still trickling down my chest in the form of blood after he'd tried to kill me.

Hayden had just opened his mouth to speak when an overly loud, familiar voice rang out from around the corner. His jaw snapped shut as he shot me a questioning look and ticked his head towards the noise, indicating I follow as he started off as quickly as his stiff body would allow.

'—and then the bloody bomb went off right by my ear!'

'What the hell . . .' Hayden muttered in confusion as we rounded the corner, making sure to avoid the tongues of flames that leaped out at us.

Once cleared of the flames, we saw a group of about thirty people gathered with none other than Dax in the middle, shouting at the rest of them. I blew a sigh of relief at the fact he was alive, followed by another as a thoroughly blood-soaked Kit came into view.

'What's going on? What happened?' Hayden demanded as we joined the circle, which parted easily for us.

'*Someone set off a bomb*—'

'Will you stop your damn shouting? Jesus,' Kit muttered, cutting him off with a roll of his eyes.

'*What?*'

'I said shut up, you oaf!' Kit repeated a little louder. He shook his head and I thought I saw the tiniest hint of a grin before he turned back to Hayden and me. Dax apparently understood this time because he stopped shouting.

'Will someone please explain?' Hayden said impatiently.

'Everyone was fighting and we were kind of getting over-run because we were outnumbered when Perdita appeared and set off this flash bomb. Of course, it went off right by this idiot, so it appears he's having *difficulty hearing*,' Kit explained, raising his voice on the last two words while throwing a pointed look at Dax. 'Scared the hell out of them all and they ran for it.'

It was only then that I noticed the tiny, frail old woman standing amongst the crowd. The gaps from her missing teeth were obvious as she grinned widely at us, clearly satisfied with her work. Hayden's description of her – old, slightly insane tattoo artist and bomb expert – flashed through my mind.

'Boom,' Perdita said simply, nodding eagerly.

21

'Boom,' I repeated quietly, as if to myself. That explained the sudden flash of light and heat I'd felt before it had knocked me out momentarily. This crazy, wrinkly old lady had potentially just saved countless lives and stopped the fighting. At least, stopped it for now.

'And they all just left?' Hayden said dubiously, frowning in confusion.

'Yeah, mate, they scattered. Good thing, too. It was getting bad,' Kit answered, cutting off Dax's attempt to speak, or rather, shout, his reply.

'*I'm not getting mad!*' Dax protested indignantly, mishearing Kit's explanation. Kit simply waved an arm at him, silencing him further. I hoped Dax's hearing would come back eventually because this new, loud Dax was going to be markedly less stealthy.

Despite everything going on, I felt a small surge of amusement. Things were still very much unsettled, of course, with fires burning and bodies still littering the ground. We were exhausted, but nowhere near done for the night.

'How many are dead?' Hayden asked grimly, a deep frown pulling at his features.

'I don't know yet,' Kit admitted. The rest of the crowd, who had remained largely silent, let out a few low murmurs.

'Okay.' Hayden paused and pushed his hand through his hair. 'All right, so, if you're badly hurt, go and see Docc to get fixed up. Tell others that aren't here that as well. If you're able to help, start lining up bodies. Us and them, keep them separate, but treat everyone as a human being, got it?'

Quiet murmurs of assent rolled through the small crowd while Hayden scanned their faces. 'Some of you get started on trying to put out the fire in the tower – hopefully we can save that. We don't really have enough water to put out the rest of the fires, so just let them burn out, but be careful not to let them spread. And everyone stay alert. You never know if they'll come back.'

With that, he ended our dismissal, causing people to disperse to their assigned tasks. Turning to me, his burning gaze locked on my own, he said, 'You should go back to my hut, Grace. This'll be hard for you since you're probably going to know some from both sides.'

It wasn't until that moment that I realised this was true. Not only would I most likely know some of those killed, I had killed someone myself. The man chasing Jett had been the first person from Greystone I'd killed. I hadn't given it a second thought. I didn't want to know what that meant.

'No, I want to help,' I said, shaking my head. I knew the impact this would surely have on Hayden, but I wanted to be there for him. 'Come on, let's get started.'

I reached out to briefly squeeze his arm, where some of the black smudges from the smoke had mixed with sweat and rubbed off onto my own skin. He was absolutely covered in sweat and black soot. I knew I didn't look much better with the blood splattered across me. We had a lot to discuss, but now was not the time.

We didn't have to move far before we came across the first body – a man of maybe thirty lying face down along the side of the path. Hayden stooped without a word to press his fingers into the man's wrist, checking for a pulse he would not find. With a sigh, Hayden straightened up and turned him over to reveal his face, which thankfully was not one either of us recognised.

I was reminded of our raid on the city when we'd shot the Brutes after our jeep broke down. Hayden and I secured his limbs to bring his body to the already growing line of those from Greystone. The same blush of cold had started to settle into the flesh, and his face held the blank lifelessness

23

I'd seen countless others times. At least four other bodies had already been laid down by the time we placed his body in the dirt, and I could see other pairs bringing even more to the area.

This was only a taste of the war to come, but already so many lives had been lost.

Hayden let out a deep sigh but didn't speak as he moved to search for our next body, which once again didn't take long to find. This grim task seemed to stretch on forever as Hayden and I hauled body after body to their respective piles. My luck ran out as I recognised the third body – a woman from Greystone only a few years older than me who'd once been close with my brother. I studied her with an odd sense of detachment as we laid her next to the others.

After carrying our tenth body, my arms started to feel slightly shaky. After the fourth person I'd recognised from Greystone, I'd stopped looking at their faces. I didn't want to know who had gone from my former life. I tried to think of them as merely bags of flour, perhaps, that I was helping to haul to Maisie. It was the only way I could keep myself from having a slight breakdown. The most I did was look to make sure none of the bodies were that of my brother, but I did not see him. It appeared he'd managed to get away.

Hayden moved methodically, as if he, too, had tried to mentally check out of the task, though I knew he was not quite successful. It didn't matter what pile the body went into – Blackwing or Greystone – every body we lifted darkened his spirit, weighing him down physically and emotionally. He was retreating further and further away from me as he lurked in the depths of his memory.

After nearly an hour of searching the grounds of Black-wing, it seemed we were done. Two unnervingly large lines of bodies had been collected, stretching further than I could measure easily. It seemed as if, for tonight, my friends were safe. I'd caught glimpses of most of them – Dax, Kit, Docc, Malin – as they helped with the carnage. Only one small person remained in the back of my mind to worry about – Jett.

I stood next to Hayden, hands resting on either side of my hips as sweat poured down my back. The fires, thankfully, had started to burn themselves out, and the crew assigned to putting out the tower fire seemed to have been successful, though it remained to be seen if the tower was repairable.

'So that's twelve from Blackwing, twenty-three from Greystone,' Hayden concluded, drawing my attention. Thirty-five people in total had died tonight, seemingly for no gain at all. A shudder ran through me as the weight of this realisation sank in.

'Jesus,' I muttered. Hayden seemed deflated as he stood next to me, unable to tear his eyes from the faces of those lined up from Blackwing. Some were older with wrinkles creasing their skin, some relatively young in their thirties and forties, while some, most shockingly, were even younger than me. Too young to be out here, dying for something they did not ask for.

'Come on, Hayden,' I said, reaching out to gently tug on his hand in the hope of getting him away from all this. 'You've done enough.'

But he stayed firmly planted to his spot. His hand dropped from mine before falling limply by his side as if he were in a type of trance. He didn't even react as members of Blackwing moved behind us to start preparing to burn the bodies of those from Greystone, keeping with the tradition I knew Hayden had started. Those from Blackwing would be buried.

'Hayden,' I tried again, moving cautiously to stand in

25

front of him and cut off his view. His eyes were slightly glazed and he had to blink several times before he managed to focus on me. 'Come on. You should see Docc to make sure you're all right.'

'No,' he said instantly, shaking his head. 'I'm fine.'

'But—'

'I said I'm fine, Grace.' His words sounded harsh, but there was no conviction behind them. He just sounded flat, hollow, lifeless. I frowned softly as the reaction I'd been expecting started to show. Predicting its arrival didn't make it any better.

At least he appeared to be relatively okay physically, aside from some stiffness and a persistent cough that had kept up throughout the night. He let out a deep sigh as I silently pleaded with him to call it a night. He needed to rest and escape from the darkness that had settled over everyone tonight.

'Let's go, come on. You can have a shower and just . . . relax, okay? You need it,' I coaxed, reaching to grab his hand tentatively once more. He resisted only slightly this time, before giving in and taking a step away from the gruesome sight before us. Once I got him moving, I dropped his hand as I remembered that our 'relationship' was still relatively secret to most members of Blackwing.

I could vaguely hear Dax shouting unnecessarily loudly in the distance. I knew he and Kit would make sure things kept moving in camp in Hayden's absence. There wasn't much left to do, anyway, so we wouldn't be missed.

I felt a sigh of relief as yet another familiar face greeted us as we turned the last corner before arriving at Hayden's hut, having emerged from where I'd made him hide.

'Grace! Hayden!' he said excitedly, a large grin plastered on his face.

'Jett,' I replied with relief, managing a soft smile at him. It was hard to smile for real after what we'd just done. 'You're all right.'

'Yeah I am! Rainey and her sister, too. I protected them just like you said even though no one came!' he said, beaming up at us. Hayden remained stoic next to me. It was only when Jett pulled the gun I'd given him from behind his back that Hayden finally reacted.

'Where the hell did you get that?' Hayden demanded, taking it from him immediately. Jett looked slightly surprised as he cast a guilty look at me before refocusing on Hayden.

'Grace gave it to me,' he admitted sheepishly.

'What?' Hayden snapped, throwing a glare in my direction.

'He's fine, Hayden, look at him. We were in the middle of a raid and he needed *something* to protect himself.'

'You let him run around here with a gun during all that?'

'No, of course not,' I retorted. 'I put him in a hut with two very scared little girls. He helped.'

'Did I do something wrong?' Jett piped up.

'No.'

'Yes.'

Hayden and I both spoke at the same time and turned to glare at each other momentarily. His eyes studied my own before he seemed to give in. He sighed and turned back to Jett as he stowed the gun in his waistband along his back.

'Just . . . be careful,' he said gruffly. 'And go back to Maisie. You don't need to see what's going on over there, you hear me?'

Jett's eyes widened in surprise. It was obvious he'd just emerged from his hiding place and had yet to see any of the devastation.

27

'Okay,' he said quietly, nodding once as he took a step backward. 'See you guys later!'

'Bye, Jett,' I called half-heartedly.

I rolled my eyes before grabbing Hayden's arm and forcing him to move. His steps were stiff and jerky as he forced the door open to let us inside. He only made it a few steps inside before he stopped and let out a slow, deep breath. It was like I could see him mentally fighting off the things that were haunting him, and I wanted nothing more than to take that burden away from him.

Without a word, I went to where he stood. Gingerly, my hands reached out to grip his sides, where my thumbs ran lightly across his ribs. I watched as he squeezed his eyes tightly shut one last time before his head tilted back down to look at me. My heart beat a little harder against my ribs under the intensity of his gaze as tension swelled during the silent moment. He seemed torn between conflicting emotions, none of which seemed particularly positive.

'Come here,' he whispered lowly.

Finally, after what felt like forever, his arms reached forward to wrap around my shoulders and haul me into his chest. My arms responded immediately to wind around his torso, locking us into a hug as my face tucked into his chest. He smelled of smoke, sweat, and blood, but I revelled in the comforting warmth of his body pressed into my own. I could feel his lips press lightly to the top of my head as he held me.

'I'm so happy you're okay,' I murmured, my words stifled by his chest as I continued to hug him. His arms tightened even more around me as if terrified I would slip away.

'That's because of you,' he replied softly. 'You saved me.'

I shook my head. If there was one thing I was certain of,

it was that he would have figured it out one way or another. He hadn't needed me to save him.

'No, I didn't.'

The hug lingered for a few more seconds. His face was only a few inches from mine as he hunched his shoulders to bring him to my level. His gaze ripped through my body and shot all the way down to my toes as it connected with mine.

'Yes, you did. You saved me, Grace. In every way possible.'

Three: Anguish

Hayden

Grace stood with her back to me, completely oblivious. My careful gaze slid down her body, bare now except for the thin material of her underwear. I noticed the way her body curved inward at her waist before widening at her hips, and I noticed that even though she was covered in dirt, soot, and blood, her skin looked devastatingly soft.

My breath hitched in my throat as she turned, smirking softly as she caught me staring at her. She turned once more and removed her final layer, leaving her stark naked as I stood waiting. The cold water from the shower pelted down on me, though the temperature seemed to rise when Grace joined me beneath the spray.

'It's cold,' I said flatly as I stated the obvious.

'Yeah, a bit,' she said. She let out a soft laugh as she stepped closer to me, and I felt the warmth of her hands land on my chest. 'You're filthy.'

'So are you,' I noted.

The streams of water were tainted near black as they lifted the grime from her skin. Most of it remained, however, as the water alone wasn't enough to clear her body. She began rubbing her skin, but it didn't have much of an effect.

'Here, let me . . .'

My voice trailed off as I reached for a rag, wetting it before

I poured some soap onto it, and dragged it over her body.

Darkly stained water slid off her wherever my hands covered, and slowly, bit by bit, her beautiful skin was restored. My heart sped up when the rag revealed the jagged scar that had formed over her ribcage. It seemed like so long ago that she'd sustained the injury that had broken it, but the proof was written there forever.

A soft sigh pushed past my lips as I raised my rag one last time to clear away the dirt from her chest, careful to avoid direct contact with the cut over her heart. My eyes studied it, taking in the tear in the skin and the thin line of blood that refused to stop. Carefully, I ran my thumb beneath the cut to wipe away the last remaining stain.

'You should get that stitched, Grace,' I said softly. 'It'll scar if you don't.'

'I don't mind,' she said slowly. 'I kind of want it to scar.'

'Why?'

She already had too many scars, and I didn't like the reminders that she'd once been in pain. This scar would join the faint one on her thigh from when she'd been shot and the long, jagged one covering her ribs, along with countless others from before I knew her.

She didn't answer me right away as she pursed her lips. Our eye contact broke as she let her gaze fall to my chest, where her hands resumed their soft work of clearing my skin when she took a rag of her own to my body.

'Why, Grace?' I repeated gently, ducking my head to force her to look at me.

'I need it as a reminder.'

'A reminder of what?' Confusion washed over me as I tried to understand.

'A reminder that . . . people can change. No matter what they are to you.'

I did not like the sound of that one bit and couldn't understand why she'd want such a grim reminder permanently on her beautiful body. She had my skin cleared now, and she set her rag down as she let what little remained of the clean water wash over us both. My hands landed on her hips as I pulled her closer.

'What happened, Grace?'

She didn't answer right away as she blew out a deep breath. Finally, her gaze flickered back to mine as I studied her intently.

'It was Jonah . . . My brother did this to me,' she explained slowly, watching for my reaction. I felt an instant flash of outrage and fury: her own brother had tried to kill her.

'Are you kidding me?' I seethed. 'He did this to you? What the hell—'

'Hayden, it's okay—'

'No, it's not!' I said loudly. Too loudly for the small space we occupied. 'You're his sister!'

I could not fathom what type of despicable person would attempt to kill any member of their family, no matter what they'd done.

'I betrayed them,' Grace said, shrugging. She appeared far too nonchalant.

'That's no reason to try and *kill* you,' I retorted quickly.

'In his mind, it is.'

'No,' I muttered, shaking my head angrily. 'That's pathetic.'

'Hayden—'

'Jesus, Grace, I'm sorry, but your brother is a dickhead.'

'I know,' she replied softly. Her hands smoothed up my chest before landing on either side of my jaw suddenly, as if fighting for my attention. 'But I'm fine, okay? Don't stress about it.'

32

'Are you really? Don't lie to me, Grace, if you're not fine, tell me,' I said urgently, searching her eyes for the truth.

She took a deep breath and brought my face down to hers. She surprised me by pressing her lips into my own, kissing me for the first time since everything had happened. My heart panged in my chest as my hands on her hips pulled her closer, and warmth seeped through my body. Much too soon, she pulled back to separate our lips as I let my forehead drop to hers.

'I'm fine, Hayden, I promise.'

I watched her, unsure if I believed her or not, as the water ran out of the shower. She aimed a soft smile at me before pulling away to grab two towels, handing one to me before wrapping one around her body. I accepted it and tucked it around my waist. She turned to leave the small bathroom.

'Wait,' I said, reaching to grab her arm lightly and tug her back. I moved to the small shelf I'd put in and pulled out a few white bandages before coming to stand in front of her again. 'Hold still,' I instructed quietly.

I unwrapped one and placed it gently over her cut, making sure to close it the best I could before placing another bandage in position. My fingers gently smoothed over the area to make sure it was flat and securely in place. Once I was certain it would stay, I ducked down to press my lips lightly over the newly covered area. I lingered for a few seconds before straightening up. As always, tension sizzled between us as the moment carried on.

'I know you want it to scar so you can remember that people change but . . . I won't. This thing between us, how I feel about you . . . that'll never change. Understand?'

Her jaw quivered slightly with the quick breath she drew, and her eyes widened in surprise. I could practically feel her heart pounding in her chest, as my own was.

'Do you understand, Grace?' I repeated softly. My hands rose to hold either side of her face gently between my palms.

'Completely,' she finally said. Her voice was slightly breathless as she spoke. 'I love you so much, Hayden.'

'And I love you.'

My soft words were followed by a sweet, tender kiss. I didn't try to deepen it, just revelled in its simplicity. It was like every time she let me kiss her, some of the crushing weight I felt lifted from my shoulders.

She lingered in my grasp a few moments longer before leading us back into the main room. From the dresser, I quickly pulled out a pair of boxers and slipped them on. I sat on the edge of the bed while Grace got dressed, drying her hair quickly and depositing her towel next to mine. I reached forward to wind my hands around the backs of her legs to tug her closer.

'Are you okay, Hayden?' she asked softly. She brushed the hair from my face gently. I nodded slowly as my fingertips trailed lightly over the backs of her thighs a few times. She turned so her legs fell between my own, resting her weight on my thigh while her arm hooked lightly around my neck.

'I'm just fine,' I said slowly. It wasn't the truth – even in those few blissful moments since arriving back at my hut, I felt the heavy darkness that had settled over us. So many lives had been lost earlier, and I'd failed at the one thing I'd promised them: to keep them safe. Grace was the only thing keeping me from practically disintegrating into dust, though the fractures were already starting to cleave me apart.

She studied me doubtfully, and it was clear she didn't believe me. She parted her lips to speak again before I cut her off.

'Look, Grace, I appreciate it but I just don't want to talk

about it, okay?' I tried to keep my tone even and light. I didn't mean to shut her out, but talking about it would only shatter the fragile sanity I was clinging to. I couldn't do it. Not tonight.

She pursed her lips as if it pained her to accept this. 'Okay. But if you change your mind . . .'

'Shh.' I leaned forward to press my lips lightly into hers to silence her. 'I know.'

She tried to hide her disappointment and aimed a soft, almost credible smile at me before she stood from my lap and pulled back the covers of the bed. She crawled in and scooted to the other side before patting the space next to her.

'Come on, then,' she said softly. 'You need to sleep.'

I shifted my weight and crawled to join her under the covers. My arms reached out for her, tugging lightly until her chest was pressed to mine, allowing one of her legs to tangle with my own. Her head rested on my bicep as my arm snaked beneath her, cradling her to my chest, where she fit like a perfect puzzle piece. I felt her warm hands land against my bare chest as she snuggled into me.

I could have spent eternity like that, beyond content to dwell in the warmth of her presence, her mere existence, for the rest of my life. If only the world would allow it.

'Goodnight, Hayden,' she murmured softly. Her lips brushed over my skin before they pushed purposefully against my neck in a gentle kiss.

'Goodnight, Grace,' I whispered in response. My fingers brushed lightly along her back as I felt her melt into me even more, settling in to fall asleep.

I, on the other hand, allowed my thoughts to continuously bombard me. My attempts to focus on the slow rhythms of Grace's breathing were drowned out by the screams of pain and the cries of the dying from earlier. When I tried to feel the comforting warmth of Grace's body tangled with my own, all I could feel was the burning heat of the flames. Her beautiful face that I tried to picture in my mind was pushed out by those that had been wiped clean in death, their blank stares haunting me, blaming me, torturing me.

Twelve people from my own camp had died tonight.

Twelve people I was supposed to keep safe.

Twelve people I had failed.

I squeezed my eyes shut and held Grace tighter, but my mind was so preoccupied that I could hardly feel her there with me. Beats thumping too quickly sounded in my chest, and an uncomfortably tight knot formed in the pit of my stomach.

I deserved to feel this way.

I hadn't been aware of it, but at some point my hands curled into fists and my body grew impossibly stiff as if it were resisting the comfort of Grace being right there. The masochist in me wanted to reject it, to move further away from her and dwell in the darkness shrouding me, while the weakness in me wanted nothing more than to cling to her desperately and try to fight off the demons that haunted me now.

Now that she was asleep, there was nothing to distract me from my thoughts. My body felt jittery, and I was surprised when I found myself untangling my limbs from hers, moving slowly and carefully so as not to wake her. I slipped from the bed and pulled the covers up around her to disguise my absence so she would remain asleep. I took one last glance at her and let out a tense breath before I shook my head and moved to my desk.

I cringed as the chair squeaked loudly when I sat down, but a quick glance back at Grace told me she was still sound asleep. A soft light flickered in front of me as I lit a match to light the lone candle on my desk.

I pulled out the bottom drawer to retrieve the item I was looking for. Soft leather passed beneath my touch as I removed the journal and opened it, flipping to one of the last pages. My eyes passed over the list and I remembered writing in the last name there; I was not looking forward to adding more. Twelve more.

It didn't seem right to add these names to the list with no further clarification; simply writing them down didn't seem to do them any justice, but I didn't know what else to do. I pressed the pen to the page and let my hand scrawl below the last name listed to write a single word: *war*.

Almost automatically, the names started to flow from the pen, each and every one accented by a mental image of their blank, lifeless faces as they lay in the dirt. I would remember every single one of them for the rest of my life, and I knew I would feel this guilt just as long.

After writing the final name, it was done. Twelve names were written on the page, marked forever in the measly excuse for a history.

Jim Rutter.

Bart Gregory.

Annie Jakobs.

Kellan York.

Travis Hendricks.

Jasmine Rossburg.

Fred Smith.

Quentin Brooks.

Julian Redfield.

Savannah Healer.

Ned Townsen.

Robert Underwood.

I scanned over the pages painfully as I read each and every name. The pen bounced shakily in my hand as I fidgeted with it, tense and on edge after committing my memories to paper. I couldn't stop the horrible sense of foreboding that this would only get much worse.

I jumped when I felt two hands land on my shoulders, squeezing gently as she tried to work the tension out of my muscles. She'd been silent as she approached and I hadn't even noticed she was awake, too consumed with my own thoughts. I felt her duck down as her chest pressed to my back, and the warm spot of heat along the side of my neck told me she'd pressed her lips lightly into my skin.

'Oh, Hayden . . .' she trailed off quietly in resignation. I knew she didn't like finding me like this.

I remained quiet as her hands moulded gently over my shoulders, kneading into the knots in my muscles. I let out yet another deep sigh as I tried to enjoy the touch, but it was difficult. Her hands pushed down my chest as she wrapped herself around me from behind, hugging me into her chest as her lips landed lightly on my shoulder.

'Come to bed,' she requested softly. I knew she could see the journal as it lay open before me, but I made no move to cover it. She was smart enough that she already knew exactly what I was doing.

'I can't sleep,' I told her.

Grace's body was warm as she continued to hug me, and the soft tickle of her breath over my skin was comforting as her lips rested against my shoulder. I allowed one of my hands to reach up and grasp her forearm lightly as it folded over my chest, holding back from giving in even though all I wanted to do was hold her to me and let her relax me.

'I know what you're doing,' she said quietly.

'What's that?' I tried to soften my words by letting my thumb run over the soft skin on her forearm.

'You're blaming yourself.'

I didn't answer, confirming her guess with silence. She was right.

'Hayden, this is not your fault,' she said firmly. I didn't believe her. I felt her sigh against me before she unwrapped herself from around my shoulders and moved to stand by my side. She grasped my hand in hers and tugged, pulling me from my seat so I stood in front of her. 'I know you don't believe me, but it's true. The only thing you did tonight was save lives,' she said earnestly, peering up at me intently. Her hands held mine firmly and she squeezed them as if to accent her words. I felt slightly hollow despite her insistence that it wasn't my fault.

'Even if it's not my fault, so many people died tonight, Grace. On both sides. For what? What's the point?'

It didn't make sense to me. I couldn't seem to wrap my head around the damage humans could inflict on each other in order to survive. We were left to rely on our most barbaric instincts as our world reverted to that of our ancestors, and we were no better for it.

'I don't know,' she said honestly. 'It's more about the end, I think. Eventually . . . someone will lose, and it will all be over. It's not who can win the fastest, it's who can last the longest.'

How could there be a winner when the cost of survival was so high? What price would we pay to linger on in this sham of a world?

'I just . . . I can't help but think this can't end well. This is bad, Grace. This is the end of us all.'

'Hayden, please . . .' she trailed off. Her face was tight with emotion and it was clear it pained her to hear me speak

39

in such a way, but I couldn't help it. Her hands dropped mine as she reached up to hold my face between her hands before allowing her thumbs to trail lightly over my cheeks.

I stood dejectedly in front of her and tried to soak in her warmth, her strength, her love.

'I know that this hurts right now, and I know you won't just get over it like that because you can't. I know you're too good a person for that, but I need you to *try*, Hayden. I need you to believe me when I say that this will end. Wars don't go on forever, and yeah, people get hurt and people die, but it *will* end. We'll get through this together. You, me, Dax, Kit, Docc, everyone. We'll be here now, we'll fight, and we'll move on.'

I drew a deep, shuddering breath as I stared at her intently, clinging desperately to her every word that I so badly wanted to believe. My heart yearned to trust her words and willed them to come true, and my body physically ached at just the thought of the relief such an ending would bring. I hardly dared hope for it as I tried to clear my racing thoughts.

'Do you really believe that?' My voice was impossibly deep, affected equally by smoke and emotion.

'I really do,' she said sincerely, stepping even closer to me and letting her hands fall from my face. She tried silently to convince me, and for the first time I felt a flicker of hope. If Grace truly thought that, surely there was a small possibility of it being true.

'We'll get through this,' I said slowly, testing how it sounded. She nodded and allowed a soft, understanding smile to pull at her lips.

'We will, and I'll be with you every step of the way.'

I vowed silently to stop these dark thoughts from taking over again. I would become stronger, more resilient. I would continue to remember those that were lost, but I wouldn't dwell on it. I wouldn't let it destroy me, because so many others still relied on me to be strong; I had to be strong.

'I really don't know what I would do without you,' I said honestly. I shuddered to think of where I'd be if I didn't have her.

'You'd be just fine,' she said, shaking her head with a hint of a smile on her face. 'And you'd have your whole bed to yourself.'

'I don't want the bed to myself,' I replied. For the first time, I felt a stirring of warmth in my heart that battled the unrelenting cold. The support Grace provided was helping, just as I knew it would.

'No?' A full smile pulled at her lips now as she gazed up at me, allowing her fingers to tickle lightly over the skin on my chest.

I shook my head slowly, holding her warm gaze as I felt the strange urge to smile.

'No. I want you in it every single night.'

'Oh you do?' She smiled even wider as she stepped closer, pressing her chest to mine as her head tilted back adorably.

'Mmhmm.'

I looped my arms around her waist and smiled softly down at her. I had no idea how she'd done it, but she'd lightened my mood and made me feel ten times better simply by talking with me. She was absolutely incredible.

'Let's go to bed, yeah?' I suggested quietly. Her eyes remained fixed on mine as she beamed up at me, pleased my mood had shifted.

'Good idea.'

With that, she leaned up on her tiptoes to press a soft kiss along my jaw that lingered only a few moments before she pulled from my grasp and blew out the single candle I'd lit on my desk. My hand was taken by her smaller, warm one as she tugged me silently through the dark towards the bed, where I heard the soft creaking of the mattress as she climbed back in. She never let go of my hand as she pulled me in after her and under the covers.

She let out a contented sigh as we settled into the mattress, resuming our position from before as we became hopefully tangled in one another. Again, I felt the warmth of her body against mine, only this time, I felt myself accept it. The soft pattern of her breathing was just that, and the image of her lying next to me was untainted by any unwelcome images. She was healing me from the inside out simply by being herself.

'I love you, Bear.'

My voice was a murmur and it was nearly lost between the sounds of our soft breathing, but the tiny squeeze of my torso from her one arm that had roped around me told me she'd heard.

'I love you, too. More than you know.'

The last thought I had was of how lucky I was to have someone like Grace to call my own before sleep finally pulled me under, ending the turmoil that I'd been unable to escape for so long without her.

Four: Haunted

Grace

The world was eerily quiet as I moved through the darkness, careful not to disturb the silent blanket that had fallen over everything. It was impossible to view more than a few feet in any direction. All I could hear was the soft panting of my breath and the incessant thudding of my heart.

I was alone, unsure of where the others had gone, as I searched for something I couldn't seem to find. My feet carried me soundlessly, and I was aware of the dirt growing even softer when I sank a few inches into it with every step. A sudden wave of a familiar stench hit my nose, causing it to wrinkle in distaste, though I couldn't see a source anywhere. Nausea rolled through me as the foetid scent of rotting human flesh registered, increasing the fear I'd been trying to subdue.

The darkness around me intensified as it suppressed any light; I felt like I was being shut into a hole in the wall with no way out. Then the toe of my boot caught on something, and my body lurched forward to land in the dirt. I noticed for the first time that the dirt was no longer dirt, but mud.

Mud caked my fingers, though it wasn't water that had transformed it – it was blood. I began to panic as I tried to push myself to my feet, but my efforts only caused me to sink in deeper and deeper.

The mixture of blood and mud seemed to creep higher up my body as I tried to sit up, and I just felt myself being dragged under. I opened my mouth to shout for help and drew a deep breath only for a mysterious hand to clamp down over it, silencing me. My eyes widened and fear flooded through me as I felt the cold, clammy palm cut off my cries for help.

'Thieves.'

It was no more than a whisper that floated through the air. I couldn't see who'd said it, but the voice sent a chill down my spine. Frustrated grunts came from my throat, but that was the only sound I could make as the impossibly strong hand restrained me. Every move I made to try and throw it off only made me sink further into the sticky blood, and I felt like it was seeping into my skin forever.

I thrashed around in panic, desperate to free myself from these horrors. I stopped as I caught sight of something else moving – the bloody dirt that was quickly encasing me. About a foot away from me, the ground heaved once, as if something were moving below it. I watched in horror as other patches of ground started to do the same, pulsating around me.

If I could, I would have let out a terrified scream when I saw what had disturbed the ground break through. All around me, rotted limbs were bursting forth to start reaching for me. Arms, hands, and most horrifyingly, arms with no hands attached, all of them reaching for me.

My skin felt like it was freezing wherever they grabbed hold of me, securing their grip before dragging me under again.

'No!' I managed to shout into the hand that still held

onto me. I realised in a flash of terror that the hand was not attached to anything else and was rotting away before my very eyes.

Tears of fear leaked from my eyes as my entire lower half was dragged beneath the bloody surface. I thrashed and fought in an attempt to throw off the disembodied limbs, scratching and clawing at whatever I could reach, but it was useless. My body was disappearing inch by inch beneath the surface, and there was no way I could stop it.

'No, help me!'

My voice was muffled and strangled as I fought, but no one came. The blood was up to my shoulders now, and I could feel the deadly cold grip of two hands around each of my wrists as I sank deeper. I attempted one last shout before my chin tilted up to avoid choking on the blood.

'Hayden . . .'

My last word was the weakest yet as I felt the blood pour over my face, suffocated from all sides. There was nothing I could do but wait until it was all over; I prayed it would be soon.

The arms shook me, as if trying to drown me. I felt hands at my face now, rubbing over my cheeks between shakes of my body. I could hear a muffled voice, though it was indistinguishable as I sank further and further into the blood.

'Grace . . .' I could faintly hear my own name but was too terrified to respond.

Again, hands prised at my cheeks, so I jerked my head to the side to try and throw them off. My heart hammered harder than ever and I found it impossible to draw a breath.

'Grace!'

Another shake of my body.

'*Grace!*'

My eyes popped open suddenly. I was confused when the sticky blood I'd been dragged under didn't immediately blind me. I gasped a lungful of air so large it almost hurt, and I was suddenly aware that a cold sweat had settled over my forehead. Blinking furiously, I slowly started to focus on what was in front of me. Rather than a pool of blood and countless rotting bits of human, I was met with a pair of concerned, narrowed green eyes.

'Hayden,' I breathed, shocked and relieved all at once. My heart still rammed incessantly as I tried to come down from the panic I'd felt. Hayden's hands ran over my cheeks again before smoothing back my hair – the same hands I'd felt in my dream, only this time they were warm and comforting rather than cold and terrifying.

'Grace, it's okay,' he said softly. He peered down at me, hair kinking out oddly on one side because of the way he slept. I noticed I was lying flat on my back while most of his weight rested to my side.

'It's just a nightmare,' he said calmly, his voice low. I blew out a deep, shaky breath as his fingers tickled lightly across my skin when he smoothed my hair again and again.

My chest rattled as I tried to calm down, but I finally managed to lift my arms and rope them around his neck to haul him down to me. I held Hayden impossibly tight as I hugged him, and felt one of his arms snake around my neck to draw me to his chest. I was shaking as I felt the steady firmness of his body against my own.

'It's all right, you're okay,' he murmured softly into my ear. I still was unable to respond, but he continued to murmur softly, 'You're here with me, Grace, it's all right.'

I felt so weak to let such a silly thing as a nightmare have such an effect on me, but the images were crystal clear in my mind. What was most unnerving was that the images were derived from real life. What we'd seen in the Armoury – the dismembered hands tacked to the walls, the rotting corpses, the word written in blood on the walls – was haunting me now.

Finally he pulled back, though no more than a few inches as he hovered over me and studied me closely. 'Are you okay?'

I nodded slowly before I managed to speak. 'Yeah, I'm fine.'

He cocked an eyebrow sceptically as he let his fingers resume their gentle, soothing action of smoothing my hair back again and again. 'Really?'

'Yeah, really,' I said honestly as I blew out yet another deep breath. 'It was just a nightmare, like you said.'

It was the truth. Now that I was fully awake and back in Hayden's arms, I felt the panic subsiding and my heartbeat slowly went back to normal. The warmth of his body was erasing the chill that had set in, and his gentle touches were helping me forget the way the cold grip of the hands had felt as they dragged me beneath the surface. It was still dark now, as it was the middle of the night, but this darkness didn't terrify me because I was with Hayden.

'Do you want to talk about it?' he asked gently, watching me closely.

I pinched my lips together in thought. Did I want to talk about it?

'It was just . . . stuff from the Armoury. Like limbs and

hands and blood and stuff . . .' My voice trailed off and I suddenly felt like talking about it in detail would only make things worse.

'Oh, Grace . . .' he said, frowning in concern. 'I told you not to think about it.'

'I know,' I responded quietly. 'I really hadn't been, but I guess it stuck there anyway.'

'Are you sure you're okay?'

'Yeah, promise. Shouldn't we tell the others about that? What we saw?' I asked. My hands were still looped around his neck, reluctant to let him go.

'Probably. We can talk about it tomorrow, okay? Don't worry about it tonight.' Hayden's words were soft and calming, matching his gentle actions.

'Okay,' I agreed.

I lifted my head from the pillow to press my lips to his. Warmth immediately flooded through me, erasing the final remaining chill in my body with his gentle kiss. He let his tongue swipe gently across my own before he pressed one last lingering kiss to my lips and pulled away.

'Get some sleep, Grace,' he said softly.

Sleep was the very last thing I felt like doing thanks to the way his simple kiss had woken up my body.

'Love you.'

I would never get tired of hearing him say that.

'I love you, Hayden.'

This time when I closed my eyes, all I focused on was the warmth of Hayden's chest pressed to my back, the comforting way his arms held me close, and the rhythmic *whooshing* of his breath as it blew past my neck. I allowed sleep to pull me under, which thankfully this time was peaceful and free of any nightmares.

Hours later, I awoke gently. Soft sunlight streamed into

the hut, and my entire body felt warm as I allowed myself a few moments of peace and quiet. I kept my eyes shut, blocking out the sunlight as I snuggled further into the warmth.

A soft, low groan rumbled from Hayden's chest, telling me he was awake as well.

'Morning,' he mumbled. His voice was deep and raspy, and he still sounded like he was half asleep.

'Good morning.'

'How'd you sleep? The rest of the night, I mean,' he asked softly.

'Perfectly,' I answered honestly. My sleep had been undisturbed, thankfully.

'Good,' he said, nodding once.

I suddenly felt like doing nothing but spending the entire day in bed with him. I still felt the pull of desire I'd started to feel last night.

Hayden didn't allow me the chance to act on those feelings, however, before he pulled himself from me to rise from the warm confines of the bed. He stretched once, raising his arms above his head to ease the muscles in his back, before rising and loping gracefully across the hut. I let out a deep sigh as I let my eyes roam over his body before giving up and climbing from the bed as well.

'We should probably go and find Kit and Dax to fill them in,' Hayden said.

'Yeah, all right,' I agreed, crushing the tiny remaining hope that we'd be able to avoid everything for a day and just stay in. Hayden was too responsible to allow that.

He shot me a small smile before disappearing into the bathroom. I was being selfish by wanting to keep him all to myself. I noticed the plank of wood nailed to the wall and I remembered the night Jett had given it to us. The painting of three stick figures, one for each Jett, Hayden, and me, sent a flash of warmth through my heart as I smiled at the memory. I hoped to see Jett today, as our last encounter hadn't exactly been cheerful right after recovering from the start of the war.

Fifteen minutes later, Hayden and I had both changed and got ready for the day. We walked down the path towards the mess hall. The fires had all burnt out, though the air still held a faint hint of smoke as they smouldered to ashes. We passed the tower, and I was pleased to see a small crew of people working on repairing it. They hadn't accomplished much yet, but at least there was hope of salvaging it.

The mess hall was about half full of people eating breakfast. Maisie looked flustered as she stood behind the counter and served. She hardly managed a greeting to Hayden and me as we took our food and searched for a table. Before long, however, an overly loud voice drew our attention.

'*I told you, mate, I can hear you just fine,*' Dax's voice insisted, clearly heard from all the way across the mess hall.

'Bloody hell,' Hayden muttered with a gentle shake of his head. He cast me a wary glance before moving to the table I now saw held Kit, Dax, and Docc.

'*Morning, guys,*' Dax shouted while Kit and Docc winced at the volume.

'Hello to you,' Docc said with a gentle nod. His voice level was much more appropriate, as was Kit's as he greeted us.

'Hey, everyone,' I said as we sat down. 'Still can't hear, Dax?'

'*What?*'

I laughed and rolled my eyes in response while Hayden and I ate our food. Dax opened his mouth to speak, or rather, shout, again before Kit punched him lightly on the arm.

'Shut up, will you? Correct, Grace, he still can't hear. I

thought it was getting a little better, but it's hard to tell, really.'

'Will it come back?' Hayden asked, directing his question at Docc as he shot a sceptical look at Dax. Dax squinted around at all of us as if he knew we were talking about him but couldn't quite grasp our words.

'*Stop talking shit about me,*' he grumbled loudly.

'I think so,' Docc said calmly. 'His left isn't as bad as his right, from what I can tell, and he seems to hear a bit better today than he did yesterday, even though he remains painfully unaware.'

'That's good news,' I said sincerely. As oddly amusing as it was, I hoped for Dax's sake his hearing would go back to normal soon.

A loud clang sounded through the mess hall, jerking everyone's attention towards the source. Even Dax, who appeared to have given up trying to participate in our conversation, heard and turned his head. Jett stood near where Maisie was serving breakfast, dishes and food alike scattered around his feet from the tray he'd apparently dropped. A deep blush settled on his cheeks as he saw everyone gaping at him, and his eyes widened at the attention.

'Sorry,' he muttered in embarrassment.

'Go on, Jett,' Maisie said patiently. 'Get another and go and eat. I'll clean this up.'

He nodded sharply and did as she said, darting away from the mess he'd made as he moved to grab another tray of food.

'I feel bad,' Hayden said softly, directing his words only to me as Docc and Kit began talking about something else. Dax continued to pout.

'What? Why?' My eyes watched Jett for a few more

seconds before flitting to Hayden, where I saw him focusing on Jett with a frown on his face.

'I haven't . . . Uh, I wasn't very nice to him the other day.'

I frowned at Hayden's words. At first, I'd thought he meant last night when he'd snapped at him for carrying a gun.

'What do you mean?'

'Erm,' he paused, casting a guilty look in my direction before he bit his lower lip. 'I said some stuff to him while you were gone that I didn't mean. I dunno, I shouldn't have said it but . . . I wasn't thinking straight.'

'I see,' I replied. What had he said to Jett? 'Well, if you feel bad, you should apologise.'

'Apologise,' Hayden repeated doubtfully.

'Yes, you know, people do that when they mess up,' I said with a hint of amusement. I'd never heard him apologise to anyone other than me, as far as I could remember, and I knew it wasn't a very familiar thing to him.

Our conversation was cut short, however, by the subject himself as he wandered up and placed his tray on the table.

'Hi, everyone!' he said excitedly. Kit and Docc greeted him before diving back into their conversation, and Dax settled for a small wave.

'Hi, Jett,' I greeted with a smile. 'How are you today?'

'I'm okay. I want to, um, thank you. For saving me last night,' he said, blushing once again as he suddenly became very interested in his food and avoided looking at me. A soft smile pulled at my lips as I watched him.

'You're welcome.'

I was glad he didn't appear too shaken up by what had happened when I'd shot the man chasing him, because at the time, he hadn't handled it very well. I could feel Hayden watching me speak with Jett, and I could feel him resisting joining the conversation. My elbow nudged into his rib lightly, encouraging him. His gaze met mine and he frowned before rolling his eyes when I ticked my head towards Jett. A deep sigh pushed from his lips in resignation.

'Hey, Jett . . .'

'Yeah?' He looked up at Hayden with slight apprehension on his face.

'I'm sorry about last night. I shouldn't have yelled at you about the gun, but you need to know, that was a one-time thing. Just because you got one then doesn't mean you get one from now on, got it?'

I frowned at Hayden's attempt at an apology; it didn't sound much like one to me. He sought my approval, but frowned when he saw me shake my head minutely.

'What I mean is, I shouldn't have yelled at you. I'm sorry,' he continued.

'It's okay! I'm just glad I got to help,' Jett said honestly. He looked from Hayden to me and back as he shovelled food into his mouth.

'Just that once,' Hayden emphasised.

Jett nodded, unable to speak thanks to his mouthful of food.

Hayden glanced at me once more. He frowned when he saw I was still unsatisfied.

'And?' I muttered, edging him along.

'*And* I'm sorry for what I said a few days ago. When you asked about Grace being gone and all that . . . I was just upset and I took it out on you.'

My heart thumped heavily in my chest at his confession. I still had no clue what he'd said, but I didn't really need to. I knew if it had to do with me being gone, it probably wasn't pretty.

'It's okay, Hayden,' Jett said easily. He wiped his mouth with the back of his hand before shooting us a grin. 'I'm just glad Grace is back now!'

I gasped when Hayden's arm looped loosely around my shoulder, hauling me into his side momentarily before releasing me. I glanced around to see if anyone had noticed the casually affectionate gesture, but it appeared no one had.

'So am I, little man. So am I.'

Five: Squad

Dax

I glowered at everyone around me. I could see their lips moving and hear a vague, muffled murmur when they spoke, but most of what they said was lost as they carried on around me. After attempting to participate in the conversation with little success, I gave up and ate the rest of my breakfast in silence. Everyone else had finished, too, yet we all still sat around the table.

Thankfully, my hearing was returning, just not as quickly as I would have liked. Sometimes it seemed almost back to normal before it reverted and I felt like I was stuffed under a pile of blankets. Between that and the gash healing on my arm after stitches from Docc, I was practically falling apart.

My eyes roamed around the table to take in Docc, Kit, Grace, and Hayden, all conversing easily with each other. Jett had disappeared after eating, staying only briefly to say something to Hayden and Grace I could not hear. Docc seemed pensive beside me as his gentle gaze drifted between Hayden and Grace. I could see Kit's mouth moving as he said something, though I heard nothing more than a stifled murmur. He appeared to be speaking to Docc, however, because it seemed Grace and Hayden were not paying attention.

I watched with an odd satisfaction as Hayden ducked down slightly to bring his lips to Grace's ear. Whatever he said to her brought an instant grin to her face. It was like I could almost see a physical connection between them, as if some sort of haze surrounded them and drew them into each other without even realising.

Grace's grin was reflected in Hayden's as they beamed at each other, completely oblivious to whatever was going on around them. A flash of movement drew my eye, and I saw Grace's hand move as if to run down Hayden's back before she stopped herself and settled for a tiny brush of her hand against his forearm. They might as well have been suffering from the same hearing loss I was for all the attention they paid to us.

It seemed so obvious that they were desperately in love with each other, and it baffled me that the rest of camp couldn't see it. The change in Hayden was impossible to ignore to anyone who knew him personally, though few had that luxury. Very seldom did he reveal any of himself to those around him, but when he did, he revealed he was a far better person than the rest of us. He and Kit had been like the brothers I'd never had, the family I'd never had, and it was clear to me that he'd started to change the day he rescued Grace.

Even the subtle way they leaned into each other when they sat side by side practically screamed love to me. I had no doubt in my mind that he, of all people, deserved to feel that way. He'd sacrificed so much of himself for everyone around him and never once complained. Never once had he acted selfishly, put himself before others, or done anything that wasn't for the benefit of the camp. He'd proved himself over and over again, though it had been at great cost; he had given up the simple things in life he was so reluctant to indulge in, taking away from so much of what made life worth living.

Grace had changed that. I could see it mere days after her arrival, probably before he was even aware. It was surprising how quickly he grew so protective of her, and even more surprising how much she had opened him up. He was selfless, as ever, while managing to take a little for himself, opening up and experiencing things as he should have all along. Grace had given him *life*, a reason to truly live rather than just exist, and I could never be more grateful to her for that.

My best friend, my brother by choice rather than blood, was finally happy because of her.

A soft tinkling of laughter burst through the haze in my ears, ripping me from my thoughts. My eyes landed on Grace as she sat across from me, smile pulling wide at her cheeks as she cast yet another glowing look at Hayden. Whatever he'd said had amused her, and it was easy to see that Hayden was pleased with her response as he gazed back at her in adoration.

I let out a deep sigh and tried not to feel annoyed that I was missing out on so much of the conversation. It was difficult to enjoy the time spent with my makeshift family when I had no clue what was going on.

I settled my gaze on Grace once again. There really was no denying she was beautiful, but I didn't fancy her. She'd come to be like a chummy best friend or maybe even a sister, which had surprised me as well. Maybe in another time or situation, I'd have felt something along romantic lines, but it was impossible. She was, in every single way, made for Hayden, as he was made for her.

'*Hey!*'

The shout registered in my mind as I blinked and

refocused. Everyone at the table was staring at me, as if waiting for my response to a question I had not heard.

'*What?*' I could feel myself shouting but I couldn't help it. Besides, their exasperated looks were quite amusing when I insisted on shouting unnecessarily.

'We're heading to the raid bu . . . to talk . . . *something*,' Hayden said. His voice faded in and out as I squinted at him, but I got the gist.

'*Okay*,' I returned. A dull thud landed on my arm as Kit slugged it with an amused chuckle.

'You better hope your hearing comes back soon,' he said, shaking his head.

'*You're telling me. You all miss my intellectual input, I know.*'

I grinned as they all rolled their eyes. Again, I didn't miss the subtle brush of Hayden's fingers along Grace's lower back as they all stood up.

My mind flashed to the night of the bonfire when they'd danced together. What had started out innocent enough had quickly deteriorated as they got too wound up in each other, making my intervention necessary to protect their relationship. It wasn't my business, but that wouldn't stop me from meddling when necessary anyway. Besides, I couldn't just let them blow their secret before they were truly ready.

Damn, I am an awesome best friend.

My smug thought brought a self-satisfied grin to my lips as I followed everyone outside and down the path to the raid building. Kit walked next to Grace and Hayden while Docc fell into step with me. I was surprised to hear his voice through the buzzing in my ears.

'Oblivious, aren't they?' he murmured.

'Who?' I replied with a chuckle, keeping my voice down.

'Hayden and Grace. They have no idea how they are together.'

I smiled. They didn't touch or even look at each other, but still I could practically see the connection sizzling between them.

'You're right.'

'When did you notice?' Docc continued gently. We dropped behind enough to remain unheard, and I was grateful for his deep voice.

'I think it was after Greystone raided, right after she got here . . . I just had this feeling but never thought I was actually right.' It didn't seem as though Docc was going to comment, so I continued. 'When did you?'

'Before that . . . after she saved Kit. Something about the way he is with her,' Docc mused.

'Ah, the ever-perceptive Docc, one-upping me again,' I said, feigning disappointment.

We arrived at the raid building, and that was the end of our thoughtful conversation.

Grace

The raid building was dimly lit as we all filed in after one another. The woman on duty nodded once at Hayden before stepping outside to give us our privacy. Hayden, Dax, Kit, Docc and I gathered around the table in the centre of the building. They knew, to an extent, what we'd found in the Armoury, but they didn't know the gruesome discovery that Hayden and I had unveiled and which had haunted me in my dreams – the bodies missing their hands that were tacked to the walls, accented with a bloody message meant to warn off those like us.

59

Thieves.

The comforting pressure of Hayden's hand landing momentarily on my back seemed to chase off the cold.

'Don't think about it,' he said softly, loud enough for only me to hear. I shot him a smile and nodded, determined to remain strong, and he returned his attention to the group.

'All right, so, I didn't want to discuss this in the mess hall but . . . we may have a problem.'

'*What?* A *problem?* But things have been going so well,' Dax said loudly, the sarcasm ringing clear. We all shot glares at him. Being in the midst of a war was hardly what anyone considered to be 'going so well'.

'What? Too soon? Okay, okay,' he said, raising his hands in surrender. Hayden stiffened beside me; he was clearly not amused.

'You make the worst jokes, Dax,' I said with a light shake of my head. My mind flashed to the day he'd told me Hayden hadn't made it, only to reveal he'd been 'joking'. I didn't think I'd ever fully forgive him for that.

'You mentioned a problem, Hayden?' Docc interrupted, getting us back on track.

'Yes,' Hayden replied. 'Obviously you guys know about all the Brutes we ran into on the raid. We know they appear to be living in the Armoury. We know about all the supplies they've gathered, but there's one more thing.'

The tension in the room was palpable. Four pairs of eyes were fixed fervently on him as they waited.

'Those Brutes . . . the ones we stole from . . . they've been killing.'

'What do you mean?' Kit questioned, furrowing his brow in thought. Dax was concentrating very hard on hearing. Docc's expression was difficult to read.

'There was a pile of bodies in there,' I interrupted. 'A pretty substantial pile . . .'

Another chill shot down my spine as I saw the tiny hands nailed into the walls. Tiny hands that could only belong to children.

'But . . . I mean, is that really a surprise? We kill,' Kit said bluntly. Hayden tensed even more beside me and I threw a glare at Kit for reminding him. I didn't want him to think about it if he didn't have to.

'This was different,' Hayden interjected. 'We kill those attacking or trying to harm us . . . These men, they didn't just kill them . . . they disfigured them afterward. Cut off their hands and nailed them to the wall because they got caught trying to steal. Children's hands.'

Hayden's voice was hollow, as if every word he uttered were paining him. A grim silence settled over everyone. The realisation of what type of men were being spoken of was almost too horrific to consider, but the sights burned into my brain and the words we'd all heard them utter about women and getting what they wanted from them were concrete proof.

'So what do we do, Bossman?' Dax finally said, his voice sombre.

'I don't know,' Hayden admitted. 'Maybe nothing for now, but we'd be stupid to ignore it. They have enough supplies down there to last a long time, and enough weapons to wipe us off the map in a blink of an eye.'

'Maybe we could scout it? Send in a small group to get more information?' Docc suggested. His brow furrowed and his thumb and forefinger cradled his chin as he thought deeply.

'Maybe,' Hayden mused. 'I think we got lucky, though. I have no idea why it was empty when we went, but I can almost guarantee that won't happen again.'

'Why is that? Why wasn't anyone there when they're clearly living there? You're right, that seems odd,' Kit questioned. He, too, frowned as if stumped by the circumstances.

'I don't like it,' I admitted. We had far too many questions and not nearly enough answers.

'It's a lot to take on,' Docc murmured. 'This war with Greystone, keeping camp running, and now these mysterious Brutes from the Armoury? Maybe we should just let things be for a while but keep an eye on it. Focus on what we can actually do.'

It seemed like the most logical option, but judging from everyone's unease, the idea of doing nothing didn't sit well with anyone. This wasn't a group to sit around passively when danger was potentially brewing not far off.

'Look, maybe they're not planning anything and they're just trying to survive like we are,' Dax said hopefully.

'Do you really believe that? After the way they came after us? That doesn't seem like men just trying to survive, to me,' I said. I hadn't been planning to speak, but the words were out before I could stop them.

'Well, what do you suggest we do, then, huh? Run back there into a death trap and see what happens?' Dax said in frustration. It was by far the most anxious I'd ever heard him.

'I don't know, but we can't just sit around and do nothing and wait for them to come after us!' My voice rose as I allowed some of the anxiety I was trying to suppress leak through.

'Well that's not—'

'*Enough!*'

Hayden's voice rang out in command, silencing Dax and

me as we bickered. An exasperated sigh pushed past his lips as his hand dragged tensely through his hair. Fear of the unknown was getting the better of us, putting everyone on edge.

'Enough,' he repeated softly.

My eyes turned to observe him, but his gaze was fixed on a point on the table as he leaned over it. Both of his hands splayed flat on the surface and his back hunched.

'Okay, here's what we'll do. If you have a better idea, speak up, but hear me out first,' he shot pointed looks around the circle. He paused a few moments longer on both Dax and me, and I felt a slight blush creep into my cheeks. It felt like he was reprimanding me for being a disobedient child. When no one spoke, he continued.

'We're not going to start anything, but we're not going to ignore them, either. We'll keep an eye on them, but from a distance. We're not risking anyone getting hurt if we can help it, and we definitely can't spare anyone to do anything more aggressive. *If* we have reason, we'll act, but only if they're a threat to us. Got it?'

'Yes . . .' Docc said slowly, nodding once. 'Yes, that sounds like the best plan to me.'

'Me, too,' Kit agreed.

'Yeah, agreed,' Dax said, still somewhat too loudly.

Silence once again fell over us for a few moments before I felt everyone's eyes land on me. I blinked in surprise as I realised they were waiting for my opinion.

'Grace? What do you think?' Kit asked.

I was slightly taken aback that they wanted my opinion. It was like they considered me not only as one of their own but as a leader.

'I think that's the best possible plan,' I said.

My stare met each of theirs, before I finally met Hayden's.

His expression was difficult to read, but I couldn't miss the flash of pride there.

'It's settled, then,' he responded, addressing the group once more as he tore his gaze from mine. 'We'll check up on them every week or so and focus on what's going on here. We've still got to get that tower back up and figure out if we can rebuild what burnt down.'

'I've been working with Malin on that,' Kit announced. 'Girl's a genius when it comes to that stuff.'

My stomach twisted at the thought of Malin as I was reminded of what she'd accidentally revealed — that she and Hayden had history — but I waved it off. Obviously he'd been with others before me, just as I had before him, and it wasn't my business.

Or so I told myself determinedly. I wouldn't be the one getting upset about things that didn't matter.

'So we're done here?' Dax said. 'I've got places to be, people to see, you know?'

His wide grin was back as he rubbed his hands together in front of him, earning an exasperated groan from both Hayden and Kit.

'Always the charmer, Dax,' Docc chuckled.

'Yeah, we're done,' Hayden replied.

'See you guys later,' Kit said as he threw a nod at both Hayden and me. He and Dax began chatting to one another as they filed out, leaving Hayden, Docc, and me alone.

'Hayden, could I have a moment alone with the girl?' Docc asked respectfully.

Hayden's lips pouted slightly as he cast a questioning look in my direction. I just shrugged, unsure of what Docc wanted but fine with being alone with him.

'All right, I'll just . . . be out here,' Hayden said slowly.

As soon as the door shut behind him, Docc turned to smile softly at me.

'Sorry, I'm not sure if you mind him hearing or not, but old habits die hard . . . Patient privacy, and all that,' Docc explained. I blinked and shook my head.

'It's all right. What is it?'

'I'm not sure if you wanted to keep up with it, but if you did, you're due for your next birth control shot. It's your decision, but I thought I'd remind you.'

A hint of embarrassment flooded my cheeks but was quickly stamped out by a rush of gratitude. In the midst of everything, the timing of my shot had slipped my mind.

'Yeah, I'd like to keep up with it,' I said, blushing. Docc simply nodded.

'Do you have time now? We could head over and get it taken care of, but really you just need to do it sometime this week.'

'Yeah, we can go now,' I answered. 'And, erm, Hayden can come, if he likes. He knows about it so . . .' I trailed off, feeling awkward. Surely Docc knew by now that my lie about using it just for my period was just that – a lie – but it was still slightly uncomfortable to talk about it with some-one who had known Hayden since he was a child.

'All right. If the lad's still out there he can tag along.'

I nodded with an awkward smile as we moved to the door. I wasn't surprised to see Hayden waiting just outside, reluctant to stray more than a few yards even though I was with Docc.

'Ready?' he asked as soon as I stepped outside.

'Yeah, um, we've got to head to the infirmary quick. You don't have to come if you don't want to,' I said evasively.

'Why? Are you hurt?' he asked immediately, concern crossing his features.

'No, Hayden,' I replied. Relief washed over his face. 'It's for my shot.'

'Oh,' was all he said. 'Yeah, all right.'

The infirmary appeared to be empty, which was surprising considering the amount of people who had been injured in the start of the war.

'No one's here?' I questioned as I sat on one of the benches reserved for patients.

'Nope. Everyone's healed up enough to get home. The supplies you got from the Armoury did wonders,' Docc said calmly. Hayden hovered beside me as Docc pulled a vial from his cabinet. He scrubbed the top with alcohol before he plunged a needle through the rubber and withdrew the medicine.

'That's good.'

'Indeed.' His eyes focused on his syringe before setting down the vial and approaching. I felt the cool wetness of alcohol as he wiped a swab over my upper arm. 'One, two . . . three.'

I felt the slight sting of the needle as he pierced my skin and the burn of the medication. I could see Hayden watching closely from beside me. It was just a shot, after all, and I was more than capable of handling it. Docc pulled the needle out and tossed it in the bin.

'Now, you probably won't get your period anymore,' Docc said after casting a wary glance at Hayden. Hayden cleared his throat awkwardly and suddenly became very interested in something on the other side of the room. He moved away from us without a word as if to give us some privacy. 'If you do, I suspect they'll be very light before they stop altogether.'

'Okay,' I replied. 'Anything else I need to know?'

'As long as you come back in another three months

for the next one, you're all set.'

'Thanks, Docc.' I smiled as I hopped off the bench, not even bothering with a bandage on my arm because it had already stopped bleeding.

'Any time, girl. Any time.'

With that, he turned to head to his familiar desk. I went to Hayden, who stood peering into one of the many cabinets Docc had to house his supplies. My hand landed on his back and he turned to look at me with a somewhat surprised expression.

'Ready?' I asked, holding back a laugh.

'Mmhmm,' he nodded.

'Come on, then. Let's get out of here.'

He offered me a lopsided smile.

'Yes, ma'am.'

Six: Tranquil

Grace

'Ma'am, huh?'

'Mmhmm. Bossing me around and whatnot . . .' he trailed off, amused.

'Please,' I scoffed playfully. 'Like I could ever boss you around.'

'Bit of a power struggle, innit?'

'Sure is, *Sir*,' I replied, grinning widely as the involuntary frown that always creased his face at that word appeared. I giggled when he leaned sideways and nudged his shoulder into mine while we walked.

'Don't call me that,' he said lightly. A small smile remained on his face.

'Sure is, Herc?' I tried. His grin widened more this time.

'There you go, Bear,' he said in satisfaction. I was pleased with the light-hearted nature of our conversation after the slightly heavy morning we'd had. It was only then that I realised we were not, in fact, heading back to Hayden's hut. The path we trekked down was leading us in the opposite direction, away from the main part of camp.

'What are we doing?' I asked curiously. The huts here looked the same as all the others in camp, and there was nothing particularly spectacular about this area.

'We need to stop and see Barrow,' Hayden answered

gravely. My heart seemed to drop in my chest.

'What? Why?'

'Just . . . I have some things to ask him,' Hayden said mysteriously. I frowned at his evasiveness.

'Like what?' I couldn't keep the distaste from my tone.

'Just stuff, Grace,' he said impatiently.

My frown deepened as we approached an unassuming hut. Hayden nudged the door open with his shoulder and disappeared inside before I followed. A man sat on a chair at the edge of the room, armed with a gun and a frown as he guarded Barrow, who was tied to a ceiling support. Scowling, I took in his dishevelled appeared when he turned to look at us in surprise. The surprise was wiped from his face almost immediately, however, when he registered that Hayden was not alone in his visit.

'Lovely,' he muttered bitterly as we came to stand in front of him.

'Barrow,' Hayden greeted flatly. Barrow and I glared at each other while Hayden waited patiently for his attention.

'Yes, Master?' he said sarcastically, the edge clear in his voice.

'It doesn't have to be like this, you know,' Hayden told him sternly. With Barrow seated on the ground and Hayden and I standing, we towered over him. I felt a flare of satisfaction at our dominance.

'You've made it pretty clear that it does.'

I felt the urge to lash out at him, but I held my tongue. Hayden surely had a purpose for visiting him and I didn't want to interrupt.

'But see, it doesn't. You're the one who can't accept that Grace is a part of Blackwing now. She's done absolutely nothing but help us from day one and you've never considered anything other than her being our enemy.'

Barrow frowned even deeper at Hayden's words before tossing another scowl in my direction.

'Think back to a year ago. Would you even have let her live if she'd been someone else? Say she wasn't such a pretty little thing, say she hadn't caught your eye, would she be alive?' Barrow spat, venom in his voice. He didn't give Hayden the chance to respond. 'No, Hayden. She would not be alive.'

'That's not true,' Hayden said evenly. I could tell he was resisting the bait for the fight Barrow was trying to start.

'Of course it's true! You saw her and wanted a piece of ass so you went soft and—'

His words were sharply cut off, however, by Hayden's hand at his throat as he lunged forward to pin him to the post.

'She's alive because she saved my life, Jett's life, the very first night I met her. She's alive because she's proved herself, over and over, that she's here for us. *How* you can't see that is beyond me,' Hayden growled, losing his cool momentarily.

His arm jerked forward as he pressed even tighter on Barrow's throat for a second, causing him to choke and sputter weakly, before he released him and resumed his full height as if nothing had happened. Barrow coughed a few times and shook his head before sneering up at us once more.

'Then why did Greystone attack, huh? Why did they start all this if not because of her?'

'Because everything is running out, you idiot. We all knew this would happen eventually and it finally is. We couldn't keep raiding forever. Have you forgotten how things work?' Hayden said impatiently. 'You're just *so wrong* on everything that it kills me.'

Barrow was silent as he seethed on the floor. Throughout

70

this entire exchange, both the man on duty and I had remained silent. I suspected this was not why we had come here, which Hayden confirmed.

'I *was* going to consider letting you free again, but you've blown that now,' Hayden informed him. Our light, playful mood from before was nowhere to be found.

'Sure you were,' Barrow muttered bitterly.

'It's true,' Hayden said. I tried not to feel slightly betrayed, but I had to remind myself Barrow had once been like a father figure to Hayden. It wasn't fair to anyone, really.

'Not truly free, mind you, but at least not tied to a pole like you are now. It's clear I still can't trust you not to hurt her.'

I blinked as I realised he was talking about me. Barrow didn't deny his statement. It was quite obvious he still very much wanted to hurt me, despite everything Hayden had said in my favour.

The feeling was mutual.

'If you're done sulking, I need to ask you something,' Hayden pressed. Barrow, who had gone between glaring at me and at the floor, returned his attention to Hayden.

'What?'

'Did you see the attack from Greystone before they got here?'

'Yes,' he growled. That must have been why he'd been raising hell on the tower the night the war started.

'How many did you see?'

'I don't know, I was tied up, wasn't I?' Barrow spit reproachfully. Hayden cocked an eyebrow impatiently at him. 'A hundred, maybe.'

'Did they come from one area or around the camp?'

'Thought the leader would already know this information.'

71

'Shut it and tell me.'

Barrow let out a heavy sigh. 'They came from two main areas, one on the south and one on the east.'

'Anything else you can tell me?'

'No. Woke up on the ground and that's the last thing I remembered.'

'Yeah, you know how you got on the ground?' I spat, anger rising once more, no longer able to keep silent.

'I'm aware,' he said flatly. His gaze bore into mine steadily.

'You still haven't thanked him, you know,' I pointed out furiously.

'It's not your business,' he sneered.

'He risked his life to save *you*. He could have died saving *you*.'

Even if he hated me, it was no reason to treat Hayden the way he was treating him.

'Thank you,' he muttered bitterly, dropping his gaze to the ground.

'You're such a fuc—'

'It's fine, Grace,' Hayden interrupted.

'It's not, Hayden!' Anger was heating my blood in my veins now.

'I said it's fine,' Hayden said firmly. 'We're done here. Enjoy your time, Barrow.'

Barrow didn't reply other than an indignant scoff and a minute shake of his head. I bit the inside of my cheek to stop another outburst. It was only when I felt the gentle pressure of Hayden's shoulder nudging into mine that I was able to move and follow him out the door. He called goodbye to the guard, and we were once again out on the path of Blackwing.

I seethed silently as we moved down the path. Hayden was silent, too, though he didn't seem to hold the same anger I did. He moved deftly beside me and I could feel his

72

gaze on me as he studied my profile.

We were walking up the short path that led to Hayden's front door when he finally broke the silence. His tone was light as he spoke.

'Oh, Grace . . .' he murmured softly. If I wasn't mistaken, I thought I caught a hint of amusement. I wasn't sure what was so amusing to him, so I ignored him as he allowed me to push open the door to his hut.

Inside Hayden's hut was dark and cool, and the familiar environment did little to soothe the lingering anger I held onto. Without meaning to, my feet carried me in a sharp line before turning around, pacing to try and work out my aggression. I could feel Hayden's gaze on me again as he stood leaning against the door he'd closed after entering. Unintentionally, I threw a glare in his direction, only to see him grinning in amusement once again.

'What?' I said, a bit harsher than I intended.

'You need to calm down, Grace,' he said smoothly.

'I am calm,' I snapped, very unconvincingly. My pacing feet and the tight clench of my hands by my sides contradicted my words.

'Sure you are,' he countered.

'Shut up, Hayden,' I muttered. It was so strange to be so worked up over something that essentially had nothing to do with me, but I supposed that was what happened when you loved someone. I turned away from him.

I jumped slightly when I felt Hayden's warm hands on my arms, his touch sliding slowly over my skin as he raked them up to my shoulders. The muscles were tense as his fingers kneaded over my skin beneath my tank top, though I could feel the heat of his touch relaxing them already.

'Relax,' he murmured quietly.

I sighed deeply as I felt the soothing warmth of his lips

73

at the base of my neck, pausing momentarily as he let his lips linger there. His firm chest pressed to my back and I felt his hands slide back down over my arms before one landed on my hip. He pulled me back against him gently while his other hand massaged light circles into my hip.

'That's it,' he breathed as he felt my body starting to melt into his. It was like the tension was leaching out of me as I tipped my head back to rest on his shoulder. He pressed warm kisses in a chain along my neck until he reached my ear, where he tugged it lightly between his teeth.

I felt my body press back more firmly against him, where he stood strong and steady to return the pressure. This time when his lips moved down my neck, I felt the wet heat of his tongue as it darted out against my skin. His fingers curled upward to increase the pressure while his lips attended to my neck and his other arm held me firmly against me, forcing my body to surrender completely to his will.

'Are you calm, Grace?'

His voice was impossibly low and laced with desire as he murmured in my ear.

'Yes,' I answered, practically panting. I was anything but calm as my heart thudded heavily, but it was for a different reason than it had been moments ago.

'Promise?'

The heat between my legs deepened as he ran his palm over me again, moving in time with his lips on my now bare shoulder.

'Promise,' I said weakly. I sounded like I was begging, but I didn't care. He was driving me insane.

'Good,' he muttered.

Pulling his hand from between my legs, I turned fully around to press my chest to his while he met my lips with a kiss.

He backed me into the desk a few feet away, where he then pressed his hips to my own. I gathered his shirt in my fists and tugged it over his hips, desperate for more contact with his bare skin. He pushed my own top upward, lifting the fabric as his tongue smoothed against mine. He pulled back suddenly, creating enough space to lift it easily over my head and toss it to the floor. The second it was gone, he dove back in to reconnect our kiss.

His lips didn't stay on mine long, however, as he gently tilted my head to the side with his knuckle to allow him to trail his lips down my throat once more. Every kiss he placed on my skin dipped lower and lower until he reached the swell of my breast, where the cut inflicted from my brother was still healing. One tiny kiss was pressed over it before he rose once more, reconnecting his gaze with mine while I panted slightly from the way he was making me feel.

His lips parted, as if about to speak, but I shook my head to cut him off. I didn't want to talk — I just wanted him.

Without hesitating, I reached for the hem of his shirt and tugged upward until it pulled free. My palms ran down his warm, jagged skin before he pushed forward, forcing my arms to loop around his neck as his hips pressed me back into the desk once again. His hands slid beneath my thighs to hoist me up onto the desk.

He slipped a hand between my legs again, before easing the pressure. It was a momentary disappointment, then he slipped his fingers back beneath the layers of clothing. His warm fingers dragged smoothly down my centre, before he put pressure on my clit. My body jerked forward at the touch I had been so desperately craving all day.

I could feel how ready we both were, and I knew Hayden could as well, but his fingers continued to circle over the nerve bundle, stoking the fire already burning inside me. It was difficult to continue kissing him as I felt a finger at my entrance, circling around lightly before pushing inside to stretch me. I gasped at the pressure, and Hayden took the chance to move his lips to my neck once again.

'Hayden . . .' My voice was no more than a breathy whisper.

I wasn't even aware of his free hand moving behind my back until the clasp was released from my bra, letting it fall loosely between us. I wasted no time in tossing it to the floor along with my top. Hayden ducked his lips even lower, continuing the torturous movements of his hand between my legs as his lips closed around my nipple. His tongue circled around it a few times before he trailed back up, where I tugged his face back to me.

Every time his thumb circled over my clit, every twitch of his finger inside me, was building me up, preparing me to come crashing down. My arms looped around Hayden's neck as I hauled his bare chest to mine, kissing him fervently as his hand continued to work between us. My breathing grew even more unsteady and my eyes squeezed tightly shut as I felt my high approaching, and one last circle of my clit with his thumb sent me crashing over the edge as I held my mouth firmly against his.

Heat coursed through me at my release, and my body sagged into his. Then he pulled his hand from me and promptly yanked me off the desk. His arm around my waist was the only thing that kept me from collapsing. Suddenly, his free hand dug beneath my waistband to push my shorts and pants down over my hips, leaving me naked in front of him.

He grinned at my surprise. He ducked forward again to kiss me once.

'Relaxed now?' he murmured against my lips. I nodded weakly as he steered us backward onto the bed.

My hands floated down his sides, feeling the rough skin covering his ribs before landing on his hips, above his athletic shorts. As Hayden's tongue pushed into my mouth once again, I allowed my palm to slide over his hips and run over the prominent bulge on his front, earning a low groan.

I slipped my hand beneath the layers he wore to grasp his firm length. His hips shifted forward, and the pace of his kiss reflected the way he was feeling as his lips moulded against mine. The silky skin covering his shaft slid along with my touch, and his hips continued to press downward as if craving more contact, just as I was.

Without further hesitation, I pulled my grasp from him to push the layers down his hips. He took over when I couldn't get his shorts and boxers any further. With the final layers between us removed, I could now feel all of him as he pressed his hips into me once more, as he pressed at my entrance.

'Ready?' he murmured against my lips. My hands raked down his back while one of his tangled in my hair and the other supported his weight. Our kiss continued for a moment before I responded.

'Yes, Hayden.'

Our kiss was interrupted as my lips parted involuntarily when he pushed slowly into me, stretching me further than his fingers had moments ago. A low, gravelly moan of satisfaction ripped from Hayden's throat as my head fell back against the pillow, revelling in the feeling of being fully connected with him once again.

'God, Grace,' he groaned deeply.

His hips pulled back slowly, drawing out of me before pushing forward once again. I whimpered as he moved; his body fit perfectly with my own, as if meant to come together this way. Hayden made me feel things on so many levels that I'd never felt before, and I was certain that would be something I'd never get used to.

Heat and pressure were already starting to build up inside me as he rocked smoothly forward, and the feeling was only increased by the burst of love I felt for him.

Looping my arms around his neck, I pulled him as closely as I could while still allowing his hips to move fluidly to push in and out of me. Hayden rested his weight on one elbow by my head, fingers tangling into my hair wherever he could reach, while his other hand roamed freely down my body.

He gripped my hip momentarily in his large hand as he guided me in rhythm, creating a perfect symphony of movement. Next, his touch trailed upward, heating the scarred skin over my rib before he reached my breast and allowed his thumb to roll over my sensitive nipple.

Finally, his hand reached my face, where he cradled my jaw gently as he continued to rock into me. My legs rose to wind around his waist, drawing him in even closer as he kissed me fervently. He was everywhere, covering me completely in the best way possible.

'Ha-Hayden,' I managed to gasp between pants.

'Hang on, baby,' he murmured against my lips once again. He'd never called me 'baby' before, but it seemed so fitting for the moment. I moaned again as he pushed impossibly deep inside me, sending my nerves fizzling through my body and setting me on fire from the inside out. My hips jerked upward involuntarily as I tried to hold out on giving in to my second release.

The pace of his hips increased as we both drew near our ends, and I could feel the thin layer of sweat that had formed over his body. I had no control as my legs locked as tightly around his waist as they had yet, and any power I'd had to hold off on my second orgasm crashed down around me as I felt it rocket through me. A half gasp, half moan ripped from my lips as I felt the sizzling relief, and my head fell back into the pillow once again as I lost control of my body.

'Ahh, Grace,' Hayden gasped tightly as he pushed into me one last time. His muscles contracted as he held himself there, and I felt the tension in him as he came. His hand gripped mine tightly and my legs were still locked around his waist, though we didn't kiss as fine movement seemed impossible while such intense satisfaction roared through both of us.

Finally, Hayden relaxed and let his weight rest on me as he started to come down. I continued to pant beneath him as I relished the moment, practically melting into the mattress. My legs loosened their tight grip around him and my free arm lazily looped around his neck while he still held my other hand. Hayden allowed his head to duck down by my throat as he breathed heavily, and I felt a warm spot of heat on my skin as he pressed a lingering kiss into my neck while he rested there.

'I love you, Grace,' he murmured softly, his voice laden with both love and satisfaction. My heart practically leaped in my chest, rejoicing in the beautiful words after the incredible way we had just come together. A soft smile pulled at my lips as I let my fingers rake gently through his hair.

'And I love you, Hayden.'

Seven: Duality

Grace

The room was dark now, all light gone save from the glow that seemed to be emitting from my heart. Hayden had shifted his weight off me and was now lying on his side, where I faced him; every tickle of his fingertips over my skin sent a calming wave down my spine. The blanket had been pulled up around us, cocooning us in the warm afterglow of what we'd done together.

There was a comforting familiarity in the silence, and it was clear we didn't need words to fill the space at all times. Our breathing had both returned to normal, and I could feel the soft pulsing of his heart beneath my touch as my hands rested on the warm skin covering his chest.

'It's still early,' I whispered, finally breaking the soft silence. It had only got dark less than an hour ago, and it probably wasn't even past nine.

'Hmm,' was all he said, the tones low and rough as they rumbled from his throat. His lips appeared a darker pink than usual and slightly swollen from our activities.

'We don't have to do anything else?'

'No, not tonight. Tonight I just want to be here with you.'

I smiled and shifted my body even closer to his. His hand flattened out against my back as he pulled me against him before resuming his gentle tracing of my skin.

'That sounds perfect.'

He didn't respond, though his lips pulled into a smile and his eyes practically radiated happiness. A few more moments of contented silence passed before I spoke again. There had been something on my mind for a while now that I wanted to discuss.

'Hey, Hayden?'

'Yeah?'

'I've been thinking about something . . .'

'Oh no,' he joked lightly. My hands on his chest shoved lightly, though he didn't move as he pulled me even closer. 'What have you been thinking about?'

I paused, taking a deep breath. I didn't know how he would react.

'Do you think . . . now that I'm officially back forever . . . that we shouldn't live together?'

He blinked in surprise.

'What?' he responded flatly. It was clear he had not been expecting that.

'Do you think I should get my own place to live?' My heart thumped heavily in my chest as I rephrased.

'You don't want to live with me anymore?'

It was impossible to miss the obvious hurt in his voice.

'No, Hayden, no, that's not it at all,' I backtracked. Lord knew I never wanted to be away from him ever again. 'It's just . . . before, I lived here because I had to, right? You had to keep an eye on me, and I get that, and then we started . . . whatever, so it just kinda transitioned over but . . .'

'But what, Grace?' he said, voice strained. His hand had stilled on my back and he felt significantly less relaxed than he had moments before.

'But I don't want you to feel like you *have* to let me live here with you, you know? I don't want to . . . smother you,

81

or whatever,' I said. I felt stupid as a blush crept over my cheeks.

'Are you serious?' His tone was hard to read as he spoke. Then he forced me to look up at him once more. 'What's this about, Grace?'

'It's just that we're together like all the time . . . I don't know if you want space or . . . I just don't want you to get sick of me.'

I felt embarrassed to admit it, but it was true. Very seldom did I voice such concerns or even think about them, really, because it felt like such a weak and girly thing, but I couldn't deny that fear had started to creep up ever since I'd returned to Blackwing. The very last thing I wanted to do was drive him away.

'Is that really why or do you not want to live with me anymore?' he pressed. My stomach clenched at his question. I wanted to be with him every second of the day.

'No, that's really why,' I said, my voice suddenly urgent. 'I never want to leave you, but I just want you to know that if you wanted your own space, I'd give you that.'

A flicker of something crossed through Hayden's eyes, but it was tough to decipher. His hand slid up from my chin to gently cradle my face, and his fingers tucked my hair behind my ear.

'You're crazy,' he said quietly. 'I don't know why you would ever think such a thing.'

I blew out a deep breath. 'That's just . . . that's kind of how everyone is at Greystone, you know? They want their own space.'

Hayden shook his head slowly, brows furrowed and serious as he watched me. I could feel my heart beating anxiously.

'I just want you, Grace. I've spent most of my life sleeping

82

alone, and I don't want to do that ever again. You hear me?'

Relief flooded through me. He'd just placated my fears, though I didn't dare fully believe him until he confirmed it one last time.

'You sure?' I dared to ask. I'd give him one more chance to speak up.

'I've never been more sure of anything in my entire life. I meant it when I said I want you in our bed every single night.'

A soft gasp sucked between my lips. Had I heard him right?

'Our bed?' I asked as my grin widened. Hayden blinked, as if he hadn't even realised he'd said it.

'Yes, ours,' he repeated slowly. He paused as if really letting that sink in before nodding once. 'Our bed, our hut, our everything, all right? You live here, too. With me.'

'I love that,' I admitted. My grin was so wide by now that it practically hurt my cheeks. Hayden's hand remained on the side of my face as he held me close, his own stunning grin revealing a dimple in his cheek.

'Yeah?' he asked happily.

I nodded blissfully, unable to speak as my happiness threatened to smother the words in my throat.

Our blissful moment was interrupted by a sudden knock at the door.

'You've got to be kidding me,' Hayden muttered, his tone laced with disappointment. He pressed one more kiss to my lips before reluctantly separating from me and pulling himself from the bed. *Our bed*.

Both of my hands rose giddily to run down my face at the thought, unable to wipe away the smile even though we'd been interrupted. I tugged the blanket up around me, bringing it to just below my chin as Hayden pulled on a pair of shorts. He cast a wary glance at me before turning to head to the door, where another knock sounded out.

'I'll talk to them outside,' Hayden told me, taking in my still naked state.

'Okay.'

A quiet creak sounded as he opened the door just enough to slip outside before pulling it shut behind him.

I could hear quiet murmurs from outside but couldn't make out any definitive words, so I decided to just snuggle under the blanket and relax. The residual buzz from my high still lingered in my veins, accented by Hayden's declaration. No longer did I need to consider this *his* hut, *his* bed. It was *ours* now, and I could not have been happier.

As happy as I felt, I couldn't ignore the lingering dark cloud in the back of my mind. No matter what I tried to tell myself, I knew it was inevitable – eventually, this blissful reprieve would end, and we'd be thrust back into the turmoil of the war. This quiet lull would not last forever, and I could feel it creeping closer and closer to the end by the day.

The door opened once more, and Hayden slipped back inside and closed it behind him. His tight torso was still bare, and I saw the way his hips shifted smoothly as he walked back to the bed.

'Who was that?' I inquired. Hayden sat on the edge of the bed but did not crawl back under the covers with me, dimming my hope that we'd be able to spend the rest of the night together as I'd thought previously.

'Dax,' he murmured softly. Something had dragged him down a bit, and I frowned at the change.

'What did he want?' Nerves started to creep up in my chest.

'He and Kit were talking and they had an idea.'

'And . . .?' I hated that I had to drag it out of him.

84

'They think that we should go to Greystone and try to scout it out to get some information . . .' he trailed off, watching closely for my reaction. 'And I agree.'

I knew this would come eventually – the inevitable involvement with Greystone – but I wasn't prepared for it. I probably should have felt a sense of betrayal, fear, defensiveness, *something,* but all I really felt was flat. It was like any lingering connection I'd held to Greystone had been obliterated the moment my own brother tried to kill me.

'Just to get information?' I questioned after a long pause. I sat up in bed, keeping the sheet tucked under my arms to keep me covered.

'Yes. No violence unless we get caught,' Hayden answered. 'What do you think?'

I tugged my lower lip between my teeth in thought, dropping my gaze to the space between us on the bed. Even though my brother had tried to kill me, I still had people I cared about there, Leutie, my best friend, being one of them. I felt like a horrible person for not even thinking of her until now, but I'd been too selfishly wrapped up in making sure Hayden and those I cared about here were still alive and well to spare a thought for anyone else.

'I think you're all right. We have no idea what they're planning from here on out. We need to go.'

'You can sit out, if you want,' Hayden offered, drawing my gaze back to him.

'You already know I won't.'

He just shrugged. 'It's not going to stop me from offering.'

'When do they want to go?'

'Now.' He grimaced apologetically as he spoke and was unable to stop his gaze from drifting down my sheet-clad body.

'Right now?' I asked in surprise.

'Unfortunately.'

I nodded and started to crawl out of bed, disappointed. Hayden rose to put on more appropriate clothes, allowing me space at the dresser to do the same. Reason prevailed — this was important. Greystone was the most vulnerable at night, as I knew from growing up there, so this was the best time to go.

A few minutes later, Hayden and I were fully dressed and on our way to meet Kit and Dax at the raid building. We would be walking and carrying only a few weapons among us for protection, though hopefully they wouldn't be necessary.

'You don't have to go,' Hayden reminded me one last time. We were nearly to the raid building now, and I could hear Dax and Kit's voices coming from inside.

'Shut up, Hayden,' I teased lightly, shooting him a soft grin. He just shook his head playfully before pushing the door and holding it open for me. I jumped slightly when I felt his hand pinch lightly on my bum as I slipped past him, shooting him an amused and surprised glance. His eyes glowed as he grinned innocently at me.

'Look who decided to show up,' Dax said, shooting conspiratorial grins at the both of us. He was no longer shouting, which I took as a good sign.

'Hearing back, Dax?' I asked, ignoring his statement.

'Not fully, but I can at least hear you when you talk,' he said happily. With his quick progress, I hoped he'd be fully back to normal soon.

'Should you really be going, then? If you're not at one hundred per cent?' Hayden questioned. He raised an eyebrow at him as he crossed to the gun case to retrieve his 9 mm pistol before tucking it behind his waist like he usually did.

'I can hear enough. If you think I'm sitting out, you're insane,' he said with a wide grin.

'What about your arm? You just got shot,' I pointed out.

'Docc fixed me up, didn't he?' he said brazenly. 'I'm good to go.'

'All right . . .' Hayden said doubtfully. Kit let out an uncharacteristic chuckle as he slammed a fully loaded magazine into his gun.

'Ye of little faith,' Dax said haughtily, as if insulted by our concern.

I laughed as I copied Hayden and moved to the gun case to pull out a weapon of my own. Usually, I carried a .22, but today I chose a 9 mm like Hayden. It was a stronger gun, and the weight of it was comforting in my hands as I loaded it.

'So what's the plan?' Kit asked as we all gathered around the table. Each of us took a switchblade to stow in our pockets.

'I'm not sure. I don't know what the best place to look would be and—'

'I do,' I interrupted. All three of them jerked their gazes to me. It suddenly occurred to me that this was the first time I was willingly giving up information on Greystone. 'I know where to look.'

They were all silent as if they, too, were having the same realisation as I was. There was no going back now. I was truly, one hundred per cent, on the side of Blackwing.

'Where should we look, Grace?' Dax asked calmly, his light nature from before sobered a bit.

'Well, they might have changed things from when I left but . . . I'd say the best place to look would be my—Celt's office,' I said.

My heart panged painfully at the thought of my father, something I'd got very good at blocking out.

Kit and Dax hadn't seemed to notice my slip, but Hayden had. The muscles in his arms tensed, and he shot me a reassuring sideways glance before wiping his features blank once more.

Something told me this trip would be more taxing emotionally than physically.

'It'll be towards the centre, so we'll have to be careful, but that's your best bet for information on anything.'

'It's as good a shot as any,' Kit muttered, nodding. 'You can show us where it is?'

'Yes,' I said, resigned to let this happen. Not only let it happen, assist it.

'Remember, this is a low-key raid. We don't want anyone to know we're there, and we don't want any violence unless it's absolutely necessary. Got it?' Kit and Dax both murmured in agreement, as I did. 'Okay, good. Let's get going, then.'

'It's been a long time since we've gone on a raid without intending to take something,' Dax mused as we filed out the door.

'Yeah it has. Remember the last time we went to Greystone?' Kit responded. He chuckled before he seemed to remember that was the night I'd caught Hayden and Jett.

'I do,' I said. A soft smile pulled at my lips at the memory. I remembered how protective Hayden had been over Jett and how obviously furious he was that Jett had shown up. I remembered how even then, when I was supposed to be killing him, that it had registered how much power he commanded. And, of course, I couldn't deny that I remembered exactly how attractive he was even that first night I met him.

He was just some stranger then.

That seemed like a lifetime ago.

'Quite the change since then, yeah?' Dax pondered.

'You could say that,' I chuckled. Hayden was quiet beside me as we walked through Blackwing, but I caught the soft grin he aimed at me.

After that, we fell silent as we made our way through the outskirts of camp and into the forest that surrounded it. I couldn't help but remember the last time I'd gone down this path how horrifically it had ended as Hayden sent me home, but I reminded myself he'd done it for me.

Because Greystone really wasn't that far from Blackwing, it didn't take long for us to reach the treeline that allowed us to see the edges of my former home. Our footsteps grew even quieter as we were more cautious, and we gathered around to observe what lay out before us. Hayden hovered next to me, and I could feel the warm heat of his shoulder as it pressed into mine while we stood hidden amongst the shadows of the forest.

'What do we do, Grace?' Hayden murmured softly. Kit and Dax alternated between examining Greystone and looking to me for instruction as they hovered a few feet away.

'Wait for the guard to go by, then go in along the left side. I'll lead us from there.'

'How long between guards?' Kit asked.

'Ten,' I said softly. 'Or at least it used to be. I don't know if they've changed it or not . . .'

'All right. Everyone stay alert. Let's get in and get out, yeah?' Hayden whispered from beside me.

'You got it, Boss,' Dax said in a hushed tone.

I jumped slightly when I felt Hayden's arm snake lightly around my neck, hauling me loosely to his side. Kit and Dax made no notice of his subtle action as they focused on Greystone. I felt his lips press lightly into my temple, kissing my skin gently before he tucked his lips low against my ear.

'I love you. Be careful.'

My arm looped around his torso to return the hug, and I pressed a light kiss along his jaw. This was the part that always came – the cautionary goodbye that hopefully would not be necessary.

'You be careful, too. I love you, Hayden.'

This was it – my first official raid on my former home. Everything I'd grown up learning was flipped now as I lurked in the shadows. Things were different now, and there was no going back.

Eight: Contrast

Grace

I watched the back of Hayden's shirt billow out behind him as he ran in front of me, paving the way for Kit, Dax, and I. My muscles revelled as they pushed my body on, determined to keep pace as we flew silently through the night.

We approached the first building to hide behind. The guard had just passed by before we'd sprinted from the treeline, giving us the opportunity to advance our position. My eyes scanned what I could see now as I leaned over Hayden, and I could feel his gaze trained tightly on me as he waited for my word. A cool breeze pushed the wisps of hair that had escaped my ponytail off my face, and I could feel the heat of Hayden's chest in the close proximity.

'I think we're good,' I whispered when I saw no other guards or potential threats. I tried to think of this like any other raid, but it was impossible to forget the familiar setting and the knowledge that everywhere I looked, there were people I knew just out of reach.

'Lead the way, Grace,' Hayden murmured. I nodded sharply.

'Let's go.'

I pushed myself off the wall, gun raised and ready, and began to slink through the dark pathways that wove through

Greystone. We were still on the outer edge that was made up mostly of huts where people lived, but it wasn't really that late and the odds of someone happening to wander outside were higher than made me comfortable. It felt odd to be leading the way as I was used to following Hayden, but it made the most sense.

A glance over my shoulder told me Hayden, Dax, and Kit were right behind me, eyes scanning constantly for incoming threats. We stayed hidden amongst the shadows, avoiding the sparse patches of light that appeared here and there along the path.

A sudden shifting shadow caught my attention as the outline of a body appeared on the ground, indicating someone about to merge onto the path we currently stood on.

'Get back,' I hissed quietly.

Immediately, the four of us melted into the shadowy space between two huts, pressing our bodies flat against the stonework. Heat leached into my skin where Hayden's arm pressed to my shoulder, contrasting with the cold metal of the gun in my hand and stone at my back. My ears pricked as I listened closely, and soon I heard the telltale crunching of boots along the path.

I turned my head slowly, to fix my gaze on the path we'd just retreated from. The footsteps were even louder now, and it wasn't long before the figure they belonged to passed into my line of vision. It was a thickly built woman, heavily muscled and armed with a large gun, who thankfully did not notice our presence as we observed from the shadows.

Clearly, Greystone had increased their guard presence as it hadn't even been ten minutes since we'd seen the last one. We would have to be even more careful than we'd previously thought necessary.

'Shit,' Hayden muttered softly beside me. It was clear the

same thing had occurred to him as well.

'We'll be fine,' I murmured encouragingly. I suddenly felt even more pressure to get the four of us in and out in one piece. If this was how Hayden felt all the time, then he dealt with it much better than I was. My leg jittered anxiously up and down, bouncing on the ball of my foot as I waited for the woman to disappear.

When I could no longer see her form or hear her footsteps, I dared to lean forward to glance down the path. She was about thirty yards away now and about to turn a corner to head down a different path. A quick glance in all directions told me it was clear.

'Okay,' I whispered, ticking my head towards the path to indicate they follow me.

Again, the four of us slinked along the edge of the path. Each step we took brought us closer to the centre of camp, and each step added to my growing trepidation. Twice more, we had to duck into the shadows to avoid a guard or a member of Greystone. Each time, Hayden's shoulder pressed into mine reassuringly, reminding me that he was right there with me.

Protecting me, as I protected him.

Something else twisted at my gut now as we got even closer, and the source of my discomfort became clear as we turned down a very familiar path. My eyes were immediately drawn to it despite my best intentions to look elsewhere. A soft glow shone in the window, proof that someone lived there after most of the previous members had left, one way or another.

The hut where I'd grown up stood before us as we paused behind a large bin. I should have been looking for guards or incoming threats, but all I could do was remember the place where my family had once been whole, happy, complete.

It was the place I realised at a young age that my brother didn't think of me as equal. The place my mother had slowly withdrawn from the world only to succumb to her illness and pass on.

The place my father had died while I held his hand.

My throat suddenly felt tight and raw as I stared, and I jumped when I felt the soft pressure of Hayden's hand on my lower back. His lips appeared at my ear as he leaned over me, chest pressing into my back from behind.

'You okay?'

I blinked furiously a few times. I drew a deep breath and finally managed to rip my gaze away. My body leaned into Hayden's, drawing the comforting warmth from him, his lips at my ear, and his chest at my back.

'Yeah, let's keep going,' I murmured. I knew he wouldn't believe me, but now was hardly the time to discuss what I was feeling.

Hayden's hand shifted to land on my hip before squeezing lightly in reassurance.

'Okay.'

If we were at my old home, we were nearly at Celt's old office. I hoped the fact that there was a light on in my previous home meant that Jonah was in there and not in my father's old office, but we couldn't be sure until we arrived.

This time, instead of creeping along the edge of the path, we chose to dart along the rear of the huts. There was too much light now and too many noises to make us comfortable staying on the paths. The sparse grass that managed to break through the bleak dirt cushioned our steps as we slinked along. Soon the target came into sight.

I held up my hand silently and everyone came to a stop as I peered around the corner of a building to get a full look at it.

'Shit,' I muttered.

'What?' Hayden whispered. He leaned forward, pressing his chest to my back again as he tried to see what I was. It was clear he did when he muttered bitterly, 'Great.'

A large, bulky man stood outside the door of the office, which was dark inside. He looked vaguely familiar to me, but I couldn't place his name. A long, dangerous-looking knife hung off the man's belt and a powerful gun occupied his hands, making it clear he was on guard.

'Can we sneak around the back and jump him?' Dax murmured, appearing by my hip as he crouched down to see around us.

'We could go around the back then come out the other side,' I mused, considering Dax's option.

'But if we kill him, won't they know we were here?' Dax questioned. He had a point.

'We don't have to kill him, just knock him out,' Hayden said. 'If he doesn't see us, they won't know who it was.'

'It's not hard to guess,' I said, grimacing.

'Still,' Hayden said, shaking his head. 'We have to get in there. We could sneak around the back, knock him out and drag him in after us so nobody sees him, and leave before anyone knows we're here.'

Everyone frowned in thought. It wasn't a great plan, but Hayden was right: we had to see if we could find information.

'I think we should just kill him,' Kit said bitterly. I suddenly remembered the way he'd saved me the night the war started. He'd appeared out of nowhere, knocking my potential killer to the ground and slashing his throat without a second's hesitation. Kit was brutal, but he was also very valuable.

'No,' Hayden said firmly. 'We'll go round and I'll knock

him out, then we get in and search while someone keeps watch. Got it?'

'Yeah,' everyone murmured in reply. Hayden nodded sharply, taking over the point position as we took another quick glance around the corner. The man still stood, facing away from us as he guarded the door.

'Go,' Hayden whispered before streaking off into the night, flying quickly towards Celt's old office. The three of us followed silently, and very soon we were now at the back of our target. 'Cover me,' Hayden murmured.

Kit, Dax, and I raised our guns as Hayden tucked his into his waistband and started to creep around the building. A nervous pang shot through my body as I realised this man was much larger than Hayden, with at least fifty pounds of muscle more packed onto his body. I wanted to whisper to him to be careful, but I couldn't risk him hearing and giving us away. It was with an anxious heart and a twisting stomach that I watched Hayden move in.

Suddenly, Hayden lurched forward. His actions were quick, silent, and undeniably powerful as his arm looped around the man's neck to drag him backward into the shadow. Hayden's arm curled around his neck, bending at the elbow where his other wrist pulled back on it tightly to cut off the man's air supply. The man struggled against Hayden, dropping his gun to the ground to clutch desperately at his arms, but with every passing second, it became clear that he was growing weaker and weaker.

With one final futile effort to remove Hayden's arms from around his neck, the man's body slackened as he passed out. Hayden exhaled a heavy puff of air as he dropped the body to the ground.

'Come on,' Hayden said casually, as if he hadn't just single-handedly taken down a much larger, probably stronger man. He stooped to take the man's gun and knife, handing the knife to Kit and the gun to Dax to stow away.

He took one quick glance back out towards the path, but no one was there. Hayden returned and ducked to pick up the man's arms while Kit rushed forward to grab his legs. They heaved him off the ground while I darted around the corner to open the door to the office, which was surprisingly unlocked. Ducking inside, I held the door open long enough for Hayden and Kit to slip through with the man's body and for Dax to follow. Dax closed the door and peered out of the window cautiously.

'I'll keep watch, get searching,' he whispered.

A heavy thud sounded as Hayden and Kit dropped the man in the corner and straightened up. It was almost pitch-black in the office, but I didn't dare risk lighting a candle for fear of someone seeing us. I jumped when the scratch of a match being dragged across something rough sounded before a soft glow appeared, though it was immediately covered by Hayden's body as he turned away from the window. His hand curled around the flame, dimming its brightness enough to still be discreet but usable.

I went to the desk and my heart gave a painful pang as I pictured Celt sitting behind it. The last time I'd seen him, his face had been so gaunt and emaciated, not at all like the man I'd grown up with. It was like I could feel his eyes on me now. Hayden moved towards me, stirring the air that brought a scent to my nose and memories. Stale tea, gunpowder, and the smell of old paper combined to form the smell that always reminded me of my father.

'What's wrong, Grace?' he murmured softly, still shielding the quickly burning-out match while Kit began riffling through the papers on the desk. Dax continued to watch the door.

'It's just . . . This place . . .' I whispered quietly. I tried to force the words out of the way so we could do what we came to do. Surely Hayden understood how difficult this would be when he still couldn't find the strength to go to his old house.

'Jesus . . .' Hayden muttered. 'I'm sorry, Grace, I didn't even realise . . .'

His voice trailed off with obvious guilt, but it wasn't his fault. I'd volunteered to take us here in the first place. I shook my head vigorously, wiping away the memories.

'It's okay. Let's just get what we need and leave before he wakes up,' I said determinedly, ticking my head towards the unconscious guard piled in the corner.

While there were countless papers on the table, none of them appeared useful. There were lists of items that needed fixing or replacing, lists of supplies that needed moving, and drawings of improvements to be made around Greystone, but nothing that pertained to Blackwing. Kit let out a huff of frustration beside me as it became apparent he was finding nothing useful, either.

The soft ruffling of papers and the quiet pattern of our breathing was the only sound to be heard, though every moment that ticked by seemed to increase the thudding of my pulse in my ears as my anxiety grew. I cringed as a thud sounded from behind me, but I calmed as I realised it was only Hayden pulling a box of papers from the shelf.

'Finding anything?' I asked.

'No,' Kit muttered bitterly. 'It's all just shit for Greystone.'

'Same here,' Hayden assented quietly. I frowned. If this trip didn't result in anything beneficial, then we had just risked an awful lot for nothing.

After shifting some of the cluttered items on the desk, a scrap of paper caught my eye. It was difficult to tell exactly what it was, but the general outline of Blackwing was clear as my eyes pored over it. That was all I managed to take in, however, before my thoughts were cut off by Dax's urgent voice.

'Get down!'

We were plunged into darkness as Hayden blew out the third match he'd lit after the first few had burnt out, and my body dropped to the floor behind the desk. Kit landed next to me and Hayden filled the space on my other side as a nearly silent curse slipped past his lips.

Dax hardly had time to duck behind a shelf along the far side of the wall before I heard the squeak of the door as someone tried to open it. It didn't move at first, and whomever it was had to throw their shoulder into it before the door gave way. I vaguely remembered how it always used to stick but didn't have time to ruminate on it as my heart all but stopped in my chest.

There was a low creak as the door pushed open, followed by the single set of footsteps that carried whomever it was inside. A soft glow filled the room from the candle the person held, not quite bright enough to reveal Dax skulking in the corner or the passed-out guard. My heart threatened to pound out of my chest as I waited to be caught, and it only beat harder when a few more footsteps sounded deeper into the room.

My gaze flitted quickly to Kit to see him silently mouthing something at Dax, still blocked from view by the large desk we all hid behind. It looked as if he were indicating Dax to jump whoever it was, so I turned to look at Hayden. He grimaced at me before looking around me to Kit and nodding once. He raised his hand so we could all see while allowing Kit to signal to Dax. We had to act, or we'd risk getting killed.

Three fingers on Hayden's hand were raised before us.

One finger ticked down.

Two fingers left.

Another finger dropped.

My heart felt like it was about to fall down to my feet with nerves as I waited for the signal, gripping my gun tightly in my hand.

The last of Hayden's fingers ticked down, causing a lot of things to happen at once. Hayden, Kit, and I sprang into standing position, guns raised and aimed at the threat. Dax leaped forward from his hiding place, locking his arm around the neck of the unsuspecting intruder and holding his knife to their throat. A surprised whimper echoed from the person who had interrupted us as they dropped their candle and plunged us into semi-darkness, and it was only then that I realised I recognised them.

Pale blue eyes framed by long, light brown hair stared at me in shock, mouth dropping open probably in surprise and terror as she felt the sharp blade of the knife at her throat and took in the three guns aimed straight at her.

My best friend from Greystone.

Leutie.

'Grace?' she squeaked, voice clearly filled with fear. Leutie did not handle things like this well. She didn't even carry weapons, much less knew how to defend herself. She was too soft for that, but she had other strengths that had nothing to do with physicality.

'Leutie?'

I stared at her in awe, and my gun automatically dropped to my side. No one else moved, however, as Hayden and Kit held their guns and Dax continued to press the knife against her throat as he held her tightly to his chest. My eyes darted quickly to the door to see if anyone was coming after her, but it appeared she was alone.

'You're alive.' She was clearly frozen in terror and hardly dared to move as her eyes darted around the room nervously. When her gaze landed on the man in the corner, her eyes squeezed tightly shut and a petrified whimper escaped her throat.

'Are you alone?' I asked, ignoring her statement. While the sight of Leutie had momentarily stilled my nerves, the anxiety was quickly rising again. Anyone else could be coming through the door at any second.

'Yes,' she answered weakly. The fear in her eyes made it clear she was telling the truth.

'Let her go, Dax.'

'What—'

'Let her go!' I hissed, cutting off his protests. He shot me a glare over Leutie's shoulder before he released his grip and lowered his knife. Immediately, she darted to the side of the room and pressed her back to the wall like a frightened mouse in a cage trying to escape a hungry, prowling cat.

'Grace . . .' Hayden said warningly in a low tone. I raised my hand slowly to cut him off.

'What do you mean, "you're alive"?' I pressed.

'We all thought you were dead,' Leutie answered. Her eyes never lingered on me for long as they flitted between Dax, Kit, and Hayden, all of whom still had their weapons out and ready. 'You just disappeared and Jonah wouldn't tell anyone what happened to you so we just assumed . . .'

'You just assumed I was dead?'

'Grace, we have to get out of here,' Hayden murmured in my ear as he ducked over. Leutie's eyes flickered to him in confusion. I nodded, acknowledging him without looking.

'Why are you here?' Leutie interrupted. I could feel the tension from all the boys as they willed me not to answer, but something in Leutie's eyes and my knowledge of her gentle nature told me she would understand. This war was affecting her as well, after all.

However, that wasn't enough for me to explain, even though it was fairly obvious. I was a traitor and she had no reason to trust me or to keep my secrets any longer. I just stared at her, feeling the seconds tick by while we wasted time.

Leutie's blue eyes widened suddenly as she looked past me out of the window.

'Someone's coming,' she whispered, eyes flashing back to me.

I whipped around. Sure enough, dark shadows could be seen a long way off, their pace was slow and causal, as if they hadn't spotted us yet. Hayden cursed beside me. My eyes went back to Leutie; she appeared to have an internal debate about something.

'Get out of here,' she whispered sharply.

'Can we trust her?' Kit asked hurriedly, shifting to stand alongside the window to peer out of it anxiously.

I stared at her for a second, and she stared back. She had been my best friend, after all, and she was never the type to stray towards violence.

'Yes,' I murmured. Dax muttered something unintelligible before shifting towards the door. Hayden moved quickly beside me to grab a few papers off the desk, including the one I'd been studying, before folding them up and stuffing them hastily in his pocket.

'Hurry,' Leutie urged, waving her hands at us. 'I'll tell them I found him like this and didn't see anyone . . . just go, please.'

'Come on, Grace,' Hayden said sharply, moving forward to take my arm in his large hand.

He pulled me towards the door, where Kit and Dax had gathered, but my gaze remained on Leutie. She shot me a small, sad smile that I couldn't return. My mind seemed clouded with confusion as Dax pulled the door open and slipped outside, quickly followed by Kit. Hayden was about to pull me out when Leutie's voice stilled my action.

'Grace,' she called suddenly, her voice still a whisper. 'I'm glad you're still alive.'

My chest caved in once at her kind words, and I was hit with a wave of sadness all over again as I remembered I'd left more behind than an asshole brother and a dead father. I'd had a real life here, too, but it was gone now.

'Thank you, Leutie.'

With that, Hayden pulled me through the door and back into the dark shadows between the buildings. The guards were approaching now, but they didn't raise any alarm, so I knew they still hadn't seen us. Hayden's hand grabbed my own, forcing me to keep moving.

'Come on, Grace,' he murmured gently.

I let Kit lead us out of Greystone, bringing up the rear with Hayden, whose hand never left mine. My mind was too preoccupied to be on alert, but I trusted the rest of my team to get us out. We darted silently through shadows, lurked between huts, and skulked around the buildings until we were at the edge of Greystone, where we had first entered.

After a quick glance around in all directions, we started running towards the treeline. My training kicked in as my body carried me without my conscious decision, yet still Hayden held my hand to guide me along. He squeezed it once reassuringly as we sprinted the last few yards to the trees, and we didn't slow down until we were under the thick cover provided by the woods.

I couldn't stop thinking about what had just happened, and while I trusted Leutie, a small part of me now feared she had been lying. Would she reveal us and put yet another target on us? Would she keep her word? My mind whirled in a thousand different directions as we moved quickly through the brush, away from Greystone.

Nine: Consolation
Hayden

Grace's hand was warm as I held it tightly, clinging to her in a desperate attempt to pull her from the depths of her mind. We moved silently through the trees, still very much in stealth mode despite being nearly back to Blackwing now. Kit and Dax moved ahead of us while Grace and I lagged behind, though neither of us spoke. I knew the trip had been loaded with painful reminders of what she'd lost or left behind.

I glanced sideways for what felt like the hundredth time to see her listlessly scanning the ground to avoid tripping without really seeing. I wanted to bring her back to me, hold her to my chest and tell her things would be all right, but there was little I could do at the moment as we trekked back to camp.

I squeezed her hand once, earning her attention as she redirected her gaze at me. She blinked, as if just realising I was there, before she forced a soft smile that didn't reach her eyes. I returned it, but it was hard to make it look sincere when my emotions matched hers. It killed me to see her like this.

'We'll have to go to the raid building to talk with Kit and Dax when we get back, but after that we'll go home, all right?' I told her gently. If she wanted to talk, we could talk, and if she wanted to just go to sleep, we could go to sleep. I would do whatever she wanted if it helped with what she was feeling, but first we needed to address what had happened on the raid.

'That sounds fine,' she said evenly, masking whatever she was thinking inside.

I squeezed her hand again and leaned closer to press a soft kiss to the top of her head in an attempt to make her smile for real. It worked somewhat as she turned to me and sent me the first real sign of happiness since we left, but it still wasn't her usual radiating smile.

The moment ended when we broke through the trees back in Blackwing, which was lit sparsely here and there by candles and lanterns as it always was at night. Grace dropped my hand but remained beside me, hiding our private relationship from anyone who might have been outside. I had almost forgotten that not everyone knew, and was glad for the privacy.

Kit and Dax walked to the raid building first. A woman in her mid-thirties was on duty. She held a sleeping child in her arms, a rare sight for Blackwing. While people did continue to have children, it was at a considerably lower rate than before everything fell apart. Jett had been born into our recent past, delivered by Docc himself. His mother died from a haemorrhage during childbirth, and his father died a few months later from an infected wound obtained on a raid, leaving him to be raised most of his life by Maisie. There was always a sense of wonder around children because they were so rare: without them, the human race would die out.

The woman stepped outside to guard the door and give us privacy. As usual, we gathered around the central table, and I found myself beside Grace once again.

'So how about that raid, huh?' Dax started, opening the conversation.

'Seriously,' Kit muttered in agreement.

'What did you get, Hayden?' Dax asked.

'I don't really know,' I muttered.

All three of them looked at me as I pulled the few papers I'd managed to steal from my pocket. Everyone leaned in as I smoothed them out on the table. The first was a list of supplies it appeared Greystone needed; the second was a list of repairs needed to be made. The third scrap of paper was difficult to decipher, because it consisted of random scribblings as if someone had jotted them down quickly. The fourth paper was perhaps the most interesting, and it was the one Grace had been studying before we were interrupted.

A very clear outline of Blackwing was sketched, with details added here and there. I was reminded of what Grace had described when she told me about the plans she'd come across, perhaps this was an updated version. A few buildings were labelled with things like 'food' and 'weapons'. A sketch of the tower had a large 'X' drawn over it. Other buildings were crossed out, though they were mostly the huts that had burned down in the start of the war.

'How do they know where our stuff is?' Dax questioned as he studied the page. Kit frowned deeply across from me.

'Well, they were spying on us . . .' Grace murmured, speaking for the first time. I looked at her and she shot me a guilty expression. 'They knew I was here so . . . They obviously found some stuff out from just watching us.'

I frowned. I didn't like the idea of the enemy knowing so much about our camp, especially details about where we kept such essential items.

'Is this like the map they had before?' I asked Grace.

'Yeah, pretty much. This one is just updated.'

'Looks like they think the tower is down,' Kit observed, pointing at the 'X' covering the sketch of the tower. 'Malin said it should be safe to use, so that's an advantage, right?'

'Right,' I agreed. While the others focused on the map, I was suddenly less concerned with it. It sounded like they had that information before, and it didn't really help us in terms of the war. What could help us, however, were the lists. 'What about this? If this is a list of things they need, couldn't we do what we can to prevent them from getting it rather than leading an attack?' I mused aloud. If we could stop them from getting supplies, we could *maybe* avoid leading an offensive attack that would surely result in more lives lost.

'And if this stuff is damaged, couldn't we make sure it's unfixable?' Kit added, following my train of thought.

'And we could add to the list of broken items . . .' Dax murmured thoughtfully.

This was it. This was how we could win the war. We were outnumbered, but the war didn't have to be decided entirely by battles fought. We probably wouldn't be able to avoid fighting completely, but maybe we could find other ways to fight other than physical attacks.

'This could work,' I muttered quietly. 'This . . . we could do this. Sneak into their camp, break down what they need, cut off their supplies . . .'

'It won't work,' Grace said, cutting me off. She had been very quiet throughout the exchange and now had all three pairs of eyes focused on her.

'Why not?' Kit asked, a bit harshly, even though I felt his frustration.

'Jonah won't let that stop him. If you do that – destroy everything they have – he'll only be more determined to break you. He'll only fight harder.'

Irritation flashed through me at her argument. I wanted to believe what we'd started to construct would work, but Grace had just shot it down in a few short sentences.

'What else are we supposed to do? Kill them all?' I said sarcastically.

'That's what he's trying to do to us,' Grace said, her voice gravely serious. 'We can't both survive on what's left. He'll risk people dying to win, because if he doesn't, they'll die anyway.'

'So what do we do?' Dax asked.

I felt a heavy wave of frustration wash over me. No matter what we considered, it seemed like there was no way out. If we fought battle for battle, we'd lose countless precious lives for something that was not guaranteed in the first place. If we tried to sabotage them and take out their supplies but spare lives, they'd only fight harder, bringing the danger we were trying to avoid. Peace was impossible, because there wasn't enough to sustain both camps, and the bitter hatred between us only made things worse. There was no solution, no way to end things without devastation and loss of life on both sides.

How had we come to this?

I sighed deeply as I hunched over the table. Grace was hunched similarly, her elbows resting on the surface, her face in her hands as if she were trying to block everything out.

'We don't have to decide tonight. We got some information and that was the point,' I said evenly.

'All right,' Kit said. 'But we have another problem.'

Confusion flitted through me before I realised what he was talking about. I'd almost forgotten that we'd got caught on the raid.

'Grace, your friend . . .' Kit continued.

'Leutie,' she filled in. Her voice was muffled by her palms.

'Yeah, Leutie. Can we trust her?'

Grace let out a deep sigh before pushing herself off the table. She looked exhausted as she glanced around at us each in turn. 'I don't know. I think so.'

Her voice was unconvincing, causing everyone to frown.

'You think so?' Dax repeated sceptically.

'Yeah, Dax, I think so,' she snapped harshly. It was clear she was still very affected from her trip to Greystone and I didn't blame her. It was how I felt every time I visited my old neighbourhood: helpless, frustrated, and perhaps the worst of all, heartbroken.

My hand snaked across the surface of the table to claim hers. My palm rested over the back of her hand and I allowed my thumb to drag slowly across her knuckles. Her gaze turned to me, which was hardened and clearly stressed, before it softened slightly when her eyes found mine. Kit and Dax ignored the gesture, for which I was grateful. Now was not the time for Dax's teasing.

'I think we can trust her,' Grace said. 'She's not the type to want to start trouble, and she hates violence. She's terrified of her own shadow, so I can't imagine her trying to stir up more conflict between us . . .'

'She did seem terrified,' Dax mused. 'She was shaking like a leaf.'

'Yeah, well, that's probably the first time she ever had a knife to her throat,' Grace told him. 'You probably scared the hell out of her.'

'To be fair, she also had two guns pointed at her,' Dax said with a wry grin.

'So not everyone over there is as badass as you?' Kit asked, a rare grin on his lips as he looked at Grace. I was pleased to see a small grin tug at her lips but disappointed I hadn't been the one to earn it.

'No, not everyone,' she said humbly. 'Leutie doesn't do raids. She's pretty soft, so I think we're going to be all right. She'll keep her word.'

She nodded once as if trying to convince herself, and the ghost of a smile slipped from her features once more.

'Let's call it a night, guys. It's late,' I said. I reached to grab the papers and fold them back up before stuffing them into my pocket. My hand pulled from Grace's as I did so.

'Yeah, all right,' Kit agreed.

He and Dax moved to return their guns to the case, taking the weapons Grace and I handed them as well. They chatted quietly about something I couldn't be bothered to listen to as I moved closer to Grace. She was quiet and subdued, avoiding my eye contact while tangling her fingers together in front of her.

'Hey, Bear,' I said so only she could hear. My heart fluttered as a soft smile pulled at her lips and her head rose so her green eyes could find mine.

'Hey, Herc,' she returned softly. I tried to read her thoughts. She pulled me closer, catching the fabric of my shirt in her fist, but nothing more, as if my mere proximity comforted her.

'See you, guys,' Dax called.

I hadn't even noticed, but he and Kit had finished putting their things away and had moved to the door. I managed a quiet goodbye before they left, leaving Grace and I alone. I cradled her face gently and let my thumbs run lightly across her soft skin.

'Are you all right?' I asked, knowing full well she was not. She drew a deep breath into her lungs, pausing before she blew it out.

'Can we go home?' she asked. Her use of the word 'home' sent a small wave of happiness through my veins, though it was quickly extinguished by the pressing need to comfort her.

'Yes,' I answered simply.

Grace moved past me to head towards the door, where the woman on guard and her still sleeping child met us. I murmured a soft 'goodnight' to her as we moved past into the pitch-black night. It was very late now, past midnight probably, and all I wanted to do was crawl into bed and pull Grace into my chest. She was still very much stuck in her head, a fact that was clear to me as we walked silently back to our hut.

Once inside, Grace immediately went to sit on the edge of the bed, while I lit a single candle to give us some light. The soft glow warmed the space, but I could still feel the obvious chill from Grace's mood. Turning to glance at her, I saw she'd hunched forward to hide her face in her hands once more as her elbows rested on her knees.

I undressed down to a pair of athletic shorts, leaving my torso bare. Grace was still fully clothed despite surely being exhausted. I pulled another one of my shirts from the drawer before crossing to her on the bed. It was only when I stopped in front of her that she lifted her head and locked eyes with me.

'Arms up,' I said softly, holding the T-shirt out in front of me.

A small half-smile quirked her lips as she allowed me to slip my larger shirt over her head, where it pooled around her waist. My actions were slow and gentle, meant to calm and relax her rather than start something physical.

'Come here,' I murmured as I knelt in front of her to rest on my haunches. My hands gripped her knees momentarily and tugged lightly.

She scooted to the edge of the bed to let my fingers undo the buttons on her shorts. I could feel her gaze on me as I worked, heating my skin as she watched me undress and redress her. My fingers dug beneath the band of her shorts and tugged them down her legs, leaving her in just her underwear.

'Good?'

'Perfect,' she responded.

I nodded once before climbing onto the bed and inching behind her. My arms wrapped around her shoulders and tugged her backward, until my back leaned against the wall. She giggled quietly until we were both propped up together. She settled between my legs, leaning back against me while her hands came up to hold my forearms that rested over her chest.

'Do you want to talk about it?' I asked. I saw a frown pull at her lips.

'I don't know,' she said slowly. 'This has to be how you feel, right? When you go back to your neighbourhood?'

We both had places we'd left behind now, places we'd lost people, places we had memories that would not be expanded.

'Yes, Grace.'

'I'm sorry you ever have to feel like this,' she murmured, ducking her chin down to press a light kiss into the skin covering my forearm.

'Hey, this isn't about me, all right?' I replied lightly. 'Don't worry about me.'

'It's just weird, you know? Seeing my old house and where he died . . .'

'That was your house?' I knew exactly which house she was referring to because I specifically remembered the look that had fallen on her face the moment she'd laid eyes on it.

'Yeah,' she said, nodding. 'It's easier to block it out here, but when it's right there . . .'

'It's tough,' I said, finishing for her. 'It'll get easier, but I can't tell you it goes away, because I'd be lying.'

My mind flitted briefly to my own memories of my parents. I'd lost them when I was five, but Grace had shared a few more years with her mother, and her entire life with her father. Was it worse to lose your parents early with hardly any memories or to share a lifetime of moments only to have them ripped so suddenly from you?

Both.

Each was bad.

'When will it get easier?' she asked, her voice laced with desperation. 'Because I thought I was doing all right until it was all back in front of me. Seeing everything I've lost or left . . . it's hard.'

'I don't know, love,' I murmured into her shoulder. My lips puckered against her skin to press another kiss gently there. 'But I'm here with you. You know that, right?'

'I know . . . I just feel selfish talking about it when you've lost so much,' she said, twisting suddenly in my grasp to face me. Her legs looped over my thigh as she sat sideways, twisting at the torso so her gaze could connect with mine. My arms loosened from her shoulders to fall around her waist, keeping my hold on her.

'Don't say that,' I pleaded.

'It's true, though . . .' she trailed off, frowning.

'It's not, Grace. We've both lost people and it hurts no matter when it happened or how long we got to be with them. Don't feel selfish for talking to me about what you're feeling . . . What can I do if I can't be here for you, huh?'

Her eyes studied me intently, as if she wanted to believe my words but didn't quite dare let herself.

114

'I mean it,' I promised.

She let out a heavy sigh before looping her arms around her neck, hugging herself into my chest. My hand around her waist tightened to hug her against me while my other hand shifted to the back of her head to trail over the soft strands soothingly.

'I love you, Hayden,' she murmured quietly. Her warm breath tickled over my neck, and I could feel my pulse beating against where her body pressed to mine.

'And I love you, Grace,' I returned easily. I pressed a kiss into her temple as I continued to hug her to me. 'You'll be okay, I know it.'

'You're right,' she agreed softly. Her lips pushed lightly against the base of my throat before she pulled back just enough to look me in the eye once more. 'You know how I know that?'

'Tell me, wise one,' I said lightly. I smiled when I saw a real grin pull at her lips.

'I'll be okay because I have you.'

'You do have me.'

She had no idea just how much she had me.

Ten: Perceive

Hayden

A soft breeze picked up the hairs at the back of my neck as I walked through Blackwing. The sun was glowing in the late afternoon sky, and melodic tweets from birds were accompanied by the soft crunching of my boots in the dirt and the light tinkling of children's laughter as I passed a family's hut.

My companion was so different to the one I was used to, and I'd found myself tuning out several times already.

'. . . and then I told Maisie that I don't want to go to school anymore because Rainey keeps trying to sit by me and it's weird,' he said as I tuned back in. I was amused by his traditional boyish fear of girls. My mind flashed to what Grace had told me about that night the war started and he'd suddenly found his bravery when it meant protecting Rainey and her younger sister.

'You have to go to school, Jett,' I said evenly. 'How else will you learn stuff, huh?'

'It hardly counts as school,' he grumbled, frowning in exaggeration.

The 'school' in Blackwing was really just a man in his mid-sixties who taught the children the essentials of a wide variety of topics and educated them on survival skills, but it was the best we could do and better than nothing. Most kids stopped going once they mastered all the basics, and Jett probably had a year or two left before he could stop.

'You know, Grace told me something,' I said, flashing a rare grin down at him. His head jerked up as he looked at me anxiously, tripping over a divot in the path before righting himself. He had to jog a few paces to catch up to me.

'Wh-what did she tell you?' he stuttered.

'She said she thought you might like Rainey a bit more than you let on.' My tone carried a hint of amusement as I watched him squirm uncomfortably beside me.

'No I don't! Girls are lame,' he said, crossing his arms tightly over his chest. 'I don't even like Rainey a little.'

'Girls aren't lame,' I told him lightly.

'Yes they are.'

'You like Grace, don't you? She's a girl,' I pointed out.

'Yeah, but she's like . . . your age. Old. I don't like her like you do,' he said, sticking out his tongue as if the idea grossed him out. I blinked in surprise, as I hadn't realised Jett was really aware enough to notice my feelings for Grace.

'How convenient, then, that Rainey is your age,' I said smoothly, ignoring his previous statement.

'I don't like her, Hayden!' he said a bit too loudly. He looked around to make sure no one had heard before shooting me a quick glare.

'Methinks thou doth protest too much,' I said with a shake of my head and a wide grin.

'What?' he asked. His nose wrinkled up in confusion as his head cocked backward.

'Never mind,' I murmured. It was something Docc used to say to Kit, Dax and me when we were younger and tried to lie about sneaking off. Our overreaching denial only confirmed our guilt.

'I don't like her,' he said yet again, frowning at the dirt

117

as we continued to walk. A low chuckle rumbled from my chest.

'Whatever you say, pal.'

He then mumbled something I couldn't quite make out. It felt odd to be in such a light mood, but it was nice. It had been over a week since our visit to Greystone, and there had been no trouble. Each day, we grew a little less anxious and a little more reassured, though we never let our guard down.

Grace, who was currently with Docc to learn some more advanced medical skills, was back to her old self again. With Grace's spirits up once again, mine had risen as well, leaving us both in remarkably good moods.

'Where are we going now?' Jett asked.

'Raid building,' I replied. He'd been following me around all day and my good mood had made me much more tolerant of him and his incessant questions than usual. And, I had to admit, it was fun to playfully tease him a bit.

'Why?'

'We're doing our first surveillance run tonight,' I told him. He didn't know about the situation with the Brutes, but he nodded and acted like he knew what I was talking about.

'Ohh, yeah,' he said unconvincingly.

Our conversation ended as we arrived at the raid building.

'Best run along now, Jett. I'll see you later, all right?'

'Okay, bye, Hayden!' he said before waving once. I got the impression he was all right with parting ways after I'd interrogated him about Rainey.

I pushed to let myself into the building. I could hear voices from inside, followed by the familiar beautiful sound of Grace's laugh. Once inside, I could see she was talking to Kit, Dax, and Docc. I tried to ignore the tiny flicker of jealousy upon seeing her laughing with everyone else.

'Hey,' I said as I joined them around the table as usual.

'Now, Abraham,' Dax started, leaning over to rest on his elbow in an overly casual manner. 'Just because you're the boss around here doesn't mean you can be late to our meetings.'

Grace stood directly across from me, locking eyes on mine as she chuckled at Dax's words. Her eyes practically glowed as she looked at me, and I couldn't help but return her grin. It felt odd to have been separated from her for most of the day.

'Sorry, I have actual work to do unlike you, so you'll have to forgive my tardiness,' I joked, raising a sarcastic eyebrow at Dax. He placed his hand over his heart as if offended.

'You wound me,' he said dramatically. It wasn't true – I knew Dax worked as hard as anyone, trying to repair the jeep that had been damaged the day we discovered the massive group of Brutes – but it was still Dax, and he deserved it for how much he dished it out.

'So,' Docc interrupted, refocusing everyone.

'Right, yeah,' I muttered, shaking my head once. 'I don't think all of us should go, because I don't like leaving camp so vulnerable without at least one of us here.'

My eyes darted from person to person to see them all nodding in agreement.

'We could just rotate? Take turns doing it?' Kit offered.

'Yeah, I think that'd be best. At least two, if not three of us go, one stays here with Docc?'

'Yeah, that sounds good,' Dax agreed, nodding.

'And you'll be leaving soon?' Docc asked. He would never go along on the raid, but he was a respected member of our camp and often the one left in charge, so he was included in the meetings.

'Yeah, as soon as we're done. I got the jeep packed earlier

today,' I answered. 'Who wants to sit this one out?'

Everyone stared at each other, reluctant to volunteer to miss the action. My eyes landed on Grace and she immediately shook her head no. Of course.

'Well obviously you two are going,' Dax said, rolling his eyes as he gestured between Grace and I. 'Can't split up the happy couple, so rock, paper, scissors, Kit?'

'Shut up, Dax,' I muttered. As much as I didn't want Grace to be put into danger, I felt more comfortable taking her with me where I knew I could protect her than leaving her behind. She didn't need my protection, but there would never come a time where she didn't have it.

Kit and Dax both leaned over the table to figure out who was coming with us while I ignored them. Docc let out a low chuckle as he refereed between Kit and Dax. I joined Grace on the other side of the table.

'Hello,' she greeted brightly. Her blonde hair was pulled back into a loose braid, and wisps of hair had fallen around her face.

'Hello back,' I returned. 'How was your training with Docc?'

'Very educational,' she laughed. 'A lot of it went over my head, but I think I learned a few things.'

'Good,' I said simply.

'*Ha!*' Dax shouted suddenly, interrupting our small conversation. 'Guess who's stuck with me?'

'Great,' I joked, rolling my eyes.

'You lot have fun,' Kit said, giving a small wave. 'See you tomorrow when you get back.'

'And be careful,' Docc added calmly. We all agreed and waved as they exited the raid building.

After gathering our weapons, Grace, Dax and I headed to the garage. The sun was starting to go down, now, and

I knew I wanted to have our surveillance place picked out and settled before nightfall. A single lantern lit the garage, illuminating our jeep. Dax had tried to patch the countless bullet holes in the vehicle and had been only partially successful, though luckily most of the damage was only superficial, meaning we could still use it.

The back was already filled with our supplies, which were more extensive since we planned on staying the night in the city, when Brutes tended to be most active. I was reminded of the last trip in the city when Grace, Dax, and I had had to sleep there, only this time, it would be on purpose. This time, we were prepared.

Dax had already claimed the front seat. Before long, the three of us were loaded up and driving out of Blackwing. As always, I could feel Grace's presence behind me. The smile she aimed at me as I drove brought a grin to my own lips.

'So once we get there, we'll stash the jeep somewhere and find a building to hide in around the Armoury,' I said to both of them. 'We can take shifts on who watches and who sleeps, but I think we should have two on watch at all times so we don't miss anything.'

'Sounds good,' Dax said.

'What are we watching for?' Grace asked.

'Anything, I guess. How many come and go, if they bring anything in or out, whatever you can see, really.'

They both nodded again. I was surprised to see we were already on the edge of the city. All three of us grew more alert as we started to pass through the tattered streets, keeping an eye out for Brutes or anyone else who might want to harm us. I drove as quickly as I could without drawing too much attention, increasingly cautious as we approached the Armoury.

'Keep an eye out for somewhere to set up for the night,' I instructed.

With one more turn, the small auto body shop that led to the underground bunker came into view. There were several buildings around it that would provide a good view of the entrance, giving us several options.

'What about there?' Grace asked, leaning between the front seats to point at a tall building of maybe twenty stories across from the auto body shop. 'If we go up to the fifth or sixth floor maybe?'

'And look – there's a garage on the lower floors where we could hide the jeep,' Dax added.

I stilled the car, leaning forward over the wheel to squint at the building. It didn't really stand out much and had a good view of the entrance, making it our best option.

'Yeah, all right,' I said. 'Keep a good lookout, now. They can't know we're here.'

Adrenaline spiked in my system as I drove towards the entrance to the parking ramp, making sure to avoid the debris that littered the streets and might make noise to alert the Brutes below ground. I was relieved when we disappeared up the shadow of the ramp, which was darker thanks to the quickly setting sun. My eyes constantly scanned the route for enemies, but I didn't see any as I drove all the way to the highest level, although the building itself continued upward, for several stories.

I directed the jeep into a far corner behind a pillar, hiding it from view as best I could before turning off the engine and pulling out the key.

'Everybody grab some supplies, then we'll scope it out. Keep your guns ready.'

With that, we all jumped out of the jeep, putting on our own backpacks that contained all of our equipment. Grace and I stood on the same side of the car while Dax secured his items on the other. I was about to turn to her to fulfil our promise when she surprised me by leaning up to press a kiss along my jaw.

'Love you. Be careful,' she said with a soft smile.

'You be careful, too. I love you.'

Her grin widened a bit more before she turned to move around the jeep. I followed, but took the lead as we moved towards the door that led to a staircase that I assumed would bring us to the upper levels. All three of our guns were raised as we made our silent way up the stairs. Once we reached the next level, we found ourselves in the lobby; it was clear that this had once been an apartment building.

A thick layer of dust had settled over everything, and much of the place had been torn apart by those who had been here before us, but it was pretty clear that had been a long time ago. Nonetheless, we continued silently as we swept through the area, checking each of the rooms on the floor but finding no signs of life.

'Clear,' I murmured. 'Next one.

The second floor housed four apartments, all of them looted of anything useful, though devoid of any life. The third and fourth floors were about the same, but the fifth floor appeared to be less damaged. The doors still worked on the apartments, and it looked as though no one had bothered coming up this high after stripping the lower floors. We continued one floor higher, just to be certain. Yet again we found no one. My heart, which had been beating a little faster with adrenaline, finally started to slow down a bit when it was obvious no one was present.

'Try that one,' Grace said, pointing to a door along the left.

My hand closed around the handle and turned it. I was surprised it wasn't locked but pleased as I opened the door slowly, leading with my gun. The sun was nearly completely down now, making it relatively dark inside. My eyes scanned the apartments. The main room appeared to be a living room, a small dining room, and a kitchen all in one, with two doors leading to what I assumed to be a bedroom and a bathroom.

Slowly, I led us inside, making sure to keep Grace behind me. I focused on keeping my breathing even and quiet as I approached the first door, listening closely for any signs of life. A quick glance over my shoulder at Grace and Dax behind me told me they still had their guns ready. I reached for the handle on the first door. It turned just as the front one had, opening the door slowly.

A bedroom was revealed, featuring a double bed, a few dressers, and even a TV, not that it would work without electricity. After ducking down to check below the bed and opening the closet doors, I declared the room cleared as well.

Dax checked the last door, pausing to listen before opening it. A sudden flash of movement caused all three of us to jump, and Dax's free arm whipped upward violently in surprise. I darted forward to tug Grace clear, but it quickly became clear we were not in any danger.

'Jesus,' Dax muttered, letting out a deep breath as he looked at us wildly.

The flash of movement happened again, this time streaking towards the front door before disappearing down the hall. It was no more than a common brown rat, escaping those who had invaded its apparent home in the bathroom. After it was gone, Dax moved to the front door to close and lock it.

'Just a rat,' I murmured. I released my grip on Grace's arm as she glanced at me.

'So is this where you want to set up?' she asked.

'I think so,' I replied.

The three of us returned to the main room and headed to the window to glance out. A clear view of the street below and the entrance to the auto body shop that hid the door to the Armoury were visible from our vantage point, making it an excellent place to observe. The apartment wasn't in too bad shape, either, which was an added bonus. The furniture was a bit dusty, but it would be more than satisfactory for our purpose.

'It looks good to me,' Dax assented. 'Who wants first watch?'

'I will,' I offered. I still felt the adrenaline of our journey up here and wouldn't be able to sleep.

'I will, too,' Grace said. I was glad, because I felt like I hadn't seen her all day.

'Bed it is for me, then,' Dax said as he rubbed his hands together. He shrugged off his backpack and set it on one of the lounge chairs in the living room. 'I'll leave the door open just in case. Keep it down out here, will you?'

Grace chuckled. 'We'll try.'

'Much appreciated,' he said with a mock bow before he headed into the bedroom. Soon the springs of the mattress squeaked under his weight, then silence settled as Dax got comfortable, leaving Grace and I alone in the living room.

'Shall we?' I asked, ticking my head towards the window. She nodded.

'We shall.'

I grabbed one side of a love seat along the wall as Grace grabbed the other, and we brought it to the window so we could sit and keep watch. We piled our bags nearby in case we needed anything but didn't bother lighting any candles or lanterns. Grace stowed her gun on the window ledge, and I set mine down on the armrest of the love seat before settling into it.

Without a word, I reached up to grab Grace's hand and tug her down next to me.

'This place seems so nice,' Grace said, keeping her voice low so as not to disturb Dax. I blinked and glanced around, nodding.

'I guess so, yeah. Weird, isn't it?'

I'd noticed things I hadn't seen the first time. Another TV, as well as a large, expensive-looking stereo. There was a glass case filled with trinkets and knick-knacks, and a massive decorative vase in the corner. These were things people didn't need to survive but had, at one point, owned anyway. Maybe in a different time, I would have had stuff like this too, but now I couldn't possibly wrap my head around it. It all seemed so superfluous.

'Very weird,' she agreed. 'Why would anyone need this stuff?'

'I have no idea,' I murmured.

We heard a soft squeak from the bedroom as Dax shifted on the old mattress, reminding us of his presence.

I glanced out of the window but saw no movement coming from the street below. My fingers continued to tickle across Grace's skin absent-mindedly, tracing little circles along her legs.

'Hey, Hayden?' she started softly.

'Hmm?'

'This might sound weird but . . . has Dax ever . . . had someone?' she asked, lowering her voice even more.

'"Had" someone?' I questioned.

'Yeah, like, I have you, you have me . . . Has he ever had that?'

My brows furrowed low as I thought back. Dax had always been fairly light-hearted, but there had been a time a few years ago when his sunny outlook had dimmed. A girl's face swam in my mind, and I pictured her strawberry blonde hair and light brown eyes as she grinned at Dax.

'He did once,' I said slowly. My eyes focused on the windowsill in front of me as the memories came back.

'Really?' She sounded surprised as she spoke. 'Who?'

'It was a girl named Violetta,' I answered. 'She was a year younger than us, I'd say, and they were together for about twelve months when we were eighteen or so.'

I felt a sudden wave of sadness as I remembered how things had ended, a feeling that only intensified as I pictured myself in that same situation with Grace. My hands squeezed her legs lightly, as if to remind myself that she was right there.

'He loved her?' Her voice was soft as she spoke, as if she already knew this story did not have a happy ending.

I nodded slowly.

'I think so. She wasn't into him at first, but you know Dax . . . wears people down. Eventually she gave in and they were pretty inseparable from then on.'

I remembered seeing them together and feeling confused by their relationship. It had seemed so strange to me, to tie yourself to one person and put yourself in that vulnerable position, but I couldn't deny the hint of jealousy I felt when I noticed how obviously happy they both were. There wasn't a day she wasn't laughing at something he said, and there wasn't a day he didn't look at her like she was the sun.

I could feel Grace holding back from asking the question I knew was coming. My fingertips trailed down across her soft skin once more.

'Go ahead, ask,' I said softly.

Grace frowned gently and pulled her brows together. Her voice was quiet and laced with emotion as she spoke.

'What happened to her?'

'She died,' I said simply. 'Ran into some Brutes on the first raid she ever went on.'

I chewed my lower lip, mind buzzing with these sad memories I hadn't thought about in ages. Grace remained quiet as she mulled over my story, and all the while my fingers never ceased their actions.

'I think he blamed himself. He was out of it for a long time, and since then he hasn't really taken much seriously,' I explained quietly.

'That's very sad,' Grace said, sincerely. I nodded, unsure of what else to add.

A voice that startled us both. 'Yes, it is.'

We whipped our heads towards the source, and I immediately was filled with guilt. Dax leaned in the doorway of the bedroom, arms folded loosely across his chest. His gaze was fixed on a random spot on the floor, but his pained expression made it clear he'd heard every word we'd just spoken. I tried to think of something to say, but nothing came to mind. It didn't matter, though, because Dax spoke once more.

'Quite the bedtime story, yeah? Sweet dreams.'

Eleven: Discrepancy

Grace

'Quite the bedtime story, yeah? Sweet dreams.'

My heart plummeted in my chest as I heard Dax utter those words. His tone was laced heavily with hurt. He didn't look at us as he let his gaze linger on the ground, unfocused and unseeing. A heavy silence hung around us for a few tense moments before he let out a deep sigh and heaved himself off the door frame. Finally, his gaze flicked up to look at Hayden and me, flashing a small grimace before he started to turn to head back into the bedroom.

'Wait, Dax,' I blurted, unable to stop myself.

He paused and turned back to me, his expression blank.

'I'm sorry,' I said lamely. 'I – we – we shouldn't have been talking about it . . .'

'There's nothing to be sorry for,' he said calmly, shrugging. His voice sounded honest, but it was impossible to miss the pain there.

'Yeah but . . .' I trailed off weakly.

Surely it had hurt to hear us speaking of Violetta. It had nearly ripped me in half to talk about Hayden after he sent me back to Greystone and he was still alive; I couldn't imagine the pain of losing someone you were in love with. It was a different pain to losing a parent – it was like losing half of your soul. I was suddenly acutely aware of Hayden's fingers brushing softly over the skin on my ankles and resisted the urge to hug him.

'Mate, we really didn't mean for you to hear,' Hayden said. I could tell he felt guilty from the way his brows pinched together and from the tightness his jaw held.

'It's fine, really,' Dax said. 'Violetta has been dead three years. Talking about her won't make her any more dead.'

His tone was flat now, as if he were withholding emotion. My heart clenched painfully for him as his eyes swept between Hayden and I, noting the intimate way we were seated. A soft, sad smile pulled at his lips.

'I'm sorry, Dax,' I said quietly.

He nodded once, knowing I wasn't apologising for our whispered conversation; I was apologising for his loss.

'Yeah,' he said calmly. 'I'm going to head back to bed, all right? Wake me in a few hours for my turn.'

With that, Dax nodded once more and retreated back into the bedroom. I heard the squeak of the mattress again as he climbed back onto the bed.

'Jesus . . .' I muttered guiltily.

Hayden didn't speak but squeezed my ankle lightly in acknowledgement. Then he reached for my hand that rested on my thigh, grasping it gently to pull me forward. He touched my cheek, guiding me to his face so he could press his lips gently onto my own.

The kiss was soft, gentle, and simple, but I could feel the weight behind it. After being reminded of how easy it was to lose the one you loved, he needed reassurance that I was there with him. I felt it too at that moment.

When Hayden pulled back, his hand remained on my cheek. His eyes were closed as he lingered there, allowing his thumb to drag gently across my skin. We remained silent as he pulled back with a soft smile to resettle into our previous position. He knew how much I loved him, as I knew how much he loved me. We didn't need to say it and risk Dax hearing it; I didn't want to upset him any more than he already was.

I should have been keeping watch like Hayden, but all I could think about was Dax and Violetta. He'd always seemed so happy, so carefree, but this discovery that he hadn't always been that way was shocking. As Hayden explained it, he'd lost his natural light-heartedness after losing Violetta, a thought that broke my heart.

It explained so much about him. He joked around so much because he had to in order to fight off the pain. He didn't take anything seriously because the one thing he probably had taken seriously had ended tragically. He'd been so supportive of Hayden and I before we even admitted to anything because it probably reminded him of how he felt with Violetta. He wanted that for Hayden, because he knew how it felt.

With every realisation, my heart broke a little bit more. I'd always known Dax was a good friend to Hayden, more like a brother than anything, but I'd had no idea about this dark memory that probably haunted him. He seemed so happy and carefree, but this information made me realise that he, too, had suffered. Even the happiest of people weren't always truly happy.

My gaze, which had been aimed unfocusedly at my knees, shifted up to study Hayden, who was looking out of the window, watching below for disturbances, while absent-mindedly letting his fingertips trail over my skin. My gaze had just travelled over his slightly unruly brows when he leaned forward, suddenly attentive.

'What is it?' I asked, turning to look out of the window.

'There's one,' Hayden said softly, pointing towards the entrance to the auto body shop.

I squinted as I tried to take in as much detail as possible. Sure enough, one man appeared, walking down the pavement, quick and alert. He swept a large gun around him as he searched for enemies.

'Guard?' I questioned.

'Probably.'

My eyes shifted to the other side of the building as I waited for the man to reappear. My leg bounced up and down nervously as anxious jitters settled in. A few more tense moments passed before the man reappeared exactly where I'd been looking, continuing his rounds and confirming our suspicions. With one last sweep of the area around him, he arrived at the door and disappeared back inside.

Hayden let out a deep breath and leaned back in his seat, nodding once to himself. 'Now we wait for another one, I suppose. Then we'll know how often they do rounds.'

'Sounds good,' I agreed. I relaxed and resumed my position, allowing Hayden to place his hands on my legs once more. We fell into comfortable silence, and my thoughts returned to Dax, Violetta, and the strong reminder that it could very easily happen to Hayden and me. The adrenaline spike that seeing the Brute had caused carried over now into my fierce determination to prevent that from happening.

After about an hour, Hayden moved again, noting another Brute emerge from the opening of the auto body shop. He copied the previous guard by sweeping all the way around the building once before disappearing. This happened again an hour later.

'Looks like they go every hour,' Hayden whispered.

'That's good to know,' I said, and some of the trepidation lessened now that we knew what to expect.

I shifted around momentarily to try and get comfortable after sitting in the same position for several hours. Hayden hadn't moved much, though he showed no signs of discomfort. Only a few minutes had passed since the last guard, and I was preparing myself for another quiet hour when Hayden leaned forward suddenly, moving faster than he had all night.

I jumped at his sudden movement and jerked my head to the side to look out of the window as well. I squinted through the darkness, unable to see what Hayden had at first. As I looked closer, however, I saw a medium-sized group of people slinking along the street.

'Brutes,' Hayden murmured.

I pulled my legs from his lap and turned so I could get a clearer view as we both got as close as possible to the window. We were too high up for them to see us, and we still had no source of light to give us away.

'How many?' I whispered. I tried to count as they moved, but it was difficult. My eyes slid over each one as they moved towards the entrance to the auto body shop that led to the Armoury, and I managed to count seven of them before I saw something that made suck in a surprised gasp. 'Wait . . .'

'Oh no,' Hayden muttered tensely.

The seven Brutes I counted were accompanied by several more, numbering probably twelve or thirteen, but what had surprised Hayden and me wasn't their relatively large number. Between them, held firmly by two large men, was a struggling girl who was clearly trying to break free. Her feet dragged every few steps as she fought, but she was unable to free herself from their tight grip as they moved along the pavement. I'd never seen her before, but she looked to be a few years younger than us, and very unwilling to be going with the Brutes.

A flash of movement to my right jerked my attention towards Hayden, where I saw him straining to open the window. The muscles in his arm bulged and his face contorted in a grimace as he tugged upward, but the window seemed to have rusted shut with age and wouldn't budge.

'Hayden.'

'Help me open the window,' he requested sharply, grunting once as he strained against it again.

'Hayden, we can't do anything to help her,' I said softly, shaking my head.

'What? Yes we can, help me,' he argued quickly. He struggled against the window some more, but too many years had passed and made the feat impossible.

A quick glance out the window told me the Brutes and the girl were nearly at the door now, lessening our opportunities to help her. She thrashed roughly, trying to rip her arms from their grip, but it didn't work. One of the men walking behind her raised his hand to shove her roughly, causing her to stumble and nearly fall before the men holding her arms yanked her upward again.

'Hayden, we can't,' I repeated.

'We have to help her, Grace!' he said angrily.

He gave up on the window with a frustrated grunt and slammed his fist down on the windowsill before he grabbed his gun and took a step towards the door. I sprang to my feet instantly, grabbing him by the wrist to jerk him back towards me.

'No, Hayden,' I said firmly. 'We can't help.'

A pained expression crossed Hayden's face, where it mixed with the frustration already there. His intense gaze was trained on the events down below, but I couldn't tear my eyes away from his face to look. His hands clenched to fists by his sides, and he blew out a shaky breath, causing his nostrils to flare because of his tightly clamped jaw.

'Why not?' he spat, finally jerking his gaze back to me. He glared down at me, and I figured the Brutes must have disappeared into the building with the girl by now.

'Did you see how many of them there were? At least twelve, and you know there are way more hiding in the Armoury. There is no way we could help her, Hayden.'

'But—'

'No!' I said, raising my voice in exasperation. 'I'm not letting you get killed to try and save some stranger.'

'Do you know what they're going to do to her?!' Hayden growled, raising a tense hand towards the window.

I swallowed harshly and blew out a deep breath. I remembered the night we'd barely escaped the Armoury and hid in the auto body shop as some Brutes had walked by. The tone of their conversation made it very clear they were hungry for some female company, and that they didn't care how they got what they desired. I squeezed my eyes shut as I tried not to picture what they would force that girl to do, but images of hands tearing at her clothes and forcing her down appeared anyway. My heart pounded almost painfully hard in my chest, but I shook my head to dislodge the thoughts. My eyes opened and I was met with Hayden's intense glare. I drew a deep, determined breath.

'Still,' I said softly, 'there's nothing we can do, Hayden.'

'She's right, mate.'

Both of us jumped as Dax reappeared. 'Can't risk any of us dying for some stranger.'

It was harsh, cruel, inhuman even, but it was the truth. If we were to try and save that girl, there was no way we'd all make it out alive. We were vastly outnumbered, and they were probably already in the depths of the Armoury now. As bad as I felt for that girl, it wasn't bad enough to risk losing Hayden.

Hayden, on the other hand, didn't seem to agree with Dax and me. While we were both selfish enough to stand by and let it play out, Hayden seemed to be struggling with sitting by and doing nothing. He would risk his life for a stranger, something he'd already proven once by rescuing me ages ago.

'This is wrong,' he said finally. He pointed out of the window and glared down at me. 'That girl . . . something awful is going to happen to her and we're just going to let it?'

'Yes,' I answered coldly. 'Because I'm not losing you for her. I don't care about her. I care about *you*.'

Hayden scoffed and shook his head. My stomach twisted tightly at his obvious disappointment, but it wasn't enough for me to take back what I'd said. It made me sound cruel, callous, but there was no denying the truth. No matter the situation, I'd pick the ones I loved over a stranger every single time. They were what mattered to me, not strangers.

'She's a human being,' Hayden argued through his clenched jaw. His brow ticked up as if he was having a hard time controlling his emotions.

'She's a stranger,' I replied. He was only a foot away from me, but somehow he felt out of reach. We stared each other down, both refusing to give in.

'You were a stranger,' he stated, his voice suddenly deadly calm. 'Imagine if I'd followed your advice before I'd saved you after everyone else had gone.'

'That's not the same and you know it.'

My voice had lost some of its conviction, and I felt my

136

chest cave in a bit. But when he'd saved me, there hadn't been twelve or thirteen Brutes around me with more waiting. And if I hadn't spared him that first night, he maybe wouldn't have saved me. If he hadn't had Jett with him, maybe I wouldn't have let him go. All the 'what ifs' and 'maybes' in the world weren't enough for me to let him go now.

'I can't lose you, Hayden,' I said quietly, my anger gone.

Hayden studied me intensely for a few moments. Finally, I saw some of his resolve melt away as he blew out a deep breath.

'You're not going to lose me, Grace,' he murmured. My eyes sought his, desperately trying to get him to see my reasoning and understand why I'd said the things I had.

'You're not losing me either, guys, don't worry,' Dax said from the side. I had completely forgotten about him in the heat of the argument. A wry smile tugged at his lips, but it didn't reach his eyes as if his mind was still wounded from our conversation earlier.

But I was grateful he'd sided with me. That way, at least I wasn't the only selfish asshole.

'Thank goodness,' I managed to say.

'Hayden, why don't you get some sleep? Grace and I can take watch for a bit,' Dax offered.

Hayden, who still appeared very uneasy with our decision to do nothing, pushed his hand roughly through his hair before he let it drop back down to his side. A sigh of frustration pushed past his lips before he nodded sharply. My hand drifted out as if to touch him, but he took a step backward out of my reach. I tried to ignore the tiny sting of rejection and told myself he just needed some time to cool down a bit.

'Yeah, all right.' His voice was deep and low, and oddly

void of emotion. His gaze flitted to mine briefly before he headed towards the bedroom, trading places with Dax. 'Wake me if you see anything.'

'We will,' I said softly.

I already knew, however, that he wouldn't sleep. He would lie there and mull over what we'd just seen, tearing himself apart because we hadn't been able to do anything even if it was the only way to ensure our survival. He'd feel guilt he didn't deserve, while all I felt was relief.

Hayden simply nodded and moved into the dark room, leaving Dax and I alone in the living room. I felt off about how things had ended, as if we hadn't resolved the fight, but in that moment I was just glad he remained in the safety of the apartment instead of on his way into the depths of the Armoury where almost certain death awaited him.

It was what was the best for us, even if Hayden didn't like it. We were, momentarily, safe, and that was all that mattered.

Twelve: Altruism

Grace

Dax and I sat in silence for what felt like ages, though truthfully it probably hadn't been more than a half hour. It was so different to when I'd been keeping watch with Hayden. Dax and I sat as far apart as we could, while my legs curled up tightly beneath me. He didn't speak, as if he didn't want to break the silence.

I was reluctant to speak to him, as I knew Hayden was probably lying there right now, mulling over the decision to do nothing and hating himself for it. I wanted nothing more than to go to him and try to comfort him, but part of me feared he'd reject me again. The only thing that managed to keep me calm was the fact that even though Hayden might resent me for it now, Dax and I had won, keeping us all safe.

'Brute,' Dax muttered, ripping me from my thoughts.

I blinked and shook my head to refocus as I stared out of the window. After leaning forward, I could see yet another Brute making the rounds just as others had before. It was the first we'd seen since the large group had disappeared with the girl. Dax and I watched him until he reappeared on the other side of the building. Just as before, he went back inside the front doors.

'Like clockwork,' I murmured quietly.

I relaxed back into the couch, curling into the ball I'd

been in before. Dax resumed his previous position. Silence enveloped us once more, and I found myself fidgeting with a loose thread on the arm of the couch, twisting it around my finger over and over again as I tried not to picture what was happening to the girl. She'd looked years younger than me, seventeen or eighteen maybe, and entirely too young to be in such a situation.

'Did we do the right thing, Dax?' I frowned. The thread twisted around my finger, cutting off the blood supply momentarily and turning the tip of it a dark reddish purple before I untwisted it again.

'Depends what you mean by "the right thing", I suppose,' Dax answered quietly.

'I don't know.'

'Hayden was probably right,' Dax started. 'But in terms of what's best for us and Blackwing . . . *we* did the right thing. We would have all died for someone we don't know, and she still wouldn't have made it out.' He went on, 'We had no choice, Grace. Hayden will come around, don't worry.'

'I don't think he will,' I replied with a small shake of my head. 'But I hope you're right.'

'I am. Better one person than four, right?'

I couldn't tell if he truly believed it or if he was just trying to make me feel better, but there was no denying that logic. One life condemned was better than four.

'Right,' I agreed quietly. I jumped when I felt his fist nudge my shoulder lightly like I'd seen him do to Kit or Hayden so many times before, turning my gaze to him.

'Look, I know I'm not the one you probably want to be talking to about this but . . . we're friends, yeah? I'm here for you.'

It was a nice feeling to know that Dax included me as a part of their makeshift family.

'Thank you, Dax. Same to you, all right? You guys are like my family now,' I replied honestly. The only member of my family left alive had tried to kill me, sharply severing that tie.

'Aww,' Dax said sarcastically, flashing a wide grin at me. I extended my arm to shove him playfully.

'Shut up,' I said with a light shake of my head.

My smile faded, however, as I realised what he said to be true. Of course I appreciated Dax's friendship and support, but he was right.

'Go talk to him,' Dax said. My gaze flicked up from where it had fallen to look at him again to discover him studying me closely.

'I don't think he wants me to,' I answered honestly. My voice was tight and my stomach flipped over anxiously.

'He'll talk to you,' Dax said assuredly. 'You're his *lover*.'

A surprising snort of laughter escaped from my throat as my face pulled into an expression of disgust. 'Oh god, please never say that again.'

Dax's grin was wide, though his eyes still held a hint of sadness in them as he smiled at me.

'All right, all right. Seriously, just go and talk to him. You'll both feel better if you do.'

I sighed, and forced my finger to release the thread I'd been playing with. I felt jittery as I gathered myself and nodded to Dax. Hayden and I hardly ever fought, and if we did, it was relatively short-lived, so this situation was stressing me out considerably. My joints felt stiff as I rose from the couch and started to move towards the bedroom before I paused and turned back.

'Thanks, Dax.'

He nodded at me. 'Any time.'

I gave him a small smile before taking a deep breath and

reaching the bedroom door, where it was still cracked open. I paused outside, resting my hands on the frame as I tried to calm my nerves, but it did little to help. I slipped quietly through the door, hesitating a moment before shutting it softly behind me. The more privacy, the better; I didn't expect this to go very smoothly.

The room was dark, but I could see the rough outline of the bed through light that filtered in through a tiny, grimy window. Hayden didn't say anything, but I could see the slope of his shoulder as he lay on his side, his back to me. My hands twisted nervously in front of me as I approached the bed, pausing on the side furthest from him.

'Hayden . . .'

I hovered awkwardly by the bed, unsure if I should sit down or move to the side he was on. He didn't respond at first. This wasn't a promising start.

Cautiously, I sat down on the edge of the bed, causing the old mattress to squeak and depress under my weight. I desperately wanted to reach out and touch him, but I didn't for fear he'd flinch away again.

'Hayden—'

'What, Grace?'

I cringed at the tone of his voice, but it wasn't as angry as I had been expecting.

'I just . . . wanted to see if you're okay,' I said softly.

'I'm fine.'

'No you're not,' I pressed softly. Again, he remained quiet for a long time before he responded.

'What do you want me to say, Grace?' His voice was hard and cold.

'I don't know, Hayden,' I answered honestly. I didn't expect him to forgive me so easily, but I at least hoped he would understand my point of view.

Despite my better judgement, I climbed onto the bed, drawing my legs up beneath me, and faced him. A foot or so of space still remained between us, and he didn't move despite surely feeling the shift of the mattress. When it became clear that he wasn't going to respond, I spoke again.

'Look, Hayden . . . I know you don't agree with Dax and me but—'

'"Dax and me", huh?' he said, cutting me off. I rolled my eyes at his back before he flipped over to glare in my direction.

'Really, Hayden?' I replied, raising a sceptical eyebrow at him.

'I could hear you, you know,' he said accusingly as I sat beside him.

'Then you'd know we were mostly talking about *you*,' I pointed out. Of all the times for his jealousy to arise, now was not it.

He sat up and leaned against the headboard, his arms folded over his chest. His legs sprawled out before him as he cast me another glare.

'I don't think that's what you're really upset about,' I told him. I forced myself to keep my tone calm and even. He let out a short sigh before tugging his lower lip between his teeth and releasing it slowly.

'No,' he finally agreed. 'It's not.'

'I know you don't like it, but it had to be that way, don't you see? We couldn't save her.' He stared straight ahead, jaw clenched tightly and arms folded over his chest.

'We would have died . . . and it would have been for nothing,' I continued. I took a deep breath and cautiously reached out to rest my hand lightly on his thigh. A sting of rejection flitted through me as he flinched away slightly, though he didn't remove my touch from him.

'You don't know that,' he said stubbornly. Still, he didn't look at me.

'But I have a pretty good idea, and you do too, you just won't admit it,' I said. 'You're so brave and selfless, Hayden, and I love you for that, but you can't be that reckless with your life. You might not care if you get hurt for someone else, but I do, all right?'

I was reminded of something he'd said to me long ago after I retrieved the family photo album for him and put myself in danger to do so.

You might not give a shit if you get hurt, but I do, okay?

How the tables had turned.

'I know you care, Grace,' he said slowly.

'It's not just me. What about Jett? Kit? Dax? Everyone at Blackwing needs you, Hayden. You can't just throw your life away.'

'I'm not trying to,' he said, a hint of irritation to his voice now.

'That's what you would have done tonight if we hadn't stopped you,' I pointed out. He didn't say anything but scoffed quietly. 'You can't put yourself in danger for someone you don't know.'

For the first time since sitting up, his gaze flitted to meet mine. 'I did for you.'

My heart thumped heavily in my chest at his words. They hurt just as much as they did the first time he said them. I remembered that day so vividly when he saved me, coming back for me when my own brother left me behind, but it wasn't the same.

'I know you did, but you know it's not the same . . . I was alone and wasn't surrounded by twelve or more Brutes . . .'

Hayden's hard, narrowed gaze remained trained on my own as I waited tensely. Finally, he shook his head and let

144

out a deep breath, the first good sign so far.

'I know,' he agreed. Some of the tension leaked out of his posture as he relaxed slightly. 'And . . . you saved me first.'

A small, sad smile pulled at my lips, pleased we'd at least agreed on something.

'I know you want to save everyone, but you can't. People need you . . .' I paused and took a deep breath. My heart felt like it was suddenly trying to break out of my ribs. 'I need you, and I'm too selfish to let you go.'

A sense of relief flooded through me as he turned his hand over in mine. My gaze fell to our entangled hands as I found it suddenly difficult to hold his eye contact.

'You're not selfish, Grace,' he said quietly.

I frowned deeply as I shook my head, certain he was wrong. 'I am. I'm selfish and I won't apologise for what I said earlier, because I stand by it. It kept you safe and that's what's important to me . . . I'm not perfect and I know that, but *you*, Hayden . . . *you* are.' I trailed off, suddenly overcome. I'd known forever that I wasn't as good a person as Hayden, but to be confronted with such a stark reality now unsettled me. I didn't deserve him.

'You think too highly of me,' he said slowly. My heart leaped when he squeezed my hand gently. I shook my head determinedly.

'I don't. I see you as you are . . . What you can't or won't see. You're just . . .' I paused, searching for the right word. There only seemed to be one. I shrugged. 'Perfect.'

Again, he shook his head. 'I'm not. I have flaws, trust me.'

'I haven't seen them.'

'You will,' he replied softly. 'Sooner or later, you will.'

This conversation, while no longer angry, was doing little to ease the tension I felt. I didn't like his absolute certainty that there would come a time where he would let me down.

145

'No,' I said stubbornly. 'You can say that all you want but
. . . it doesn't change anything. I still need you. I need you
safe and alive.'

'You have me, Grace,' he reassured me. 'I'm not going
anywhere.'

'You promise?' I asked quietly. I hated how suddenly
vulnerable I felt as I watched him beneath lowered brows.

He nodded slowly and squeezed my hand once more.

'I promise.'

He surprised me by raising my hand to his mouth so he
could press his lips lightly into the back of it, sealing his
promise with a soft kiss.

'I know you guys were right, it's just hard to accept,'
he finally said. He lowered our hands to his lap, where
his fingers toyed with my own. He still appeared unsettled but much calmer than he'd been at the start of this
conversation.

'I know, Hayden.'

We were both quiet for a long time, and the tension we'd
slowly started to lift lingered around us as it refused to dissipate completely.

'We wouldn't have died, you know,' he said suddenly. I
frowned as a frustrated huff forced its way through my lips.

'Hayden—'

'*We* wouldn't have. I'd never have let you go with me,'
he replied sharply, cutting me off. I blinked in surprise;
that hadn't been the point I'd been expecting him to
make.

'No?'

'Of course not,' he said, shaking his head as he reconnected our gaze. 'I'd never put you in danger like that.'

'But you'd put yourself in it?'

'You didn't let me, now did you,' he stated, a tiny ghost

of a smile pulling at his lips. I mirrored him and felt a small smile of my own forming.

'No, I didn't.'

He leaned forward, and the distance between us shrank.

'Do you know how many people have the power to make me listen to them?'

'Not many,' I guessed.

'No, not many,' he agreed. 'One person, in fact.'

'She must be quite important to you,' I murmured quietly as I attempted to rein in the smile trying to spread across my face. Hayden nodded, an eyebrow quirking up as he did so. I could feel the heaviness evaporating around us.

'Very, very important,' he agreed sincerely. 'It sounds quite pitiful but . . . I really need her, too.'

I sucked in a small breath and felt the knot in my stomach vanish. His words were playful, but there was no ignoring the obvious truth behind them. I leaned towards him as his free hand rose to land softly on my face, allowing his thumb to drag lightly across my cheek.

'I love you, Hayden,' I whispered, dropping the little game. Relief wasn't a strong enough word for what I felt after resolving our tense conversation.

'Oh, I wasn't talking about you,' he said in mock confusion, very clearly amused with himself. 'Talk about awkward,' he continued as he pretended to grimace and bit his lower lip into his mouth.

'Shut up, Hayden,' I replied with a shake of my head.

My hand rose to touch his jaw, and I pulled him forward to close the space between us before pressing my lips into his.

'Say it back, Herc.'

The space closed again as he pushed forward, kissing me once more. He allowed his lips to mould lightly against my

147

own for a few moments before pulling back.

'I didn't mean you,' he lied. The wide grin on his face made his statement very unconvincing, and it became even more unconvincing when he dove back in to kiss me once more. I giggled into the kiss as he captured my lips with his over and over again.

'Say it back,' I mumbled against his mouth.

Both of his hands had risen to cradle my face now, holding me to him as he kissed me. His shirt was gripped in my fists as I held him close, and I found it difficult to kiss him through the smile on my face. When I felt his tongue push lightly into my mouth, I summoned every ounce of willpower I had to push backward on his chest, separating his mouth from mine. His chest rose and fell quicker than usual, and he leaned forward as if breaking off the kiss had set him off balance.

'Say it.'

My voice was no more than a whisper now as my gaze connected with his.

'I love you, Grace. So much.'

The widest grin yet settled on my face at his words, and I was unable to stop myself from tugging on his shirt once more to bring him back to me. The distance between us disappeared as his lips landed gently on mine again, healing the ache and soothing the damage done by our fight. My heart pounded happily in my chest as he kissed me contentedly, and in that moment, all felt right again.

Thirteen: Reluctance

Hayden

The sun was just starting to rise, casting a soft glow around the apartment, picking out the superfluous items as if determined to show the stark contrast between how we lived now and when things had once been so luxurious. I'd quickly grown tired of looking at them, as it was impossible not to think of my life before the fall of civilisation. I didn't want to feel that pain on top of the ache I still felt at abandoning the girl.

Despite the light nature of our conversation after we'd resolved our fight, I still felt off about the whole thing. It didn't sit right with me to abandon someone helpless, even if I could clearly see the logic why it had to be that way. Guilt had been tearing me apart inside all night, and no amount of holding Grace and studying her beautiful features could fully eradicate that. After she'd fallen asleep, I was left alone with my dark thoughts for company. I was determined, however, to keep that from her. I'd meant everything I'd said to her, and I didn't want her to doubt that.

I squeezed my eyes shut, forcing away the images from last night. The sun would be fully up soon, and we had to get back. As always, I felt myself wishing things could just be like this forever – cuddled against each other, secluded away from the harsh realities of our world, settled into the silence together – but I knew they couldn't. That was impossible, because there were always things to worry about. I allowed a few more moments to drink in the feel of her warm body pressed comfortingly against my own before I decided to wake her.

I bent my arm that served as her pillow at the elbow to curl upward and brushed my fingers slowly through her soft hair. I flattened my other hand across her lower back and pulled her tightly against me as I ducked forward to press a light, lingering kiss into her temple.

'Grace,' I murmured softly. A quiet whine left her throat as she stirred, though she didn't wake. My hand ran up her back before raking back down gently. 'Wake up, love,' I tried again.

I glanced down at her face to see her eyes squeezing tighter shut and felt her hands twist into the fabric of my shirt. A sudden deep breath told me she was reluctantly awake before she buried her face in my neck, as if hiding from the light of the day. A deep chuckle rumbled from my chest as my arm tightened around her momentarily, indulging her.

'Morning,' I greeted quietly. Even though I hadn't slept, my voice was deep and gravelly.

'Morning,' she replied. She sounded exhausted.

'Sleep all right?'

'Mmhmm. You?'

'Just fine,' I lied. My hand trailed lightly down her back once more before she finally squinted in the light and cast me a sleepy smile. Even now, she was so beautiful it hurt.

'Do we have to go?' she asked quietly.

'Soon, yeah.'

She sighed heavily and nodded. 'Let's just stay here forever.'

A soft smile pulled at my lips as my gaze met hers. Her fingers tickled lightly over my ribs as she let her hand drag up my side.

'Right here? In this apartment?'

'Hmm, yes,' she murmured. Her eyes drifted lazily closed as a small smile spread across her face. 'Right here.'

For a moment, I pictured sitting on the couch with Grace curled into my side, television on as we watched. I imagined the smell of food cooking in the oven. I heard the soft whirr of the air conditioning that pumped cool air throughout the space. I saw the traffic on the street below as people casually went about their day, devoid of any worry about being shot simply for being out. I imagined how vastly different our lives could have turned out had the world taken a different path. I shook my head once. That was not our world, and it never would be.

'I'm not sure this one is to my taste,' I replied lightly.

'We'll fix it up,' she joked easily, reconnecting our gaze as her eyes opened.

My thumb moved slowly over her skin. I knew she was kidding, but I couldn't help but feel a small part of her genuinely wanted that. A small part of me did, too.

'Maybe someday, Grace.'

Her gaze dropped mine momentarily as something indecipherable flickered across her face, but I was stopped from assessing further as a voice interrupted.

'Will you two shut up in there already?'

Another giggle escaped Grace as she shook her head. I'd almost forgotten he was just in the other room.

'Good morning, Dax,' she called.

I jumped as the door to the bedroom burst open with

no warning knock, though I made no effort to separate myself from Grace. I wasn't quite ready to part with her just yet.

'Morning, pals,' Dax said as he leaned casually against the frame.

Despite his sunny tone, I noticed the dark circles under his eyes. He probably hadn't slept either, as his turn to sleep had been interrupted by Grace and I talking about Violetta, and he'd spent the rest of the night on watch. He'd probably sleep when we got back.

'We'll be right out,' I told him. I noticed the tick of his eyebrow as he took in the tangled position we were in, even though we were both fully clothed.

'Right,' he said sarcastically. 'Just hurry it up, would ya? *Some* of us have been working all night.'

I rolled my eyes as Grace laughed again and replied, 'Such dedication.'

'You bet,' he responded. 'I'll get the stuff packed while you two laze about.'

'Oh shut it,' I mumbled.

Dax let out a quiet chuckle before retreating. I allowed myself to press one last kiss onto Grace's forehead before untangling myself from her to rise from the bed. I extended a hand to Grace, which she tugged softly to lead me from the room, never releasing her grip. It was something we hardly ever did, as the secret nature of our relationship demanded, but it felt nice to be free to hold her hand now as we walked into the living room. Dax had our things piled and ready to go.

'See anything else last night?' I questioned.

'No. Just a guard every hour like before.'

I nodded, relieved to hear of no more disturbances like the one we'd witnessed. 'Ready?'

Grace and Dax murmured their assent and readied their weapons, prepared to repeat the process we'd done on the way up to this apartment. I allowed Dax to head to the door first. Grace stood behind me, and I felt the soft heat of her breath on my skin as she whispered. 'I love you. Be careful.'

A light kiss on my neck just below my ear sealed her fulfilment of our promise.

'And you, yeah? I love you.'

'That's sweet and all, but I'm exhausted, so let's move,' Dax interrupted once more, grinning widely at the front door.

After making sure things were clear outside, I opened the door and moved into the hall. Our careful descent through the building was without incident, and I was relieved to see the jeep in the exact same condition we'd left it in at the parking ramp. After loading our supplies, I pulled out of the inconspicuous parking spot and drove down the ramp.

There were no signs of movement on the streets, but we were careful to keep watch for any enemies. I hadn't expected to have any trouble as it was very early in the morning, but the risk was still there.

Finally, we reached the limits of the city. It seemed like we reached the trees in no time at all, and soon we found ourselves driving beneath their shade. Dax had dozed off, thanks to his sleepless night, but every once in a while I saw the flash of green from Grace's eyes in the rearview mirror.

When we finally arrived back into camp, I was surprised to see a rather large number of people gathered in the centre. It was relatively early, making it strange for so many people to be out. My nerves spiked, as did Grace's. When we drew even with the large gathering, I stopped the jeep and jumped outside, waking Dax as I slammed my door shut.

All the people were studying something on the ground. Adrenaline buzzed through me as I pushed my way to the front, ignoring the stares slowly turning to me. I could see Kit at the front of the crowd now, and I worked to get to him with steps that grew hastier by the second.

'Kit,' I called.

Kit turned at the sound of his name. He grimaced as he saw me draw nearer. Finally, I pushed through the last few people to see what everyone was staring at.

On the ground, laid side by side, were three men ranging from late teens to mid-forties, and all three of them were dead. My heart plummeted in my chest as I took in the grey pallor of their skin and the stiff lifelessness that only came with death. I felt only slightly relieved when I realised I did not recognise them. Whoever they were, they weren't from Blackwing.

I felt the light touch of Grace's hand at my back before she withdrew it to stand beside me.

'Shit,' Dax muttered, announcing his arrival as well.

'What happened?' I demanded, tearing my gaze away from the bodies to look to Kit.

'They raided early this morning,' Kit explained. 'They got all the way to the raid building before anyone saw them.'

I swallowed harshly. They'd got far too deep into our camp before being detected, and much too close. Something needed to be done about this, and fast.

'We need to talk. Kit, get Docc and meet us in the raid building,' I instructed. After a quick glance around, I realised far too many people were staring as if it were some kind of spectacle. 'A few of you need to take care of the bodies

154

and burn them. The rest of you, go on with yourselves. There's nothing to see.'

People jumped to action, obeying my orders without question. I glanced at the bodies once again. My eyes lingered on the face of the youngest one, who was probably only a few years younger than me. His reddish-brown hair was sheared close to his head and freckles covered his now grey skin. Who had he left behind? A mother? A father? A girl he loved, perhaps? A shudder ran down my spine as I realised how that could easily have been me on so many occasions.

'Hayden.'

The soft voice jolted me.

'Let's go, yeah?' said Grace.

I suddenly wondered if she recognised these men, but I refrained from asking until we were in a more private location. Dax followed, though he didn't speak. We were silent as we walked, but luckily we arrived at the raid building quickly, where Kit and Docc were waiting. The man on guard nodded to us as we went inside.

'Okay, tell me what happened again,' I requested as we gathered around the table as always.

'I don't really know,' Kit started. 'Like I said, they got all the way to the raid building before the person on duty saw them and started shooting. They didn't have any real weapons besides these little knives, so they went down pretty quickly.'

'Do you know them, Grace?' I asked as I turned to look at her. She frowned.

'No, I don't recognise them at all,' she replied. 'They weren't from Greystone.'

'So if they weren't from Greystone, where were they from?' Dax questioned.

'They definitely weren't Brutes. They're way too clean for that,' Kit said.

'It must have been Whetland,' Docc said, speaking for the first time. He looked pensive as he stood across the table.

'Have you guys been raided by Whetland before?' Grace asked with a frown.

'No,' I answered quickly. 'Never. We've raided them, but they're usually so non-confrontational and haven't really been known for fighting or raiding . . .'

'Yeah, that's what I thought. They've never raided Greystone either. At least not while I was there.'

'So why now?' Kit questioned as he frowned at the table.

'They're probably facing the same issues we are, things running out and such,' Docc mused. Everyone was silent for a few seconds as they thought.

'Yeah, but they grow their own food, right? Like, we have some but nowhere near what they have . . . why would they raid us?' Dax pressed.

My mind felt like it was whirring a thousand miles an hour. I'd been prepared to come back to troubles from Greystone, but I'd honestly never even given a second thought to Whetland. I had a bad feeling creeping up; I'd always known Whetland could be dangerous thanks to their self-sufficiency and smart leadership, and it looked like the time was finally coming.

'They weren't raiding for food though,' I said, as the idea came to me. 'They were raiding for weapons, right?'

'And all they had were knives, so that would make sense,' Grace agreed as she caught my train of thought.

'Why do they suddenly need weapons when they've never needed them before?' Dax muttered. I was wondering the same thing.

156

'I don't know,' I admitted reluctantly.

This new development unsettled me when we already had enough to worry about. Greystone, the Brutes, and now Whetland? It seemed like the world was ending all over again.

'Did any of them get away or did they only send three?'

'Just the three,' Kit answered. 'I got there right as the last one went down.'

'Did they say anything?'

'Not that I'm aware of.'

'Well, no matter why they were here, they got way too close. We need to be more careful. What if that had been Greystone leading another attack?'

Grace sighed heavily beside me, drawing my attention. She stared at the table with her brows pulled low over her eyes as she leaned on her elbows. As if she could feel me watching her, she allowed her gaze to flick to meet mine. A small grimace pulled at her lips as she shrugged.

'We got lucky,' Docc said slowly, recapturing my attention.

'Lucky won't cut it,' I said sternly. 'Add another guard to the shifts, and make sure there are at least three people in the tower at all times. We can't have this happen again.'

'Yes, sir,' Dax said. I threw him a dark look as he grinned at me; he knew how much I hated that. 'I'll set it up now, but then I'm going to bed for a bit. I'm exhausted.'

'All right. Thanks, mate.'

'And I'll head up the tower now. There's only one person, I think. I'll do the first watch until Dax sets up a schedule,' Kit added. I nodded in agreement.

'I'll go with you,' Grace said, surprising me by offering.

'What?' I asked before I could stop myself.

'You said you want three, right? Kit and whoever else is up there is two. I'll be the third,' she explained.

'No,' I said flatly.

She let out an exasperated huff.

'Hayden—'

'Aren't you tired? You should sleep,' I said gruffly. I could feel everyone watching our exchange and I didn't like it.

'I slept just fine last night,' she said with a shrug. 'I'll be okay.'

'I'll come with you guys then—'

'No, Hayden, you should get some rest. I know you didn't sleep,' she said gently.

'You really should get some rest, Hayden. At least for a few hours,' Docc chimed in gently. I glared at Grace for a few more seconds. They were all right and I knew it, but that didn't mean I liked it. Grace nodded once reassuringly and offered a small smile.

'Fine,' I grumbled. 'But I'm coming up in a few hours.'

'Deal,' Grace said with a smile. She rolled her eyes playfully at me when I did not return it and continued to frown.

'Right, well, now that that's settled . . .' Dax said as he clapped his hands together once. 'I'll get to work now. See you later.'

'You know where to find me if you need me,' Docc said. He and Dax moved towards the door and waved goodbye before exiting.

'Ready, Grace?' Kit asked, raising his brows at her.

'Yeah,' she replied. Kit nodded and moved across the building to get his usual gun. Grace took the chance to move to stand just a foot away from me and peered up at me. 'Go get some rest. For real this time.'

'I don't like this,' I told her, ignoring her words. Again, she rolled her eyes at me.

158

'Hayden, it's impractical to be together all the time,' she said gently before continuing. 'Even if we want to be.'

She had a point and I knew that, but it didn't change my feelings. Now, more than ever, I wanted her by my side at all times.

'So?' I muttered stubbornly.

She sighed and looked up at me endearingly.

'Just get some rest, Hayden, please,' she pleaded quietly.

I studied her for a long time, a frown firmly on my face, before I let out a deep sigh of resignation.

'Fine.'

I knew what came next – the promise. 'I love you. I'll see you in a bit.'

'And I love you,' I murmured. When I made her promise me to always say goodbye, I never imagined we'd have to uphold it so often.

Kit reappeared by our side as Grace took a step back. She shot me one last smile that I again did not return before turning and heading towards the door with Kit. I tried to ignore the uneasiness in my stomach as she got further away from me. Kit was already out the door and she was about to follow when I finally managed to speak.

'Grace,' I called, halting her progress. She turned to look at me. 'Be careful.'

'Always am,' she replied lightly.

With that, she whipped around and headed out the door. The soft wisps of blonde hair were the last I saw of her as the door drifted shut, cutting me off from her. I shook my head once and tried to clear away my thoughts.

You're being overprotective, Hayden.

I knew I was being overbearing and probably too protective. How could I call myself a man if I didn't do everything in my power to protect the one I loved more than anything?

159

She twisted my rationale and overrode every thought in my mind, but there was absolutely nothing I could do about it. With a deep sigh, I trudged from the raid building. I retreated to my hut, fighting my instinct the entire way.

Grace was right. We couldn't be together all the time, and I would just have to learn to accept that.

Fourteen: Ignorance

Grace

It felt strange to be walking beside Kit rather than Hayden as we moved through camp. His hair was dark like Hayden's, though it was much shorter, and his eyes were such a dark brown I had trouble distinguishing his pupil sometimes. He moved differently, too. Hayden walked with a naturally graceful stride and a slight sway to his hips. Kit walked as if he were always in a hurry to get somewhere, each step purposeful and strong.

'How long will we be up there?' I asked as we arrived at the foot of the tower, which was blackened from the flames, though its metal structure remained intact. I guessed it had been there long before Blackwing was around, and doubted it would go anywhere any time soon.

'Dunno. However long it takes Dax to set up the new schedule, I suppose.'

I nodded in reply as we started to climb the stairs. I liked Kit, but he wasn't as easy to talk to as Dax or Docc. He was naturally serious and quiet, which I could understand, but it didn't make for easy conversation. It was quite odd, because we'd both saved each other's lives at one point, but I hardly knew anything about him. Hayden seemed to get jealous every time I talked to him, so our chances for chummy exchanges were pretty much non-existent. One thing I knew about Kit, however, was that he was fiercely loyal and willing to do whatever it took to survive, even if that meant being brutal sometimes.

'Do you know who's up there now?' I asked as we climbed. We'd just passed the third storey. I glanced sideways at him and saw the thick scar that ran down his neck. It seemed like so long ago that I'd had to plunge my fingers into his artery to stop the bleeding.

'I don't,' Kit admitted. 'Hopefully someone tolerable.'

I caught the slight kink to his lips telling me he was joking. On the rare occasion that he did show humour, it was dry as could be.

'How was the raid?' he continued. We passed the fourth flight of stairs, making us about halfway up.

'It was . . .' I paused in thought. 'Rough.'

'Rough?'

'Yeah. We saw some girl get taken by the Brutes but couldn't do anything about it,' I responded. My stomach twisted uncomfortably again at the thought.

'Bet Hayden didn't like that.'

'Not at all,' I agreed.

'Hmm.' We were a floor below the top now. 'Hey, I've been meaning to say . . . I'm sorry about your dad.'

I blinked in surprise. I hadn't been expecting him to mention that at all and it caught me off guard as a jolt of pain clenched at my chest. 'Thank you.'

'Yes, sorry to hear about your father, Grace.'

My blood ran cold as I recognised the sarcastic voice at the top of the tower. None other than Barrow sat with his hands tied behind his back to one of the bars, and he was sneering right at me.

'What the hell is he doing up here?' Kit demanded of the other man atop the tower.

'I-I thought someone said he could be held up here as long as he was tied up?' the man stammered. He sounded very unsure of himself now.

'Who told you that?' Kit snapped angrily. I was frozen in place, locked into a heated gaze with the man I hated so much. I wanted to go and kick that stupid sneer off his face.

'Well, Barrow did . . .'

'Barrow did,' Kit repeated flatly. 'Do you really think *Barrow* is the best one to be getting orders from considering *he's* the one tied up?'

'I, um, well . . .' the man stuttered, clearly embarrassed as he fidgeted with the hem of his shirt. 'I'm sorry, I'll take him back down.'

'Forget it,' Kit snapped. 'We'll watch him until you find someone to help. I don't trust one person to handle him.'

The man stood sheepishly in front of us as his gaze flitted between Kit and Barrow.

'Well? Go find someone to help you!' Kit ordered. The man jumped and mumbled something before rushing down the stairs, leaving Kit and I alone with Barrow, who smirked at us.

'What a coincidence seeing you two here,' Barrow said smoothly.

'Shut up,' Kit said with a roll of his eyes.

I was slightly surprised with how blatantly rude Kit was being to Barrow. He'd taken ages to warm to me even after I'd saved his life. I got the sense that if you betrayed Kit once, that was it. Barrow had practically raised him, but he didn't care because he'd tried to overthrow Hayden, who was like a brother to Kit.

'Sorry, Grace,' Kit added quietly to me. I was still frozen in place and unable to look away from Barrow's derisive sneer. As if I didn't have enough reasons to hate him, now he was going to throw my father's death in my face?

'It's fine,' I finally managed to mutter. I forced my feet to move to the very opposite side of the tower, where I perched myself behind one of the mounted guns. One last glare was thrown over my shoulder before I made myself look away and take a deep breath.

'Surprised you're not running Greystone, Cook,' Barrow spat. 'Now that your daddy is gone and all.'

Ignore him, Grace.

I seethed in silence as I stared out around me, unable to appreciate the view because of the fury ripping through me. Kit grumbled something as he situated himself behind another gun and surveyed around us as well.

'Nothing to say? Or did Daddy not even pass on the rights to you?'

Shut up.

'That's it, isn't it? He didn't even pick you, so you came crawling back.'

I could feel my hands starting to shake in rage, but still I remained silent.

'She came back to warn us about the war, you idiot,' Kit spat. 'And you already knew that, so why don't you just shut the hell up?'

I felt a small flash of gratitude for Kit, but it was quickly smothered by anger again as Barrow snickered scornfully. Barrow's burning hatred for me confused me, but I now suspected it had a lot to do with jealousy of Hayden's position, and he was taking it out on me since he couldn't to Hayden.

'So you and Hayden still playing house then?' Barrow asked, ignoring Kit as he continued to pick at me.

'What did I ever do to you?' I demanded. My self-control snapped as I spun around to glare at him.

'You're the enemy,' Barrow growled, dropping his feigned casual tone from before.

'Is that your only argument?' I demanded, crossing my arms defiantly over my chest.

'I don't like anyone who comes in here and thinks they're better than us,' he snarled. 'You've only got worse as you've got more comfortable and it makes me sick.'

Kit scoffed, as if angered by this entire situation. That made two of us.

'You're deluded. You're just jealous because Hayden's in charge and you're not, so you're using me as an excuse,' I spat. I hadn't meant to, but I'd taken a few menacing steps forward, towering over him thanks to the way he was tied up. 'It's pathetic.'

'I'm deluded?' he challenged.

'Yes.'

'Oh no, I don't think so. You think you love that boy?'

I refused to reply and continued to glare down at him. My jaw ticked angrily and I focused on stopping my limbs from shaking.

'You do. You think you love him,' Barrow inferred. He let out a humourless chuckle and shook his head as if he thought I was a fool. His stone-grey eyes locked on mine. 'You think you know everything about him? Every secret and every dark moment in his past? You find out a bit more about him and see how much you love him then,' Barrow muttered.

'I don't need to hear any of your bullshit,' I told him confidently. He could say what he liked, but I knew Hayden. He didn't have dark secrets in the way the rest of us did. Hayden was *good*.

'You can call it that if it makes you feel better. Haven't you asked him how he knew your father was dying?'

My stomach dropped like a rock. I'd been able to dismiss everything so far as bitter jealousy and resentment, but I'd thought about this before. Hayden had only told me that he'd known my father was ill when he sent me home, but he'd never mentioned how. I'd never asked because it hurt too much to talk about, but that didn't stop the question from appearing in my mind.

'I'll take that as a no,' Barrow continued, interpreting my silence correctly. I glared at him once more.

'That's enough, Barrow,' Kit snapped in exasperation.

'Better question, has he told you it's his fault your father's dead?'

I felt the colour drain from my face as my blood turned to ice in my veins.

'Barrow!' Kit hissed angrily. 'Shut the fuck up!'

'Another no,' Barrow said smugly.

I took a step back and tried to think clearly, but the world seemed to be swirling around me. Kit's lack of denial wasn't helping, and I suddenly felt like I was going to pass out.

Could it really be Hayden's fault?

My breaths grew more and more shallow, and I stumbled until my back collided with the rail. I gripped it tightly, blanching my knuckles as I tried to think clearly. It couldn't be Hayden's fault. My father had endocarditis. An infection. Hayden couldn't have anything to do with that.

But . . .

The question still remained — how had he known he was dying?

'Grace.'

I blinked furiously once and forced myself to look up. Kit was staring at me, and I got the sense it wasn't the first time he'd said my name before I'd heard.

166

'What?' My voice sounded weak, so I cleared my throat in determination. My leg jittered anxiously on the ball of my foot and I forced it to stop, though I still felt shaky.

'Don't listen to him. He wasn't even there and has no idea what he's talking about.'

I nodded as I tried to quiet my brain, but I couldn't stop myself from speaking again.

'How did you guys know my father was dying?' I demanded sharply. Barrow snickered in satisfaction, but I ignored him as I stared determinedly at Kit.

'Well, I didn't know he was your father then,' Kit said, avoiding answering. 'Neither Dax nor I did.'

'But you knew Celt, the leader of Greystone, was dying,' I urged. Anger simmered beneath the surface and I felt my leg start up the anxious bouncing again.

'Yes,' he admitted.

'How?'

Kit drew a deep breath and pushed it out slowly. His brows were pulled low over his deep brown eyes as he studied me and stalled. I was about to repeat my question when he finally answered me.

'I think you should just talk to Hayden.'

My heart plummeted in my chest. That was not what I wanted to hear. I wanted to hear him say Barrow was making things up, that his words were all lies, but his reluctance to talk about it made me fear the worst. It seemed as though Hayden had been keeping a few things from me.

'Whatever you're thinking . . . I'm sure it's worse than the truth,' Kit said as he tried to reassure me.

His words did little to comfort me, however. I nodded stiffly and forced myself to turn back around to man my gun. I stared unseeingly out across my side and tried to ignore the upheaval rolling through my stomach. What did Barrow mean? Did Hayden really have something to do with my father's death?

My dark ponderings were cut off, however, by the arrival of the previous guard and another man. I wanted nothing more than to rush across the tower and push Barrow off the top as they untied his arms from the railing, but somehow I refrained. He spoke one last time in his disgustingly oily tone, sending a jolt of rage and hurt right down my spine.

'Looks like the honeymoon's over.'

'Take him out of here,' Kit muttered bitterly.

The two men nodded and started to drag him down the stairs, where his cynical cackle floated up to my ears. Tension lingered in my muscles as I stiffened and tried to calm down, but it was almost impossible. He'd dug into the two things I cared about the most – Hayden and my father.

I jumped when a tentative hand landed on my shoulder, forcing my eyes open to look at Kit once more.

'Hey,' he said. It was the gentlest I'd ever heard his voice. 'Just . . . talk to Hayden before you assume anything, all right? It's not my place to discuss with you but . . . don't freak yourself out.'

I nodded and forced a deep breath from my lungs. The last thing I wanted to do was get ahead of myself, but I could feel it happening anyway. Kit didn't say anything else as I battled internally; it was clear this wasn't his forte, but I was glad for his silence.

I desperately wanted to talk to Hayden about what Barrow had said, but a large part of me was terrified that I'd discover something I didn't want to know. I wanted to live in blissful ignorance and not give another thought to the subject, but I couldn't. The tiny, nagging voice in the back of my mind told me that, in some way, Barrow had been telling the truth.

I didn't know how long I sat up there in stony silence. It could have been minutes or it could have been hours, and I was only aware that time had passed when the sun started to drop towards the horizon. Kit let out a soft groan as he stood and stretched his back, telling me we'd probably been up there longer than I suspected in my anxious haze.

'Someone's got to be coming soon to switch shifts . . .' Kit muttered.

I couldn't tell if he was talking to me or to himself, so I remained silent. Part of me wanted to stay up there forever and avoid the inevitable talk I'd have to have with Hayden, while the other part of me wanted to sprint down the stairs that very second and get things figured out.

Just when I thought I was about to crawl out of my skin, I heard quiet murmurs of voices ascending the tower. A mixture of relief and even more anxiety flooded through me as I realised the end of my shift must have finally arrived.

'Hey, Kit,' a voice called from the top of the stairs.

Three people had appeared. I vaguely recognised them all, though I didn't know any of their names. The one who had spoken nodded calmly at me in greeting.

'Hey,' Kit replied. 'You our replacement?'

'You got it,' the man answered easily. He had light brown hair and a large bald spot on top of his head, as well as a bristly-looking moustache on his face.

'All right. We didn't see anything, but it was daytime, so keep your eyes peeled. It'll be dark soon,' Kit said as he passed along our report. I still could think of nothing

169

to contribute as my mind roved over and over the many questions I had for Hayden.

'We will. Head on down, now,' the man said with a nod.

I jumped when Kit appeared beside me, jerking me out of my haze. My eyes met his as he spoke calmly. 'Let's go.'

I gave a stiff nod and followed him as he started to descend the stairs. Twice on the way down, he opened his mouth as if to speak before cutting himself off yet again. The third time he did it, we were nearly at the ground and I couldn't stop myself from snapping.

'What, Kit?'

He shot me a disapproving look. 'Look, I know you're pissed off or whatever, but just try to take a few deep breaths before you freak out.'

I barely managed to hold back the offended scoff fighting to break through my lips. 'Pissed off' only seemed to be a tiny bit of the emotion I was feeling, but I had to remind myself that Kit was not Hayden, and that he didn't know how to read me the way Hayden did. Kit saw an angry girl, that was it, but I knew Hayden would see so much more. There would be no hiding this mood from him.

'Right, yeah,' I said stiffly. My attempts to sound calm failed as we reached the bottom of the stairs. We started off in the same direction before he paused.

'I've got to go this way but . . .' he trailed off uncertainly. 'Good luck.'

A frown pulled at my features before I managed to wipe it away.

'Thanks,' I replied evenly. Kit nodded and started to walk away before I stopped him. 'Hey, Kit?'

'Yeah?'

'Thanks for what you said . . . about my father,' I said sincerely in a brief moment of clarity. Kit was not the type to express emotions through his words, so for him to say it meant a lot.

'Sure thing,' he replied casually.

With that, he sent a small wave in my direction before turning to leave. I stood planted into the dirt, hands fidgeting with the hem of my shirt as I chewed my lower lip. I wasn't far from our hut, but I didn't know if I was ready to go in just yet. Hayden hadn't appeared for watch, which told me he probably hadn't woken up yet. I suspected he was exhausted, so this didn't surprise me, but I didn't relish the idea of waking him up only to confront him with this.

At that moment, I wanted to forget I'd ever heard what Barrow had said. I wanted to pretend Kit hadn't avoided the subject so shadily. I wanted to return to the hut and find a peacefully sleeping Hayden, where I could crawl under the covers and press into his body. I wanted to feel the way his arms would inevitably wind around my waist to haul me against him. I wanted to go back to the blissful ignorance when I'd been so happy with him just this morning, but the nagging thoughts in the back of my mind prevented it.

With a determined nod, I uprooted my feet and forced myself to move. Much too soon, our hut came into view; every step I took carried me closer and added to the mounting anxiety rolling through my stomach. It was like I could feel the edge of a cliff approaching but did nothing to stop myself from running for the plunging depths.

When I reached the door, I paused outside. My hands rose to rest on either side of the frame, and my eyes closed as I blew out a deep, uneven breath. My mind continued to whirr loudly inside my skull, bombarding me with negative thoughts and anxiety-inducing uncertainties. A shaky hand

171

was pressed into the wood of the door as I forced my eyes to open and pushed my way inside.

I had to know.

I had to know the truth, even if it was about to rip me to shreds.

Fifteen: Catharsis

Grace

It was dark inside, and it took my eyes a moment to adjust before they settled on the bed. I saw the slope of Hayden's shoulders as I took a few steps inside, closing the door silently behind me. Unlike the last time I had walked into a room to find him, he was actually asleep. My stomach clenched tightly as I thought of ripping him from his much-needed slumber, but I felt like I was going to disintegrate if I waited a moment longer without knowing the truth.

I arrived at the side of the bed. Now that I was closer, I could see the finer details of the sleeping man that I loved so dearly. His arms were curled around a pillow, as if they'd tried to find me only to settle for the poor substitute. Soft, brown strands of his hair fanned out around him, leaving a few waves to fall haphazardly across his forehead, and his full, pink lips were slightly parted as deep, even breaths drifted out.

An unhappy frown settled over my lips as I observed him quietly before sitting gently on the edge of the bed. I hated myself for doubting him even for a second, but it was impossible to ignore the quiet nagging voice that I'd stifled for so long. The questions I'd managed to push down rose up now, screaming in my head and refusing to be suppressed any longer without being addressed. I'd been able to ignore them up until now, but they'd been disturbed and multiplied after hearing Barrow's spiteful words that carried a strange ring of truth.

I reached out, as if to touch him, but paused, my hand stilling in the air between us. With a deep sigh, I let it drop into my lap.

Hayden would explain it, and we would be fine. I just had to get this out of the way. My eyes opened to a still sleeping Hayden as I opened my mouth to speak.

'Hayden . . .'

My voice was soft and quiet, as if my body were rebelling against what I was about to do. He didn't move, and his breath remained as slow and even as ever. My stomach flipped anxiously as I reached forward again to let my hand land lightly on his shoulder. His skin seared hotly through his shirt when I moved my hand to wake him up.

'Hayden.'

I spoke a little louder this time, the combination of my words and touch causing him to stir.

'Hey, Bear,' he mumbled deeply.

He squinted one eye shut and a lopsided smile pulled at his lips as he looked up at me sleepily. The use of my nickname only served to send a jolt through my heart, so opposite from the wave of warmth that usually washed over me. I almost lost my resolve to bring it up when he reached for me. His long fingers curled gently around my wrist as he tugged, trying to pull me down to him how I so desperately wanted, but I resisted. He looked confused at my resistance.

'Hey,' I said quietly.

'What's wrong?' he asked. 'Did something happen while you were on watch? Are you all right?'

I broke our eye contact. The truthful answer was *yes*,

174

something had happened and, *no, I was not all right*, but not for the reasons he would think.

He grew impatient with my silence, and sat up fully and leaned forward, forcing me to look at him.

'Grace, what's wrong?'

'Nothing's happened in camp,' I reassured him gently.

'Okay . . .' he said slowly, obviously confused. 'So why are you upset?'

There was no hiding this from him even if I wanted to.

'I went to take watch with Kit, but when we got to the top of the tower . . .' I paused. It seemed difficult to put things together how I wanted. I shook my head, determined to start over.

'Yeah?' Hayden urged softly. His thumb ran soothingly over my wrist and I resisted the urge to pull my hand away.

'Hayden . . .' I felt jittery and unbalanced as I stared into his loving eyes. 'How did you know my father was dying?'

There. I'd asked. Now it was up to him to answer and potentially shatter my fragile heart.

Hayden's jaw fell open in surprise and his brows raised momentarily before he regained control of his features and frowned. His hand fell from my face as if too surprised to keep it there.

'What brought this up?' he asked, avoiding answering.

'Just tell me,' I begged quietly. My voice was breathless and, unfortunately, desperate.

'Grace—'

'Hayden,' I cut him off, my voice suddenly stern.

He caught the change in my tone, but his avoidance to answer was not helping me believe his innocence. The despicable doubt I felt grew stronger, and I hated every second of it.

'Where is this coming from?' he pressed, shaking his

head. His lips remained parted and his brows were furrowed in confusion.

'Just tell me,' I pleaded. 'Please.'

After a few long seconds of searching my gaze, he blew out a deep breath that seemed to cause him to sag a bit under the weight of his body.

'You remember that raid when I forced you to stay behind? And things didn't go as planned and we took longer than we thought?' he said slowly, watching me keenly the entire time he spoke.

'Of course I do,' I replied quickly. Like I could ever forget those traumatic days.

'And you remember how I told you we ran into some people from Greystone before the Brutes showed up?'

'Yes . . .'

My heart seemed to pound faster with every word he spoke, desperate and terrified for him to continue all at once. He squeezed my knee, but I was almost too jittery to feel it. Hayden looked nervous as he watched me closely, which only added to my growing worry.

'Well, there were a few moments before we saw them . . . They were just around the corner, you see, and they didn't know we were there, so they were talking loudly . . . And I sort of overheard them speaking.'

Hayden paused to draw a deep breath as he looked guiltily at me. He looked as if he would literally rather be doing anything other than having this conversation. He was so close to revealing everything and I forced myself to sit still until he finished.

'What did you hear?' My voice was stiff and unfeeling as I asked, as if it came from someone trying their best to sound like me rather than coming from my own throat.

'Grace,' Hayden whispered quietly. He shook his head,

more to himself than at me, as he placed his other hand on my leg. I tried not to flinch as I waited; I was surprised the thick tension hadn't drowned me yet.

'What did you hear, Hayden?'

'I . . . I heard them mention that they needed to get medicine back to Celt before it was too late . . . and that his sickness was getting worse.'

My heart all but dropped out of my chest. That was it – that was how he knew. He'd overheard people talking about my father, making it abundantly clear that he was nearing the end of his life. This wasn't what made my blood run cold, however. No, what caused my despairing was the realisation of what had happened after he'd overheard this information.

'You killed them.'

My voice was hollow and flat. I found myself unable to hold his gaze any longer. I leaned backward, desperate to separate myself from him.

'Grace, please,' Hayden begged. He didn't even bother denying it.

'Oh my god,' I choked out suddenly.

His hands suddenly felt like ice on my legs, and I found myself stumbling out from beneath his touch as I landed clumsily on the floor. My feet took uncoordinated steps backward, increasing the distance between us, while Hayden watched me dejectedly and guiltily from the bed.

'You . . . Those people, from Greystone . . . they were getting my father medication that could have saved him and you . . . you killed them.'

My vision blurred as Hayden's upset face swooped in front of me, and I found myself stumbling sideways until I managed to catch myself on the chair behind his desk. My hands trembled as I gripped the chair so tightly that my knuckles blanched.

'Grace,' Hayden said as he started to rise from the bed.

'No!' I said loudly.

Too loudly, but I couldn't seem to control my voice as I held up a hand to still his actions. I couldn't be that close to him when I was trying to think clearly. He paused and looked hurt at my rejection, but in that moment all I could register was the overwhelming sense of betrayal I felt.

'Barrow was right,' I murmured quietly as my hand pressed to my forehead. The words tasted like acid on my tongue, but I couldn't deny them.

'Barrow?' Hayden repeated in confusion. My eyes flitted to him for a fraction of a second before a gasp of a breath ripped through me, forcing me to look away. 'Grace, I don't know what Barrow has to do with this . . . but I'm so sorry,' he said sincerely. He looked as though he wanted to reach out to me, but his touch was the last thing I wanted.

'I can't believe he was right,' I said, ignoring Hayden as I spoke more to myself.

'What are you talking about? Please tell me, Grace, talk to me,' he said urgently as he took a step forward. He was halted by the sharp glare I threw in his direction, where he raised his hands as if surrendering.

'He said it was your fault my father died . . .' I started. The words fought for attention as they rammed into one another, making it almost impossible to form a coherent thought. 'You didn't . . . you didn't kill him, but you stopped them from saving him . . . he died so quickly after that . . .'

'You're right,' Hayden said softly.

For the first time, my gaze jerked to his and stayed locked on him, only this time, he was the one not returning it.

'I can't deny any of that,' he said with a submissive shrug, eyes focused on the floor. 'Those men were trying to help your father and I helped kill them.'

That was the thought repeating itself over and over in my head. I couldn't think of how they probably had no choice. I couldn't think of how it might not have mattered anyway. I couldn't think of how much this information must have tortured Hayden. My selfish nature was shining through as that one loathsome thought pounded my brain over and over again: Hayden had, in some indirect way, aided in my father's death.

'I'm so sorry, Grace, believe me,' Hayden repeated.

My eyes refocused from the blurred chaos I had been seeing as I looked at him standing ten feet away, frozen as if fighting with himself. My eyes squeezed tightly shut as my resolve crumbled and a choking sob ripped from my throat.

My submission to my breakdown shattered any self-control Hayden had as he rushed forward, closing the distance between us quickly. I felt his strong arms wrap soundly around my shoulders as he hauled me to his chest, but the hug was one-sided; he clung to me desperately, trying so hard to comfort me, while my arms crossed tightly over my chest, blocking me from melting into him the way I usually would.

My one source of never-ceasing comfort, my steady rock, my unimaginably captivating love, was now the very person who I could not allow to fix me. No matter how I tried, I could not let him pull me back together. I remained stiff and unfeeling as I caved in on myself, crying tears his hug could not dry as he remained wrapped around me despite my resistance. It broke my heart in so many ways, and I feared the pieces had suffered too much damage to ever fit back together.

It could have been ages that we stood like that – Hayden

wrapped around me while I kept my arms folded over my chest like a barricade and sobbed – but he never released me, even though I didn't return the hug. He murmured quiet things in my ear, but I couldn't make them out thanks to the buzzing that seemed to have settled over my brain.

Barrow had been, at least partially, correct. My father's death was in part Hayden's fault, and it was shattering me to pieces.

'I'm so sorry.'

I believed him, but it didn't mean anything. He was sorry, yes, but that didn't change what had happened.

I felt my hands form into fists, and I was surprised when I found them pushing firmly against his chest. Still, however, he didn't loosen his grip on me, even though my fists pounded weakly against his chest once more. Each time I moved, my actions grew stronger and more combative, and the dull thuds as my fists landed against his firm chest grew louder each time.

'Let me go,' I choked out, struggling against him as I pushed and shoved against his grip. I was reminded so strongly of the time he'd returned from the very raid we were just discussing, only then, I'd been fully prepared to let him catch me before I fell apart, whereas now I so desperately needed to get away from him.

'Grace, no,' he said gently but firmly.

I pushed again, fighting to hold down the tears I was so tired of crying. My throat burned with the effort, and my hands shoved at his chest with all the strength I could muster. Finally, I broke his grip on me and stumbled backward a few feet. Gasping breaths ripped from my chest as I stared at him. His face held no traces of anger or resentment – only concern, sadness, and, undeniably, guilt, were featured there as he watched me sombrely.

I found myself staring blankly at him, as if all of my emotions had suddenly crashed to the floor, where I was pretty sure my heart had already fallen. A strange calm settled over me as I held Hayden's intensely concerned gaze, and an odd void seemed to rush in to fill the gaping spaces left in my chest where my heart had been.

'I'm sorry, Grace. I'm so, so sorry,' he said softly. His voice was so quiet that I almost couldn't hear him even though he was just feet away. My face remained unchanged as I watched him.

'I know you are,' I replied honestly. Hayden hesitated a fraction of a second before speaking again.

'I didn't want to do it,' he continued cautiously.

'I know you didn't.'

Hayden drew a deep breath and took a tentative step forward, as if afraid any movements would scare me all the way across the room. When I didn't move, he took another few steps until he was standing right in front of me, where he towered over me as always. His deep green eyes locked on mine as he held my gaze, though he didn't try to touch me.

'I wish it wasn't true,' he whispered. 'But it is.'

I didn't speak as I stared up at him with the same odd calm from before. His eyes pleaded with me silently, begging for forgiveness I so desperately wanted to grant. I could practically hear his heart hammering in his chest, feel the heat radiating off his body, see the desperation for me to let him back in, but I couldn't give in, no matter how much I might have wanted to.

'I love you so much, Grace,' he murmured. The first flicker of emotion flared through me momentarily before the cold settled back in and smothered it.

'I know you're sorry, and I know you didn't want to do it,' I paused and closed my eyes for a few seconds before opening them to reconnect our gaze. He seemed, if possible, even closer than before. 'And you know that I love you, but . . .'

Hayden's face fell, dropping the tiny bit of hope that had started to show on his features as he heard that fateful word: but.

When I took a step back, his chest caved in as a breath was forced from his lungs.

'But I can't forgive that,' I said truthfully as I shook my head slowly. 'I can't forget that you might have hurried my father's death.'

'Grace . . .'

Another step backward increased the space between us. The pain I'd seemingly lost suddenly returned at full force as my heart clenched painfully when I took in the broken expression on his face.

My voice was as weak and shaky as ever as I finally spoke, answering his unspoken question to forgive him.

'No, Hayden. I can't.'

Sixteen: Rumination

Hayden

No, Hayden, I can't.
  I can't.
  I can't.
  No, Hayden . . .
  I can't.
Grace's words echoed in my head as I stood cemented to the ground. Minutes or hours had passed since she'd left, but my brain had lost the ability to process time. The image of her turning from me, shattered and filled with gut-wrenching disbelief, was burned into my brain. Her echoing words were accompanied by the footsteps that carried her away, the creak of the frame that let her slip past, and the quiet thud of the door closing to finalise her departure.

How many times would I have to watch her walk away from me? How many more experiences like this could I tolerate before she truly was lost to me forever? We'd been in fights before, resented each other before, but they'd been brief and fleeting. The single true test to our relationship had come full circle after I'd sent her home and she'd come back to me, but something about this felt different.

This wasn't something I'd done for the best for her, and it wasn't something I could easily fix. A heavy uncertainty weighed in the pit of my stomach that sent waves of aching anxiety through me with every breath. I couldn't process much besides horrific guilt and uneasiness; she was right – there was no denying it – and I couldn't blame her for leaving. I'd hurried her father's death, and I knew she would have a difficult time forgiving me, if she ever did. It was my fault, as she'd so dejectedly said, and I couldn't deny it.

No, Hayden, I can't.

I squeezed my eyes tightly shut and ran my palm down my face as I blew out a deep breath. Every instinct I had was screaming at me to chase after her, to calm her down and explain myself, but I knew I couldn't. She didn't want to see me, something she'd made abundantly clear with her final departing words and defeated posture. How could I fix her when I was the one who'd broken her?

The worst part was that I didn't know what this meant. Was she out there, right now, going over how much she hated me? Did she mean she just needed space for the night? A week? A month? My stomach churned and I suddenly felt like throwing up as another thought crossed my mind.

Was she done with me forever?

I couldn't even entertain that idea or I'd lose it for sure. Surely she'd see after some time that I'd had no choice.

There was nothing I could do. In the chaos of running into the members of Greystone and Brutes all at once, it had been hard enough to even understand what was going on, much less process the implications. It wasn't until after things were over that I realised what I'd done and what it meant, but I didn't have it in me to go to Grace with my weak explanation. No matter what I said, it didn't change the fact that I was, at least partially, responsible for her father's death, and I hated myself for it.

All I could do was wait and desperately hope that she would see things differently after some time alone. I'd wait until she was prepared, because I respected and loved her too much to pressure her into coming back to me before she was ready.

If she was ever ready, that was.

If there was anything I was certain of, it was that I loved her with every cell in my body, every breath in my lungs, every beat of my heart. Every action and thought I had went into keeping her safe, happy, alive. All I wanted was to be hers and to let her take full control of my heart, but it seemed my life was making every move possible to keep me from that. My life had never been more complicated and stressful now that Grace had entered it, but there was no doubt in my mind that she was exactly what I needed. Every hardship was worth it if it meant I got to be with her, and I prayed this would only be another bump in the road to our happiness.

I tried to ignore the dark, ugly weight that had settled over me. There was a nagging in the back of my mind that I couldn't ignore; it lingered there, whispering dark thoughts that I so desperately did not want to hear that chipped away at me word by word.

You don't deserve her.

You've ruined it forever.

She's going to leave you.

You're going to go back to being alone.

If you lose her, you lose everything.

My body shot upward in a desperate attempt to quiet the thoughts. My shaky hands pushed roughly through my hair as I leaned forward, resting my elbows on my knees as I squeezed my eyes shut again. That last thought sounded too familiar, and a memory sparked of Grace and I sitting at the top of the cliff after our trip to the Armoury.

It sounded familiar because it was something I'd said to

her, and seemed to be playing out in a cruel irony at this very moment. I could practically see her face in the soft moonlight, feel the breeze that had tickled over our skin, and hear the quiet buzz that had fallen over us before I said the words I knew to be true. When I'd said them, I never expected them to come back and haunt me as they were now.

'If I lose you, I lose everything.'

The words had been absolutely true the first time, and they remained so now. Her absence allowed the words to reverberate through my skull and send a chill through my veins, like the very warmth had been stolen from my body the moment she'd walked out. It was practically impossible to process anything at that very moment, but one thing I knew was absolutely certain – if I truly had lost Grace, I'd lost everything.

Grace

The world swooped in front of me as I staggered away from the hut, my steps growing less coordinated and jerkier by the second. It was like every inch of space that appeared between Hayden and me cooled the temperature in my body until I felt absolutely chilled to the bone. I couldn't even begin to process what had just happened; all I knew was that I needed a place to sit and think to try and absorb everything that seemed so determined to interfere with my life.

I didn't make it very far before I dropped to sit on a small grassy patch of land on the edge of the huts. I could see ours from where I sat, but at least it was far enough away that I couldn't feel Hayden's presence. My body drew into itself as I focused on taking deep breaths, determined to regain my calm after losing it so spectacularly.

It took a lot of effort, but I finally managed to get my breathing back to a semi-normal rate. My heart didn't seem to get the message, because it continued to pound wildly. Every muscle in my body felt tight and uncomfortable as I sat curled into a ball, but at least the shaking had stopped. These physical changes, however, did nothing to calm the chaos raging inside my head.

All I wanted was to go back to before I knew any of this, when I could look at Hayden without feeling this sting of betrayal and hurt. I wanted to let him hold me, let him take away that hurt he'd caused, and I wanted to understand what he was probably feeling at this moment. I wanted to be there for him, to calm down, think clearly and stop behaving irrationally, but my emotions were clouding my judgement.

It had grown completely dark now, and a soft breeze tickled across my face as I finally lifted my head from my arms. I uncurled my arms from where they'd been locked around my knees. I was about to get up when a flash of movement caught my eye. I tensed and reached for a weapon I did not have before I looked a bit closer.

Two small shadows were walking down the path, separated by a small distance, while one of them fidgeted nervously. I prayed they'd take no notice of me on the small grassy slope. When I recognised them, I felt concern – it was much too late for them to be out.

It was Jett and Rainey, the girl around his age I'd put him in charge of protecting the night the war began. My silent pleas to remain ignored were not answered, however, when I saw Jett do a double take in my direction. He glanced quickly at Rainey as if he'd been caught doing something he shouldn't have been before they turned towards me.

'Grace, what are you doing?' he asked. A confused, concerned frown creased his face. Rainey sent me a small, slightly scared smile as she stood next to Jett.

I sighed heavily, hoping he couldn't tell that I'd been crying earlier. 'I should ask you the same thing.'

His brown eyes widened as he glanced guiltily at Rainey. I was positive they'd just been walking around together, but in Jett's mind, that was comparable to much, much worse. He was too young, too innocent, too naïve to ever do anything further, and would see this as something incredibly embarrassing.

Sure enough, a deep blush crept up his cheeks and he took a deliberate step away from Rainey, who looked slightly put out by his subtle rejection.

'I was just . . . um . . . walking her home because . . . it's not safe?' The end of his sentence drifted upward as if questioning his own reasoning. 'With the war and all . . .'

'If you say so,' I said with a shrug. As much joy as I normally would have got out of this situation, I didn't have it in me to press him. I just wanted to think.

'Where's Hayden?' Jett glanced around as if expecting Hayden to be lurking in the shadows nearby.

'Inside,' I said vaguely. My stomach clenched involuntarily at the mention of his name.

'But—'

'Let's go, Jett,' Rainey said. My eyes flitted to her to see her watching me closely. She appeared to have noticed my mood despite my attempts to hide it, unlike Jett who remained fairly oblivious. I gave her a small, appreciative nod. While she clearly wasn't the bravest of girls, she seemed rather intelligent and observant for a girl of probably eleven or twelve.

Jett nodded once and cast another embarrassed glance at

Rainey as they started to walk away before he paused and looked back at me.

'Are you okay, Grace?' he asked quietly. His brown eyes were filled with concern.

'Yeah, Jett, I'm fine,' I lied, flashing a weak, reassuring smile. He looked as if he didn't quite believe me but got distracted when Rainey tugged on the sleeve of his too large shirt. He was obviously flustered by her action and he stumbled away, blushing harder than ever.

'Bye, Grace,' he called softly.

'Bye, Jett.'

I watched with a sad expression as they retreated, disappearing down the path towards where I knew Jett lived with Maisie. They were about thirty feet away when a second voice called out, making both of them jump.

'Jett, you sly dog!'

My eyes shifted towards the source to see Dax exiting his own hut with a wide grin on his face. I couldn't see Jett's face but didn't need to in order to know he was blushing harder than ever.

'Shut up, Dax!' he shouted before he picked up the pace, practically running away from Dax's teasing. Rainey followed after him, apparently less concerned by Dax's words.

A low chuckle sounded through the air as Dax moved further outside. Once again I found myself hoping I'd go unnoticed, and once again, I was disappointed. Years of training had taught Dax to be observant, and I caught his attention almost immediately. As he drew closer, the amused grin on his face faded to be replaced by a look of confusion.

'What's up?' he asked casually as he glanced down at me. I sighed heavily and pushed my hand down my face.

'Nothing.'

'Okay, well that's obviously a lie, so let's try this again,'

Dax muttered. My face remained pressed into my hands but I could hear him sit down next to me and feel his eyes on me. 'What's wrong?'

I tilted my head sideways to peek out at Dax, forehead resting on my forearms over my knees. His lips pinched together and his brows rose as he waited expectantly.

'You don't have to be here, you know,' I told him.

'I know,' he said with a shrug. 'But something's obviously happened with Hayden or you wouldn't be out here so . . . spill.'

I turned to block out him and the world again, but it did nothing to sort out my thoughts. Maybe it would help to talk to Dax. Maybe he could tell me something to help placate the sting of betrayal and hurt I still felt so severely. My head rose slowly from my arms as he leaned sideways to nudge my shoulder gently.

'Come on, out with it.'

I took a deep breath and prepared to talk; it felt quite strange to trust someone other than Hayden with such personal things, but Dax had said we were friends.

'You remember that raid you guys went on when I couldn't go with you? And you came back and told me Hayden hadn't made it?'

'Of course I do. You punched me in the face for that,' he said with a low chuckle. I raised my brow warningly, which flattened his smile. He cleared his throat and continued. 'Sorry, not funny. Go on.'

'Do you remember running into those people from Greystone?'

'Yeah,' he nodded. 'There were a whole lot of them. Then a bunch of Brutes showed up. It was nuts.'

'Did you hear what they said before . . . before you guys attacked them?' I questioned quietly. As much as I didn't

190

want to hear it, I wanted as many details as possible.

'Yeah, something about their leader being sick and—' he paused and blinked before focusing intently on me. 'Holy shit, I just now realised . . . that would have been your father.'

I couldn't meet his gaze so I just stared straight ahead, jaw clenched and determined not to show emotion. 'Yes, it would have been.'

'Wow, I never even put that together until now . . .' he trailed off. I remembered that, at the time, Hayden had been the only one who'd known that Celt, leader of Greystone, was actually my father. To Dax and Kit, he would have just been the leader of the enemy camp.

'Yeah,' I said flatly, unable to think of anything else to say.

'So what does that have to do with what's happening now?' Dax continued.

'They were getting medicine for my dad and you guys killed them. He could have lived longer if he'd had it.' My voice could have sounded accusatory, but it was more of a detached monotone.

'That's why you're mad at Hayden?' I could practically hear him frowning even though I didn't look at him.

'Mad . . .' I repeated, testing the word. Mad didn't sound right. Hurt, betrayed, shocked, yes. But mad? No. 'No, not mad. But I can't stop thinking it's at least somewhat his fault that he died . . .'

'Well, if it's Hayden's fault, it's mine and Kit's as well,' Dax told me. For the first time, I looked at him to meet his gaze. He was studying me closely, watching for my reaction. He had a point, but it didn't register that way.

'It doesn't feel the same,' I said. I liked Kit and Dax and I trusted them, but I wasn't in love with them. Their actions didn't make me feel the same aching hurt or burning betrayal. I just felt nothing.

'Grace, I'm going to say some stuff, and I don't want you to get mad and hit me again, okay?' Dax said slowly, keeping his voice calm and even.

'No promises,' I said as the corner of my lips quirked up slightly. He shrugged and grinned.

'I'll take it. Look, I know this is probably all really shocking for you, because it's shocking for me even, but Hayden loves you and he'd never do something to intentionally hurt you. The entire time we were on that raid, he was an absolute mess because he was clearly stressed about leaving you here. He never said it, but it was obvious.'

I could feel my throat tightening. My fingers picked at the blades of grass by my side as I waited for him to continue.

'What happened that day . . . it was all so fast and chaotic that even if he'd thought of all that could happen after killing those men, it probably wouldn't have mattered. We didn't have time to think, we just had to act. Between the Brutes and us, it's impossible to even say if Hayden killed anyone from Greystone at all, but if he did, he did it so he could come back to *you*. Everything he does is for you.'

I sniffed once as a single, hot tear streaked down my cheek. I didn't bother to wipe it away as I listened, frozen into place. Dax had given me details I'd been craving to hear, and they made me feel both better and like a piece of shit all at once. According to Dax, Hayden had to either fight and kill, or be killed. When he put it that way, I couldn't possibly blame Hayden for this.

'He didn't tell me any of that . . .' I trailed off weakly. To my surprise, Dax let out a low chuckle beside me.

'I'm not surprised,' Dax muttered lightly. 'He doesn't often make excuses. I told you, he's better than the rest of us.'

An odd sense of relief washed over me. 'He really is.'

We were both quiet for a few moments before Dax spoke again.

'I'm really sorry about your dad, and that honestly sucks how things played out, but . . . would it even have mattered? If he'd got medicine?'

'Yes,' I answered honestly. With medicine, the sooner you got it, the better your chances were. Days made a huge difference, much less an entire week. 'It probably wouldn't have saved him, but he might have got more time.'

'Damn,' Dax murmured. He shook his head sadly. 'Life is cruel.'

I nodded weakly. I could feel my tumultuous emotions subsiding, but I still didn't feel ready to face Hayden. Dax's words had helped tremendously, but the dark clouds lingered over my mind. One night away, that was all I needed.

'Would it be weird if I asked to stay on your couch tonight?' I glanced sideways at him.

'Hayden would kill me,' he said lightly, only half joking.

'Hayden doesn't control me,' I reminded him.

He shrugged once again and nodded.

'If anyone controls anyone, it's you over him. I wish I could explain how much he's changed since he met you,' Dax surprised me by saying.

My brows furrowed.

'How so?'

'Not in a bad way at all, he's just . . . different,' Dax said. I noticed his eyes drift towards Hayden's hut. 'He's happy. Like, he actually enjoys life now rather than just living to protect people.'

'That's because of me?' I asked in slight awe. Guilt stirred in my stomach.

'Absolutely. Like I said, he loves you. It's pretty amazing to see, honestly.'

'I love him, too,' I admitted quietly.

'I know,' Dax replied casually. 'You two softies say it enough.'

He chortled as he nudged me once again, earning a wider smile.

'It's obvious though, even without that,' he said, suddenly sincere. 'I know it'll probably take time to fully get over this, but you will. You guys will be okay.'

I sighed and leaned sideways, resting my head momentarily on his shoulder. His presence was comforting, and he was very quickly becoming like the brother I'd never had in Jonah.

'Thanks, Dax.'

'Welcome. Just don't break my mate's heart or I'll have to be tougher on you,' he teased.

I laughed. 'Never.'

'Good. Still want to stay at mine tonight? Clear your head a bit?'

'Yes, please,' I said, relieved he'd brought up the offer himself.

'All right,' he said with a nod. He pushed himself off the ground to stand before offering me a hand to help me up. 'You good?'

I nodded. Dax offered me a small smile as he led the way to his hut, where I was determined to settle my mind once and for all. Even after everything that had happened, I was still absolutely certain of how much I loved Hayden; that was something indestructible, and no amount of opposition from the world could destroy that.

Seventeen: Concomitant

Grace

I'd never been to Dax's hut, and while he was someone I'd come to trust completely, I felt a weird sense of uncertainty as he pushed the door open. It was dark inside, but he lit a lantern to cast a soft glow around the room. I saw a bed, a very small couch, and a dresser. I was surprised to see it wasn't much smaller than Hayden's; even though he was the leader, Hayden didn't have it much better than anyone else.

Dax cleared his throat and shot me a self-conscious smile as he saw me surveying his home. 'It's not much, but it'll do, right?'

'Yeah, thank you again,' I replied quietly.

'I'll take the couch if you like,' he offered kindly as he gathered a blanket off the end of his bed.

'No, no, I'll take it, don't worry,' I said, shaking my head.

I was reminded of my first month or so in Blackwing when I'd stayed on Hayden's couch. Even after we'd shared several moments together, it took a long time for Hayden to offer to share his bed.

Dax handed me the blanket, and I moved to the couch to set up. 'Feel weird?' he asked as he sat on the edge of his bed.

'Yeah,' I admitted with a grimace.

Even though Dax was like a brother to me, it felt like I was betraying Hayden. Surely he wouldn't like the idea of me staying in another man's hut, even if it was only Dax. A thought occurred to me as I sat down on the couch.

'Hey, Dax?'

'Yeah?'

'Could I ask you a favour?'

'What, staying on my couch isn't enough?' he joked lightly. I knew he was kidding and trying to make me feel better, but I felt guilty for asking so much of him. 'I'm kidding, what's up?'

'Do you, um, do you think you could tell Hayden I'm staying here? I don't want him to worry or . . .' I trailed off, unsure of how to continue.

'Or think we're getting it on?' he finished. A wide, cheeky grin pulled at his lips. The idea amused him and there was no way it'd ever happen, but it wouldn't stop Hayden from thinking about it. His jealousy often got the better of his judgement, and this certainly was not a good time for it to flare up.

'Basically, yeah,' I said. My fingers fidgeted with the blanket.

'You should be so lucky,' he laughed, quickly dismissing the thought just as I had.

'Ha ha,' I replied dryly.

'Yeah, I can do that. But if I don't come back in a half hour, you better come and check to make sure he didn't kill me.'

'He won't kill you,' I said with a shake of my head. Despite his attempts to make me laugh, my smiles were superficial and didn't quite warm the cold that had settled into my body.

Dax snorted disbelievingly and shot me a doubtful look

but rose from his bed and moved towards the door. 'Be right back.'

'Thanks, Dax,' I repeated quietly. He nodded once and slipped outside, leaving me alone once more.

I sighed as I melted back into the couch, which was, unbelievably, even less comfortable than I remembered Hayden's being. A spring seemed to have broken through the fabric and was poking into my shoulder blade, but I didn't care enough to move. In the silence, I tried and failed to think of anything but Hayden, and soon he was swarming my mind all over again.

Absent-mindedly, my hand drifted to my chest, where I felt the now-jagged, raised edge on my skin directly over my heart. It had scarred, just as Hayden had said it would, just as I wanted it to. It was evidence of what my own brother had tried to do to me, and it was my reminder that people can change. The nagging in my head was suddenly drowned out by a different voice – a deep, lulling tone that belonged to the one man in control of my heart.

This thing between us, how I feel about you . . . that'll never change.

I heard the words he'd said so clearly now as my finger ran over the scar, pretending it was Hayden's touch instead of my own. The echo of his voice calmed and comforted me, and allowed me to make a decision right then and there: I would give myself one night to sort this out. One night to feel the ache and wrap my head around everything that had happened, and then I would move on. I would forget about the 'ifs' and 'maybes' and carry on with life.

One night, and I could go back to him. One night, and I'd be back where I belonged.

197

Hayden

The walls of my hut seemed to be closing in on me, trapping me there and threatening to suffocate me. I was determined to stay inside, because I knew if I so much as went out the front door, I wouldn't be able to stop myself from trying to find her.

I stared unseeingly at the ceiling while my fingers tapped an irregular beat into the mattress beside me. I had no idea what time it was, nor did I care. All I cared about was getting this night over with and hopefully getting Grace back. It was driving me insane not knowing where she was, and every instinct I had was screaming at me to go and find her, but I had to remind myself that she was strong enough to take care of herself. It was like my heart and mind were at war with each other, and I was pretty sure both sides were losing.

I practically jumped out of my skin when a knock sounded at my door; my body jerked upright so quickly that a wave of dizziness swept through my brain, though I didn't wait for it to pass before throwing myself at the door.

'Don't look so disappointed,' Dax said lightly when he saw my face fall.

'It's not a good time, Dax,' I muttered flatly as I turned and retreated into my hut. He let himself in and closed the door behind him.

'I know,' he replied, surprising me.

I let out a deep huff and sat down on the edge of my bed. My fingers resumed their odd drumming pattern on the blanket. When I didn't speak, he continued.

'I, uh, I know you and Grace are having a . . . rough patch,' Dax told me. I glanced at him with furrowed brows to see him tug anxiously on the hem of his shirt.

'You could say that.'

My voice was flat and low. Dax took a tentative step away from the door.

'Listen, don't kill me but—'

'That's not a promising start,' I said with a cocked eyebrow.

'I know, okay, but it's necessary,' Dax continued. He cringed and nodded like he knew he was right. 'Like I said, don't kill me . . . but Grace is staying in my hut tonight.'

'*What?*' I hissed, unable to hold back the flare of jealousy and anger that I felt.

'Hey now,' Dax said, raising his hands in surrender. 'Better with me than outside alone, right?'

I didn't reply as I clenched my jaw tightly. The muscle in my cheek ticked once, and I could feel my nostrils flare.

'Or with someone else . . .' Dax continued, raising his brows.

'Stop.'

My voice was practically a growl. I knew he was right, but that didn't mean I liked it.

'Come on, mate, she just needs a little break. She'll be back in no time.'

I sighed heavily and ran my hand down my face in an attempt to wipe away the scowl.

'You don't know that she will,' I said stubbornly. I was surprised when I heard him chuckle.

'Shut up, you know she will. She just needs a night away, that's all,' Dax replied assuredly.

'I don't like it,' I muttered belligerently.

'Yeah, well, she doesn't either, but that's life. You guys are going to have fights. It wouldn't be real if you didn't fight once in a while.'

I bit down on my lip gently, eyes focused on the floor as I

thought. I'd already promised myself to give her space, but that didn't mean I wasn't dying to find her and pull her into my chest. I wanted to hug her, to hold her so tightly against me that I could feel her heartbeat through her ribs, to feel that she was right there with me, but I couldn't. Not yet.

'Yeah.' The word rumbled from my throat as if it had to fight its way out. Dax was quiet for a bit before he spoke again.

'I know this is hard for you and all and I know how it feels to love someone, but just . . . trust me when I say, this isn't the worst thing that could happen. She's still yours, you're still hers.'

My heart gave a sharp, painful thud, but for the first time, it wasn't for myself or for Grace. Heartbreak for Dax flooded through, because I knew exactly what he was talking about. I'd lost the one I loved for a night, while he'd lost his forever. His love, Violetta, could not come back to him. It was shocking that he had any sympathy and understanding for me at all.

'I'm sorry, man—'

'Don't be,' Dax said lightly with a shrug and a calm shake of his head. 'I didn't mean it like that. I'm just saying that you guys will be all right.'

I nodded and suddenly felt very selfish. 'Thanks, Dax.'

'You got it,' he replied easily with a hint of a smile. He turned to head back towards the door when I spoke, stilling his actions.

'And Dax . . .'

He paused and turned to face me.

'Yeah?'

'If you touch her, I'll kill you,' I warned, half joking. The corner of his lips quirked up in an amused smile.

'Don't worry. She'd kill me, first.'

For the first time, a full grin tugged at my features. He couldn't have been more right, and it was impossible to ignore the sense of pride I felt. 'She would indeed.'

With that, he chuckled once and pulled the door open before disappearing into the darkness, leaving me alone once again. It was a small relief to know that Grace was, for the most part, safe for the night. If there was one person I trusted her to stay with, it was Dax.

I was about to head back to my bed when something caught my eye. The bottom drawer was cracked open, revealing the few sentimental items I owned. I leaned down to pull it all the way open. There was my journal and something I'd stored away but not yet had the courage to open: the family photo album Grace had retrieved for me.

Slowly, I reached inside and picked it up, and sat at the desk. I set it down gingerly as if it might bite me and stared at the charred, once handsome cover. Even though the thought of opening it was causing my stomach to twist anxiously, something about this felt like the right time. Maybe now, at my most vulnerable, was the best time to reopen this old wound. Surely it would hurt, so why not try when I was already hurting?

Part of me had wanted to do this with Grace, but another part of me feared whatever reaction I might have. I didn't want her to see me like that – weak and vulnerable. I wanted her to be proud of me, but I also wanted her to know what she'd done for me wasn't for nothing.

I slowly opened the album, careful not to further damage the already damaged pages. I sucked in a quiet gasp as it fell open to the first photo, which showed my mother and father holding a tiny bundle that could only be me as an infant.

It was so surreal to see their faces. They looked just how I remembered them, as they'd died only a few years after this photograph was taken. Blissful smiles were planted on both of their faces, each framed by dark hair. It was impossible to miss the resemblance between my father and me now that I'd grown, but some of my mother's features looked quite familiar too. Happiness radiated off the photo, but all I felt while looking at it was a devastating sense of loss.

I shook my head quickly and flipped the page, determined to keep going. I wanted to feel happy looking at the photos, but I wasn't off to a good start. The second photo appeared to be from my parents' wedding. My mother's hair was curled softly around her radiantly happy face as she held a piece of cake near my father's mouth, though he was too busy beaming at her to notice the icing that had dripped onto his shirt.

There was no doubt that they were deeply in love, which only reminded me of Grace. Was that how we looked to others? Was that how Dax had known for so long just how in love with her I was? If my parents felt for each other even a small amount of what I felt for Grace, I would be happy to know they'd experienced such a thing. The photo certainly seemed to prove so, and I was relieved to feel a small flicker of warmth for the first time.

I turned the next page and felt something shift. It wasn't until the album lay flat again that I could see what it was. I remembered it so clearly, even though it was such a small detail from my childhood. The fine gold chain was one my mother had worn around her neck nearly every day of her life. Two circles linked together in the centre, one slightly smaller than the other. Her voice suddenly filled my head, answering a question I'd asked long ago.

'What are they for, Mum?'

'They're for you, love. One for you, one for your father.'

My eyes squeezed shut at the memory. That was what

she'd always said – the small circle for me, the larger for my father, linked together and worn by my mother so we would always be together. I reached to gingerly pick it up. Despite being pressed tightly between the pages of the photo album, surprisingly it was in perfect condition. It appeared as though the flames that had charred the cover hadn't managed to reach inside.

All these years, it had been right there in my house. I'd thought it was lost long ago, either consumed by the bombs dropped in my neighbourhood or gone like my mother's body. I shook my head in disbelief as my finger ran down the fine chain before feeling the linked circles. This was a piece of my life, a piece of my family, that I could tangibly hold, and it was all because of Grace.

I toyed with the chain, beyond grateful for what she'd done for me. She'd risked her life and endured a broken rib to get it without a second thought. It made sitting there even harder, because I wanted to go and find her all the more now that I'd found this. My thin self-control was dwindling, and I didn't know if I'd have the willpower to make it through the night.

My thoughts were suddenly interrupted, however, by the unmistakable *bang* of a gun being fired. My head jerked to the side as I listened closely, body tensed and ready to spring to action. The sound of a second gun being fired had me hastily placing the necklace back between the pages before I slammed it shut unceremoniously and jumped to my feet. Hammered beats of my heart pounded against my chest as I retrieved my gun and ran to the door, throwing it open before bolting into the night.

It didn't matter what I'd decided earlier. I had fully planned to give Grace the night away, but this changed things. The sound of even more shots going off only urged me on to Dax's hut, determined to get to her before anyone else could. I had no idea what was happening or who was shooting, but I wasn't about to let Grace out of my sight at a time like this.

I should have known it was coming. Things had been quiet for too long, and it was only a matter of time before the next phase of the war arrived. I was almost positive the gunshots I was hearing were from Greystone, and if that was the case, it was even more important I got to Grace as quickly as possible.

Dax's hut was in sight, and I was closing in quickly on it. My heart pounded as I sprinted, my veins filled with adrenaline, determination, and fear. If there was one thing I knew, it was that I had to get to Grace first, no matter what.

Eighteen: Rage

Hayden

I could hear muffled shouting in the distance and there was a definite buzz in the air that promised danger. My pulse pounded in my ears, each beat of my heart hard and heavy. My body reacted so quickly to the threat of danger that I didn't even have to think before I moved, though now my attention was entirely focused on finding Grace.

Another series of bangs echoed through camp. To be so close yet still unable to see her sent waves of anxiety through me that only pushed me faster. My eyes were trained tightly on Dax's front door, willing myself to get there. I let out a frustrated growl. Fifty feet remained now between me and Dax's hut, and I didn't dare think what I'd do if Grace wasn't there.

She'll be there.

I felt like my heart was about to beat out of my chest as I repeated that phrase over and over again in my head. I couldn't quite convince myself of it, as too many things had gone wrong in our past to allow me to fully believe it.

She'll be there.

Suddenly, there she was. A wave of relief so huge washed through me that it nearly knocked me over when I saw her throw open the front door, face set in determination as she sprinted out towards me. Her eyes locked with mine and I could feel her own relief match mine.

The distance between us evaporated so quickly that I hardly had time to realise my eyes weren't playing tricks on me. Before I could draw a full breath, I felt her body slam against me. Her arms locked around my neck as mine wrapped around her waist. Her feet left the ground momentarily as I held her, beyond relieved that she was there with me.

'I'm sorry,' she gasped immediately. Her words muffled by her lips at my neck as she clung to me, and I could feel her heart pounding erratically in her chest.

'No, I'm sorry,' I replied, shaking my head. I knew time was short and we had to move, but I couldn't resist indulging in that quick moment before I risked losing her all over again.

'I love you,' she continued, voice strained with emotion. 'God, I love you, Grace.'

I pulled back just enough to allow my hands to grasp either side of her face to get a clear look at her. My heart all but exploded at the contact, thrilled that she was not only safe and with me, but that she'd kissed me.

The kiss was short-lived, however, as yet another bang of a gun broke us apart.

'Be careful,' I said quickly. She nodded sharply, brows pulled low and face set determinedly.

'And you,' she replied. 'Let's go.'

We both turned to head towards the source of the noise. A sudden voice from behind caused my head to jerk backward. Dax ran towards us. He carried a gun in each hand.

'You're going to want this,' he panted. He practically shoved one of the guns he held into Grace's hand, and I noted the switchblade she had stashed in her pocket, so similar to the one I always carried.

'Thanks,' she replied. Her hands moved deftly to load the bullets into the chamber.

'All right, come on.'

With that, the three of us turned to run side by side through camp. My eyes scanned constantly as we ran to catch glimpses of people here and there, but so far all I could see were members of Blackwing rushing to help just as we were. Now that Grace was with me, I could focus on fighting and keeping my people safe.

'There,' Grace muttered, pointing towards the edge of camp where shadows could be seen.

I had my gun tucked behind my back but didn't dare take a shot when I couldn't see who was who. Dax peeled off, heading towards someone streaking between two huts. Suddenly, two more shadows appeared in front of us, halting our progress. I saw Grace react as she ducked a potential blow before I turned to focus on my attacker.

A man of around thirty faced me now. He aimed a kick at my side that I managed to dodge. My fist swung around to counter his blow, connecting with his jaw. He was hardly fazed, however, and I felt a searing heat ripping at my upper arm. Blood leaked from the gash he'd created with his knife, soaking through my sleeve and dripping to the dirt.

His moves were too quick for me to grab my gun, as hand-to-hand combat so often turned out. My heart pounded as I ducked a second swipe of his knife and managed to throw my knee into his ribcage. The kick connected with a solid thud and he hissed in pain, but it didn't stop him from advancing again. This time he lunged forward, leading with his knife that I just managed to dodge. I wasn't quick enough, however, to miss the heavy punch he threw at my jaw, snapping my head to the side momentarily before I recovered. I ignored the slight throbbing that erupted from the contact and the stinging of the gash in my arm as I lurched forward to tackle him to the ground.

We landed in the dirt with a heavy huff, and in the corner of my eye I could see Grace fighting with another mysterious individual. It gave me a small amount of relief that she was okay, before I refocused on the struggling enemy attacking me. His body was pinned beneath mine, but his strength was impossible to ignore as he landed a strong punch to my side as he tried to throw me off. With a quick swipe of my hand, I managed to knock his knife from his grip to send it sprawling across the dirt.

Sweat had formed on my brow now as I struggled, and I managed to land two heavy hits in a row on his jaw and cheek. The blows seemed to stun him a bit, and he stopped trying to attack me as he tried to regain his strength. My fist pulled back, muscles flexed and tight, before I let one more hit fly. A sharp sting reverberated up my arm as my blow connected with his jaw, knocking him out cold in the dirt beneath me. Blood trickled from his mouth, and his eyes flickered once before he went slack and passed out.

My eyes jerked up as soon as I saw he was out to see Grace, who had just landed a solid kick to the ribcage of the man she was fighting. I saw a thin line of blood leaking from a cut somewhere in her hairline, but other than that, she appeared relatively unharmed. She held her knife firmly in one hand, but her gun was nowhere in sight, and I assumed she'd lost it somewhere during her fight.

'Grace.'

I heaved myself off the ground, determined to help her, even though she was holding her own. My foot slipped in a pool of blood in the dirt, but I righted myself and started to sprint towards her. I watched as they circled one another and felt a surge of pride when I saw the man was more

208

bloodied than Grace, his nose clearly broken. My pride turned to horror, however, when he lurched forward and collided heavily with her chest to knock them both to the ground.

I had just about reached them and was about to dive in to drag him off her when a solid body collided with my own, sending me stumbling a few feet off my trajectory. My gaze jerked towards the new arrival to see none other than Grace's brother, Jonah, as he leered back at me. I'd hardly had time to take in his sudden appearance when his fist swung forward to connect with my temple, stunning me momentarily as bright white lights burst in front of my eyes.

'You,' he spat angrily as he glared at me.

Another punch was aimed at me, but this time I was ready and ducked it expertly. A quick glance to my left showed that Grace was still struggling with the man that had tackled her, but a heavy thud followed by a deep hiss told me she'd landed another solid hit. Jonah's face refocused in my line of vision as I stared at him. This man was the reason for so many of my problems, and now he was right in front of me.

'Jonah,' I seethed angrily.

I noticed he carried no weapon, which led me to believe he was either incredibly skilled or very reckless. Both, possibly. My gun still rested safely behind my back, but again I didn't have time to reach for it as Jonah advanced, aiming two consecutive punches that I managed to deflect with my forearms before launching my counter-attack. He ducked my first blow, but my second landed solidly along his jaw, snapping his head to the side. His chest heaved angrily as he spit out a mouthful of blood and cast me a derisive sneer.

'Jonah, stop!' Grace yelled, clearly distracted from her own fight to observe what was going on in mine. I glanced quickly at her to see her pushing with all her might on the chest of the man hovering over her, who was doing his best to subdue her on the ground. It struck me as odd that he didn't appear to be trying to kill her but simply trying to restrain her.

I paid for my momentary distraction with another solid blow to the head, followed by a punch that landed right over the deep cut in my arm, causing me to hiss in pain as the searing-hot sting ripped through me. I could feel the blood dripping down my arm as I moved, but it didn't stop me from throwing another punch at Jonah. If I could just get to my gun, this whole thing could end, but I didn't dare take the time to grab it between hits flying in both directions.

'Why don't you just give up already?' Jonah growled as he aimed a kick at my side that I softened with my forearm.

'After you,' I spat.

I could feel the skin on my knuckles tear as I landed a double hit, with my left hand before my right. It was impossible to tell if it was his blood or mine now mixed with sweat as blow after blow landed on each of our bodies. Heavy thuds, deep huffs of breath, and the occasional grunt of pain filled the air. Every hit I landed spent a little more of my strength, and every blow I endured added a little bit of haze to my mind.

'Hayden!'

Grace's voice rang through the air, thick with fear and tension, but I couldn't break away. It was like I was locked into that moment with Jonah, too entrenched in our fight to even think clearly. I managed to duck another blow, but my actions were slowing. When I straightened up, my eyes landed on Grace, where I saw something that made my blood run cold.

Her arms were pinned above her head by the man that held her down, and while her body thrashed beneath him, she was unable to throw him off. I froze, and my vision started to blur as fury ripped through me when he reached the top of her chest and tugged her shirt down before stuffing his hand beneath the hem. She screamed in what could only be fury and fear as she squirmed, snapping me out of my horrified trance. My feet shifted in the dirt, completely forgetting about Jonah and our fight as I sprinted to Grace.

'Get the fuck off her!'

My voice was an enraged snarl as I launched my body at the man's, knocking him off Grace to send us both sprawling into the dirt. I didn't feel any pain or hurt as I quickly righted myself and re-entered the fight, pinning his body down with my own as I towered over him. He lay on his back, a stunned expression crossing his face as if he hadn't realised I was there. He looked to be about my age, but that was all I took in before my fists started flying.

'I'll fucking kill you,' I growled through gritted teeth as blow after blow landed on his face.

His head snapped to the side whenever I landed a blow, and he only lasted one or two hits before he succumbed and blacked out. That didn't stop me, however, from raining punches down on his face. Blood flew out around us as it poured from his nose and mouth, but still I didn't stop. Fury blinded me, and my body was burning with the effort of attacking him, but there was nothing that could stop me from beating him to a bloody pulp.

'Hayden!'

Grace called my name, but still I didn't stop. The squelching thuds of my fists on his face became like a rhythmic mantra in my head, as if the more hits I landed, the more I'd be able to erase what he'd done, but the images stood starkly in my mind as I lost control of my body.

'Hayden, stop!'

An urgent hand landed on my shoulder in an attempt to pull me off, but I ignored whoever it was trying to stop me and remained entirely focused on the bloody mess now below me. Heavy panting filled the air, joining in the rhythmic sounds of my punches, and everything around me started to blur. It was like I'd fallen into a deep trance.

'*Hayden!*'

Two hands wrapped round my bicep and tugged, finally managing to jerk me out of the trance I seemed to have fallen under. I felt wild and feral as I looked around, gasping and soaked with blood. Grace ducked down to tug on my arm again. My body went limp as I allowed her to pull me off the unmoving man, eyes trained in full concentration on her as I rested on my knees in the dirt. It was like I was suddenly aware of the world around me, although I couldn't look anywhere other than Grace to see what was going on.

'Grace,' I breathed, slightly stunned by my own actions. She dropped to her knees so she was level with me and placed two hands gently on either side of my face.

'Are you okay?' she asked desperately.

My hands, which were covered in blood and jagged flesh, rose to touch her as if to make sure she were real. She nodded once as if reading my thoughts. I didn't seem to be able to speak as my chest rose and fell in deep, uneven breaths.

'Hayden, are you okay?' she repeated more urgently.

'Did he hurt you?' I managed to ask, ignoring her question. My fingers coursed lightly down the side of her neck as if feeling for injuries I couldn't see.

'No,' she said with a sharp shake of her head. 'No, he didn't hurt me.'

My eyes drifted closed for a second in momentary reprieve. When I opened them, Jonah and the first man I'd fought were nowhere in sight, and it was only then that I realised that silence seemed to have fallen over the camp. No more bangs from guns echoed, and the muffled shouting I'd heard earlier was no more.

'What happened?' I questioned. I still felt shaky with anger as I managed to pull myself to my feet, hauling Grace up with me. She stood in front of me and peered up at me intently.

'As soon as you tackled that guy, Jonah got up to attack you again, but I pulled a gun on him,' she explained. My brows furrowed as I listened closely, jaw set tensely.

'Did you shoot him?'

I didn't know what I wanted her answer to be. She paused in silence for a while and chewed on her lower lip before giving a small shake of her head.

'No.'

Both relief and disappointment washed through me at once. Relief that she hadn't had to kill her own brother, disappointment that he was still alive.

'All right,' was all I managed to say.

'He ran and called off the attack. I don't know what's going on anywhere else, though,' she finished. I nodded as I tried to absorb her words.

'Okay.'

I wanted to touch her, hold her, and feel that reassuring heat of her body, but the bright red blood covering my hands stopped me. She saw my hesitation as I realised what all that blood probably meant. My head turned towards the motionless man on the ground, but Grace's hands drew me to look at her instead.

'I love you, Hayden,' she reminded me.

It was as if she could read my mind; that was exactly what I needed to hear before I faced what I had possibly just done: killed someone. I reached to grasp her wrist lightly to pull her hand from my face and turned my head to press a light kiss into her palm.

'And I love you, Grace.'

Her eyes narrowed with concern as I gently lifted her touch from my body to look again at the jagged, swollen flesh covering the man's face. At first I thought he was dead, but the near undetectable movement of his chest told me he was, somehow, still alive.

Again, I felt the odd mixture of disappointment and relief. The image of his hands on Grace's body flashed through my mind again. Her hand landed lightly on my lower back, calming me with her presence. She squatted by the man, and pressed her fingers into the inside of his wrist to feel for a pulse.

'He's alive,' she confirmed quietly.

'Shouldn't be,' I muttered bitterly.

'We should take him to Docc,' she said, ignoring my statement.

'*What?*' I hissed. Of all the things I wanted to do to this man, that was the absolute last action I would have taken.

'Yeah, Hayden. If he lives, we could question him about stuff,' she explained. 'Maybe he'd tell us something if we don't kill him.'

'Doubt it,' I grumbled.

Grace stood up and took a step back.

'It's worth a shot. He might not make it anyway,' she said. She appeared to be thinking out loud as she frowned down at him. Usually I was so against loss of life, but I found myself wishing I'd got a few more hits in before Grace had stopped me to finish the job.

'He tried to— He touched you, Grace,' I seethed, unable to find words to express how horrific his actions truly had been. I felt myself getting furious all over again.

214

'I'm fine, Hayden,' she reassured me calmly.

I finally managed to rip my gaze away from the man to focus on her. Aside from the thin line of blood leaking from her hairline and a few smudges of dirt, she appeared to be unharmed. I, on the other hand, was still bleeding profusely from the gash in my arm and surely had many other injuries I had yet to even notice. The throbbing in my knuckles was just one indicator of the damage I'd done to my own body.

'Let's go and check on everyone else, yeah? Then we'll take care of him and get you cleaned up,' she suggested calmly. Surely she was more stressed than she let on, but her focus was on fixing me.

I closed my eyes and forced myself to take a deep breath. 'Yeah, okay.'

Even though I had Grace beside me, I wasn't sure I was ready for whatever we were about to find.

Nineteen: Alleviate

Grace

Hayden's hand, warm and sticky with blood, remained clasped around my own. The blood didn't bother me; I'd dealt with far too much of it to sacrifice that small point of contact after everything that had just happened. I found it difficult to form one clear thought, so instead I chose to ignore everything and focus on the warmth of his touch and the way it felt to be back beside him where I belonged.

Hayden had stopped someone from Blackwing as they went by and told them to take the unconscious man to Docc. I recognised my attacker but we'd never spoken, nor did I know his name. It was odd, because he knew who I was, too, yet he'd still done what he had. I shivered at the thought of his hand on my body. I forced myself not to think of it. There would be time later to process and sort things out, but now, we had to make sure the rest of Blackwing was okay. My brother, the fighting, and everything else could wait.

I glanced up at Hayden to see the way his jaw was set firmly, as if forcing himself to remain hard on the outside. A bruise was already forming along his cheek, and there was an alarming amount of blood splattered across his face, though I suspected most of it wasn't his. What concerned me most was the wide gash along his upper arm; blood was still leaking fairly profusely from it, and I knew he'd have to have it stitched or it would never heal. I didn't bother mentioning it yet, however, because I knew there was no way he'd consider taking care of it before checking on everyone else.

My heart picked up speed in my chest as we neared the source of the noise. People were milling around, but it was hard to make out much else. Instinctively, I slipped my hand from Hayden's as we always did whenever others were around. I was surprised when he resisted and clamped my hand firmer in his own. He shot me a sideways glance before speaking quietly.

'I don't care anymore, Grace. Let them see.'

His voice was nonchalant, but the meaning behind it was anything but that. He didn't care if his entire camp knew the truth that we were together. I hardly had time to be nervous about the reaction we'd get before an entirely different kind of nerves set in. Hayden and I had been so wrapped up in our own individual fights that we hadn't had a chance to see what else was happening. A horrible thought struck me as we drew nearer to the small crowd gathered.

What about Dax? Kit? Jett? Docc? Were they all okay, too?

I blew out a deep breath and squeezed Hayden's hand as people's faces started to come into view. A wave of relief washed through me so quickly that it almost knocked me down when I saw Kit talking to one of the people gathered nearby. He looked remarkably unscathed, so I scanned the crowd for the rest of my friends.

'Kit,' Hayden said with obvious relief. We drew even with him.

'Glad to see you two are alive,' Kit replied honestly.

'And you,' Hayden nodded. 'Is anyone—'

'Holy hell, Hayden, what happened to you?'

The second voice interrupted Hayden's question and brought a second wave of relief crashing down on me. I turned on the spot to see Dax strolling towards us from between two huts. He carried a gun and had hair sticking up oddly on half of his head, but he was alive and only slightly bloodied.

'War, I guess,' Hayden said with a shrug. It would have been easy to miss the small smile now that he knew his two best friends – his brothers, really – were alive.

'Looks like you took a shower in blood,' Dax commented. Kit gave a low chuckle with a shake of his head.

'Yeah,' Hayden muttered distractedly. 'What happened over here? Is anyone hurt or . . .?'

I could tell he didn't want to ask, but the way his words trailed off hinted strongly enough: had anyone died?

'There weren't many of them, honestly,' Kit started. 'Couldn't see them coming from the tower because it's so damn dark out tonight, but one of the guards on patrol saw them and started firing. They came into camp, but I figure there were only ten or so.'

'Yeah, okay, but did anyone get hurt?' Hayden pressed, frustrated with the information he was getting.

'Looks like you did,' Dax said as he nodded pointedly at Hayden's arm.

'Jesus, did anyone from Blackwing get hurt or die?' Hayden demanded. He was clearly fed up with how long it was taking for his questions to be answered.

'Chill, mate,' Kit said exasperatedly. 'Look around, will you? Everyone's fine.'

I didn't fully dare believe Kit until I saw for myself. It was surprising but a massive relief to see that, this time, there were no bodies crumpled to the floor. I had been expecting death, so to not have it felt like a wonderful treat that we did not deserve.

'*Everyone's* fine?' I repeated disbelievingly. 'Jett, Docc, everyone?'

'Yeah,' Dax nodded. 'Just ran into Jett, actually. Popped right out of Maisie's hut as I ran by to ask what happened.'

'Thank god,' I muttered with relief.

It hadn't sunk in that, for once, things seemed to have gone all right. That wasn't true, however, because there had been a lot of damage done, just not in terms of lives lost. Hayden was very clearly upset by what had happened, and he still needed to be fixed up before we could begin working on anything else.

'I can't believe no one got hurt,' Hayden murmured as if reading my thoughts.

'Well, a few people got a bit cut up or banged around, but they'll be fine. I've sent them to Docc, so I expect he'll be quite busy for a while,' Kit said with a shrug of his shoulders.

'All right, good,' Hayden nodded.

He then looked at the small crowd of people watching expectantly, as if waiting for instructions from him now. I suddenly became acutely aware of my hand still claimed by his, though no one else seemed to even notice it.

'Okay, guys. If you're not hurt and don't need to see Docc, head back to bed or to your duty if you're on. Good job keeping everyone safe, and stay alert.'

As always, his voice resonated with authority while somehow managing to still sound respectful of others. It was no wonder he was still trusted even after all that had happened. People gave silent nods and quiet murmurs of assent before dispersing into the night to head home. Hayden and I were left with just Kit and Dax.

'Need anything from us, Bossman?' Dax asked.

Hayden shook his head.

'No, it's all right. Thanks, guys.'

'Sure thing, mate. See you both later,' Kit replied. He nodded at both of us and turned to head home.

'Get yourself stitched up, Hayden. Bleeding all over the place . . .' Dax trailed off, shaking his head disapprovingly as he walked away.

Hayden and I were alone now, and I had to agree with Dax.

'It's fine,' Hayden negated unconcernedly. I frowned.

'Hayden, we really should take care of your arm,' I told him. He wasn't going to bleed out from it, but I didn't like having to wait longer than was necessary to fix it.

'They just said Docc's going to be busy for a while,' Hayden said, attempting to shrug off my concern. 'It'll be fine, don't worry.'

'No, you definitely need stitches, don't be crazy. I can do it,' I replied matter-of-factly. I'd stitched up people before and would have no problem fixing Hayden.

He frowned down at me uncertainly.

'You sure?'

'Of course. What, you think I'm going to stitch "Grace" into your arm?' I said with a small grin. I was pleased when he let out a low chuckle accompanied by a gentle squeeze of my hand.

'You never know . . .'

My smile widened even more, then I shook my head. 'If I promise not to do that, will you let me? I don't want it open longer than it has to be.'

Hayden nodded. 'All right, Grace.'

I flashed him a small smile as we turned towards the infirmary. Things seemed so oddly calm now that those from

Greystone had left, but I needed to focus on fixing Hayden up before I could address my thoughts, and there was a lot to address: Jonah, the guy Hayden had nearly killed, my feelings about what had happened between Hayden and me.

It had been my intention to stay the night away from him, but the moment I'd sensed danger in the camp, all my previously conceived notions came crashing down. Everything I'd been so uncertain and confused about was viewed with a sudden clarity. Despite everything that we'd gone through, all that mattered was that he was safe and that we loved each other. It had taken fear of the unknown for me to realise that what we'd gone through was temporary, and that, over time, we would heal.

'I can't believe they just *left*,' Hayden murmured softly, pulling me from my thoughts.

'I can,' I replied honestly. He frowned and cast me a questioning look.

'Why?'

'Because Jonah's selfish,' I said with a shrug. 'He'd rather call off the raid than die when I pulled the gun on him.'

'But you wouldn't have shot him,' he inferred gently.

I shook my head.

'No, I don't think I could.'

We were nearly to the infirmary now, and Hayden squeezed my hand gently. Despite knowing he wouldn't hesitate to kill me, I just couldn't bring myself to kill my last remaining family member, no matter what he'd done.

'I understand,' Hayden replied softly.

He said no more, however, as we reached the entrance. I could feel his body tense up as he opened the door for me, following quickly behind as our linked hands demanded. There was an obvious buzz in the air, and tense voices could be heard as we neared the area Docc always worked in. Once

221

inside, we could see five people gathered, all with wounds of varying degrees of severity, while Docc flitted between them. Hayden suddenly stiffened even more and let out a low growl. I followed his angry line of vision to the very corner, where the bloody mess of the man I'd been fighting with lay unmoving on one of the cots.

'Hayden,' I said in an attempt to stifle his anger. I tried to pull gently on his arm to take him to the other side of the infirmary, but he stayed firmly rooted to the spot.

'Hayden,' I repeated.

'I can't do this, Grace,' he said tightly, still focused on the man whose chest was rising and falling slowly, but the amount of damage done to his face was very extreme and I didn't know if he'd survive the night. Docc was focusing on members of Blackwing first, leaving the man for last.

'Yes, you can,' I told him. 'He didn't hurt me.'

'That's not it,' he said through gritted teeth.

'Hayden, look at me,' I requested calmly but firmly. He forced himself to meet my gaze. 'I promise you I'm fine. Please just try not to think about it so we can get you better, okay?'

He was still clearly upset about whatever was going through his mind. His brows were pulled low over his stunningly intense eyes, and his breathing was slightly quicker than it should have been. I squeezed his hand and tugged, hoping to coax him into moving. Stiffly, he obliged, and allowed me to pull him into the corner by a single cot. Some storage shelves and a medicine cabinet cut us off from view of everyone else.

'Sit here,' I instructed, leading him to the cot. Reluctantly, he obeyed, though he was clearly still on edge. 'I'm going to get the supplies I need.'

He nodded but didn't speak as I turned to head to the main treatment area.

Docc shot me a small wave as he finished suturing a cut in someone's eyebrow.

'All right, you're all set,' Docc said dismissively to his patient. Four others remained, though none of them appeared to be in any urgent danger.

'Docc, anything I can do to help?' I offered as I started rummaging through one of the cabinets to find what I needed.

'Take care of Hayden,' he said quickly. His back was to me as he started examining the next person. 'I'll take care of these people.'

I nodded, even though he couldn't see as I stuffed my arms full of equipment. I returned to Hayden, careful not to look at the man in the corner.

The gash was on Hayden's upper right arm, and most of the skin beneath the wound was covered in thick, red blood that had started to congeal. The wound itself was still wet as fresh blood leaked out.

He remained sitting on the cot as I came to stand beside him, making us just about level. I started to feel nervous now that we were in a better lit area. His usually pink lips appeared very pale. I set my supplies down on the bed next to him and pressed my fingers to the inside of his wrist. Just as I expected, his pulse hammered, much faster than usual.

'You lost a lot of blood,' I said anxiously.

'I'm fine,' he said stubbornly.

I didn't even bother arguing with him as I prepared my supplies. My hands hurriedly twisted off the top of the disinfectant and poured a good amount onto a large gauze square. I was about to press it into the cut before I noticed his ragged, dirty shirt.

'Shirt off,' I requested.

He nodded and accepted my help. His flat stomach was exposed as I pulled the shirt upward and allowed him to pull his good arm through before I helped work the dirty fabric over his head and finally over his damaged arm. Bruises were already starting to form along the side of his ribcage, but he took no notice of them.

Hayden was quiet as I worked, but his gaze was trained tightly on me with every move I made. I could practically feel him watching me as I gathered up my disinfectant-soaked gauze once again and brought it to his cut. I tried to ignore the sizzling tension between us.

'This might sting a bit,' I warned, flitting my gaze to meet his.

'Okay,' he said quietly. I nodded once and refocused on the cut.

I pressed the gauze down into his wound, wiping away any dirt or clotted blood that had formed since he'd endured it. He made no sound, nor did he flinch, despite the sting he surely felt. Very quickly, the pristine white gauze was stained dark red, and I had to four more squares in the disinfectant before I'd cleaned the cut to my satisfaction. Now that it was cleaned up, it was easy to see that the cut itself was fairly straight, which was a good thing for me. It would be easier to suture than a rough, jagged one.

'You all right?' I asked quietly. It reminded me so much of the last time I'd cleaned him up, only then, all I'd dealt with were a few tattered knuckles and some smaller cuts.

'Yes, Grace,' he replied evenly.

I grabbed a small vial and syringe.

'What is that?' he asked as he saw me preparing it.

'Lidocaine. It's a local anaesthetic for when I suture it back up.'

'Save it,' he said, shaking his head. His uninjured hand rose to still my actions.

'But Hayden—'

'That's rare, right? We don't have much of it left?' he pressed.

'Yeah . . .'

'So save it. Don't use it on me.'

'But—'

'Save it, Grace,' he repeated firmly. He took the vial from me now and placed it on the other side of him out of my reach. 'I don't need it. Just talk to me.'

I let out a frustrated sigh. He was so selfless all of the time, and he deserved to indulge in something once in a while. A small shake of his head had me rolling my eyes in exasperation before finally accepting his request.

'Fine,' I grumbled. I picked up the fine needle and suture, making sure to keep it from touching anything else.

'Fine,' he repeated archly. I shot him a playfully reproachful look as I prepared to start my first suture.

'One, two, three.'

I threaded the needle through his cut and tugged. I had to make the sutures deep inside the cut, as it was too deep to stitch only the skin. I had to do two layers, both inside and outside. I noticed his arm tense as he felt the poke, but again he made no noise or complaint. My hands had completed about four stitches before he spoke.

'Thought you were going to talk to me?' he asked lightly. My eyes stayed focused on my work as I shook my head and let out a soft wisp of a laugh.

'Sorry,' I apologised. 'How do you feel everywhere else? And don't lie.'

'Fine,' he replied automatically.

I stabbed the needle through his skin a little less gently,

earning the first reaction out of him as he let out a quiet hiss. 'I said don't lie.'

'All right, woman, don't stab me,' he grumbled playfully. 'I'm really fine. Just need to clean up my knuckles a bit, maybe . . .'

'Yes, I agree. What about your ribs?' I asked, nodding to his side briefly.

'Just some bruises, I'll live.'

'You sure?' I asked sternly. He was so reluctant to admit if he actually was hurt that I didn't want to miss anything.

'*Yes*,' he said in exasperation. I pulled the needle through another stitch, marking the halfway point in the first line of sutures. Every now and then I had to raise a gauze square to catch a drip of blood that leaked from the cut.

We fell quiet again for a few moments as I focused on my work, though I never stopped feeling Hayden's eyes on my face. It was like he was trying to think about anything other than the needle threading in and out of his arm, so he'd chosen to focus on me instead. His tone, which had been almost playful before, was heavier as he spoke again.

'Are you sure you're okay?'

I'd never felt more helpless in my entire life than when that man had held me down and put his hands on my body. I had a feeling that I hadn't really absorbed what had happened, and that more feelings would come, but for now, I was carrying on.

'Yes, Hayden. It could have been worse.'

'That doesn't mean you have to be okay,' Hayden said quietly.

'I know, but I am,' I said honestly. 'For now, at least.'

'Well, I'm not,' he told me seriously.

This managed to draw my gaze to his once again, where the concern and emotion was clear in his eyes.

'God, Grace, that killed me,' he carried on. 'I can't even imagine what . . . what could have happened . . .'

His arm suddenly tensed even more beneath my touch, and I placed my free hand on his back.

'Hey, don't do that, Herc,' I said softly. 'Nothing happened because of you. You stopped it.'

'I know but—'

'But nothing. You saved me.'

His free hand moved to my hip as I stood next to him, and his thumb moved slowly over my side in a soothing motion. I held his gaze for a few more seconds before returning my attention to my work. He didn't speak to acknowledge my last statement and appeared to fall into his own thoughts for a while. I felt a flash of accomplishment when I finished the first line of inner sutures, cutting off the line after tying it a few times.

'Halfway done,' I told him as I prepared another suture.

'You're good at this. It hardly hurts,' he said. I couldn't tell if he was lying or not. Surely it did hurt, but perhaps the pain in the rest of his body was distracting him enough from it.

'I've done my fair share of stitches,' I replied. It was something I'd learned years ago and had only got better at.

Hayden's free arm had relaxed and fallen from my hip, but his hand remained in contact with the side of my leg as he let his fingers trail lightly across my thigh. He moved rhythmically, as if unaware of his actions.

'Lucky for me,' he murmured.

I was pleased by his compliment and smiled. I finished up the last of my sutures and tied the final knot. After swiping a clean gauze over the now finely stitched cut, I was happy with my work.

'What do you think?' I asked.

'Beautiful,' he commented before flashing me a small grin.

I was surprised when I felt his finger tuck under my chin to tilt my head backward, allowing him to duck down to press a light, lingering kiss to my lips, holding it long enough to send a comforting wave of warmth through me, before he pulled back.

'Thank you.'

'You're welcome,' I replied, voice hardly louder than a whisper. His lips quirked up to one side in a small smile.

'Let's go home. We can do the rest of this there, right?' he asked softly.

'I guess so, I'll just have to bring some stuff with me,' I replied.

'Take what you need, then,' he said gently. 'I just want to be alone with you.'

I hoped he'd stay like this when we left the infirmary. To be alone with him sounded like the perfect remedy. Nothing could quite heal me like he did, and I knew it was at least somewhat the same for him. Alone, we could work on healing each other after the damage inflicted on both our minds and our bodies. He'd voiced exactly what I wanted, and I was more than willing to oblige.

Twenty: Longing

Hayden

It was late, easily past midnight, as Grace and I made our way back to our hut. She carried a few items so she could finish cleaning me up under one arm, but the other nestled in mine once again. I could ignore the slight stinging in my upper arm if I focused on the warmth of her hand in mine.

All I wanted to do was go back home with her. I wanted to let her finish what I knew she would be determined to do. I wanted to feel the gentle way her fingers feathered over my wounds, feel the way she cared for me so tenderly like no one ever had before, feel the way she healed me both physically and mentally simply by being there. I'd grown so very protective over her that nothing could quite break me like she could, just as nothing could quite fix me like she could. It was a cycle that I could do nothing to stop even if I wanted to.

She was pensive as we walked, and she hadn't said much, but I knew we had unfinished business to attend do. Despite our reunion, issues remained. Her father's death. Her brother. The pathetic excuse for a human who had dared touch her. The raid.

I hoped we'd be able to settle it soon so I could do what I really wanted: just be with her.

'Weird, isn't it?' she murmured softly.

I glanced down at her and saw the light breeze push back the free wisps of hair that had fallen around her face.

'What's weird?'

'Being out in the open like this . . .' she trailed off and squeezed my hand, indicating what she meant. Even though it was very late and almost everyone had gone to sleep for the night, the potential for someone seeing us no longer bothered me.

'I guess so,' I shrugged non-committally. 'It's a relief not to care anymore.'

'It is,' she agreed, just as we arrived home.

I'd just touched the handle, more than prepared to disappear inside and fully let myself relax with Grace, when she spoke.

'What is that?'

She was frowning at something on the ground, eyes squinting against the darkness. My eyes followed her line of vision to see something small and white in the dirt resting against the wall of our hut.

'I don't know,' I muttered before taking the few steps necessary to bring me closer. Grace's hand fell from mine as I bent to pick it up with very bloody fingers, tainting the white a bit.

'Let's go inside and get some light,' she suggested.

She lit a candle as I closed and locked the door, casting us in a soft glow. We sat on the couch and I held out the object, a folded-up piece of paper − not something just anybody had access to in our world now.

'Open it,' Grace urged gently.

Slowly, I unfolded the paper, careful not to stain it any further with blood.

'It's a note,' I observed, once I'd smoothed out all the creases. It took me all of three seconds to read the four words that were written on the paper. The handwriting looked hurried, as if the person hadn't had much time to write it out.

Come find me – Leutie

'Where did this come from?' Grace questioned.

'I dunno . . .' I trailed off in thought. Four small words weren't much to go on.

'Do you think one of the raiders put it there? From Greystone?'

Grace's brows were pulled low in thought when I glanced up at her.

'I don't know how else it would have got there,' she muttered. She appeared just as stumped as I was. 'Why though?'

'I don't know,' I muttered. My brain felt tired from all I'd had to think about lately.

'And who? Did Jonah know they did it? Why does Leutie want me to find her—'

'Hey—'

'What if it's not even really from Leutie—'

'Grace—'

'It could be a trap, too—'

'Grace!'

My hand tilted her face as I forced her to look at me rather than letting her gaze dart around distractedly. I ran my thumb along her jaw once as she drew a deep breath, and her eyes locked on mine.

'Let's not worry about it tonight,' I told her softly yet firmly. If I was already fried, I knew she had to be as well. 'We're not going to figure it out now, and we can talk about it with everyone else tomorrow, yeah?'

'But what if—'

'No,' I said with a firm shake of my head. 'Even if we

231

knew what it meant right now, there's no way we'd actually do anything yet. It can wait.'

She let out a deep breath and nodded slowly in acceptance of my decision.

'Okay,' she said simply. As if my touch had reminded her, she pulled my hand gently from her face to claim in her own. 'We have to finish cleaning you up, anyway.'

I didn't respond as she gathered her supplies up again and led me to the bathroom. My knuckles felt stiff thanks to the amount of blood that had dried over them, as well as across my face. I wasn't surprised when she set her supplies down again and steered me into the shower.

'You going to join me or do I have to undress you, too?' she dared. Her hands worked to undo the fastenings of her shorts, where they soon joined her shirt on the floor.

'Wouldn't mind . . .' I quipped truthfully.

Dressed only in her bra and underwear she stood before me. She placed her warm hands on either side of my hips. Tension sizzled between us as her hands drifted down my sides, catching in the band of my shorts on the way.

'Okay,' she breathed quietly.

She leaned forward to press a delicately light kiss to my throat as she tugged down on my clothing, letting them drop to the floor. I didn't care in the least about cleaning up, because she was driving me absolutely insane. She reached behind her back to undo the strap on her bra, then moved to drop her underwear. I almost lost all self-control on the spot.

'Come on, then,' she said softly, taking my hand and pulling me under the shower. I followed, like a moth to a flame. When she pulled the lever to start the shower, I could practically feel steam rushing off my skin because of the heat that had suddenly accumulated there.

The water pelted down, plastering her hair to her cheeks as she let her eyes close for a moment to enjoy the feeling. Her lips parted invitingly, and she gasped as if taunting me. I let my eyes travel from her face to her neck, across her collarbone, down her chest . . .

I was about to cave in to my urges and kiss her when she shot me a smile with a hint of mischief lurking beneath it.

'Give me your hand,' Grace requested. She took a small step backward to allow me to place my palm in hers. She started to clear away the blood under the running water, dropping her gaze from mine to inspect her work.

'You're not playing fair,' I grumbled quietly. A soft, uncharacteristic giggle trailed from her lips as she shook her head innocently.

'I don't know what you mean . . .'

'Bullshit,' I muttered. The faster I allowed her to clean me up, the faster we could move on to other things.

Again she laughed as she cleaned my knuckles, always so careful not to hurt me. Once she finished the first hand, she brought it to her lips and pressed a soft kiss that lingered long enough to send a wave of heat up my arm. She started on my other hand, repeating the process until that, too, was cleared. This time when her lips pressed to my skin, her eyes flitted up to catch mine, sending me a gaze that sent a shudder down my spine.

My body was waking up, and the warm buzz I felt leached any pain that remained. I drew her closer to my body, pressing small circles into her skin with my thumbs.

She gave a tiny, almost imperceptible shake of her head as if clearing her own thoughts before raising her arms to start clearing the blood from my face and hair. I felt like my gaze was practically burning through her, because every few seconds she'd abandon her work to look me in the eye. I could feel her body react beneath my hands as they shifted lower on her hips, and it took everything in me to stop myself from dropping a hand between her legs.

Wait, Hayden.

I tried to be patient, but the gentle way her fingers were running down my scalp and the heat of our bodies pressed together was tearing apart my already fragile self-control.

'All done,' she murmured. I knew from the flush on her cheeks and the way her lips parted when she breathed that she was feeling what I was, and that was all it took for me to allow myself to duck down and finally kiss her.

The water poured over us, surely about to run out any second. Her lips melded softly with mine, fitting in the gaps like the perfect solution to a puzzle. The warmth of her hands settled on my chest, allowing her fingertips to tickle lightly at the base of my neck as I kissed her gently. It felt so good to kiss her, really kiss her, after all that had happened, and I wondered if I'd ever be able to stop.

Just as I predicted, the water ran out just as she parted her lips to allow my tongue to push lightly against her own. The sudden change caused her to pull back as she sucked a quiet gasp, and I found myself trying to follow her instinctively. She allowed me to press one light kiss into her lips before she spoke.

'Hayden.'

My name. That was all she'd said, just my name, but hearing it roll off her tongue in such a breathless whisper was like taking a jackhammer to my self-control. I wanted to hear her say it over and over again, breathless and desperate and needy for me. Again, I tried to kiss her, and again, she stopped me by placing a gentle hand on my chest.

'You're killing me, Grace,' I murmured in frustration. Why did she have to keep stopping me?

'Hayden, you're still bleeding,' she noted.

I honestly couldn't have cared less, because all I wanted in that moment was to lay her down on our bed and show her how much I needed her.

'See?' she continued as she picked up my hand. While it was cleared of dirt and clotted blood, it was easy to see the jagged skin still slightly oozing as she held it in her hand. She let my hand go and moved to grab two towels. One was wrapped around her chest before she handed me the other, which I carelessly roped around my hips.

'What are you going to do?' I asked, trying and failing to force the impatience out of my voice. I watched as she sorted through her equipment and pulled out a few gauze squares and some medical tape.

'Just bandage them. Give me a minute.'

She raised a finger and beckoned me to her, taking my hand once again. I watched as she pressed a gauze pad into my knuckles to absorb the blood that was still slowly leaking out before taking the tape to wrap around my hand a few times. She repeated the process quickly on my other hand, securing the second square of gauze across my knuckles. It looked like she'd taped them for some type of boxing match, and it appeared her work would be more than effective in stopping the bleeding.

'You done now?' I asked with a cocked eyebrow. She drew a deep breath as if she knew what was coming before nodding.

'Yes.'

'Thank god,' I muttered.

The words had hardly slipped from my lips before I ducked down once again to her lips. This time she responded instantly by wrapping her arms around my neck, hauling her body tightly against mine. My freshly bandaged hands

235

roamed down her towel-clad sides, kneading lightly into her body as I kissed her deeply. She gasped as my hands passed over her bum before hitching under her thighs to pick her up, holding her steadily in my grasp as her legs locked around my waist.

Without further hesitation, I carried her back into the main room, where a lone burning candle provided just enough light to find my way to our bed, where I was careful to set her down gently. Her back was pressed to the mattress as my body followed, hovering over her and never disconnecting our lips.

She squirmed beneath me as my hand that wasn't propping me up dropped to her thigh. My fingertips slipped over her skin and beneath her towel. When my touch reached her centre, I couldn't resist dragging the pads of my fingers devilishly slowly up her core until I reached her sensitive bundle of nerves. A dangerously sexy whine escaped her lips as I put pressure there, relishing the sounds she made when I touched her.

Our kiss broke as her head tilted back to let another breathy gasp fly from her lips when my fingers circled over her. I took the opportunity to trail my lips hungrily down her neck. I could feel the weight in my groin where I ached for her, but I couldn't resist the beautiful way she reacted to my careful touch between her legs.

When my lips trailed across her collarbone and down her chest, I felt her hands tangle even further into my hair, entrenching her fingers in the strands as she tugged softly. I allowed my fingers to circle around her clit a few more times before I pulled my hand from between her legs to tug open her towel, baring her beautiful body to me now. She took a deep breath, causing her back to arch towards me and nearly drive me over the edge.

I tasted her tongue against my own as she held me to her. Her body was restless beneath me, and I could feel the way she rolled her hips towards me as if silently begging for my body to connect with hers. I wanted to make her wait just a little longer, so I ripped my lips from hers to trail across her collarbone and chest. My lips closed around her nipple and I let my tongue dance around the edge, drawing another tantalising moan from her lips.

'Hayden . . .'

There it was — the sound I'd been dying to hear since she'd first said it in the shower. My heart hammered even faster, pumping adrenaline and desire for her through my veins as I rounded her nipple with my tongue once more before closing my lips around it.

When I felt her soft hand trail down my side and unhook my towel before discarding it, I hardly had time to prepare before I felt it close gently around me. My lips released her nipple to kiss the swell of her breast.

With all the self-control I could muster, I reached between us to pull her hand from where she touched me. Her fingers tangled with mine as I pressed it above her head, holding myself up with my other elbow as I hovered over her.

'I need you, Grace,' I breathed between kisses. My hips shifted forward, so desperate to connect with her in our perfect way.

'I need you, too,' she gasped, sucking in a breath when my hips pushed against her again without actually pushing into her. A quick mental check told me she'd only got her birth control shot a few weeks ago, meaning we would be fine to carry on.

I sank my hips between her thighs now, and her legs squeezed together as if begging for me to proceed. Her hands roamed up my sides, through my hair, down my back, all while she shifted desperately beneath me. Another deep groan rumbled from my chest at the sight, and that was all it took for me to shift forward and sink into her.

Her eyes drifted closed as her head tilted back, letting another quiet whine escape her lips as her body accepted mine. I was certain there would never come a day I'd get used to the feeling of being with her, and I was shocked yet again at how beautifully perfect we seemed to be for each other as we fit together. All that paired with the desperately burning love I felt for her was enough to cast me completely under her spell.

Grace's hand squeezed mine tightly as I pulled back slowly and pushed forward again, aiming to draw as many whispers of my name as I could from her tantalising lips. I felt her other hand press into my hip and her legs close around my waist as I moved between her thighs. The way her hips rose to meet mine as I rocked slowly into her added to the already sizzling heat between us.

I could already feel sweat forming over my skin as I moved, my actions fluid and smooth. Each and every roll of my body was designed to please her, because pleasing her pleased me beyond belief. The quiet whimpers and gasps that she failed to stifle only encouraged me, and her tight grip on my hand only grew more desperate as I pushed into her over and over again.

She seemed unable to continue kissing me as I drove myself deeply into her, so I dropped my lips to her neck again. When I sucked at her skin, her grip on my hand tightened. Goosebumps rose over the surface of her body. When I pulled my hips back and pushed in slowly and smoothly, quiet whimpers accompanied the way her back arched off the mattress and into my chest.

The feel of her body connected with mine was enough to

end me, but the way she reacted and writhed beneath me as I moved was practically driving me insane. She tugged at my hair, rolled her hips in rhythm with mine, pulled at my hand, and let her touch roam across wherever she could reach. She tried and failed to quiet her sensual mewls, and her breathing was uneven and gasping as I rocked into her again and again. Best, though, was the way she sounded when she said my name.

'Hayden,' she breathed again, clutching desperately at my neck as she ripped her hand from mine. She kissed me fervently, her body practically thrashing as I drove into her over and over. I could feel my end approaching, but I refused to give in until I'd got Grace to her high.

'Yes, baby,' I groaned, unable to restrain myself from quickening the pace a bit. She gasped when my hips pushed against hers, as I made her body jump with every move of my own.

It was my turn to gasp when she tore her hands from my hair where they'd been tangled to push at my chest, flipping us so I landed on my back. Her body followed, and I let out an audible groan as she sank back down onto me, resting over my hips to give me a perfect view of her body.

'Oh my god,' I muttered as I bit down sharply on my lip.

It was almost too much to take as I let my eyes rake over her body, starting from where we came together before moving up her rolling hips, over her chest, and finally to her stunning face. She was flushed and wet with sweat, but she was practically glowing as she rose and fell over me. I pushed roughly up her thighs before gripping her hips tightly, guiding her as she moved over me. My hips rose off the bed to meet hers, and I knew my end was closer than ever.

When her head tilted back in pure ecstasy and her muscles

started to tighten around me, I knew she was desperately close. Without hesitation, my body shot upward, bringing my chest to meet hers as her arms roped around my neck. One of my hands splayed wide across her back to hold her firmly against me while we moved together, and my other managed to slip between us to put pressure on her clit once more.

The loudest whimper yet flew from her lips, and all it took was a few circles of the pads of my fingers around her sensitive nerves to send her crashing over the edge. She clung to me as her orgasm ripped through her, causing her muscles to tighten torturously around me while I continued to move inside her and push her through her high. Her breathing was shallow and quick as she started to shake around me, and I felt her starting to melt into me as her muscles gave out. My arms were all that were left holding her up as she rode out her high. I could feel her pulse pounding in her veins as I held her, and it only took one more deep push inside of her to allow myself to finally reach my end as well.

My deep groan was stifled as she pressed her lips firmly to mine, drowning out the sounds I made as I came with her. Fingers tangled into my hair as she clutched me to her, her breath still fast. Finally, after we both started to come down, I collapsed backward and took her with me so that she draped limply across my chest, too exhausted to hold herself up. I could feel her breath across my neck as she rested, and the tiny point of heat that pressed into my throat when she kissed me there was the perfect way to finish my high.

'I love you, Hayden,' she whispered, saying my name one last time in that tone I so loved to hear.

My heart pumped wildly, and my skin felt like it was tingling wherever she touched me. She seemed to still be coming down, because her body shook slightly with every breath she took. Again, I was struck with the awe that she was mine, and that I was lucky enough to be hers.

'And I love you, Grace. So much.'

Twenty-One: Crucial

Grace

Apart from the sound of breathing nearby, I was uncertain what had pulled me from the depths of sleep. My face was tucked into the warmth of Hayden's back, our hands were linked by his side. I could feel the easy expansion of his chest every time he drew a deep breath and the heat of his body pressed to mine.

He slept so soundly now, which was a relief. I'd been worried he'd have trouble sleeping after everything, but it seemed the way our bodies had come together and the few blissful moments we'd shared had allowed him to rest. Last night, after barely managing to put a few articles of clothing back on, we'd both fallen asleep very quickly. Hayden had put on just his boxers, while I'd managed a T-shirt and underwear before climbing back in bed.

I would have been more than happy to remain like that all day, but I knew we couldn't. So badly did I want just one day to spend lounging in bed with Hayden, but our world didn't allow that. We had responsibilities to uphold and a life to maintain, restricting our time for leisurely activities.

I pressed my lips gently into his scarred back. I met resistance when I tried to pull my hand from his grip, as if we were locked together even in his sleep. I succeeded at a second try, moving slowly so as not to wake him. Carefully, I pulled myself from the bed before heading to the bathroom. I hoped he would remain asleep for a while yet, because he deserved the rest. I heard no noise as I carried out my business, which I figured to be a good thing.

Once finished, I opened the door quietly and made my way back into the main room. Something out of place caught my eye. I'd got so used to the way things were in our hut that I was surprised it had taken me so long to notice. My eyes locked on it before my brain fully processed, and my feet carried me to the desk to have a closer look. There, sitting out in the open for the first time, was Hayden's family photo album.

A small smile spread across my lips as I reached out to touch it, trailing my fingers carefully across the charred cover, tempted to open it but determined not to. It was Hayden's, and I wouldn't take away some part of him because of my selfish curiosity. If he wanted to show me, I'd let him, and I wouldn't ruin it by looking first.

'Hey.'

I jumped as his voice rumbled deeply in my ear, just before his hands slid around my waist. He hugged me from behind and ducked to let his chin rest on my shoulder, hanging on me in the most comforting way. My hands covered his as they looped around my waist.

'I didn't hear you get up,' I told him.

'I'm stealthy,' he said before pressing a light kiss onto my neck.

'I guess,' I murmured distractedly. My gaze was still focused on the photo album, and I knew he was thinking about it, too. 'Hayden?'

'Hmm?'

I could feel his chest vibrate against my back as he hummed in reply.

'Did you . . . did you look at it?'

I didn't need to specify for him to know what I was referencing. He was quiet for some time, but his hands squeezed mine momentarily, still locked around my waist.

'I started to,' he admitted softly. 'I got a few pages in before the raid started and I ran to find you.'

It spoke volumes that he'd finally felt strong enough to look at it, especially considering how things had been with us at the time.

'I'm so proud of you, Hayden.'

He was quiet again as he pressed his lips into my shoulder.

'I didn't get far,' he murmured finally.

'But you opened it and that's huge,' I said honestly. I then twisted in his grip around my waist and lifted my hands to push his messy hair back from his face. 'How was it?'

'Hard,' he admitted, studying me closely as he held my gaze. 'But I think it was good.'

My smile spread even further. 'I'm so glad.'

'We'll finish it together sometime . . . if you like.'

My heart gave an extra thump at his words.

'I'd absolutely love that.'

'Good,' he said simply with a small nod. He ducked forward to press a light kiss to my lips. He lingered for just a moment before pulling back. 'Not today, though. We have a lot to do.'

He was right; we had to deal with a lot – mainly the note that was supposedly from Leutie – and didn't have time for an emotional trip down memory lane. His hands squeezed at my hips once before he released me and started to head towards the bathroom.

'Get dressed and we'll round everyone up, yeah?' he suggested.

'Yeah, sounds good.'

He nodded before disappearing into the bathroom. I took one last look at the photo album before moving to the dresser to pull out some clothes. My collection of clothing had grown quite a bit in my time here, and it was difficult to close the drawer now. I smiled; it was yet another example of how at home I truly was in Blackwing. With Hayden.

Ten minutes later, Hayden and I left his hut and were heading towards Kit's to gather him for the meeting. The note was folded and placed in my pocket, where it seemed to sizzle for attention. I was eager to hear what everyone else had to say about it. I blinked as we stopped in front of Kit's door, where Hayden raised a hand to knock sharply. Some scuffling could be heard from inside and a few moments passed before the door swung open. Much to my surprise, it wasn't Kit that greeted us, but Malin.

'Hey, guys,' she said brightly. Her dark hair was slightly ruffled and she wore a shirt that was much too large for her. It was quite obvious she'd spent the night here.

'Hi, Malin,' I greeted. I glanced at Hayden to see his steady expression. My mind flitted to the information Malin had accidentally revealed – that they had history – but I ignored the small knot my stomach twisted into at the thought.

It doesn't matter, Grace.

I took a deep breath and forced myself to smile at her, which she returned genuinely.

'Erm, is Kit here?' Hayden asked somewhat awkwardly. I wondered if he was remembering the time he caught them sleeping together in the storage unit.

'What's up?' Kit's voice sounded suddenly as he appeared behind Malin. He touched her hip lightly to shift her to the side, and I caught the small smile that appeared on her face. I suddenly felt bad for her because it seemed she cared for him more than he cared for her.

'We've got to have a meeting,' Hayden said. 'Come to the raid building in ten?'

Kit nodded. 'Yeah, all right.'

'See you guys,' I said with a small wave. 'Good to see you, Malin.'

'You too. We should . . . talk soon,' she said with a slight blush. I knew she hadn't meant to hurt me when she'd told me. I didn't know what she wanted to discuss, but I was open to it.

'Yeah, sounds good,' I said honestly. She smiled before she and Kit retreated into his hut. Hayden, I noticed, remained stoically silent throughout this exchange, a slight tension in his jaw as we started toward Dax's hut.

'What?' I asked in amusement.

'Nothing,' he replied. 'I didn't know you guys were friends.'

'I dunno if you'd call it friends, but she's always been nice to me,' I said with a shrug.

'Hmm.'

He glanced down at me thoughtfully but said no more. Hayden knocked and Dax opened the door, as expected, standing in just a pair of shorts with slightly wet hair, as if he'd just run water through it.

'Morning, lovebirds,' he greeted with a wide grin. 'You're up early.'

Was he being his usual pain-in-the-ass self or had he heard us last night? Embarrassment started to flood through me, but I was saved from replying by Hayden.

'Yeah,' he said, ignoring Dax's implication. 'We're having a meeting in ten minutes, so put on a damn shirt.'

'Such a shame to cover this beautiful body . . .' Dax trailed off jokingly. Hayden rolled his eyes. Dax moved to his dresser and pulled out a shirt before hauling it over his head. He stuffed his feet hurriedly into his socks and shoes. 'All right, let's go.'

'Should we get Docc?' I asked as the three of us set off towards the centre of camp.

'Yeah, probably,' Hayden assented. 'And maybe that pig will be awake and we can ask him some stuff while we're in the infirmary.'

I suddenly thought that wouldn't be such a good idea, because I wasn't certain Hayden would be able to restrain himself, but it was too late as we arrived at the infirmary. Sure enough, the moment the bloodied and bruised man came into view, Hayden's muscles tightened and his walk became stiff. I placed my hand on his lower back to calm him down, but it didn't seem to work.

Docc was at his desk in the corner, and I cast him a wary glance as I followed Hayden to the patient. Now that he was cleaned up, I could see each and every tear in the skin on his face, every bruise along his jaw, and the dark blue smudges around each of his eyes. He was in rough shape, and his breathing was ragged as it pulled from his chest, but he was alive.

His dark blond hair was dirty and stuck to his head in places, and his blue-green eyes looked startled as they flickered open. I guessed him to be about twenty-five, and he could have been handsome if not for the damage done to his face and the residual hatred I had for him after what he'd done to me. He appeared most afraid when his gaze landed on Hayden, whose fists were balled tightly, his jaw clenched.

'What's your name?' I asked him firmly.

'Shaw,' he replied in a deep, slightly hoarse voice.

Suddenly Hayden snapped and swung his fist into the

man's jaw, snapping his head to the side and knocking him out instantly.

'Oh shit!' Dax cried in surprise.

'Hayden!' I exclaimed. He struggled against me and ignored my words as he tried to shrug me off, but I didn't let go. 'What are you doing?!'

'I can't do this,' he growled angrily as he continued to glare at the unconscious man. I shifted around his side, putting myself between him and Shaw. His eyes were wild and dark, and I had to place my hands firmly on either side of his face before he finally looked at me.

'I love you, but that was not very helpful,' I scolded lightly. He blew a deep, shaky breath out of his nose and kept his jaw clamped shut. I knew he was picturing the way the man had touched me.

'I don't care,' Hayden muttered bitterly.

'Jesus, he's really out,' Dax commented from behind me. Hayden's eyes flitted over my shoulder to look at him and I caught his darkly satisfied grin.

'Guess we'll just talk to him later then,' I conceded while shooting Hayden a disapproving look. 'You'll need to stay calm, Hayden.'

'No promises,' he grumbled. I loved him for how much he loved me, but I wondered if he'd be more of a hindrance than a help in terms of interrogating Shaw.

'Hayden, what have you done to my patient?'

Docc's calm voice washed over us as he appeared by the bedside, a stern look on his face. Dax poked Shaw in the shoulder as if checking for signs of consciousness.

'I hit him,' Hayden muttered matter-of-factly. He showed no signs of regret, which earned a small chuckle from Docc.

'Hopefully he wakes up again,' Docc continued.

'Here's hoping,' Hayden said sarcastically as he raised his

hand to show two fingers twisted together in the universal sign for good luck. His lips twisted into a bitter, sardonic grimace.

'So, did you come just to knock out my patient or did you need something else?' Docc questioned lightly.

'We need to have a meeting. Is there someone who can watch him while you're gone?'

'Yes, let me find Frank and I'll meet you guys there.'

Hayden nodded and cast one last scathing look at the still unconscious Shaw before turning to leave. Dax rolled his eyes playfully at me behind Hayden's back before we followed his skulking figure back outside.

The trip to the raid building was silent, but I chose to let Hayden calm down on his own rather than try to force him to. Kit was already waiting for us when we walked into the building. He sat at the table in the middle and casually flipped a knife back and forth between his hands.

He looked up. 'About time,' he joked easily.

'We had a minor interruption,' Dax said smoothly.

Hayden continued to sulk as he moved to stand next to me. Docc joined us moments later.

'All right, what's happening?' Kit asked now that everyone was present.

'Show them, Grace,' Hayden said. His voice was still low and laced with anger as he spoke, but he appeared to be calming down enough to cast a glance at me that wasn't blazing with aggression.

'So, we found this after the raid . . .' I started as I pulled out the note. My fingers carefully unfolded it and set it out on the table for everyone to read. Everyone was quiet for a moment.

'Who is Leutie?' Docc questioned, breaking the silence first.

'She's my friend from Greystone,' I filled in.

'Do you think it was really her?' said Dax. 'I thought you said she didn't go on raids?'

'She doesn't.' I shook my head. 'So it couldn't have been her that dropped it off. If it was even her that wrote it.'

'Can you tell from her handwriting?' Kit asked.

'No.' I shook my head. 'We don't exactly write all the time, you know?'

'True . . .' Kit murmured with a frown.

'So . . . are we saying if it *was* her, someone dropped it off for her?' Dax questioned, thinking aloud.

'It'd have to be,' I said with a shrug. 'That's a big "if" though.'

'What would she want?' Hayden asked, speaking for the first time.

'I don't know,' I admitted when he looked at me.

'How would she know which hut is yours?' Docc asked.

'Jonah knows. Maybe he told some people and Leutie found out . . . Or whoever dropped it off?'

'If only she'd written in some secret that only you two knew to clearly identify herself,' Dax joked lightly. Hayden shot him a glare; he was not at all in the mood for jokes. 'Sorry.'

'There are two possibilities,' Hayden said sternly. His eyes passed around the circle. 'One: this actually was Leutie, and she got someone to drop it off for her who knew where you were staying. Two: it was someone else and it's some kind of trap. Personally, that first option seems like a long shot.'

'I agree,' Kit muttered reluctantly. I had to agree – it seemed too far-fetched to be credible.

'So someone is trying to lure us into Greystone so they can attack?' Dax continued.

'I think that's the more likely,' Docc said. His lips pursed together as he shot us a sympathetic look.

'So what do we do?' I asked. I was torn, unsure of what I believed and what I even wanted to believe.

Everything hinged on our decision on who the note was actually from. My gut was saying not to go, that it was a trap and that Jonah was waiting to pounce like a predator on its prey, but my heart was saying to go and find Leutie. Was she in trouble? Did she need me?

'What do you think, Grace? You know both sides.'

It suddenly became clear that whatever I decided, they would do.

If I decided to go after Leutie, they would all risk their lives to do it. If I decided it was a trap and we did nothing, I'd live with the constant questioning of whether I'd decided the right thing. What if I was wrong and Leutie really was in danger, but I chose to stay here? What if she had something that could help us, but we never got to know because we didn't take action? My heart picked up the pace in my chest, beating erratically, while my mind practically hummed with the effort of sorting it all out.

I drew a deep breath and glanced at everyone before focusing on Hayden, bracing myself for his reaction.

'I think we need to go,' I started slowly. All four of them stared determinedly back as they waited for me to continue. My stomach knotted uncomfortably in my abdomen, and I tried to calm my racing heart before I finished speaking. 'We need to go . . . But I'm going alone.'

Twenty-Two: Formidable

Grace

My words lingered in the air between us for only a split second before Hayden spoke and swatted them to the floor.

'No. Absolutely not.'

I frowned. I knew he'd say that. Every word and action until this point made it very clear he'd never go for such an idea, but he didn't control me.

'Yes,' I said calmly.

'No way,' he muttered with a shake of his head. 'You're not going alone. It's too dangerous.'

'How? One person is less conspicuous than four, and I know Greystone better than anyone,' I argued. I crossed my arms over my chest in an act of defiance.

'She's got a point, mate,' Dax dared to say. The harsh glare Hayden threw in his direction shut him up quickly before his attention was returned to me.

'Grace, you can't go alone, that's insane,' Hayden continued.

'*How*? It makes the most sense. If it really is a trap, we can't risk everyone getting caught or even killed because of it. If it's not, it'll be easiest for me to sneak in, find Leutie, and get out before anyone even knows I'm there.'

'I don't care what the situation is, trap or not, you're not going alone,' Hayden grumbled angrily.

I hadn't noticed, but he'd taken a step towards me so the space between us was less than a foot now. He glowered down at me, while I stood my ground and glared back up at him. No one else said anything as the tension simmered around us. I could feel their eyes on us even though none of them spoke.

'You're not thinking rationally,' I retorted.

'*You're* not thinking rationally. You could be walking right into a trap and you want to go alone? They could kill you, Grace. They've already tried before,' Hayden seethed. I knew it was his love for me that was making him angry, but his seeming lack of confidence in my ability was starting to feel insulting.

'I can handle myself just fine. You know that,' I spat harshly.

'You're not going,' Hayden stated stubbornly.

'You don't control me, Hayden. I can go if I want to,' I replied. My tone was angry and spiteful now. 'You don't think I can handle it?'

'That's not—'

'How about we take a step back and talk about this?' Docc said, interrupting our spat.

Hayden and I glared at each other a few moments longer, deep breathing forcing from our lungs, before I managed to tear my gaze away from him and jerk my attention back towards the table.

'She's not going alone,' Hayden spat immediately.

I shot a quick glare in his direction before glancing around the table to see everyone else's reaction.

'Now, son,' Docc began calmly, 'I know you don't like it, but she makes a good point. She does indeed know Greystone the best and stands the best chance of getting in and out, whatever the situation, without being detected.'

'But if it's a trap—'

'If it's a trap, all the more reason only one of you should go,' Docc interrupted Hayden's protest. 'We simply cannot risk sending all of you to a potential trap. Grace is more than capable of defending herself, we all know that.'

'That's not it,' Hayden seethed. 'I know she's just as strong as anyone, but that doesn't mean I'm okay with her going alone.'

'It's not your decision, Hayden,' I said quietly. It helped a bit to hear him say that he knew I could defend myself.

'It's my decision if I go with you, though,' he retorted sharply. I sighed heavily as I met his glare once again, frustrated with his insistence to protect me.

'Let's put it to a vote,' Docc said evenly.

'What, no—'

'I vote she goes alone,' Kit said quickly. Hayden looked at him like he wanted to hit him in the face. Kit just shrugged before continuing, 'She's right, mate. She's got the best chance of anyone, no matter what it is.'

'Dax?' Docc carried on.

'I . . . Look, I know you don't like it, Hayden, but I agree. She goes alone.'

'And I agree,' Docc concluded.

'What the hell is wrong with you all?' Hayden practically growled. He glared at each of us in turn.

'Hayden, can I talk to you outside?' I requested calmly. I could see that everyone going against him wasn't helping, because it was only making him angrier by the second.

'Fine.'

I went to a small gap between the raid building and the one next to it to give us a bit of privacy. When I turned around, he came to a stop about a foot away from me, hands clenched tightly by his sides in fists.

'Hey,' I started evenly.

He cocked an eyebrow defiantly and didn't return my greeting.

'Hayden, come on,' I pleaded calmly. 'You know I'm right – this is the best way.'

A short huff of frustration pushed between his lips as he gave a minute shake of his head. 'Grace, you know I can't let you go alone. I just can't.'

'Yes, you can, you just don't want to.'

'Does it matter? I don't want to let you go alone because what if something happens to you, huh?'

Finally, some of his anger started to evaporate as the fear he'd been hiding showed through. A hint of vulnerability crossed his features.

'It goes both ways, Hayden. What if you come along and something happens to you? I can get in more easily if I'm alone, and I don't want to risk you getting hurt.'

'I don't care if I get hurt,' he muttered determinedly.

'But I do,' I replied immediately. 'So stop fighting with me, please.'

'Please, Grace.' The last hints of anger had gone, leaving only the raw and vulnerable tones behind. I was surprised when he raised a hand to place his palm gently against my cheek, where his thumb traced lightly over my skin.

'Don't you believe in me?' It was impossible to hold the sting of hurt out of my voice.

'Of course I do,' he responded quickly, voice still quiet and soft.

'Then let me do it alone,' I pleaded.

Hayden looked like our conversation was physically paining him, because his brows tensed even more and his frown was deeper than ever. I needed him to trust me. He took a deep breath and gave a tiny tick of his head as if fighting with himself internally.

'Okay, Bear.'

A sigh of relief pushed past my lips as some of the tension lifted off my shoulders. Hayden watched me unhappily but allowed his thumb to trail across my cheek one last time before he ducked forward to press his lips into my forehead.

'Will you at least let me go with you until the edge of the trees?' he reasoned.

'Do you promise you'll wait there? Because I know you and I know how hard it'll be to stay there while I'm gone,' I said sternly. He hesitated to answer. 'Hayden—'

'Yes, I promise,' he agreed. 'It's better than waiting here.'

'Okay,' I conceded. 'Let's go tell them.'

Hayden nodded and dropped his hand from my face, stepping back to allow me to lead the way back inside. Kit, Dax, and Docc all stopped whatever they had been talking about when I re-entered and turned to look at me expectantly. Hayden followed close behind, closing the door after us before we gathered around the table once more.

'Well?' Kit asked anxiously.

'I'm going alone,' I told him. Hayden let out an unhappy huff beside me but didn't speak.

'Well, well, well, what a surprise,' Dax said lightly. 'We all reckoned he'd never let you.'

'He doesn't control me,' I said calmly. I didn't want to offend Hayden, but it was the truth. My decisions were my own, whether he liked them or not.

'I'm going with her and waiting along the treeline,' Hayden stated. 'You guys need to stay here in case part of the trap was drawing us out of Blackwing.'

'I think this is a good plan,' Docc assented. He nodded pensively as he studied us each in turn. 'Dax and Kit stay here, Hayden accompanies Grace to the edge of the trees, Grace goes in, yes?'

'Yes,' I agreed. It was the best possible option I could think of and it made me feel better that everyone else seemed to agree. Other than Hayden, that was.

'When will you be going?' asked Kit.

'I think I have to go tonight, don't you?' I questioned, focusing my gaze on Hayden. He looked resistant but nodded after a few moments.

'I think so, yeah,' he agreed. 'Kit, Dax, you guys take care of things here while we're gone.'

'You got it, Bossman,' Dax said with an overly serious nod.

'You be careful, girl. We want you to come back here,' Docc said to me. It was such a nice feeling knowing that he actually cared for me.

'I will.'

Docc turned to leave, then Kit appeared in front of me next.

'You've got this,' he said confidently. He looked impressed with my determination to go alone.

'Thanks, Kit,' I replied with a small smile. He gave a quick wave before disappearing out the door after Docc. Only Dax was left, and he approached me now as Hayden looked on.

'All right, Bud, do you need a pep talk?' he said with a wry grin. I chuckled.

'I don't think so, Dax, but thanks.'

'If you insist,' he conceded, raising his hands by his head in defeat. 'But make sure you come back, yeah? We need you. That one needs you.'

He ticked his head towards Hayden, who was surely already regretting his decision, but I wasn't going to let him go back on it.

'I'll come back,' I promised Dax. I was surprised when he threw his arm around me, giving me a quick side hug. Hayden, for the first time, appeared too distracted to show any jealousy.

'See you later, then,' Dax said with a quick smile. He nodded at Hayden and clapped him on the shoulder once before exiting, leaving Hayden and I together.

'You sure you want to go alone?' he asked.

'Positive.'

He nodded in defeat. 'All right.'

The rest of the afternoon passed quickly. Hayden and I grabbed a meal in the mess hall, where Maisie was more than thrilled to see us. After that, we stopped by the raid building to grab any supplies I might need. Two 9 mm handguns, two switchblades, several rounds of ammo, a bottle of water, a few first-aid supplies, and a backpack were taken back to our hut. Having so many weapons made me feel so much more powerful, so in control, and, admittedly, quite excited. The adrenaline a raid provided was like that of nothing else, and I couldn't deny a bit of me looked forward to it.

After our evening meal, Hayden and I had a little bit of time to kill before it got dark. I was surprised when Hayden insisted I rest for a while before the raid, and I was even more surprised when he accompanied me. It was something I'd longed to do for such a long time, and there was no denying I was reluctant to get up when the time finally came. Hayden and I spent a few hours in bed, doing absolutely nothing other than lying cuddled together, drifting in and out of sleep between simply taking comfort in each other's warmth.

Before I knew it, it was dark and Hayden and I were heading through camp. He carried a few weapons of his own in case things went sour, but I sincerely hoped he wouldn't need them. He was quiet as we walked, and we'd made it about halfway through the trees before I spoke.

'Are you going to stay in the trees like you promised?'

'Yes, Grace.'

'*Really?*' I raised a sceptical eyebrow at him.

'Yes, really,' he said, barely managing to hold back the exasperation in his voice. 'But if you're gone longer than an hour, I'm coming after you.'

'No, that wasn't the deal, Hayden!' I should have known he'd try something like this.

'You never said anything about that,' he pointed out. He held a long branch out of the way for me to duck underneath it.

'Two hours,' I bargained.

'One.'

'Two or I'll make you turn back,' I threatened. He and I both knew I would not win that battle, but it was worth a shot.

'One.'

'That's not much time, Hayden. I have to sneak in, find Leutie, figure out what's happening, and sneak back out. One hour will be up in no time and you'll come after me and cause more trouble,' I reasoned. He let out a frustrated huff as he saw my logic.

'Fine. Two. But after that, I'm coming after you.'

'Fine,' I said with a light eye roll and a smile.

We grew quiet then as we approached the edge of the trees. Greystone was clearly visible through the sparse branches now thanks to the lanterns lit here and there. As always, it was odd seeing my former home, but this time felt different. I felt strong, powerful, determined. I felt good. Hayden and I stood side by side, surveying what lay ahead. His hand slipped into mine gently and gave a light squeeze.

'You can do this, Grace,' he said quietly. 'I know you can.'

I couldn't stop a smile from pulling at my lips. That was what I needed to hear to give me that last bit of confidence. 'Thank you, Hayden.'

His hand left mine to slide up along my neck, where his fingers wove into the hair at the back of my head. He ducked down as he pulled me to him before pressing his lips lightly to mine. We drank in the feel of each other one last time before we fulfilled our promise like always.

'I love you. Be careful,' he murmured.

'And I love you. Be careful, and stay here,' I replied with a slight smirk. He did not return it.

'I mean it, Grace. Come back to me.'

I pulled in a deep breath to steady myself. This all seemed so familiar, yet the situations were reversed. Last time we were separated like this, I'd been the one begging him to come back to me.

'I will. Wait for me and I'll come back to you.'

A slightly pained look crossed his face before he leaned in to give one last emotional kiss. I shot him a brief smile before turning away and heading off into the darkness. True to his word, he did not follow.

I needed to focus every thought I had. Hayden's face swam before my eyes, cementing my determination to come back to him, before I blinked it away and focused on the softly twinkling lights that flickered through Greystone.

I stalked through the darkness, moving quickly to avoid being seen. I was constantly in search of guards or threats but saw none as I crept closer to the outer ring of huts. I had been expecting to see a lot of them with the war. Warning bells started going off in my brain, alerting me that this indicated a trap, but I pressed on.

Finally, I reached the first building and flattened my back

against it, pausing to plan my next move. My eyes darted back to the treeline where I knew Hayden was waiting. He probably couldn't see me anymore. I was reminded that I was on my own, as I had wanted. The success or failure of this was solely on me, and I embraced the responsibility.

My ears pricked as I heard a pair of footsteps on the other side of the building. Quietly, I edged closer to the corner to glance around, where I saw a dark shadow moving along the path. It appeared to be on guard, judging by the rifle in its hands. I had timed my run towards the building well. The footsteps began to fade until I couldn't hear them anymore, so I darted around the edge of the building unseen. A quick glance down the path told me the coast was clear, so I ran across into the next ring of huts.

So far, there were no signs of a trap, but I remained sharp and focused as I glanced around continuously. My gun was drawn and loaded, ready to fire if I needed. It didn't matter that I was in my former home – if anyone attacked me, I wouldn't hesitate to defend myself. I expected to be caught at any minute, and I felt like I was just waiting to feel the knife at my throat or the barrel of a gun on my temple.

I was near the middle of camp now, drawing ever closer to Leutie's home, and my heart was pumping adrenaline through my veins so quickly that I felt like my body was vibrating. I sprinted between the huts, and my senses seemed sharper than ever. The air seemed to be buzzing around me with an ever-growing intensity, as if urging me on. Three times, I encountered someone either on guard or just out, and each time, my presence went unnoticed.

Finally, the hut where Leutie lived alone came into view. It was very small, ten feet by ten feet at the most. A single grimy window, cracked in several places, showed no light coming from inside. I had no idea if she was even there, but it was the best place to start. I was about to dart across the final path when I heard voices, forcing me back into the shadows. Crouching down, I ducked behind a pile of metal scraps, determined to remain out of sight. My breath stalled in my lungs as I deciphered the words.

'. . . I told you, he won't listen. If he's going to continue resisting, then he'll have to be taken care of.'

My heart dropped in my chest as I recognised the voice. What had once been a source of comfort now turned my blood to ice in my veins. Jonah. I had no idea what he was talking about, but the menacing tone told me he was not very happy with whomever he was discussing.

'What are you going to do?' asked a second voice that I did not recognise.

My eyes squeezed shut as I willed them to pass. Their footsteps sounded like they were feet away from me, and I prayed they wouldn't stop. Thankfully, they continued on, Jonah's voice receding, but I just managed to make out his final statement.

'If he won't cooperate, I'll kill him.'

I drew a shaky breath, nervous for this mysterious person Jonah was very openly threatening. My head shook once to refocus; that wasn't my concern. My concern was finding Leutie, figuring out if she sent the note, and getting out. The path became clear to me once more as I stood slowly, and I made sure to check twice that no more enemies were around. I took a deep breath and darted across the path.

My silent feet skidded to a halt as I stopped, breath shaky, outside her door. I pressed my ear to the wood, listening closely for any signs of life inside. Silence greeted me, which did little to calm my nerves. If the note said to find Leutie and it was a trap, danger could very well await me inside. My leg bounced up and down anxiously as I waited.

I raised my gun, gripped firmly in my slightly sweaty palm, and twisted the knob slowly with my free hand. My teeth clenched together tightly as I willed the door to stay silent. I saw a few inches of space between the door and the frame, but inside was dark. When nobody immediately attacked me, I felt brave enough to open the door enough to slip inside.

Now I could hear the soft whispering of breath. The bed was just a few feet away, and slowly, still careful to be wary of traps, I crept forward. I held my breath as I inched closer, making it easier to hear the pounding of my own heart in the quiet area.

With my gun raised, I ducked down to get a good look at the sleeping form of Leutie. A small flash of guilt shot through me as I aimed it at her; she hated guns and always had, but it was a necessary precaution. I raised my free hand and held it in front of her face, ready to silence her if I had to.

'Leutie,' I hissed, just loud enough to try and wake her.

A small groan escaped her as if resisting waking, but her eyes didn't open.

'*Leutie,*' I repeated more urgently.

This time, her eyes drifted open lazily before blinking once and bulging open in shock. Her lips parted to let out her surprise, but she didn't get the chance as I clamped my hand tightly over her mouth. The frightened scream was stifled by my hand but still loud enough to hear if anyone was really listening.

'Are you going to be quiet?' I whispered sharply, keeping the gun trained on her.

She nodded, and I could feel her shaking as I held her down. Mercifully, she remained quiet as she stared at me in shock.

'Grace, what are you doing here?' she whispered in awe as she pulled herself up to rest on her elbows.

'Did you write me a note?' I demanded, ignoring her question.

'A note? What? No, I—'

'It wasn't you?'

'No,' she said with a confused shake of her head.

'*Shit*,' I muttered under my breath.

'Grace, you shouldn't be here,' she warned quickly. 'Jonah, he's lost it . . . they're all looking for you.'

'It *was* a trap,' I snapped more to myself than anything. I could feel anger starting to boil up inside me as my jaw clenched tightly.

'Um, Grace, could you take your gun off me?' Leutie whispered timidly. I blinked, unaware I still had my gun aimed straight at her face.

'Oh, sorry,' I murmured distractedly, lowering it but keeping it ready.

'What's going on?' she whispered. Concern was laced through her tone as she watched me intently.

'We found a note that said it was from you, but obviously not . . .'

'*That's* what they were talking about,' Leutie said cryptically.

'What is?' I demanded sharply.

'It's a long story—'

A loud voice from right outside cut her off, and her eyes widened even more as she jerked her gaze skittishly towards the door.

'You should leave,' she muttered in fright.

'Come with me,' I suggested on a whim. It was clear she was no danger to me or she would have alerted someone the moment she saw me.

264

'What? No, I can't.'

She started shaking again, clearly terrified at the thought of sneaking out and, essentially, betraying Greystone.

'Yes, you can,' I urged. 'Are you happy here? Do you feel safe?'

'No,' she admitted, brows lowered over her blue eyes.

'Then come with me. You could help us end this and we'll keep you safe,' I bargained.

Another sound from outside caused me to twitch in irritation, quickly growing impatient and anxious. She studied me closely as if battling internally with her decision. Every second that ticked by made it more dangerous for me to be here, and the sounds outside were only adding to my growing trepidation. I nodded encouragingly at her, silently pleading with her to come with. Her eyes were wide with fear as she nodded slowly.

'Okay.'

Twenty-Three: Defection

Grace

'Yes, okay, good,' I said quickly. 'Now get up, we have to go.'

'I don't know if I can do this,' she said fearfully as she pushed down her sheets and pulled on a pair of shoes before she stood up.

'Yes, you can,' I told her.

I moved to the edge of the window and looked out while staying in the shadows, searching for signs of movement. Already, her weakness was starting to grate on me, but I pushed it down. It was important to get her to Blackwing.

'Take what you need and only what you can carry,' I instructed. I pulled one of my guns from my waist and held it out to her. 'And take this.'

'I can't,' she said with a shake of her head. Her eyes darted down to the weapon as if afraid it would explode. 'I've never used a gun before.'

'You're going to learn, now take it,' I commanded firmly. 'You need to protect yourself, and we're going to need to move quickly.'

'O-okay,' she stammered weakly. Her fingers closed gingerly around the gun before she moved to grab a small bag off the floor. After stuffing a few articles of clothing and some other random items inside, she slung it over her back and gave me a nod.

'What's all that noise?' I demanded, forcing my voice to stay low.

'I don't know exactly, but Jonah was talking to someone earlier about something big they had to do tonight,' Leutie explained quietly.

'Like set a trap for me?' I muttered flatly, connecting the dots. It wasn't hard to figure out: Jonah hoped his trick would work, and planned to attack whoever responded to the note. I had managed to slip into Greystone before they were ready, but every second that ticked by took me closer to the time when their plan was set, meaning our escape would be much more difficult.

'Apparently,' she murmured in agreement.

I had so many questions I needed answers to, but now was not the time to ask. The noise from outside grew louder as more and more people began moving through camp. It was much too late for so many of them to be out, which only confirmed my suspicions that Jonah was going to try to trap me tonight. I was vaguely aware that I'd been gone nearly sixty minutes now, giving me one more hour before Hayden left his post to come and look for me.

'We have to go,' I told her quietly. 'And if someone attacks, you need to shoot. Can you do that?'

'I don't . . . I don't know, Grace,' she said with an unsteady shake of her head. Her face was starting to look a little green as she watched me with frightened eyes. Again, I had to force down my frustration.

'You *can*.'

She didn't respond but nodded meekly at me before I looked out of the window one last time. I couldn't see anyone, but I knew someone could arrive at any moment. 'Follow me, and stay alert.'

I opened the door as quickly as I could while staying

silent and slipped outside into the shadows. I cringed as Leutie followed noisily behind me, not nearly as stealthy or smooth as I was. We managed to make it between a few small buildings before I heard voices loud enough to give away their location before I could see them. They remained oblivious to us as they passed, and I barely managed to wait until their backs were to us before moving on with Leutie close behind.

Quickly, we darted to the next shadowy reprieve a few yards away, careful to stay in the shadows. I leaned around it to check for oncoming enemies. Leutie remained next to me, panting far too loudly for my comfort. As I glanced down the path, two shadows, one considerably larger than the other, appeared at the end and began to move in our direction. Their words drifted to me as I listened.

'. . . he said it could be tonight or tomorrow or even later, but we need to be ready. His bitch of a sister is bound to fall for it.'

Leutie gasped as she realised they were talking about me. Anger bubbled inside my veins.

'Shh,' I hissed almost silently, on edge with her noisiness.

'Sorry,' she whispered back, making me cringe once more.

Her free hand reached up to push her sweaty hair out of her face. As a loud crash sounded, my head whipped to the side to see a pile of wooden crates tipping over, knocked off balance by Leutie's elbow. She sucked in a gasp of surprise and shot me an absolutely terrified look. Not even a full second later, I heard the voice of one of the men who had been approaching.

'What was that?' the first one asked his counterpart sharply.

'It came from over there,' said the other. This one sound-ed younger.

'Go and look,' commanded the first one.

His voice sounded louder as they approached. It was already too late to hide, and I knew using my gun would only draw more attention to our hiding place. Leutie was shaking like a leaf as she pressed herself into the wall so tightly it was as if she were trying to melt into it, so she would be no help. If we wanted any shot at escaping, I would have to fight these two men at once.

'Get down,' I hissed at her quickly. I stowed away my gun and pulled out a knife in each hand, ready to defend us both. I could hear the crunching of the men's boots, bringing them closer. They would be here any second. I had just enough time to close my eyes and force out a deep breath to prepare and focus.

You can do this, Grace. I know you can.

Hayden's confidence resonated in my mind, giving me the last bit of strength I needed. I opened my eyes and saw the first man, the younger one, step into the area between the huts where we hid. He stood with his back to me, only a few feet away, but I was hidden by the darkness. I couldn't see the second man yet, and I knew I had to act quickly. Before I could give any second thoughts, I bolted out of the shadow, knives held firmly in each hand, as I quickly closed the distance between us.

Dirt crunched beneath my feet and alerted the man to my presence. He started to turn towards me, but not before I slid feet first into the dirt and skidded by him. Two almost simultaneous wet slicing sounds filled the air as the blades of my knives slashed through both of his Achilles tendons, dropping him to the ground as he cried out in agony. His hands clutched at his ankles, where he tried to stem the gushing blood.

'What the fu—'

His cursing transformed into a guttural groan of pain as he writhed on the ground. He still hadn't seen me, as I'd slipped back into the shadows while his pain distracted him. In that time, the second man had rushed into the darkness, just as I had wanted him to.

'What happened?!' he demanded, eyes darting around quickly before he refocused on the man on the ground. I could tell by his voice that he was the one who had referred to me as Jonah's 'bitch of a sister'. Anger simmered inside me at the sight of him.

'I don't— Look out!'

The injured man's warning was too late, however, as I darted forward. This time, my knife was aimed at the second man's throat. One quick flash of movement was all it took to drag the blade across the tender skin and spill his blood, where a stifled gurgling erupted before he dropped to the ground, dead.

'Oh my god,' gasped Leutie, absolute horror ringing through her voice. I ignored her as I approached the younger man, who was looking at me as if I were a ghost destined to haunt him.

'Please,' he gasped, staring wide-eyed at me as he weakly rolled away from me.

I stalked forward, determined to do what I had to do and make it out alive. Blood dripped from my knives, splashing into the dirt by my feet.

'Please don't kill me,' he begged weakly. His face was pale and sweaty. He dragged his body across the dirt slowly away from me. I didn't respond but continued advancing. 'Please,' he repeated. 'I . . . I'll do anything, please just don't kill me.'

'Grace . . .' Leutie whispered from behind me.

A flash of recognition crossed the young man's features as

he heard the name. He was more of a boy than a man, maybe sixteen or seventeen, I guessed.

'Grace?' he questioned. I kept my face blank and did not react. 'You're Grace . . .' He looked like things suddenly made much more sense as his eyes glanced over my face. 'You're the one everyone is looking for . . . the traitor . . .'

'I'm not a traitor,' I hissed, unable to stop myself. The fact of the matter was that I was the exact definition of a traitor, but I couldn't admit it out loud.

'Grace, let's just go,' Leutie begged from behind me.

I ignored her. The boy reached the edge of a hut now and was unable to retreat any further. He was gasping for air and grimacing in pain every few seconds, terror written across his features. I stood over him, knives poised to deliver the lethal blow that would end his life. My heart thumped heavily in my chest, as if begging me not to.

'You don't have to do this,' he continued shakily. 'I'll . . . I'll tell you anything, please.'

Do it, Grace.

'I don't know how to fight in a war. I don't want to die.'

Do it.

My jaw clenched tightly as I glared down at him, hating him for making me feel this way. I should have just pushed my knife into his heart and got it over with. Slowly, I crouched down in front of him and pressed the tip of my blade into his chest, directly over his heart.

'Oh my god, no,' he gasped, tears of fear leaking from his eyes as they squeezed shut. 'Please, I mean it, I'll tell you anything you want, just don't kill me.'

I put slight pressure on the blade, enough to dig into his muscle but not enough to break the skin through his shirt. He winced in pain, eyes closed tightly and teeth bared.

'Look at me,' I commanded quietly yet forcefully. He took a deep, shuddering breath as he forced his eyes open and looked me in the eye. 'What's your name?'

'Nell,' he answered frightfully.

'If I let you live, you're mine, understand? I'll be back, and when I am, you do absolutely everything I say, got it?'

He nodded quickly, lips quivering as he watched me.

'You don't say anything about me or Leutie to anyone. You tell them you didn't see who did this to you or him, and you wait for me to come back.'

He nodded again, absorbing my every word through pained eyes.

'You owe me your life, and if you cross me, that'll be the end of it. I promise you that.'

'I won't say anything, I swear,' he whispered shakily, swallowing harshly as he held my eye contact. 'I won't . . . I won't say anything.'

I watched him closely through suspiciously narrowed eyes, knife still pressing sharply into his chest, before I nodded once. 'Good.'

With that, I stood and returned to my full height. I cast one last derisive look at the boy before I beckoned Leutie forward. She looked nervously at the dead man lying in the dirt and avoided the injured boy altogether as she followed me. A quiet whimper of pain was all I heard from Nell as we darted into yet another shadow, slowly but surely working our way out to the edge.

Every step we took added to the tension and anxiety sitting in my stomach, and I kept waiting for Jonah or one of his allies to attack, but no one did. Three more times, we had to hide ourselves as members of Greystone passed, but no one else saw us. Leutie was as unskilled as ever, tripping over rocks and panting far too loudly, but luckily she avoided knocking anything else over. After about a half hour of sneaking our way through Greystone, we paused at the edge of the huts, giving us a clear view of the treeline where I'd started.

'We have to run, Leutie,' I whispered evenly. While I had no trouble keeping my breath slow and steady, Leutie was dripping in sweat and gasping with each breath she drew thanks to her serious lack of training.

'To where?' she asked, eyes scanning the vast line of trees.

'There,' I replied, pointing to the area I recognised. I checked one last time for enemies, but none were visible. I knew our window was small, however, due to the large amount of people we'd already encountered. 'Follow me and keep your gun ready, yeah?'

'Yeah, okay,' she whispered. She was clearly terrified, and rightfully so. There would be no cover between here and the trees, and it made her abandonment of Greystone absolute. My heart gave an extra thump, determined to get us out alive.

'Let's go.'

Instantly, I broke into a sprint. My feet flew quickly over the patchy grass and my arms pumped by my sides to propel me. I could hear Leutie's heavy, clumsy footfalls behind me and the panting coming from her lungs. A quick glance over my shoulder told me she was quickly falling behind, so I slowed my pace enough to let her catch up. We were moving very slowly, which made me nervous, though no sounds of alert could be heard from Greystone.

'Come on, Leutie,' I urged as I ran, willing her to move faster. We were nearly across the expanse now, and I prayed we'd make it without being seen.

I hadn't yet dared think of Hayden, until we neared the treeline and closed in on it. It hadn't been two hours, and

273

I hoped he had kept his word and stayed in the trees. The final ten feet towards the trees disappeared as we sprinted into the shadows, falling under cover once more.

We slowed to a stop, where Leutie bent over and rested her hands on her knees, gasping for air. I was hardly winded and much more concerned with finding Hayden. Panic started to rise in my heart as I called out quietly.

'Hayden!' I hissed, squinting into the darkness for his form.

'Who's Hayden?' Leutie whispered breathlessly with a glance in my direction.

'He's my . . .' I trailed off, unable to find a word that did our relationship justice. Any simple titles that may have existed just didn't seem like enough for what he was to me. I gave up. 'He's supposed to be here.'

I stepped a few feet further into the trees and looked around, but still nothing.

'*Hayden!*'

'Grace, look out!'

Leutie's warning was followed immediately by a firm hand wrapping around my wrist. My first instinct was to twist around and attack, but there was something gentle about the touch, something familiar. I knew who it was before I even turned around, and I didn't hesitate to throw my arms around his neck the moment that I did.

Warm arms wound around my waist, encasing me and holding me tightly to his chest as my face buried itself automatically in his neck. I breathed in the familiar smell of him and revelled in the comforting heat of his body against mine. He held me tightly but didn't speak, as if letting his contact show the relief he felt at my return. Leutie all but disappeared from my mind as I hugged him, too distracted by the release of tension I'd been feeling from when I left him to bother thinking about her for a moment.

'Herc.'

My voice was barely a whisper and stifled by the smooth skin covering his neck, but the way his arms tightened around me at the sound told me he'd heard.

'I knew you could do it, Grace,' he murmured quietly, just loud enough for only me to hear. 'You came back to me.'

He didn't give me the chance to respond, however, before he pulled back just enough to slide a hand along my jaw and pull me towards him. His lips pressed to mine, and his gaze lingered on mine for a few seconds. It was impossible to miss the pride beaming from his eyes.

'So I'm assuming this is Hayden,' Leutie said, breaking the moment. She sounded sheepish, but I couldn't find it in me to care. The relief I'd felt when Hayden had appeared was too strong for me to ignore.

Finally I broke away from Hayden, though his touch lingered on my lower back as we both took a step towards Leutie. 'Yeah, Leutie, Hayden. Hayden, Leutie.'

'I recognise you from that night,' Leutie told him thought-fully. I knew she was referencing the time she'd caught us in Greystone and covered for us, before she knew his or anyone else's name besides mine.

'Yeah,' Hayden replied slowly, apprehension clear in his voice. He watched her for a few seconds before turning to me. 'What happened? Did she send the note?'

'No,' I answered with a shake of my head. 'It was a trap.'

'Are you okay?' he pressed urgently.

'Yeah, I'm fine. We just have a lot to talk about when we get back,' I told him. My mind was already buzzing with thoughts begging to be shared.

'So if she didn't write the note, why is she here?' he asked, gesturing towards Leutie. He spoke as if she wasn't there and I was reminded of when he used to do that to me.

'She's my friend, Hayden, and I trust her,' I told him lightly. 'She can help us.'

He studied me intently for a few moments as if trying to decide if I was right or not when Leutie spoke.

'I can help,' she reiterated quietly. She seemed intimidated by Hayden but was determined to get her point across. 'I've heard Jonah and some others talking . . . I know some things. I'm on your side.'

Hayden glanced at her and thought for a few moments, lips pulled into his mouth, before he nodded slowly.

'Well, all right, then. Welcome to Blackwing, Leutie.'

Twenty-Four: Expound
Grace

The air was thick with tension as we shifted among the shadows, torn between a hasty retreat and our necessity to remain silent. Each step we took away from Greystone only added to my anxiety rather than decreased it, and I couldn't shake that feeling of impending doom. Things certainly hadn't gone as planned: I'd killed someone and brutally injured another. As despicable as it may have sounded, it wasn't the fact that I'd killed someone that was bothering me, however.

The boy I'd left behind, Nell, was maybe sixteen. He now knew exactly who I was, who Leutie was, and knew what I'd done. The assurance of our success hinged on a boy's decision, and I didn't have much faith that this boy would stay silent even after I'd threatened him. If it were me, I'd be very reluctant to protect someone who'd slashed both of my Achilles, no matter what they'd said, but I had to hope he'd stay quiet. Two words from him could see Jonah storming after us.

Hayden led us back to Blackwing while I brought up the rear, sandwiching a very inept Leutie between us. She was so loud that it didn't matter how silent Hayden and I were; between her laboured breathing, heavy footsteps, and the frightened squeaks she let out whenever so much as a breeze rustled the leaves, anyone would have been able to find us with a minimal amount of effort.

'Leutie, at least *try* to be quiet,' I hissed impatiently.

'Sorry,' she gasped, casting a fearful glance over her shoulder. 'Aren't you afraid they'll follow us?'

I was quiet for a second as we moved hastily. 'Not afraid, just wary.'

She swallowed harshly and nodded as if trying to convince herself to be brave. I could tell by the tension in Hayden's shoulders that he was on edge with her, but he never spoke. After thirty more painstakingly noisy minutes, we arrived back to camp. Leutie's eyes were wide as she glanced around, clearly intimidated to be in the infamous Blackwing. I remembered feeling the same sense of awe the first time Hayden had brought me here, but now all I felt was pride.

'We should get the group,' Hayden said finally, breaking his stony silence.

'Yeah,' I agreed.

Hayden veered off the main path to swing by the infirmary, which was near where we'd entered camp, to alert Docc. We then went to the raid building, where he quickly shooed the man on guard outside.

'Docc will get Kit and Dax,' Hayden told us as he lit a few candles in the middle of the table.

'What are we doing?' Leutie asked anxiously. She shot a fleeting glance at Hayden, though her gaze darted to me the moment he looked at her. It was clear she was terrified of him.

'You're going to tell us everything you know,' Hayden said sharply. Leutie's brows pulled even lower over her eyes in terror, but she nodded once in assent.

A loud thud sounded suddenly, causing Leutie to

practically jump out of her skin. The door bounced open to reveal Dax, Kit, and Docc. Kit looked intense, Docc curious, and Dax downright excited as they spilled inside and joined us around the table. All three of them had their eyes fixed on Leutie, and I was almost certain I heard her squeak with fear. I had to restrain myself from rolling my eyes; even though we were friends, it was girls like her that irritated me, because they only reinforced so many people's belief that girls were weak.

'Well, well, what do we have here?' Dax said slyly, eyeing Leutie with a wry grin on his face as he circled around her like a predator stalking prey. 'Fresh meat?'

Leutie let out a quiet whimper and squeezed her eyes shut as if trying to block him out.

'Stop it, Dax,' I said disapprovingly. 'She's already scared enough and we don't need your stupid ass to freak her out even more.'

'I've been told I'm charming, thank you,' Dax retorted. He stood behind Leutie now and shot a quick wink at me over her shoulder before returning to his place at the table. Leutie swallowed nervously as she dared to open her eyes once more.

'Have you quite finished?' Hayden asked sharply, raising his brows at Dax. Dax's lips quirked to the side in a lopsided grin as he shrugged non-committally.

'I suppose so.'

'Good. Grace, care to make introductions?' Hayden continued as he glanced expectantly at me. I nodded.

'Leutie, just try to calm down. No one here will hurt you as long as you don't try anything, all right?' I warned. I wanted to trust her, but we had to be safe. Hayden had taken the gun from her the moment we'd started walking back to camp.

'I-I won't try anything,' she said weakly, shaking her head quickly a few times.

'Good. So, you've met Hayden,' I said, gesturing to where he stood beside me. 'That's Docc, Kit, and Dax. Guys, this is Leutie.'

A low chorus of 'hellos' greeted us. Leutie simply pursed her lips and tried not to look terrified.

'Did you write the note?' Kit wasted no time in asking.

'No,' Leutie admitted. 'It must have been a trap Jonah set.'

'I knew it,' Kit murmured with a frown. 'Wait, so why is she here?'

'She's here because she wants to be. She knows some of what's going on over there and has agreed to help us if we keep her safe.'

'All right. So spill,' Hayden commanded, his arms crossed tightly over his firm chest.

'I don't . . . I don't know where to start,' she admitted, glancing at me once again.

Jonah's voice from earlier floated through my mind as I remembered him threatening to kill someone who wasn't cooperating. It was as good a place to start as any.

'Who is Jonah trying to control? I heard him say something about someone not cooperating . . .' I trailed off, hoping she'd understand. Leutie frowned in thought.

'I'm not sure . . . it could be a lot of people. Some people aren't exactly thrilled with how things are going.'

'Who?' I pressed. I suddenly became aware that I was leaning into the table towards her as if trying to draw answers out of her subconsciously.

'Just people,' she said with a confused shrug. 'Don't get me wrong, lots of people support the war, but there are some who don't. They're trying to get him to stop, but he won't. He's attacking everyone, not just you guys.'

'Everyone?' Dax repeated thoughtfully.

'Yeah, Blackwing, Whetland. He even tried to attack some Brutes a few weeks back, but he lost nearly everyone that went . . .' she trailed off, a sad expression crossed her features.

'If he attacked Whetland, that could be why they came here looking for weapons,' Hayden said suddenly.

Whetland was the only camp that seemed to be self-sufficient so far and thus had no real need for weapons, but if they were being attacked, their need would significantly increase.

'That makes sense,' I agreed. 'What else, Leutie?'

'I think he tried to force Renley to show him how they did everything first, but he refused,' she continued. 'That's when they started attacking Whetland, too.'

Renley was the leader of Whetland. He was a few years older than Hayden and I and had risen quickly thanks to his ability to make their camp self-sufficient. What they lacked in power and strength, they made up for in self-reliance. It was no wonder Jonah had wanted him to help him – killing him would do no good, because then they'd never get his knowledge.

'I bet it was Renley I heard Jonah talking about,' I murmured as the thoughts came together.

If he doesn't cooperate, I'll kill him.

I had sudden clarity. 'Jonah won't give up the war even though some people in Greystone want him to, so he tried to force Renley to teach him how to be self-sufficient. When he wouldn't, Jonah threatened to have him killed . . . and carried on with the war against everyone. He's trying to get rid of everybody . . .'

Jonah was ruthless, brutal, relentless. He would carry on with the war until everyone was dead before stopping, no matter how many people he lost.

'I think you're right, Grace,' Hayden agreed.

'Leutie, you said people were unhappy with the war?' Dax questioned.

'Yeah.'

'How many?' Dax pressed.

'We've lost so many that it's hard to even know who thinks what anymore.'

'How many have you lost?' Kit asked.

'At least a hundred,' Leutie said softly, as if it hurt to admit it.

'*A hundred?*' Hayden repeated incredulously. While it ripped Hayden apart to lose a single person, Jonah was continuing on with seemingly no thought to the massive loss of life.

'Jesus Christ,' Hayden murmured finally.

No one spoke for a while, as if letting the shocking truth sink in. I squeezed Hayden's hand once to draw his distracted gaze to me.

'How many are against him, Leutie?' Docc asked softly.

'There are only twenty or thirty maybe who are open about it. Some are too afraid to say anything. The rest support him. The ones resisting him were getting a little braver, but their leader died on an attack . . . here.'

'Wait, what?' I asked sharply, narrowing my eyes at her.

'Yeah, there was one guy who would stand up to Jonah, but he's dead now so . . .'

'He died raiding Blackwing?' Hayden pressed. He seemed to catch my train of thought as he leaned eagerly forward. 'When? This last attack they did?'

'No one died . . .' Kit murmured now in confusion.

282

'What was his name, Leutie?' I asked. I already knew the answer before she said it. The last time Greystone had attacked Blackwing, none of them had died, but someone never made it back. One who remained barely alive in our infirmary as we spoke . . .

'Shaw.'

'Holy shit,' Dax muttered as his jaw fell open. 'That guy Hayden nearly beat to death? He's the one going against Jonah in Greystone?'

'"Nearly" beat to death?' Leutie questioned. Her light blue eyes narrowed in thought as she glanced between Dax and me.

'He's still alive,' I told her. 'But barely. Docc's got him in the infirmary.'

'*That* piece of shit is trying to make Jonah stop the war?' Hayden muttered angrily.

'What did he do?' Leutie asked hesitantly. I frowned, reluctant to speak of it.

'He physically disrespected Grace,' Docc said regretfully.

'He fucking touched her,' Hayden spat, unable to hold back his anger.

I took a step closer to him and placed my hand on his back. He looked furious and hurt all at once as his eyes burned bright beneath tightly knit brows.

'It's okay,' I mouthed at only him. He drew a deep, shuddering breath before giving a curt nod and releasing some of the tension in his jaw.

'Oh my god,' Leutie muttered, fear leaking into her voice once again. 'I mean, he was always pretty rough, but I never thought he'd do that.'

'He's lucky I didn't kill him,' Hayden muttered darkly.

'So what does this all mean then?' Dax replied to get us back on track.

'A lot of cards just got laid on the table,' said Kit.

'I believe, from what I've gathered, that Grace's brother Jonah is quite determined to destroy everyone, no matter what the cost. He's willing to attack anyone and everyone, even though he's facing resistance in his own camp. Does that sound like him, Grace?' Docc's voice was even and smooth as he spoke, as if trying to keep everyone calm, since Hayden appeared to be struggling. His dark eyes focused on me as he waited patiently for my answer.

As much as I wanted to say 'no, he'd never do that,' I couldn't quite fool myself into believing it. Jonah had proved, over and over again, that all he cared about was himself. Even as a child, he'd put himself first, stepped on others to get what he wanted, and ignored what others had to say if it wasn't what he wanted to hear. Even I, his own sister, was shoved to the side if I posed any threat. In a way, I was grateful for it, because it was one of the major things that had made me what I was today. I was strong partially because of him, but that didn't stop it from hurting that my only brother was a complete and utter jackass.

'Yes, Docc. That sounds exactly like him,' I admitted somewhat bitterly. I had no idea why we'd turned out so differently or what exactly it was that made him the way he was, but it didn't matter now. It was Hayden's turn to place his hand on my back in a comforting gesture, and I tried to focus on the warmth of that to chase away the cold that had crept in when thinking of Jonah.

'So let me get this straight,' Dax said with a sharp shake of his head as if to clear his thoughts. 'Jonah is your brother. Jonah runs Greystone. Greystone is at war with everyone and their dog. Whetland tried to steal weapons from us because Greystone was attacking them for not helping. Shaw, also from Greystone, was trying to stand up to Jonah before Hayden beat the shit out of him and landed him in our infirmary. Shaw is also a huge creep. Oh, and the Brutes still have a massive haul of pretty much everything they could ever need to destroy us all. Did I miss anything?'

'And we're all running out of things to survive,' Kit added with a twisted, sardonic grin.

'Ah yes, thank you, Kit. And we're all about to die because we're running out of supplies. Does that cover it?' Dax raised both his eyebrows and looked around at us nonchalantly as if he'd just read off a grocery list.

'I think you got it,' I said flatly. Put like that, I was surprised we were still alive at all.

'Lovely,' Dax said with a heavy sigh.

'So what do we do?' Kit questioned, glancing around. Everyone appeared deep in thought. Even Leutie had a frown on her face and appeared to be searching for solutions.

'It's late,' Hayden said with a hint of defeat. It was probably long after midnight now. 'Let's all get some sleep and meet to discuss this later.'

'Good idea, son,' Docc said with an approving nod. 'No use trying to figure things out with tired minds.'

Dax raised his arms above his head and stretched as he let out a loud, overdramatic yawn. 'Agreed. It's a lot to process.'

'Let me know when we're meeting. Night, guys,' Kit said with a wave as he dismissed himself and moved outside. Docc followed him and paused to glance over his shoulder before exiting.

'Oh, Leutie, welcome. Have a good night,' he said lowly before slipping outside into the darkness.

'Thanks,' she said softly, too late for Docc to hear.

It was now down to Hayden, Dax, Leutie, and me.

'Well, Leutie, I certainly hope you're really on our side,

because we'd have to kill you if you were lying to us,' Dax said as he nudged her playfully in the shoulder.

I could tell he was kidding from the slight glint in his eye, but Leutie did not appear to catch that as she sucked in a quiet gasp of fear. The hint of delight that crossed Dax's face told me he very much enjoyed frightening her. I was reminded of his occasionally questionable sense of humour.

'Leave her alone, Dax,' I said with a disapproving shake of my head. Leutie's widened eyes darted quickly to me as Dax took a step away from her.

'Just being honest,' he said with a non-committal shrug. An amused grin lingered on his lips as he moved to the door. 'See you guys tomorrow. Get some sleep, Leutie, but watch out – I heard Blackwing was full of crazies just dying for fresh meat.'

He let out a hearty laugh at his own joke before disappearing outside, leaving behind a clearly terrified Leutie. I hoped she'd get over this whole 'being afraid of everything' thing soon.

'Ignore him. He's just messing with you,' I told her.

'Okay,' she replied with a forced smile. 'Where, um, where will I be staying?'

I hadn't thought of that. I turned to Hayden. He shrugged as if it hadn't occurred to him either.

'She could stay with Dax?' Hayden suggested with a twist of his lips.

'No,' Leutie objected quickly. Hayden and I both turned to look at her to see a very prevalent blush on her cheeks. 'I mean, um, please not him.'

'Why not?' I asked. 'I'm serious, he's just teasing you. He won't hurt you.'

'Just . . . not him,' she answered vaguely. Her cheeks

turned to an even deeper red as she avoided my gaze.

'Okay . . . Do you just want to stay with us until we can figure something else out?'

'What?' Hayden asked sharply, clearly not very pleased with the idea. I shot him a disapproving look.

'Just until we figure something else out,' I replied quietly. The last thing I wanted to do was make Leutie decide she would be better off at Greystone after all and send her running back.

'Yeah, all right,' said Hayden, after I silently asked for his agreement. 'You can stay on our couch,' he told her flatly. A small smile pulled at her lips.

'Thanks,' she replied sincerely.

'Yeah, yeah,' Hayden muttered unhappily.

I smiled at his obvious resentment of her intruding upon our private time. It gave me a warm glow to know he cherished it as much as I did. Even though we were together almost all day, every day, time spent truly alone was few and far between. That was when he could really let down the walls he had built up around him. It was the only time I could fully relax and feel completely at ease. It was the only time when we could focus wholeheartedly on one another. I was certain that no matter how much time I got like that with Hayden, it could never be enough.

'Come on, then,' I said quietly to Leutie as I started to follow Hayden out of the building. She obliged without a word.

It was cool and dark outside as we moved through Blackwing, Hayden on one side and Leutie on the other. Despite all the terrible things we'd figured out tonight and despite all the difficult times that were surely to come, I felt an odd sense of peace. With Hayden's hand in mine and the unwavering sense of reassurance and strength I felt from him, I felt prepared to take on whatever would come our way. I knew that if I had Hayden, I could make it through absolutely anything.

Twenty-Five: Monster

Hayden

I felt an odd vulnerability as Grace, Leutie, and I arrived at our hut. I didn't want to share that space with Leutie; it was my space to have with Grace, and it was the only place I ever felt completely open. It allowed me to let down my guard and reveal the core of myself to Grace and Grace alone, though now that was hindered by another's presence.

'This is it,' Grace told Leutie as she lit a few candles. I remained silent and leaned against the door I'd firmly closed, observing.

'It's nice,' Leutie said kindly as she glanced around.

I let out a deep sigh and pushed my hand through my hair as I reminded myself that this was necessary. Leutie could help us, and I didn't want to terrify her into leaving the first night she was here. If she felt safest staying with Grace, I would suck it up.

For tonight.

But that was it.

After tonight, she'd have to find somewhere else to stay.

'Come on, I'll show you the bathroom,' Grace said with a tick of her head. She glanced briefly at me and shot me a somewhat amused look before disappearing with Leutie into the smaller room.

I let out another deep sigh and kicked off my boots, taking

the opportunity to change into a pair of athletic shorts and clean T-shirt while Leutie was out of the room. I padded barefoot quietly across the wooden floor and sat on the edge of the bed. When the bathroom door opened once more, only Grace slipped out.

'Hey, bub,' she greeted with a soft smile.

She came to stand in front of me and I reached for her, trailing my fingers lightly on the outer side of her thighs. My head tilted back to look up at her, and her hand gently pushed my hair back off my face.

'Hey back,' I returned quietly.

'I'm sorry about this. She's just afraid, you know? I'm the only one she knows here.'

'I know,' I admitted. My eyes closed momentarily as I enjoyed the soothing feeling of her fingers raking through my hair. The skin on her thighs was soft beneath the pads of my fingertips as they feathered over her legs.

'We'll figure this out, right?'

I knew she wasn't just talking about Leutie's living arrangements. I pulled her into my lap, folded my arms around her and let her legs fall between mine.

'Yes, Grace. We'll figure this out.'

I pressed a light kiss into her temple as she chewed on her lip, deep in thought. All I wanted to do was pull her back into our bed and fall asleep holding her, but our moment was interrupted by the bathroom door opening. Leutie emerged and saw how Grace was perched in my lap before quickly averting her eyes and blushing. Reluctantly, I allowed Grace to pull herself from my lap to bring Leutie a blanket.

'You can sleep on the couch, Leutie,' Grace told her kindly. 'It's not the most comfortable, but it's better than the ground.'

Leutie nodded and settled into the couch. Grace tossed

the blanket over her and they exchanged a few quiet words I couldn't hear. I was suddenly reminded of Grace's first month here, when she'd spent every night on that miserable couch. How long ago that seemed.

'Thank you, Grace,' Leutie said softly as Grace moved to blow out the candles she'd lit. 'And . . . thank you, Hayden.'

It seemed like the first time she'd spoken directly to me and it surprised me.

'You're welcome,' I replied evenly. I wasn't entirely sure what she was thanking me for, but I accepted it.

Grace blew out the final candle before moving to the dresser, where she quickly changed into something she could sleep in. I could hear her feet padding towards me, and the heat of her touch on my shoulder could be felt as she slipped past me to crawl into bed.

She faced me and hitched her leg loosely over my hip as I pulled the blanket up around us, cocooning us away before letting my arm snake around her waist. Even if Leutie was sleeping on our couch, I wasn't going to let that stop me from holding Grace like I wanted.

Everything was quiet for a while as we all settled down. I wanted to ask Grace about the details of her trip to Greystone. I wanted to figure out a plan for dealing with all the problems we were facing. I wanted to be able to talk with her freely without worrying about Leutie overhearing.

'I wish we were alone,' I whispered after about thirty minutes of silence. It was difficult to tell if Leutie was still awake or not, but my voice was soft enough that she wouldn't hear from across the room.

'So do I,' Grace murmured softly in reply. It was like my heart sighed in response as I pulled her closer to my chest. Her warmth seeped into my skin and comforted me.

We both lay there for a long time, silent and sleepy but

unable to fall asleep. Every once in a while she'd let out a deep sigh before opening her mouth as if to speak before she cut herself off. Something was keeping her awake and I wanted to know what, but I wanted the safety of privacy before we spoke. Leutie's presence grated on me once again as it held Grace back from saying whatever she was clearly struggling with.

'We'll talk tomorrow, okay?' I whispered softly.

'Okay,' she breathed in response.

'Just try to sleep. You need it.'

Her arm snaked around my ribcage to squeeze lightly as she hugged herself to me, settling in and relaxing fully for the first time since we lay down.

'Love you,' she mumbled sleepily. A light point of heat was pressed into the base of my throat as she kissed my skin gently.

'Love you, Bear,' I replied quietly.

The last thought I had was how nice it felt to have my body pressed into the comforting warmth of Grace's before I finally succumbed to sleep.

Grace

My body felt tight, as if I was being pressed in on from all sides until it was difficult to breathe. Darkness surrounded me as I blinked furiously, desperate to see through the oppressive black that had overcome my vision. It was cold, very cold. The chill settled down to my bones, making me feel brittle and shaky all at once. Strange moisture hung on the air, and the odd metallic taste that lingered triggered the familiar, unwelcome taste on my tongue.

Blood.

Fear spiked through my system as I began to recognise elements I'd experienced before. When I lifted my foot, I saw the same thick, red-black mud that was wet with blood. When I looked to my left, what little I could see in the dim light showed a slowly shifting ground, hinting at what lurked beneath the surface. My heart hammered in my chest as I looked around, desperate for a way out before I knew what was coming next happened, but it was too late.

'*Thieves.*'

My eyes squeezed shut as I tried to block it out, and my hands pressed tightly over my ears. The sticky substance covering the ground slowed my steps as I tried to move away from the sound and, worse, the limbs, rotted and sickly green in colour, that attempted to trip me as they rose from beneath the ground. I tried to run, but my body rebelled. It was as if each step I took dragged me two steps backward instead of forward.

'*Thieves.*'

A scream of fear pulled from my lips when I felt a firm grasp wrap around my neck, jerking my body backward into an impossibly cold, stiff figure. Two overpowering arms wrapped around my body, pinning my arms helplessly to my sides as I struggled to no avail. A deep, rattling breath sucked in behind me as whoever held me easily controlled my flailing.

'*You stole from us,*' he hissed, voice low, crackly, and almost inhuman.

'No . . .'

My mouth was stifled by a hand that was equally stiff and cold as the body I was held against. No amount of thrashing could throw my captor off me. Finally I worked up enough courage to look over my shoulder. As soon as I locked eyes with my captor, I wished I hadn't.

Eyes so black that there was no distinguishing the irises stared back at me, framed by a thick layer of blood leaking down either side of his face. Instead of normal teeth, rotten, jagged stumps were bared at me. An odour that could only be described as death leaked from his mouth, invading my senses and clouding my mind. Never had I ever been so terrified and helpless, and I was certain my life was about to end. My eyes squeezed shut again, cutting off my view of the horrifying man as I prepared to die.

'Grace.'

I shook my head and kept my eyes closed, unable to face the horror that awaited me. The grip around my arms was tighter than ever, and I found it impossible to move.

'Grace!'

My body shook once and something ran down my face. It seemed my hands had been freed, so I pushed with what little strength I could muster against the body pressing into mine. My body shook once more, causing my eyes to snap open as my name sounded yet again.

'Grace.'

I sucked in a harsh breath as the world shifted around me. That scent of death and blood and decay was gone, replaced by the familiar smell of Hayden. I blinked a few times as I realised he was hovering over me, pushing back the hair from my face that was now damp with sweat.

'Hayden,' I breathed. I was shaking as I felt his body weight against mine.

'It's just me,' Hayden murmured softly. His brows were pulled low on his face and he looked saddened by what he'd just interrupted. 'You're all right.'

I nodded, unable to speak as I tried to slow my laboured breathing. Hayden's hand continued the gentle action around my face, and the soft touch helped calm me down.

'Was it the same nightmare?' he asked quietly, voice low and raspy.

'Kind of,' I whispered. 'There was a man this time . . . He was covered in blood.'

'Oh, Grace,' he murmured gently. His eyes connected with mine and he looked even more pained by this. 'I wish I could protect you from that.'

'You woke me up,' I said, shaking my head. 'That's all you can do.'

I had no control over where my mind went when I slept, and there was no predicting when it would happen. My physical training and determination could only make me so strong; I had cracks and weaknesses like anyone else, and I hated it.

I raised my arms to loop them lightly around his neck, hugging him to me for a few moments. He let out a deep sigh and held me closely.

'Can you sleep?'

I nodded. 'I think so. Thank you, Hayden.'

'Mmhmm,' he hummed softly. He shifted his weight so he covered me still but didn't let his full weight rest, allowing me to feel the comforting heat without being stifled. 'Sleep, love.'

I nodded and turned to press a kiss into his temple, which was the only part of him I could reach as his gentle breath drifted out over my neck. My eyes drifted shut then, allowing me to fall into a comfortable, uninterrupted sleep.

When we awoke the next morning, I was almost surprised to see Leutie on our couch; I had pretty much forgotten she was there. She jumped when I shook her gently to wake her and agreed to get ready to go in a few minutes.

After everyone was dressed, Leutie in a new shirt of mine, the three of us headed towards the mess hall for some food.

I still felt the overwhelming need to talk to Hayden, but I wanted to wait until we were completely alone.

The energy in the mess hall was high. People chattered all around us, though it didn't take long to identify the table full of my friends. Dax, Kit, and Docc all immediately focused on us once we'd sat down, having gathered our food from Maisie, who was in good spirits today.

'Hello everybody,' Docc said with a calm smile.

'Hey,' Hayden greeted evenly. Leutie remained silent and I nodded at everyone in greeting. I wasn't sure if I was up to dealing with everyone after the night I'd had.

'What's on the agenda for today, Boss?' Dax asked after swallowing a mouthful of food. My stomach rumbled, so I started to eat; I noticed our portions were considerably smaller than usual. It was yet another reminder of our dwindling supplies necessary to sustain life.

'I was thinking we should do some more training,' Hayden replied. 'Leutie will need to learn basic defence and gun safety. Jett and the others who have been training should keep at that as well.'

Everyone nodded in assent. The mention of Jett's name had me glancing around the mess hall. After a few moments, I spotted him on the other side of the room, sitting across from none other than Rainey and her little sister. They didn't appear to be talking, and Jett glanced around the room far too often, as if determined to look anywhere but at Rainey.

'Leutie, you ready to start training?' Dax asked her, amusement clearly written across his face. Her eyes darted to me before meeting his gaze.

'I guess so,' she said softly.

'How terrible are you going to be?' Dax continued. His grin widened even more as he watched her grow more and more flustered.

'Probably pretty terrible,' she admitted with a sheepish grin.

'That's all right. These lads will take good care of you,' Docc said with a reassuring nod. Leutie chanced an appreciative smile around the group as they all murmured in agreement with Docc.

The rest of our meal passed in a pleasant manner, but I couldn't stop thinking about everything. My nightmare, Jonah, the war, Nell back in Greystone, the seemingly endless procession of problems we faced. When everyone finished eating and got up to put away their dishes, I hung back and tugged lightly on Hayden's shoulder.

'Hey, can we talk before we go and train? I just can't focus,' I admitted. He nodded immediately, confusion and concern written across his face.

'Of course,' he replied evenly.

We deposited our dishes and moved quickly through camp. Back at our hut, Hayden manoeuvred me onto the bed. I sat and crossed my legs. I knew what I wanted to say, but I didn't know how to get there.

'What's going on, Grace?' Hayden asked gently. His hand reached forward to trail his fingertips lightly across my knee. My lower lip pulled between my teeth as I chewed on it in thought, eyes staring unfocusedly at the blanket covering the bed.

'Did I ever tell you that I had a dog?'

The words were out of my mouth before I had really decided to say them and were met with a surprised look from Hayden.

'No, I don't think you did,' he replied, having managed to wipe the look of surprise away.

'Yeah, I didn't think so. I had this dog when I was younger, ten or eleven maybe. His name was Farmer.'

'That's an interesting name,' Hayden said with a soft smile.

'We had just finished learning about farmers in our version of school and I thought they were so interesting. My dad brought him back from a raid one day and gave him to me.'

Hayden listened, as if he suspected there was more to this conversation than me simply telling him about my dog.

'He was this mangy little thing. Black, patchy fur. Legs that were way too long and made him clumsy. Some kind of mutt, I'm sure, but I thought he was the best. He was just a puppy when Celt gave him to me.'

My heart thumped painfully as I pictured the little mess of fur. He'd wiggled happily from the very first moment my dad put him in my arms, and I'd been subjected to relentless licks from his little puppy tongue.

'I took him everywhere. To school, to training, on raids. He even slept on the edge of my bed.'

I had to blink a few times and shake my head to get rid of the images surfacing.

'He grew into his legs eventually and got to be pretty big. I swear he was the smartest dog – always knew when it was time to eat, or when we were playing versus actually being in danger. There was this one raid where he stopped this Brute from attacking me before I even saw him. I loved that dog more than I loved almost anyone else.'

Hayden's hand claimed mine and squeezed once. The emotion I'd been fighting to hold back had started to creep into my voice, and my lip was starting to feel numb where I kept biting into it.

'Then this one day in the middle of summer . . . It was really hot and he had so much fur that I was afraid he was going to overheat, so I wanted to give him a haircut, you know? I didn't want him to get sick or something. So I found this pair of scissors in Jonah's room and took Farmer outside to give him a trim . . .'

It grew more and more difficult to keep my tone steady. I felt hot tears stinging at the backs of my eyes, but I forced them down. Hayden was watching me closely, a saddened frown, as if he already knew this story didn't have a happy ending. I took a deep breath, determined to continue.

'I was about halfway done when Jonah came home and found me. He saw that I was using his scissors and he got *so mad*. I couldn't understand why he was so mad. They were just scissors. I wasn't hurting anyone . . . I was just trying to take care of my dog. I didn't know why he was so mad.'

I swallowed harshly, and squeezed my eyes shut to fight off the images assaulting me now. Each breath I drew was shaky in my chest.

'He came over and ripped the scissors from my hand. He pointed them at me and yelled at me . . . Called me an idiot for using his things on a "stupid dog". He was so much bigger than me then, and I could never fight him off when he picked on me . . . He – he kept coming towards me and cornered me against our house—'

A shuddering breath ripped through me, cutting me off mid-sentence. The tears I'd tried to hold off now welled in my eyes. Hayden's hand rubbed soothingly over my leg, but still I couldn't look at him.

'And he put the blade of the scissors at my throat. He told me if I ever took his things again, I'd be sorry. He kept pressing it down, tighter and tighter, until I couldn't breathe. I tried to push him off, but I was so young and weak that I couldn't . . . And I was so scared and helpless and about to give up when all of a sudden Farmer—'

Another gasp ripped through me and a tear leaked down my cheek.

'Farmer attacked him . . . And he – he bit his arm that had the scissors at my throat and knocked him over. I couldn't do anything, so I just watched as my dog protected me from him . . . They fought for a while, but soon—'

Another shudder shook the breath from my lungs.

'And they were fighting and I kept yelling at Jonah to stop. I begged him to stop, *begged him*. But – but he wouldn't, and soon there was this wet sounding thud and a yelp from Farmer . . . and he stopped moving as Jonah stood up . . .'

Tears were leaking down my face.

'And Farmer was dead. Crumpled in a pile on the ground with blood leaking from his chest . . . Jonah killed my dog. Because he protected me. Because I'd taken a pair of *scissors* to give him a haircut.'

I sniffed once and sucked in a breath. I almost jumped when I felt Hayden's hands wrap around either side of my face, allowing his thumbs to collect the tears that had fallen. His eyes looked pained and deeply saddened as he studied me closely.

'I'm so sorry, Grace,' he lulled gently. 'I'm so, so sorry.'

I nodded and squeezed my eyes shut, sniffling once more.

'Don't you see, Hayden?' I pleaded desperately.

'See what, Grace?' he asked as gently as he could.

'Jonah is a monster,' I choked out, determined not to break again. 'He is now and always has been . . . He won't stop what he's doing, because he doesn't have that in him. He just doesn't care . . .'

Hayden waited patiently for me to continue. I knew what had to happen. I just didn't want to admit it.

'There's only one way we're going to end this war.'

'What's that?' Hayden questioned softly. A dark sadness etched across his face as if he already knew.

'We have to stop the one who started it all . . . We have to kill Jonah.'

Twenty-Six: Valour

Grace

Silence echoed around us, heavy with the weight of the words I'd dropped. Hayden watched me closely with pained yet understanding eyes, as if trying to see through me to what I was truly feeling. I felt nauseous and off balance, but I knew what I'd said was true. Hundreds of people had already died because of one person, and there were no signs that he planned to stop any time soon.

We had to kill my brother.

'Grace, no . . . There has to be something else . . .' he murmured while shaking his head slowly.

Hayden's words were heavy and resigned, as if he wanted to find some other way but knew I was right. He grabbed my hand in his.

'There isn't, Hayden. You know I'm right. As long as he's alive, Greystone will never stop. They'll kill everyone before he gives up.'

My voice sounded flat and devoid of emotion now. The tears I'd cried had dried, leaving an uncomfortably tight feeling on my skin.

'We can figure something else out,' Hayden insisted gently. 'He's your brother.'

'He's not anymore. Dax and Kit are more brothers to me than he ever was and I've known them what, five or six months?'

'Grace . . .' I could see his resolve slipping as he began to accept my statement. I knew he could see it was what had to be done – he just didn't like it.

'You cut off the head of the snake and the whole body dies, right? That's Jonah . . . If we kill him, odds are this whole thing will be over.'

'Not everything . . . but a large part of this, yes,' Hayden finally agreed solemnly. I let out a deep breath and squeezed his hand in return. My teeth gritted in determination and I nodded once.

'So you agree?' I dared to ask.

Hayden surprised me by reaching forward to loop his fingers around the back of my neck. He pulled me gently forward and ducked his head to press his lips into my forehead. When he pulled back, his touch remained on my neck and his thumb stroked lightly along my jaw.

'Yes, Grace, I agree.'

I sniffed once as I felt the sting of tears threatening to return, but I held them back. I needed to be strong about this.

'I'm going to need you, Hayden. More than I already do,' I admitted quietly.

'There will never be a day when I'm not here for you,' Hayden promised.

I was about to reply when he surprised me by releasing me and rising from the bed. He moved to his desk, where he bent and rustled around in the bottom drawer. When he stood and returned to me, his fist was closed gently around something. The bed shifted beneath his weight as he crawled back onto it, settling himself behind me.

'Close your eyes,' he requested softly.

'Hayden, what are you doing?'

'Just do it,' he said with a slow smile.

I shot him one last confused look before obeying. I felt him shift closer to me, and the heat of his chest at my back as I felt his hand gently sweep my hair off my neck. He brushed it over my shoulder and followed his action with a light kiss that warmed the skin on the back of my neck, sending a shiver down my spine.

'You're so brave, Bear,' he murmured quietly. 'So brave and so strong . . . But you can't do everything alone.'

Just then, something cold landed on my chest, before being looped around my neck, where his warm, gentle fingers worked to secure it. He finished with a final kiss just below my ear.

'Open your eyes,' he breathed.

Immediately, I glanced down to see he had placed a fine gold chain around my neck, two circles linked together, one slightly larger than the other. My lips parted in a silent gasp as I lifted it gently off my chest to examine it closer. Again, I was speechless.

'I know your family is basically gone now but . . . you have a family here. People who love you, care about you, look up to you . . . People who need you. And you have me, you'll always have me, but you know that, right?'

Hayden's words were slow and deep as he murmured quietly into my ear, all the while holding me to his chest where I could feel his heart hammering surprisingly fast. That was all I needed to know that this wasn't just a necklace. This held meaning for him if giving it to me was affecting him so.

'Right,' I finally managed to choke out, too stunned to form a coherent sentence.

'You belong here, and I need to know that you know that,' he continued softly. 'You're not alone.'

My eyes squeezed shut as emotion overwhelmed me. There was absolutely no way I deserved to be with such a man as

Hayden. How he loved me so much was a mystery to me, but I would accept it because I loved him too much not to.

'I love you, Hayden,' I whispered. All I could do was whisper.

'I love you, Grace,' he murmured before kissing my shoulder lightly. His arms squeezed around me. 'You want to know where I got it?'

My heart thumped heavily in my chest. 'Of course.'

'It was my mother's,' he said slowly. This admission alone caused me to suck in a breath. 'She wore it every single day. She always said it was for my father and me . . . one circle for me, one for him, see?'

He gently took the necklace from between my fingers to point out the two circles as he rested his chin on my shoulder.

'I'd always thought it was gone but . . . I found it a while ago, tucked away into that photo album. The one that you got me. The one I could only open because of you. It's all because of you, so it's only right that you wear it. It can still be for a family, just . . . a different one.'

A single silent tear streaked down my cheek. I didn't feel worthy of such a thing.

'Hayden, I can't wear this—'

'Yes you can,' Hayden said, cutting off my protests gently. 'And you will. I want you to have it. I want to see it on you.'

I let out a deep sigh and melted back into him even more as I closed my eyes in defeat. I couldn't find words to do justice to what I felt. 'Thank you, Hayden.'

'Thank you for wearing it,' he returned, pressing another light kiss along my neck.

One of his hands slipped to claim mine as he kept himself wrapped around me, hugging me from behind, while my free hand gently picked up the necklace again. All I could register was the intense love I felt for him and the weight of the meaning behind the necklace. All the things he'd said had been just what I needed to hear after coming to that conclusion about Jonah. It was almost as if he'd known there would come a time when I'd need to hear them and had waited until that moment to do just this.

I didn't think it was possible to love him any more.

Hayden and I stayed like that for a while – tangled up in one another, silent other than the quiet sounds of our breathing and the gentle thudding of our hearts. I let my body relax into his and draw strength and comfort from his warmth and reassuring touch. It was exactly what I needed in order to get back out there and face the future. Those few moments of respite gave me more peace of mind about accepting what needed to be done. I was more convinced than ever by the time Hayden and I finally stood from the bed.

'Shall we go and see how the training is coming?' I asked with a small smile, determined to focus on other things.

'If you're all right, yeah,' Hayden replied.

I nodded.

'I am for now,' I answered honestly.

It was still early afternoon, and while it was warm, clouds loomed overheard, threatening rain. My mind was still busy processing Hayden's incredible gesture, so I was quiet as we walked, though the silence didn't last long as we approached where Kit and Dax were leading training sessions.

Every once in a while, guns could be heard as people practised shooting, and some muffled grunting told me someone was getting a lesson in hand-to-hand combat. When we reached the small clearing on the edge of camp, we were greeted with the sight of more people than I had expected.

'Looks like everyone's here,' Hayden muttered with a soft chuckle.

He was right. At first glance, I could see a crowd of at least thirty spread out into little clusters. On the right side of the clearing, Kit was teaching a small group how to fight defensively. Closer to us, Malin was going over the proper way to hold a knife with a group of girls, ranging from nine or ten up to only a few years younger than me. Even more surprising was Perdita, who I hadn't seen in a while, sitting in the middle of the clearing, tinkering with some wires and what looked suspiciously like explosives. She appeared to be humming to herself with a contented smile on her face.

Dax stood on the edge of the clearing with another small group that included Jett and Leutie. He was teaching them to aim at a few cans he'd set up. I watched as he adjusted Leutie's grasp on the gun, and noticed how Leutie looked flustered when he touched her. He gave her a reassuring nod and a smile before backing away to observe as she fired at the can. She missed, but the spray of dirt behind it told me she wasn't far off. A second shot rang out from beside her as Jett sent a bullet ripping through his can, earning a small cheer and a high five from Dax.

'This is new,' I commented. Again, I felt stirrings of pride as I looked around to see so many people banding together with one common goal: protecting Blackwing. I'd seen people training before, but never all at once and with such enthusiasm.

'I don't like all the kids being here, but I suppose they need to know how to defend themselves,' Hayden said with a slight frown. He was studying Rainey and her younger sister tentatively grasping the knives Malin held out to them. Malin was careful to keep the blades away from them as she shifted their tiny fingers on the handle to the proper grip.

'Hopefully they never have to, but you're right, it's better if they know,' I agreed.

My eyes drifted over the crowd again, this time focusing in on Perdita. I watched as she twisted two wires meticulously together while bobbing her head to whatever she was humming.

'Should she be doing that? Making bombs in the middle of everyone?' I asked.

'Probably not,' Hayden said with a light chuckle. 'But never once has one gone off unless she wanted it to. She's very good.'

'Hmm,' I hummed. I wasn't about to question a woman who had been making explosives for sixty or more years if Hayden was fine with it.

'Shall we help?' he asked brightly. It was as if seeing so many people working so hard had lifted both of our spirits.

'We shall,' I agreed with a smile. 'I'll see if I can find anyone interested in first aid or something.'

'All right,' he nodded. 'I'm going to talk to Dax.'

We parted ways, heading off to assist in the training. If this many people and more were willing to do their part to survive, I was willing to do whatever it took to protect them, no matter what it meant.

Hayden

As Grace turned away from me, I caught the glint of light sparkling off the necklace. Seeing it on her made me happy; I needed her to know what it meant and what she meant to me, and I felt confident that she understood finally.

A shot followed by a small *ding* and a cheer brought my

attention to Jett on the edge of camp, so I headed in that direction. As I approached, I saw Dax line up behind Leutie. His arms looped around her shoulders as he helped her aim at the target. I saw her suck in a breath at the contact. Dax grinned over her shoulder and helped her fire, earning a second *ding* to match Jett's. Leutie grinned and turned around excitedly, beaming at Dax. He said something I couldn't hear before taking a step back to observe her try again. I shook my head suspiciously as I came to stand by his shoulder.

'What the hell are you doing?' I asked quietly so Leutie wouldn't hear.

'It's all for the greater good, my friend,' Dax replied with feigned nobility. I cast an amused glance at him, to which he replied with a wink.

I returned a light scoff as I nodded disbelievingly.

'Right.'

Dax shrugged but didn't say anything else as he watched Leutie aim with great concentration. She fired and missed, causing her shoulders to sag in dejection.

'Try again. Keep your arms straight,' Dax coached gently. Leutie nodded in acknowledgement.

I could see why he didn't mind helping her, because it was impossible to miss the parallels between Leutie and the only girl he'd ever loved, Violetta. She, too, had been quiet, soft, afraid. She knew nothing about defending herself or others, but she carried a shy, endearing gentleness that had drawn Dax to her. Leutie fired and missed again, earning a low chuckle from Dax. I hummed once in thought and chose not to comment further.

'Yes!' an excited Jett exclaimed suddenly, interrupting my thoughts. He waited until those around him stopped firing before darting forward to grab his can. His skinny

309

legs carried him back to where I stood, and he held it out proudly.

'Hayden, look! I hit it three times in a row!'

His grin was so wide that it looked like it might be painful, and he watched me with obvious pride in his own accomplishments as he waited for my reaction. Pleased, I granted him a genuine smile.

'That's brilliant, Jett,' I said honestly. He was still so small for his age because of lack of proper nutrition, but he'd got a little taller over the last few months. I still towered over him as I smiled down at him.

'I used to never be able to hit it!' Jett said in happy disbelief. His fingers ran over the tiny holes in the can and he practically bounced up and down on the balls of his feet.

'Proud of you, kid,' I said with an indulgent chuckle.

'I even taught Rainey how to shoot,' he continued happily before he realised what he'd said and blushed. His gaze darted across the clearing to where Rainey was learning with Malin before looking anywhere but at me.

'Oh, really?' I laughed. 'Spending a lot of time with her, are you?'

'No, um, just . . . just training,' he said with a defiant shake of his head that fooled no one.

'Right, okay,' I said with a sarcastic nod. He was still so childlike and innocent, yet I could see subtle changes in him as he started to grow up. Not only had he got slightly taller, but it was blatantly clear that he was starting to show interest in girls. One girl, particularly.

'Shut up, Hayden,' he said with an embarrassed grin. I laughed in return as he turned to start practising once more. I really was proud of him.

A sense of peace washed over me as I surveyed the clearing. After a few moments, I found Grace on the other side, teaching a small group how to bandage a wound properly. She already had a lot of medical knowledge to begin with, but her training sessions with Docc had made her even better. I smiled as I watched her nod encouragingly at a middle-aged woman who was practising wrapping a bandage around Grace's arm.

That sense of peace was suddenly shattered, however, when I heard a deafening round of gunfire from the other side of camp. A few people in the clearing shrieked in surprise and fear, and I whipped around towards the sound. My eyes fixed on the tower as I saw whoever was on top firing into the treeline that surrounded Blackwing. My heart plummeted in my chest as I realised what that meant; someone was attacking, and I had a pretty good idea who it was.

Twenty-Seven: Massacre

Grace

My heart all but dropped in my chest when I heard the hauntingly familiar sound of distant gunfire. Fearful voices and panicked whispers buzzed through the air like mosquitoes as they searched for blood. I forced my gaze from the tower to look around where people began marshalling the young ones.

'*What do we do?*'

'*What's happening?*'

'*Where should we go?*'

These words and more were hurled around the vicinity as people who had just been training let fear get the better of them. I sought out Hayden, who was intercepting people every few steps as they asked him for instruction. His lips moved as he responded to them, but his eyes stayed locked on mine as he made his way to me. Finally, I heard his voice as he approached me, bringing Maisie, who was holding onto Jett and Rainey, one hand in each of her own.

'—hurry and take them to your hut,' Hayden was saying to her. 'Don't worry about fighting or anything. Just stay there and keep them safe.'

'Of course,' Maisie said with a sharp, determined nod. Fear was written clearly across her face and those of Jett and Rainey.

'Hayden—' Jett opened his mouth to speak, but Hayden cut him off sharply.

'No, Jett. I need you to keep Maisie and Rainey safe, okay?' Hayden said as sternly yet gently as possible. Jett's face hardened in determination as he nodded bravely.

'I will, Hayden, I will!'

Hayden reached out quickly to ruffle his hair before allowing Maisie to lead them off, taking them to safety in the opposite direction to the fighting. She wasn't the only one; adults were slipping away here and there with children on their arms, but I was surprised to see most people staying as they waited anxiously for Hayden to speak. Gunfire sounded again, forcing Hayden to speed towards me as he finally closed the distance. Without a word, his hand slipped into mine as he pulled me towards the centre of everyone, where Kit and Malin had started dispensing weapons to anyone capable.

I noticed Dax rushing over to Leutie, where he lightly touched her shoulder and said something. She shook her head and started to speak, but he cut her off by tucking his finger gently under her chin. He said something that caused her to look pained before she nodded and darted off after Maisie. Relief washed through me as she caught up to them. She wasn't ready to be out here for this, and at least she would be safe.

'Stay with me, Grace,' Hayden murmured quickly over his shoulder. 'I mean it.'

I didn't get the chance to respond, however, before he spoke louder, his tone urgent and sharp as he hurried to give direction over the quickening gunfire in the distance.

'All right, I can't be sure, but I'm willing to bet that's Greystone,' he called to the crowd, which had fallen completely silent the moment he opened his mouth to address them. 'If you don't feel ready to fight, I suggest you go and hide somewhere. Better you're safe than dead.'

He paused and waited for people to take him up on his suggestion, but no one moved. A chill ran down my spine as I took in the eyes hanging on his every word; determination was clear in their gazes, ready to protect their home and follow their leader.

'Those on duty are probably already over there, so we need to hurry. If this is your first time fighting, remember your training. You guys have worked hard and you can do this,' Hayden reassured them. His voice was strained and rushed, but I could tell his words had an effect on them as the crowd stood a little taller. I noticed Kit, Dax, and Malin amongst them, looking strong and unwavering.

'All right, let's go,' Hayden called out. All of that had happened in about sixty seconds, though the weight of the situation made it feel like ages.

People reacted instantly, turning and running towards the edge of camp where all the noise was coming from. I was about to follow them when my arm was jerked backward, spinning me so my chest collided lightly with Hayden's. I had no time to react before I felt his hand cradle my jaw and pull me forward as his lips pressed suddenly to mine. The kiss only lasted for a second, but it was long enough for anyone to see it. When Hayden pulled back, his eyes were intense and on edge, but he took the next few seconds to carry out our promise despite the dire circumstances.

'You be careful, Grace. I love you,' he assured me.

'I will,' I promised. 'I love you and you be careful, too, yeah?'

He nodded sharply and allowed his thumb to trace once along my cheek before he dropped his hand to pull a gun from behind his back and press it into my palm. I noticed

314

he already had one of his own, as well as a knife he always carried. My knife was where I always kept it, giving me two weapons.

'Let's go,' he said with a sharp tick of his head.

With that, we both turned and broke into a sprint, catching up to the crowd easily and weaving our way to the front, where Kit and Dax were leading. Adrenaline was already flooding through my system, increasing my heart rate and bringing droplets of sweat along my hairline. I knew it was coming, and I had started to accept what needed to be done, but I hadn't expected it so soon. I had hardly spoken the words aloud, much less had time to actually prepare myself to do it. I shook my head, determined to do what had to be done if the opportunity arose: kill Jonah.

It didn't take long for us to reach where the fighting had already begun. As Hayden predicted, those on duty in Blackwing had already started defending it, and judging by the evidence on the ground, people had already started falling. Chaos took over, and I was reminded of the very first night the war had started. Everywhere I looked, people were fighting; knives slashed through the air, guns fired from every direction, fists flew with full force until they connected with sickening thuds on other people's bodies. More people than I could count had gathered in this area, fighting for the right to survive.

'Oh my god,' someone from beside me gasped in fear.

I glanced to my right, away from Hayden, to see a girl of maybe eighteen. Her eyes were wide with fear and her limbs were shaking as she hurried along. She didn't seem ready to be here, nor did she look particularly powerful, but I admired her bravery for even coming along. I was about to open my mouth to tell her to turn back when a high-pitched whistling sound rushed past my ear, followed immediately by a wet *thunk* as a knife buried itself in her chest.

My jaw dropped open in horror as her eyes widened and her hand flew to her chest before her feet stumbled, bringing her to the ground. My feet kept moving but my head jerked back to see her crumpled into the dirt, unmoving as people skirted around her. Just like that, she was dead, and it could have very easily been me.

I shook my head, clearing the harsh image from my mind, as our crowd thinned out to pair up with those attacking. Just as I suspected, I could see faces I recognised from Greystone fighting against those I knew from Blackwing. Everywhere I looked, people I knew at least by sight were joining the fray. I was acutely aware of Hayden beside me as I saw someone rush forward, fist cocked and ready to strike before Hayden dodged out of the way and countered with a blow to the attacker's ribcage, bringing him to the ground.

That was all I saw, however, before I was accosted by an attacker of my own. The glint of a knife appeared, then I felt the stinging burn of it ripping into my skin, although luckily it barely grazed along my shoulder. I swung my gun around and felt it collide heavily with the back of the person's head, causing them to cry out in pain. When they straightened up, I could see it was a man about my age, maybe a few years older, though I did not recognise him.

My blood dripped off the edge of his knife as he refocused himself, preparing to attack me again, but he wasn't quick enough. In the few moments he took to recover from the blow I'd landed on his head, I'd managed to pull my knife free and slashed it forward, slicing a fine, almost invisible line across his throat. The line became more pronounced, however, when thick, red blood began spilling from the slit. He dropped his weapon as his eyes bulged, both of his hands reaching up to grasp fruitlessly at his neck, but it didn't matter. He dropped to his knees in front of me, choking on his own blood, before falling flat to his face, dead.

I'd been here for thirty seconds and already seen two people die, one of them by my own hands. This was not going to be good.

My chest heaved as I breathed, eyes darting frantically around in search of attackers or allies in need of help. Hayden was back on his feet, after a scuffle on the ground. Whoever he'd been fighting now lay still in the dirt, unmoving and staring with blank, unseeing eyes up at the sky. A pool of blood was leaking out around him, and judging by the blood dripping off Hayden's knife, it was clear what had happened.

Hayden interrupted my staring by darting back over to me, tugging my arm to jerk me out of my daze and pulling me to find others to fight. All around us, pairs of people were fighting, killing, dying. Brutality exploded around us as we darted through the chaos, but we didn't make it far before, once again, we had to fight. A man at least twice Hayden's size appeared in front of us, leering at me in a disgusting way before Hayden kicked him heavily in the stomach, redirecting his attention.

A flash of movement to my right caught my interest, and I managed to duck just in time as a fist flew over my head. I didn't even straighten up before I raised my foot and brought it down forcefully on my attacker's, earning a grunt of pain as they doubled over. When I straightened up, my eyes landed on a girl. She looked about my age, and she wasted no time in cocking back her fist before swinging forward and connecting it heavily with my jaw. Stars burst in front of my eyes as my head snapped to the side, and I had to spit out a mouthful of blood before I refocused.

Again, she tried to hit me, but this time I dodged it and

317

lurched forward, colliding heavily with her chest to bring us both to the ground. I landed on top of her with a heavy huff, and she squirmed beneath me as she tried to throw her knee into my side. I heaved out heavy, uneven breaths as I managed to pin her down with my knees before rearing back to let two solid hits fly, each landing squarely on either side of her face. Blood spurted from her nose where it was clearly broken, and more blood gushed when she coughed. She gave one weak attempt at hitting me before her eyes fluttered a few times and she stilled beneath me, unconscious.

I heaved my body off hers, wiping blood and sweat alike off my face as I stood. A quick glance around showed Kit fighting off two men at once, his skilled actions making them both look more than inept. A man from Blackwing that I didn't know fought another from Greystone with only their hands, both of them very bloody. Horrifyingly, a young woman I recognised from Blackwing lay gasping on the ground, spitting up her own blood before her chest gave one final heave and stilled for good.

A heavy grunt brought my attention as I turned back to see Hayden still fighting the much larger man. To my horror, I saw that the man had Hayden pinned to the ground, though Hayden managed to land two heavy blows to the man's ribs, causing him to buckle long enough for Hayden to slip out from beneath him. Hayden's eyes darted in my direction as soon as he stood, and in his distraction the man hit him over the head and brought him back into the dirt.

'Grace, look out!' Hayden shouted just before the man slammed his large fist across his jaw.

I jerked around, following Hayden's line of vision behind me as I saw a large man barrelling towards me. The deranged look in his eye was one I hadn't seen for a while, but I felt my blood run cold as I recognised him. He carried some type of rudimentary spear in his hands as he sprinted towards me, eyes focused and filled with anger.

Barrow.

I hardly had time to absorb how he'd got free, much less dodge as he sprinted straight towards me. He cocked his arm back, preparing to launch the spear straight into my chest. The insane look in his eye paralysed me, rooting me to the ground and making me suddenly defenceless. His arm released the spear, and I could hardly think a cohesive thought when Barrow shouted, jerking me out of my haze.

'Duck!'

My body reacted before my mind did, dropping to the ground milliseconds before I heard the *whizzing* of the spear as it soared over my head. I heard the cry of pain that followed the wet slicing sound caused by the spear. Immediately, I twisted in the dirt, terrified to see who it had hit. My eyes were wide with fear as they landed on the spear, which was now stained red with blood, buried in the chest of the man that had been fighting Hayden. The man's eyes widened as he looked down at it before falling to the ground.

A sweaty, bloody Hayden stood hurriedly, his eyes darting in shock between the man and Barrow, who was now next to me. The slightly mad look in his eye had diminished, though he was still huffing heavily and glaring at Hayden.

'Well?' he hissed. 'Get back to fighting, you two.'

With that, he darted off to take one of the men Kit had been fighting, leaving a stunned Hayden and myself behind.

'What the hell?' Hayden muttered in surprise.

'I don't know,' I said with a harsh shake of my head.

Barrow had just come out of nowhere and potentially saved Hayden's life, as well as sparing me my own.

'Come on,' Hayden said dismissively.

His hand grabbed mine once more as he pulled me back

into the thick of things. A deafening *bang* sounded after a bright flash of light, making several people scream in fear before they were silenced by another one. This time, I knew what it was, and it didn't take me long to find a wispy Perdita lurking in the shadows as she launched yet another bomb into the distance as far as her frail body would allow. The third bang sounded different, wetter somehow, and the spray of red that showered the air told me she'd hit someone directly. My stomach churned at the thought, but I forced myself to focus on the heat of Hayden's hand in mine and the importance of staying alert.

'Let's get the fuck out of here!' someone called desperately. My eyes found the young man and saw him focusing on another while he pleaded.

My feet stumbled once as I recognised the second man, and again I felt sick to my stomach. He was busy fighting someone, but the fight was over quickly as he took out his gun and blasted a hole in his opponent's chest, dropping them to the ground to give me a clear view of him.

Jonah.

'Hayden,' I gasped, stopping so abruptly that my feet dragged a few inches in the dirt as my arm jerked Hayden's backward.

He turned sharply and looked at my face, seeing the emotions there.

'What is it, Grace?' he asked quickly, looking around over my shoulder for any incoming enemies.

'Jonah's there,' I said, pointing with a somewhat shaking hand. Hayden whipped around to look, where he saw Jonah take out yet another member of Blackwing.

'Grace, we have—'

Hayden was cut off, however, as a body flew out of nowhere to collide with him, driving them both into the side

of the building we stood next to. Hayden groaned as whoever had attacked him threw a knee into his side. Hayden
threw his elbow down sharply to collide with the back of
his attacker's head, giving him enough time to look at me
and shout a few words.

'You know what you have to do, Grace,' Hayden shouted
over the horrifying sounds echoing around us. 'You can do
it!'

I nodded sharply and took a deep breath, casting one last
look at him before I sprinted off. There was no way I'd be
able to beat Jonah in a hand-to-hand fight. As much as it
hurt my pride to admit it, I knew I couldn't. He was simply
too big, too strong, too heartless. But I could trust my skills
with a gun, and I could take him out that way.

Air ripped through my lungs as I sprinted through the
fighting, ducking a fist here and there, while landing a few
hits of my own along the way. I clenched my gun tightly
in my sweaty hand as I trained my eyes on my target – the
shadowy space between two buildings that would give me
enough cover to aim my shot. I felt the sharp sting of a knife
slash across my calf, but I was lucky again as it didn't go too
deep. I continued sprinting on and managed to leap over a
crumpled, unidentified body before disappearing into the
shadows created by the buildings.

My chest heaved with the effort I'd expended with all my
running and fighting, and sweat mixed with the blood caked
on my skin as it poured down my forehead. Adrenaline was
pumping so quickly through my veins that I thought my
heart might actually beat out of my chest, but it was nowhere near the level of mental pain that had started to creep
up at the thought of what I had to do.

Quickly, I crept around the edge, careful to stay out of
sight of anyone. Leaning forward, I could see Jonah talking

to the man who'd begged to retreat, a gun in each of his hands as he raised one and aimed at someone. He fired so casually it was like he'd been aiming at a target, as he killed yet another member of Blackwing. I had to act, and I had to act quickly.

With slightly shaky hands, I raised my gun. My heart pounding, eyes narrowed, I lined up the guides directly at Jonah's heart. He was hardly moving, which should have given me an easy shot, but I felt frozen. My finger hovered over the trigger, poised to shoot and kill, but I couldn't pull it down and complete the action.

'*Come on, Grace,*' I hissed to myself, shaking my head once to try and bring up all the strength I had.

My toes bounced anxiously, making my aim waver from the target. A frustrated growl ripped from my throat as I shook my head, furious with myself for falling apart at such a time. This was maybe the best chance I'd get at killing him and ending this for good, but I couldn't force my body to cooperate enough to aim a steady shot. My heaving breaths and shaking limbs were making it impossible to keep the guides on top of my gun in line with his chest for more than a millisecond, and anger at myself combined with a gut-wrenching pain was so strong that it was starting to blur my vision.

I forced my legs to stop their jittering, using every ounce of strength I had, mental and physical, to line up my gun with his chest once more. I held my breath and stared down the barrel, preparing to shoot. At the last second, my eyes darted up to his face. Just as I did, he turned, and I gasped as his green eyes, so similar to mine, locked on my own. His lips parted in surprise as he saw me aiming the gun at him. Instead of the sneer I was expecting, he looked taken aback, and, surprisingly, hurt. He gave the tiniest shake of his head, freezing me into place, before he opened his mouth to call out to those from Greystone.

'Let's go!' he shouted, casting one last unreadable look in my direction before turning and speeding away from the fighting.

My chest caved in as I sucked in a breath, and my arms dropped to my sides, swinging the gun with them. I watched in shock as he and what remained of his attacking party fled into the trees, leaving Blackwing behind as they retreated.

I couldn't do it.

I was too weak, and I had failed.

I stood rooted to the ground. Too many thoughts and feelings were ripping through me that I was almost certain they were physically making me bleed. My eyes glazed over as I stared at where Jonah had vanished to.

That was it; he was gone, and he was still very much alive.

A sudden scream of complete and utter agony ripped through the camp, jerking me from my haze. I sprinted from the shadows, darting over bodies and other wreckage as I sped towards the sound. Quickly, I could see a small crowd had gathered, obscuring my view of what everyone was staring at. If I felt sick before, it was nothing compared to how I felt now as sudden petrifying fear ripped through me.

'Hayden.'

His name slipped past my lips, no louder than a ghost of a whisper, as fear rocked me to my core.

Where was he? Was he okay?

Please let him be okay.

My body started to shake again as I reached the crowd. With trembling hands extended, I pushed my way through the crowd, desperate to get to the source of everyone's staring. A heavy sense of dread and foreboding crashed through me, blurring my vision and making me stumble as I pressed on desperately. Finally, I managed to break through the crowd, nearly tripping in the dirt after being freed from their oppressive and suffocating presence.

'Oh my god,' I choked out.

The words caught in my throat and felt like acid as they tumbled over my tongue. What I saw felt like an ice-cold dagger driving straight through my heart, ripping me to shreds and freezing the blood in my veins.

Twenty-Eight: Grim

Hayden

Pain.

Pain like nothing I'd ever felt ripped through me, shearing my heart from my chest. Searing agony twisted at my stomach, pricked at my skin, gnawed at every bit of flesh and blood and bone I possessed. It was like the world had been engulfed in flames, bent on destroying us all as it charred me from the inside out. Surely there was nothing more painful than what I felt right now.

There was blood, too. So much blood. Where had all this blood come from? Did a human body possess this much, or was it the world playing tricks on me, shifting reality into some waking nightmare that I had no hope of ever escaping? Surely the hot, wet, sticky red substance I was seeing so much of was a figment of my imagination, designed to haunt me.

It was like the world had fallen away around me, like someone had placed a giant glass box around me to cut me off from everything else. There was no sound. I should have heard the muffled chaos that came with fighting or even the pounding of my own heart, but all I could hear was a faint white noise buzzing incessantly in my ear, drowning out everything else and leaving me alone to feel the pain that was currently ripping me apart.

How had this happened? How had our world got to such a state that this kind of thing could occur? Humans weren't supposed to live like this. Fear wasn't supposed to rule our lives and drag us backward in evolution. We weren't supposed to fight one another to this point of such destruction, and we weren't supposed to kill one another simply to survive. Bodies were massacred and obliterated, but what was most horrifying was the damage done inside.

Surely our souls could not survive such carnage.

I hadn't seen it happen. I hadn't seen who'd done this, who was responsible for the gory sight that lay before me. There was nothing I could do, no way to attack whoever had caused this. For the first time in my life, I wanted to kill, but I couldn't as the blood flowed freely over my hands.

'Ha-Hayden.'

That sound ripped me back to reality, plunging me deeper into what my eyes were seeing but my mind could not absorb. My hands shook violently as they drifted uselessly down the blood-soaked torso, pressing down over the holes that had ripped through the skin. It didn't help, and the blood pushed past my fingertips as I failed to stop it.

People had gathered around, but they might as well have not even been there for all I noticed. I rested on my knees, collapsed in the dirt as I slung my arm around his shoulder in an attempt to keep him up. His skin was already losing its colour, and the dark brown eyes that stared back at me held droplets of water that made them glow in the darkness. His jaw shook as he struggled to pull in a deep breath, hindered by the two tiny holes that had ripped through his chest.

'It's okay, Jett,' I managed to choke out. 'You're going to be okay.'

He gasped another breath as he stared intently into my eyes, unable to look anywhere else. I held his gaze and gave him a shaky nod that was meant to be reassuring, but the tightness that burned at my throat made it feel very unconvincing. My entire body was shaking as I held him in my arms, determined to save him as the blood so essential for life continued to pour out of him.

'You're okay, it's not that bad,' I lied, barely able to speak.

I couldn't stop my hand from shaking as I pressed it desperately into his chest, fighting the sticky, warm liquid. My head snapped up to look around frantically, desperate for someone to help. Faces blurred together and I found it hard to distinguish any single one, but I saw Maisie standing in the crowd. Her fingers pressed to her lips as she cried silently. Her scream of pure agony had been what alerted me to this in the first place, and she watched in shock now as I held Jett in my arms.

'Where's Docc? Someone get him!'

Countless pairs of blank, shocked eyes stared back at me. No one moved to help or to alert anyone. They all just stood and watched, some with tears slipping down their cheeks, others with fingers pressed to their lips as they held back sobs.

'Hayden . . .'

I jerked my gaze back to Jett. His voice was weak and the desperation in his eyes faded a little as he clung to my every word. Utter panic ripped through me as his eyes fluttered once and closed, sending a chill through my entire body.

'No, no, *no, Jett!*'

Fear and agony were loaded in my voice as I shouted desperately, shaking him once. Short-lived relief returned as he opened his eyes again, sucking in a startled breath as his gaze found mine.

'Am – am I going to die?'

'No, little man, you're not going to die,' I told him, shaking my head sharply.

He nodded weakly, licking his shockingly pale lips once as his eyes drifted closed for a moment. He opened them again, but the spark behind them was quickly fading as his breaths grew shallower and weaker.

Again, I looked around the crowd, desperate for help to appear.

'Someone get Docc! Get Grace, get anyone,' I begged. Again, no one moved. They all knew what I refused to accept: help was too late already. 'Please, help.'

My voice broke on the last word and, again, I was ignored. I squeezed my eyes shut momentarily before refocusing on Jett, who was shaking slightly as I held him.

'I just wanted to be——' he sucked in a rattling breath. 'I just wanted to be brave.'

My heart all but shattered in my chest as I forced my jaw to stop quivering. He was growing so pale so quickly, and despite the heat of the blood covering my hands, he felt cold.

'You are brave, Jett. You're so, so brave,' I reassured him honestly. My eyes stung as tears crept up, threatening to spill over.

'Am I br-brave like you?'

The intensity suddenly returned to his eyes as he stared into mine. I felt his small hand close around the front of my shirt as he clung to me. I couldn't stop the tear that fell from my eye and landed silently on his chest, where it was lost in the swirling mess of red.

'You're so much braver than I am.'

His thin, white lips pulled into a semblance of a smile that only lasted a moment before he sucked in a sharp breath. My eyes widened and darted around his face, praying that the colour would return and he'd suddenly sit up, but he didn't. His features blurred as tears obscured my vision, and I ducked my head to wipe my eyes hastily on my shoulder to clear them away. My entire chest rattled as I struggled to draw a full breath, but my heart was breaking and ripping my insides apart, making it almost impossible.

'I'm sorry,' he whispered, brown eyes locked on mine. I shook my head instantly, squeezing my eyes shut and grimacing as I fought off the sob threatening to break through. I couldn't remember the last time I'd cried.

'Don't be sorry. I'm so proud of you,' I choked out, my voice tight and strained as it ripped at my throat.

'I love you, Hayden.'

His voice was a tiny whisper of a breath, and so quiet I almost couldn't hear it. I couldn't stop myself from ducking to press a light kiss onto his forehead. My shaking hands held his body as I gave up on trying to stem the bleeding. It was too late, and we both knew it. When I pulled back, I saw he could barely keep his eyes open, and his breaths were no more than soft pants that drifted weakly past his colourless lips.

'I love you, too, Jett.'

Again, that soft smile I thought I saw earlier pulled at his lips as he closed his eyes, content after hearing those final words. He released a tiny whoosh of air before his chest stilled, and his grip on my shirt went slack as his hand let go and fell limply to his stomach. The tiny remaining spark of light that had lingered in him was gone, extinguished long before it should have been as his young life came to an end.

'No,' I gasped, shaking my head in denial.

I shook him slightly, refusing to believe he was actually gone. This time, however, he did not react as I moved his thin body. His head rolled to the side on my arm where he rested, but his eyes did not open, and his chest did not rise.

'Jett,' I choked. 'No, no, no . . .'

Tears flowed freely down my cheeks now and my jaw quivered uncontrollably as I failed to draw a full breath. I felt like my entire body had crumbled to bits in the dirt only to be ground into dust and burned. I leaned forward, resting my forehead against him as I wrapped him completely in my arms and hauled him to my chest. My eyes squeezed shut in an attempt to block out the pain, but no amount of darkness could smother how I was feeling as heartbreak ripped through me. My jaw clenched as a grimace pulled at my face, obscured from sight as I hid behind Jett's tiny body.

I rocked back and forth where I was perched in the dirt, clutching Jett to me as if I thought doing so would bring him back. His body was quickly cooling as the last of the heat that remained slipped away. A sob finally ripped through my body, making me convulse while I still clung to him.

This couldn't be happening.

I felt the heat of a hand on my shoulder but ignored it, too overwhelmed to think about or feel anything other than the complete agony destroying me right now. My grip on Jett was tighter than ever as my body hunched forward, refusing to believe that he was gone.

'Hayden.'

I vaguely registered the sound of Grace's voice saying my name and knew it must have been her touching me now, but I felt nothing.

'Grace, fix him,' I begged weakly, my voice muffled by his body as I continued to hug him. 'Please fix him.'

'Hayden . . .' she trailed off weakly, ignoring my pleas. She sounded broken, and it was obvious that she, too, was crying.

'Come on, Grace,' I begged tightly. 'You can fix him, right? Please fix him . . .'

I felt her kneel behind me as her arms roped around my neck, pressing her chest into my back as she hugged me tightly from behind. I couldn't tell if she was shaking or if I was. Probably both.

'I can't, Hayden.'

Her voice cracked and I could feel her shake her head, but I could draw no comfort from her touch. All I could do was feel Jett's limp body in my arms, feel the coolness of his skin against my own where our foreheads touched, feel the obvious lifelessness in the weight of his tiny, frail body. Mine was breaking down, and I felt myself shattering to bits as I let Grace hold on to me. The relief that she was alive was not enough to heal the gaping wound that losing Jett had caused.

It was absolutely silent around us, apart from the shuddering breaths that ripped from my lungs and the gasps that sounded as I tried to calm down. I could feel wet heat at my neck that told me Grace was still crying while she held me, but her tears were silent. I didn't know if we were alone or if the entire camp was watching, but I didn't care.

It didn't matter.

Nothing mattered.

If Jett, the unyielding source of light and innocence in our world, could die, so could the rest of us.

Without deciding to, my body started to move. My joints screamed in protest as if I'd spent ages on the ground. In all reality, I had absolutely no idea how long it had been, but, again, I didn't care. Grace's hold around my shoulders broke as I rose to my feet, lifting Jett's tiny body with me. He remained limp in my grasp as I started to walk, unable to even look around to Grace. Surely seeing her face would only break me more.

It was then that I saw people had formed a circle around

me, though they parted instantly as I approached to let me through. No one said a word, and it was so quiet that I was certain every single person present was holding their breath. I managed to make it to the edge of the circle before I heard hurried footsteps following me. My eyes squeezed shut in disappointment.

'Hayden—'

I knew she'd follow me. She did it because she loved me, but I couldn't see her right now.

'Stay here, Grace.'

'But—'

'No. Stay here.'

My voice was sharp and commanding, but undeniably flat. The tone sounded as lifeless as the boy in my arms, though it showed no hints that I'd just broken down moments before. Much to my surprise, Grace listened. Her footsteps stopped while mine continued on, carrying me away from her and everyone else in the crowd. She let me go, and I was grateful. I couldn't be around anyone else right now.

Right now, I needed to just be alone and let the anguish and torment take over.

Grace

My heart shattered as I watched Hayden walk away from me. He was covered in blood, most of which probably wasn't his own, and utterly and completely broken as he carried Jett's body away. Tears stung at the cuts on my face, and my hands shook by my sides as I stood in shock. There was nothing I could do to help him.

None of this seemed possible. Jett wasn't even supposed to be there for the fight, much less a victim of the senseless carnage. He was supposed to be in his hut, safe and out of harm's way. He was supposed to be alive.

Quiet murmurs started to sound behind me, where the rest of the crowd remained frozen in place. I was stuck, rooted to the ground as I watched Hayden disappear from sight with my back to everyone else. People's voices were loaded with pain, confusion, sorrow, and countless other emotions I felt rolling through me. It was like I was incapable of feeling anything besides pain as I forced myself to turn and head back to the crowd. My throat felt absolutely raw from holding back tears, and my entire body felt like it'd been run over by a truck.

'It all happened so fast,' Maisie was saying to those around her.

Her voice was hard to decipher between her gasping sobs and choking breaths. Tears flowed freely down her face as several people tried to comfort her. I listened, desperate to understand how such an innocent boy had wound up in the middle of all this.

'We — we were hiding like Hayden said when all of a sudden—' she was cut off by a choking gasp that ripped through her chest. 'All of a sudden someone burst in and tr-tried to attack.'

My heart pounded heavily in my chest as I listened, transfixed by Maisie as she recounted her story to everyone listening.

'Jett led them outside, away from us . . . and that was the last I saw of him until . . . until now,' she choked out before breaking down and falling to her knees. Her hands pressed into her eyes as she sobbed, and those around her roped comforting arms around her shoulders as they hugged her. 'He s-saved us.'

I suddenly felt overwhelmingly sick to my stomach as

reality started to set in. My feet carried my stiff body away from the crowd until I could duck between two buildings. Bending forward, I barely had time to take a breath before the contents of my stomach emptied into the dirt. I lifted a shaking hand to wipe my mouth and drew a rattling breath, in and out, still hunched over. I leaned into the wall beside me, closing my eyes for a few moments to try and sort things out.

Jett was gone.

But Hayden was alive, and I couldn't deny that the thought flooded my body with relief. I felt sick again, however, when I thought of the others. I'd yet to see Dax, Kit, Malin, Docc . . . So many others I cared about were unspoken for. Again, I had to duck forward as I threw up once more, the acid burning my already tortured throat. I pressed my hands firmly into my eyes, causing bright lights to spring up in my vision. I had to get it together and find out what else had happened.

With one final, shaky breath, I forced myself upright. I took a wobbly step out from between the buildings. With Hayden gone and obviously desperate to be alone, I had to find the others to keep myself sane. My heart thumped painfully at the thought that Jett might not be the only one that I cared about who had been lost today. I shook my head, fighting off the dark thought.

You'll find them. They'll be fine.

But as soon as I got a clear view of where most of the fighting had taken place, my hopes plummeted to the dirt beneath my feet. My jaw fell open in shock as I fully took in the scene for the first time. Gore and death surrounded me, the grisly scene far worse than I had realised. Bodies littered the ground, some of them so twisted and mangled that I had a hard time telling if they were male or female. Blood leaked

334

into the dirt, standing in stark contrast to the usually dark brown. My vision blurred and the world seemed to swoop around me as I looked around, petrified and shocked by what I was seeing.

How could I even dare to hope those I cared about had survived this?

A cripplingly cold numbness settled over me as I forced myself to move, careful to avoid stepping in puddles of blood or, more horrifyingly, bits of human being. A chill shot down my spine as I approached the first body – that of a man. His dark hair made it difficult to tell who it was, but when I circled around, a flash of relief seared through me when I saw it was no one I knew.

The next body lay only a short distance away, but this one I recognised. It was the first man I'd killed, frozen where he'd fallen after I'd slashed his throat. His gaze was blank and lifeless, eyes stuck open at the point of his death. My feet carried me on determinedly to study the next body.

Time after time, I passed a fallen fighter, and time after time, the faces of my friends did not appear. I didn't dare hope, though, as I still had countless more bodies to examine. Every time I vaguely recognised someone, my heart clenched painfully. Some I recognised from Greystone, others from Blackwing, others not at all, but each person was dead because of this war.

All the while I searched, Hayden's face swam before my eyes, and I had to shove down the burning desire to go after him. My heart ached at the thought of him being alone, but I knew it was what he wanted. As much as it hurt, I had to respect that. He was alive, and I would see him when he was ready.

That reassurance did little to calm me, however. Every body I looked at seemed to chip away a little more at my remaining sanity. I had myself convinced that the next body would be someone I cared deeply about.

Dax.

Kit.

Docc.

Malin.

Leutie.

Perdita.

Their faces swam before my eyes, blurring my vision as I moved on. I could hardly process the reality of what I was actually seeing, desperate that their faces would elude me.

'Grace!'

I jumped when someone called my name from behind me, and I jerked around towards the sound to see someone rushing in my direction. Relief so strong flooded through me that I hardly had time to open my arms before his body collided with mine, hugging me tightly to his chest. The hug felt different, off somehow because I wasn't used to his body, but it was comforting all the same.

'Dax,' I breathed. His arms tightened around me, and I could feel his obvious relief. The sight of a familiar face set me off all over again, because I could feel my throat tighten and eyes prick with the wet heat of tears.

'I'm so glad you're alive,' he murmured, squeezing me one last time before releasing me. When he pulled back, I saw a deep gash in his brow that was leaking a substantial amount of blood and several other cuts and bruises, but he appeared to be fine for the most part. There was none of the usual spark or lightness that he usually carried; only fear and trepidation were written across his face now.

'Where's Hayden? Is he okay?' he asked, clearly terrified of the answer.

'He's okay,' I said, shaking my head quickly.

Dax sagged with relief and let his eyes close momentarily. He had obviously been expecting us to be together, so his absence must have made him assume the worst.

'Thank god,' he muttered.

'What about Kit?' I asked, equally afraid to hear his answer.

'I don't know,' Dax admitted tightly. Concern was written clearly across his features. 'Come on, let's go and look.'

It didn't appear that Dax knew about Jett. How could I tell him without breaking down? To say it out loud would make it real, and at this point, nothing felt real. I was unable to speak as I let him nudge me across camp to where a different group of people had gathered. I was relieved to see so many alive; it seemed that with the mass amount of fallen bodies, no one had survived, but I could see now that that wasn't true.

Dax and I approached the smaller group, where people turned to face us. The crowd parted and I was suddenly surprised and relieved to see Kit standing in the middle. His arms were wrapped around a sobbing Malin, and I could see his lips murmuring things in her ear that I could not hear. They stood next to a middle-aged man who had fallen on the ground. His posture was like that of so many I'd already seen – broken, immobile, and undeniably dead.

'Malin's father,' Dax murmured softly to me.

My jaw fell open in surprise as I understood. What little remained of my heart broke for Malin as thoughts of my own father came rushing back. I knew what it felt like to lose a parent, and it was something I wouldn't wish on anyone. My lower lip trembled once before I bit it harshly between my teeth, determined to be as strong as I possibly could.

Kit then noticed that we'd arrived. His head tilted back momentarily as he closed his eyes, relief evident in his posture when he saw that Dax and I were alive. When he opened his eyes once more, his hands never stopped their gentle soothing actions as Malin sobbed in his arms. His lips moved silently as he mouthed a single word in our direction.

'*Hayden?*'

Dax nodded and mouthed back, 'He's fine.'

Kit blew out a breath of relief before returning his full attention to Malin. As confusing as their relationship was, I was glad that he at least cared for her enough to be there for her at a time like this. Despite our brief upset, when I had accused him of being responsible, I couldn't imagine having had to deal with my father's death without Hayden. I hoped Kit could be there for Malin like Hayden had been for me.

Hayden.

Every thought I had of him sent a sharp dagger of hurt through me, and again I fought the desperate urge to find him. For now, I had to figure out how to help. The more I could help here, the more I'd be able to help Hayden whenever he finally returned. Hayden was clearly broken, and I had to remain strong for the both of us. Two broken people were no use, but the longer I stood and let the truth of everything sink in, the more shattered I felt. If I couldn't remain strong, we'd be left as jagged shards of people, fragmented and torn to unrecognisable bits, left to grind to dust in the wind.

Twenty-Nine: Rhythm
Grace

A soft cloud of dust rose in the air as the dull thud of a body landing in the dirt sounded. I straightened up and let out a deep sigh, pausing to wipe the sweat off my forehead with my sleeve. I closed my eyes to give myself a brief moment of respite, though the tiny bit of darkness did nothing to wipe the gruesome sights I'd subjected myself to all night from my mind. Once I opened my eyes, I was greeted with the gory sight of more bodies than I could count lined up in a neat row on the ground.

Just like last time we'd been attacked, there were two piles: one for Blackwing, one for Greystone. After each pile had reached twenty, I'd stopped counting, and that had been a long time ago. Dax stood across from me, where he was also covered in sweat and dirt. He looked slightly shell-shocked and hadn't spoken in over an hour. After I'd found him and Kit, I knew I had to tell them about Jett. They were close to him too, and they needed to know.

Kit had taken the news without a word, his frustration and heartbreak showing through as he turned to punch a wall as his only outlet of emotion. Dax had sputtered in disbelief, saying it wasn't funny to joke about things like that. It was only when a single tear slid down my cheek and I shook my head that he realised I was telling the truth. He'd fallen to the ground, where he'd pushed his hands through his short, dark hair and let out a few silent tears. Ever since then, he hadn't said much other than to mutter quiet instructions.

Neither Kit nor Dax had asked where Hayden was once they found out about Jett; they understood his absence, and didn't question it. It was still driving me insane not knowing, but I forced myself to focus on things at camp. The more I did here, the less Hayden would have to do whenever he returned. I just hoped that was sooner rather than later.

'Come on,' Dax murmured, pulling me from my reverie. I kept falling into something like a trance, where I'd stare wide-eyed at the shocking amount of bodies that were piling up.

I followed him silently as we walked along the row. Countless pairs of shoes covered feet that would never walk again, and I found myself noticing tiny details about the dead. One man had a tattoo of an orchid along his ankle. One woman wore a tiny bracelet made out of string around her wrist; perhaps a child had made it for her and she couldn't resist wearing it to make that child smile. One man had only one shoe left, the other lost somewhere in the heat of the battle.

I ripped my eyes away and shook my head. The more details I noticed, the more human they felt, and the more it hurt to lay them to rest. Each body I saw reminded me of how I had failed to kill Jonah. Each life that was lost here, on either side, could be traced back to him. These people's lives could have been spared if I had just been strong enough to do what I knew needed to be done.

I couldn't stop that thought from repeating itself in my head. As Dax and I reached another body and determined it to be someone from Greystone, we each gripped a now cold limb and lifted, making our way towards the Greystone pile. I didn't know this person, but they were still human, and now they were dead. So many were dead, and I felt each pair of blank, lifeless eyes looking at me in blame.

You could have saved me, they said.

This is your fault, they taunted.

If you weren't so weak, I might still be alive, they hissed.

It was tearing me apart and I was letting it, because the silent whispers of the dead were right. Jonah had caused this, and I had failed to stop him.

A quiet thud sounded again as we dropped the body gently. It had become familiar now.

Walk, lift, carry, drop.

Walk, lift, carry, drop.

Over and over again, Dax and I moved. It went on for hours, until sweat poured down my face and my back felt like it might snap. Despite the physical turmoil, it was nothing like the shredding that was happening inside as I felt my heart rip to pieces and disappear altogether. I needed Hayden, and I needed to be there for him, but I couldn't.

Dax and I were about to set off to find another body when a loud, frightened gasp sounded from a little way away. Fear of another attack tore through me as I jerked towards the sound, but that fear quickly subsided when I saw a ghostly pale Leutie standing near one of the piles of bodies. She was practically trembling as her widened eyes took in the shocking sight, and she stumbled backward as she took an involuntary step away from the carnage. Instinctively, I moved to her, and I heard Dax following behind me. If seeing this was ripping me apart, there was no way Leutie would be able to handle it.

'Don't look, Leutie,' I said gently, taking her by the wrist and tugging her a few steps away so the sight was cut off by the side of a building.

Her jaw quivered and her arm shook beneath my touch.

Her eyes darted around frantically as if desperately trying to orient herself, and it appeared she was unable to take a full breath. I was suddenly reminded of Hayden and myself in the depths of the Armoury, when I'd accidentally seen the gruesome mess of dismembered bodies decaying in the dark. It haunted me to this day, and I hoped that wouldn't happen to Leutie.

'How – how did this happen?' she gasped, still unable to look at me as her eyes flicked around.

'War,' Dax answered, surprising me. His voice was uncharacteristically serious as he moved to stand next to me.

'Why though?' she whispered shakily, finally looking at me before glancing at Dax.

'You know why,' I said gently. 'Everyone's running out of stuff to survive and you know Jonah . . .'

She nodded, confirming her understanding. Leutie understood Jonah perhaps more than anyone else besides me, as she'd grown up with him, too. She knew his barbaric, unrelenting nature, and she understood his irrationally reckless disposition.

'I just – I don't—'

She was cut off, however, as her hand flew to her mouth and she choked out a gasping sob, losing all control she'd been clinging to. I watched her fall apart and found myself unable to do anything. It reminded me of Hayden, and reminded me yet again of how helpless I was to help him. Leutie's sobs echoed around me as tears flowed down her face.

'She shouldn't be here,' Dax muttered to me, compassion leaking into his voice. He was right; Leutie was not prepared to see this. He surprised me again by moving forward and placing a hand on her back.

'Hey, come on now,' he said gently. 'Let's get you out of here, yeah?'

She choked out another sob but managed to nod once, leaning into him slightly as if desperate for some sort of comfort. I saw Dax close his eyes and let out a deep sigh, as if some memory had arisen, but he shook his head to wave it off.

'I'll take her to mine for the night,' he said to me. 'Hayden's going to need you and it won't help if she's there.'

I nodded again, relieved. It would be hard enough to be there for Hayden at all, much less with Leutie present. Hayden would never be able to be open about how he felt with her there, so I was grateful for Dax's intervention. I also got the distinct impression that Dax didn't want to be alone after all this and hoped that having Leutie around would help.

'Sounds good,' I told him.

He nodded once and steered her off, hand still placed comfortingly on her back. She allowed him to lead her away, all previous hesitations apparently gone. I watched them retreat, feeling slightly jealous that they got to use each other for comfort, even if they didn't really know each other. Another human presence was comforting, no matter how well you knew them.

I let out a deep sigh and turned around. As my eyes scanned the area, I felt a bit of relief to see that most of the bodies had finally been cleared. Two groups of people carried what looked like the last of them to be collected, meaning that this part of our work was done for now. A smaller group had got to work setting up an area where we could burn them, giving them as much dignity and respect as we could in such times.

A soft breeze blew through camp, carrying the stench of

blood heavily in the air. The bitter, metallic scent would linger for a while, I suspected, serving as a haunting reminder of what had happened. It also reminded me of the blood covering my own body from where I'd been wounded, and it made me realise I'd yet to see Docc. Automatically, my feet carried me to the infirmary. I hadn't seen his body when we were cleaning them up, but I hadn't seen him alive, either. Fear suddenly ripped through me as I felt the desperate urge to make sure he was okay.

As soon as I reached the door and burst through, I jumped when my eyes landed on a rather shocking sight. Five bodies were piled neatly in the entryway, with no blood or obvious wounds, though they were undeniably dead. I realised they were all from Greystone, and frowned in confusion as I tried to figure out what happened.

'Don't linger, girl, let's take a look at you.'

Relief washed through me when, ripped from the lifeless bodies, my eyes landed on Docc's dark brown ones. He stood in the middle of the infirmary, where he was wrapping a wound on someone's arm. His brow ticked upward as he beckoned me inside. I came to stop a few feet away from where he was working.

'Good to see you, Grace,' he greeted now that I was closer.

'You're alive,' I said, my voice a mixture of shock and relief.

'Oh, yes. Not for their lack of trying, however,' he said, nodding towards the pile of bodies by the door.

'What happened?' I asked, confused.

'Some of those Greystone lads came in here expecting to take us out,' Docc explained, gesturing to himself and the several other patients, including Shaw. 'I had a problem with that.'

'Yeah, but what did you do to them?' I pressed. I was confused as to how they'd all seemingly dropped dead with no injuries.

'I injected them with potassium chloride,' he said simply. His eyes were focused on his work as he finished up his bandage. 'A lot of it.'

'All of them?' I asked in surprise, brows raising.

'Years of being a doctor has made me quite steady. I can be very quiet when I choose to be,' Docc said mysteriously. I blinked, both surprised and impressed that he'd apparently killed five people before the others had noticed.

'Wow,' I murmured softly. I let that sink in for a second before I shook my head. 'Anything I can do to help?'

Docc shook his head slowly as he dismissed the man he'd been fixing up. He turned to look at me, noticing my injuries. 'Let me have a look at those. I think things are under control here.'

I nodded and allowed him to glance over my wounds, letting him direct me so he could get a clear look at the gash along my arm and my shoulder blade. He grabbed some antiseptic and a few squares of gauze, working quickly yet smoothly to clean them up.

'I don't think you'll need stitches. Just keep them clean and come see me soon,' he said after finishing his inspection. I nodded in agreement.

'Thanks, Docc.'

'Where's Hayden? I heard about losing Jett. Such a shame, he was such a precious child.'

My throat tightened at the mention of both Hayden and Jett all in one exchange, and I had to hold down tears as they threatened to fight their way back up.

'I don't know where he is,' I answered honestly,

brows lowering as I felt the pain threatening to take over again.

'Hmm,' Docc said pensively. 'And how are you doing? Be honest.'

His dark brown eyes peered into my very soul.

'Pretty terrible,' I admitted. My voice cracked on the second word, but I managed to suppress the tears.

'I'd be worried if you weren't,' Docc said with a calm, understanding nod. 'Don't force that down, all right? You're human. It's okay to feel, even if it hurts. You'll drive yourself mad if you don't.'

I nodded and blew out a shaky breath. Tears had gathered in my eyes once again as the emotion rushed back in at full force, and I blinked a few times to clear them away.

'Thank you, Docc. For everything.'

'Of course. Best get some rest, now. You take care of Hayden, all right?'

My heart clenched yet again at the sound of his name.

'I will.'

He nodded and I turned away, starting to head towards the door before his voice stilled my actions.

'And Grace,' he called softly. I paused to turn and look back at him. 'Let him take care of you, too.'

For some reason, this caused my throat to tighten even more. I blinked to hold back more tears. My feet carried me away, but there was one more thing I had to do. My hand dug into my pocket to pull out the pen and piece of paper I'd asked for earlier. The paper had crinkled after all the effort of moving the bodies, but it would still work. As I approached where the bodies were stored, I was relieved when I saw Kit. He could help me with this, and it was important to get it right.

Hayden

My muscles burned and my palms stung as I moved, but the trance-like state my body had fallen into made it easy to block out the physical pain. It was as if my mind and heart were suffering too much to feel anything else. The rhythmic sound of the shovel spearing into the dirt became like a mantra for me as I moved, determined to complete this task tonight.

I stood in a hole about three feet deep, just long and wide enough to encase someone about a man's size. The dirt shifted beneath my feet as I dug the shovel down, and I felt the familiar ache as I lifted the earth and tossed it to the side. Every bit of dirt that was removed felt like it was taking a bit of my sanity with it before it was unceremoniously deposited by the side, lost and forgotten as I sunk deeper and deeper into the ground.

I could feel him there. He lay on the ground on the softest patch of grass I could find, covered with my shirt. It was the best I could do and nowhere near what he deserved, but I had to do this now. I had to bury him before I completely lost it again. The sooner I did it, the better, because the sooner he was in the ground, the sooner he could be at peace.

Peace. Something I suspected I would never feel again.

Sweat trickled down my back as I continued to dig. I found I now relished the sting and ache caused by the shovel. It was pitch-black out, but the meagre light that managed to trickle in beneath the trees from the moon and stars above provided enough light to manage this task. It was fitting that I should dig his grave in the dark, because the darkness matched so well what I felt inside.

Bleak. Barren. Broken. Worse, I felt cold. Cold to the

world, as if my emotions had been turned off the moment I'd carried his body away. Cold in my thoughts, as I could think of nothing but bitter hatred for the one who had done this, even if I didn't know who. It didn't matter who had actually shot him, because I knew under whose orders it had been done. There was only one person to blame for all of this, and he happened to be the brother of the only girl I'd ever loved. Jonah was responsible, whether he'd physically fired the gun that had killed him or not.

I couldn't say his name. I couldn't even think it. Even in my mind, I kept referring to him as vague pronouns.

Him.

He.

His.

Never his name. Never once could I think his name. Surely the boy of that name was still running around camp, offering inexperienced help to anyone who needed it. Surely he was busy casting embarrassed, sneaky glances at Rainey as he tried not to admit his little crush. Surely he was pestering Dax right now, asking when they could have another shooting lesson. Surely these were more likely. Surely he was not the cold and lifeless body hidden by my ratty, bloodied shirt.

I'd fallen deeper into the ground now as the inches disappeared with every scoop of my shovel. The level of the pit was up to my head, and I found myself wishing it would cave in on me and bury me there. I could hide in the pits of the earth, drowning in dirt and finally succumbing to the pressures that had been trying to crack me open. I could give in to this crushing agony and fully admit defeat. There could be relief. Relief to finally be done with everything, to stop feeling all these tumultuous emotions. I could finally give in and let it all end. I could let the gripping cold that had started to creep in take me completely.

Blood leaked from my palms as the blisters there burst open, yet still I continued to dig. Only one thing kept me going. The thought of revenge drove me on, thoughts of vengeance and retaliation fuelling me forward. I could not let this end without rectifying the injustice. I would set things right if it was the last thing I did. He deserved that, and so much more.

I had never had the desire to kill. It had always appalled me. It was something to be done only as a last resort or in order to survive. Each death I witnessed ate away at me, whether it was by my own doing or not. But now, as my muscles strained and blood dripped down my fingers, I wanted to kill. I wanted to see the life leave his eyes, feel the blood as it left his body. I wanted him to know just how much suffering and pain he'd caused, and I wanted him to endure it tenfold before his life was finally over.

I wanted to kill Jonah.

The dark thoughts brewed in my head, swelling and growing more and more vengeful the longer I dug. I felt my body take over as my mind became unable to focus on anything else, letting the darkness creep through my veins and settle into my bones. It wasn't until the edge of the hole was a foot above my head that I finally stopped, tossing my shovel forcefully into the dirt before I leaned against the side. My head tilted back and I closed my eyes, relishing the feel of my burning muscles and sweat-covered skin. Dirt stuck to my body, but I didn't care.

This place would be where he rested forever. He deserved so much more. He deserved a crowd of people gathered here to say goodbye. He deserved a parade to celebrate his short but happy life. He deserved to be honoured by everyone he loved so dearly. He deserved to still be alive.

Some of those things would come. People would be able to come here and say their goodbyes. They'd be able to visit his grave and remember him fondly. They would have that chance, but for now, I needed this experience alone. I needed to be the one to lay him to rest. He'd been like my little brother, family by choice rather than blood, and I had failed to tell him that in his lifetime. I had never told him, until the very last moments of his life, how much I loved him. Never told him how proud I was of how much he'd grown. Never told him how much I enjoyed his company, even when he annoyed me at times.

I never got the chance to say those things, and now he was gone.

I sniffed once and wiped away the sweat that had trailed down the side of my forehead before I picked up the shovel and tossed it out of the grave. My muscles screamed in protest as I hauled myself out of the hole, where my eyes found his body lying a few feet away. It seemed so much brighter now that I was out of the darkness of the grave, and the air seemed cleaner as I took a deep breath.

Before my mind had the chance to stop me, I moved forward, grabbing the two ropes I'd collected when I'd taken the shovel. I moved rhythmically, systematically, because I knew if I thought about it too much, I'd break down again. I was determined not to. I'd had my breakdown and shed my tears, but that was over. After this, I would not feel anything. I'd shut it out, refuse to feel it, and I'd move on so I could accomplish my goal.

My hands finished their work, and I straightened up to examine it. One rope was tied around his ankles while the other was secured around his chest, where he was covered from there up with my shirt. To see his face would have ruined me. Again I stepped forward to collect the ropes, which I used to hoist his small body off the ground. He was so light that it was hardly any work to carry him to the edge of the grave. His body hovered over it as I stalled, pausing to close my eyes and take a determined breath. My heart hammered painfully hard in my chest, and I felt the sting of emotion creeping back in as I prepared to complete my task.

Finally, I opened my eyes and sighed before letting the ropes slide slowly through my hands. I watched as his body descended into the ground. Darkness swallowed him as I continued to release the ropes, careful to move slowly until I felt his weight hit the bottom of the grave. I squeezed the ropes tightly in my hands for a few moments, clinging to them like I'd clung to the hope that he would suddenly wake up. But he wouldn't, and my grip on the ropes slackened, letting them fall into the darkness along with my desperate wish.

Again, my body moved by instinct as I picked up the shovel once more. The cuts on my hands started to bleed again as I threw piles of dirt into the hole. The task was much easier physically, but was emotionally just as taxing. Every pile of dirt I threw into the grave only cemented the fact that he was not coming back. The light was gone, leaving only darkness behind.

About thirty minutes later, the grave was completely filled in, his body covered. Sweat was once again pouring off me as I packed down the dirt one last time before moving to place the large, flat rock I'd found at the top of the grave. I pulled the knife from my pocket and dug it into the rock, carving away until I managed a single, shaky word into the stone. His name.

Once I was done, I straightened up and took a few steps back. It looked terrible, and it was not even close to what should have been a beautiful grave, but it was the best I could do. Here he would stay, awaiting the surely many visitors he would have throughout the years. This was the place he would rest forever, the place he should not have been until he was an old, withered man, but would remain all the same.

'Goodbye, Jett. I love you.'

Thirty: Defeat

Grace

My heart felt heavy as I made my way back to our hut. It had been over an hour since I'd left Docc and had started on my task. I had finally finished, and there was still no sign of Hayden. Kit had left to tend to a still understandably distraught Malin, and I was glad he would be there for her to deal with the loss of her father. Without much idea of what to do, I had finally decided to head home in the hope of his return.

The little hope I'd been clinging to that Hayden would already have gone back to our hut dissipated as soon as I pushed through the door. It was quiet and very obviously empty. I moved inside and lit a candle on his desk. I tried to feel something other than crushing disappointment and loss, but there was nothing. I desperately wanted Hayden to return so I could relish in the simple relief of his presence. Just being in the same room as him again would do wonders at this point, but still he did not return. He'd been gone for hours now, and every minute that ticked by felt like an eternity without him.

With a heavy sigh, I moved to sit down at his desk. My fingers fidgeted together as my eyes landed on the bottom drawer, hesitating to carry out my plan. I knew what agony it would cause Hayden to have to record all the names of the people lost tonight. After walking down the seemingly endless row with Kit, I'd gathered each and every name of those who had died. Forty-two names were now written down on the paper folded in my pocket. Forty-two names I could spare Hayden from writing down in his journal.

My knee bounced up and down anxiously as I shook my head and pulled the drawer open, moving quickly as if afraid I'd change my mind. The journal was exactly where I knew it would be, buried beneath some scraps of paper and his charred family photo album. My heart pounded nervously as I set it on the desk, where I stared at it as if waiting for it to talk to me. The room remained silent as my eyes grazed over the smooth leather cover.

A shaky hand reached forward to flip it open, where I was careful to turn to the last page where the names were recorded. Even now, I didn't want to read his journal without him. Although he'd shared it with me, there were parts he kept private, and I didn't want to disrespect that, especially now. A pen was stashed between the pages, as if waiting for use as I picked it up. I pulled the scrap of paper with names scrawled across it from my pocket and placed it on the desk next to the journal, where I smoothed it out with my fingers.

I closed my eyes for a moment and allowed myself to see the faces that had lost all traces of life. These were the people whose lives were over but not forgotten. Slowly, I opened my eyes and pressed the pen to the paper, where I carefully copied down the first name on the list that Kit had helped me create. It felt odd to write because of how seldom I did, and my handwriting wasn't the best, but it did the trick, and I copied down the second name.

I carried on this way, carefully writing as neatly as I could until I had the entire page filled. My heart gave a heavy pang when I had to turn the page to continue, and panged even harder when the list spilled over onto the next. Each name I wrote down was accompanied by a visual image of their face, floating before me as if waiting to see if I recorded them correctly. By the time I was done, I was mentally exhausted and felt heavier than ever, but I had to admit it took a small weight off my shoulders knowing that Hayden would not have to endure that task. Surely it would be a hundred times harder for him, as he had actually known these people.

There was just one name left to record, perhaps the most painful of all. The pen tapped restlessly between my fingers as I stalled. Recording his name in the list would make it feel that much more real, that much more permanent. Once he was on the list, he wasn't coming off. The bit of my heart that had managed to cling to life in my chest broke as I pressed down the pen, leaving a shaky 'J' on the paper. It took every bit of mental strength I had to finish his name, only for me to realise with dismay that I didn't even know his last name. He would remain on the list as I'd known him.

Jett.

Simply Jett, as no other identifiers were needed.

I stared at the printed word for a few seconds before I had to close the journal. The longer I stared at it, the heavier my heart felt. Carefully, I returned the journal to its resting place in the drawer and stood up, needing to put some distance between it and myself. My feet immediately started carrying me across the room. I was reminded of the time Hayden had made me stay behind on the raid and I'd paced for hours in this very same hut, waiting anxiously for his return.

I had no idea how long it had been, but I soon became aware of the pattern I was wearing myself into. I paced relentlessly around the room, twisting my fingers together into knots only to undo them and repeat the process. I was aware that I needed to shower, but I didn't want to for fear of missing Hayden when he finally returned. Every tiny sound I heard caused me to jump and jerk my head towards the door, but it was never him.

It seemed like it had been hours and hours since I'd last seen him and I was starting to get even more worried than I already was when I heard the quiet padding of footsteps right outside the door. My feet froze as I once again jerked my attention to the door, waiting anxiously and silently begging him to appear. My heart jumped in my chest as the door handle turned and the door swung inward. A sigh of relief so huge washed through me that it nearly knocked me over when I saw him appear in the door frame.

'Hayden,' I breathed quickly before I bolted forward, rushing to him.

He barely managed to move through the door and close it behind him before my arms wound around his neck, hugging him to me as our chests pressed together. He was shirtless and covered in dirt, but I didn't care. I felt as though a thousand pounds had lifted off my body as I held him, but the relief was short-lived as I realised his arms remained limply by his sides, lifelessly. Pulling back, my arms still looped around his neck, I looked at his face. What I saw made my heart clench in pain.

His face looked hardened, flat, and cold as he looked down at me blankly. The pain I'd been expecting to see in his eyes was masked by a strangely emotionless stare, and his jaw was set in a firm, difficult-to-read expression. My hands drifted up the sides of his neck to gently hold either side of his face as I studied him, fearful about his lack of engagement.

'Hayden,' I repeated softly. He didn't respond, still not touching me as he stood before me. My thumbs drifted lightly over his jaw before I let my hands fall, hovering in front of him. 'Are you—'

'Did you do it?'

His voice was morbidly flat and monotone as he spoke. He didn't need to specify for me to know what he was asking: Had I killed Jonah?

'No,' I admitted quietly, shaking my head once in defeat.

His jaw tightened and the muscle ticked beneath his cheek as he nodded sharply, his disappointment clear. He remained silent as he then stepped around me, making his way towards the bathroom. I tried to ignore the sting of rejection as he distanced himself, but it felt like more than a physical distance between us as he opened the door.

'I'm going to shower. I'll leave you half.'

My stomach twisted uncomfortably as he used the same flat tone as before, shutting himself in the bathroom without so much as a glance back at me. I swallowed past the sudden lump in my throat and blinked a few times, trying to clear my head. My body suddenly felt jittery, and I unconsciously bit my lower lip between my teeth as I thought. I tried not to take it personally, but it hurt that he was turning away from me at such a time.

I heard the shower start and resumed my pacing as my mind tried to buffer my thoughts and my stomach twisted anxiously. Throughout Hayden's shower, I fought the urge to go to him. I wanted to be there for him, hug him, comfort him, but how could I if he didn't want to accept it? I'd just have to wait and hope eventually he'd allow me to be there for him like I knew he needed me to be, even if he couldn't admit it.

Finally, the water stopped and he appeared a few moments later with a towel wrapped around his still damp torso. He cast one fleeting look at the wall where the painting Jett had done of the three of us hung before the tiniest flash of emotion crossed his features. It was wiped clean, however, by the time he crossed the room and reached the dresser.

'There should be half left,' Hayden said dismissively, clearly suggesting I leave him again. I bit down on my lower lip once more and nodded. My legs carried me to the shower where I undressed and pulled the tab to start the water. My hands moved quickly to wash my body as my mind continued to race.

This was all wrong. I had been preparing for an emotionally distraught, broken Hayden. I'd been ready to comfort him, hold him, cry with him. I'd been ready to mourn the loss of such an innocent life, as well as so many others. I hadn't been prepared for this cold shell of the man I loved that had walked through the door. I'd been expecting sadness and turmoil but had been greeted with a flat, expressionless void. Surely more lurked beneath the surface than he was showing me, but it would do little good to try and comfort him if he didn't want it.

I sighed heavily as the water ran out and wrung out my hair before wrapping a towel around myself. After drying off a bit, I moved back into the main room, where I was relieved to see Hayden still there. I had been slightly afraid he'd disappear again in my absence. He wore just a pair of shorts as he sat on the bed, staring blankly at the floor from beneath furrowed brows. I moved to the dresser quickly to pull on some clothes and wrung out my hair with the towel one last time before hanging it up and moving to stand in front of Hayden.

Usually, he'd tickle the backs of my legs or pull me into his lap, but this time he didn't move. Slowly, I ducked down to crouch in front of him, placing my hands on his knees as I looked up at him. My thumb rolled slowly over the soft bristles covering his legs as I shot him a sympathetic grimace.

'Hayden, are you all right?'

Stupid question, Grace.

I shook my head, shooing away the harsh thoughts as I waited for his response. Of course he wasn't all right, but I didn't know what else to say.

'I'm fine,' he muttered.

A thousand more questions rushed through my head, but I didn't want to push him when he was clearly suffering so much. He was blocking everything out: the pain, the loss, even me.

'Do you want to talk about it?' I asked gently. I wished he'd make some reassuring gesture, but he made none.

'No.'

While monotone and hollow, his voice didn't sound mad. I'd almost have preferred him to sound mad. At least then he'd be expressing something. My heart gave a painful pang as I watched him closely.

'Okay.'

He nodded once and let out a deep sigh before pushing his hand through his still wet hair.

'I'm tired,' he said slowly.

With that, he shifted back on the bed and pulled the covers down. I watched as he slid his body beneath the blanket and rolled to his side, ignoring me completely as he settled in. I rose to my feet and watched him for a few seconds before I moved to blow out the single candle lighting the room. Tentatively, I made my way to the other side of the bed and crawled in carefully as if afraid it might explode.

Hayden's back was to me as I settled in, just visible in the faint light filtering through the window. My hand stretched silently through the air, hesitating just before I touched him. I held back, unsure of what to do and hating it, before

359

I allowed my fingers to trail lightly down the scarred skin covering his back. He was warm to the touch but felt coldly distant.

Slowly, I shifted my body until I was close enough to press my lips lightly into his shoulder blade. I lingered for a few moments and felt him inhale as my hand drifted gently down his side. If he wouldn't let me comfort him with words, the least I could do was let him feel my presence.

'You know I'm here for you, right?' I whispered gently. My thumb stroked lightly over his ribcage.

'I know, Grace,' he murmured in response. He made no moves to return my careful touch.

'And you know how much I love you, right?'

'I know, Grace,' he repeated. His tone sounded softer than it had earlier but still lacked so much of the emotion I knew he was hiding. I tried to ignore the sting when he didn't say it back.

'Don't forget that,' I said softly.

My words were muffled by his skin as I pressed another gentle kiss into his shoulder. Still he didn't react other than to shift slightly, as if to brush away my touch. My heart sank as he moved subtly to nudge my hand off his ribs. I retracted my touch and scooted back a bit, like he obviously wanted me to, feeling more and more rejected by the second as he settled back into the mattress again.

I curled up into a ball, huddling under the covers to try and soothe myself when the one source of comfort I so desperately wanted lingered just a few inches away, more out of reach than ever. I wanted to feel the warmth of his body against mine, hear the soft thudding of his heart and quiet whisper of his breath. I wanted to tangle his fingers with mine and let his arms wind around my waist. More than anything, I just wanted him to be there, but he wasn't. He might as well have never come back for all I was getting from him, and that broke my heart.

I could feel the warmth of tears creeping up yet again, surprising me as I lay on my side and stared at Hayden's back. I felt a hot tear streak down my face, running into the pillow that my head rested on. I sniffed once and tried to conceal the sound to hide it from Hayden, but if he heard, he made no move to acknowledge it. Even though I knew he was awake, he remained closed off.

I swallowed once and drew a deep, silent breath. Determined, I forced myself to stop the tears that were leaking from my eyes. I just had to focus on getting through this. It would pass, with time. Or at least I hoped it would, because this feeling was crushing me from the inside out. I closed my eyes in an attempt to block everything out and fall asleep even though I knew it would be futile. Sleep would evade me when I needed it most.

I was about to accept defeat and settle in for a long night of painful suffering when Hayden spoke, surprising me. He didn't turn towards me, move to touch me, or even move at all, in fact, but his words managed to fill some of the cracks my heart had endured throughout the night. It was enough to give me a tiny bit of warmth in the otherwise bitterly cold emotion my mind, body, and soul had been subjected to.

'I love you, Grace. Goodnight.'

Thirty-One: Cold

Hayden

Everything hurt as I lay awake in bed, back turned to Grace while she tried to hide the tears I knew she was crying. Pain in every form assaulted me from all directions, and the bitter cold that had settled into my heart didn't quite manage to numb me from that. I felt everything and nothing all at once, too closed off and broken to feel and process properly. It was like the world had shattered around me, leaving fragmented bits of my former life to mock and taunt me before spearing their way straight through my heart.

I was being selfish. There was no denying it. I knew it, surely Grace knew it, yet she didn't say anything as she let me cave in on myself like a dying star that had spent the last of its life-sustaining resources. She let me ignore her without a word, hurt her without complaint. What was worse was the fact that I knew I was doing it, but I couldn't quite bring myself to stop and snap out of it. My ability to empathise had gone with Jett's life, buried deep beneath the cold ground.

Surely she needed me. Surely she needed me to reassure her that it was all right, that we'd figure something out. Surely she was missing him just as much as I was. Surely she needed me to hold her as much as I needed her to hold me, to feel the warmth of my body, to hear me whisper comforting things in her ear, but I couldn't. It had taken all my strength to whisper that one reply, and I was spent, unable to give her even close to what she deserved.

In my broken state, I was failing her in every way possible, and there was nothing I could do to stop it from happening. My head was consumed with something else, something darker, that took over my every thought and desire. Revenge had clouded my mind, tingeing my thoughts and staining my usual guidelines. Jonah's face swam before my eyes in the darkness, a physical reminder of everything that had happened. No matter what logic told me, I couldn't stop equating the entire blame of losing Jett with Jonah's actions.

This was Jonah's fault, and Jonah had to pay.

I stewed silently, clenched and locked into my position as my mind turned over the possibilities of the ways I could exact my revenge. My muscles grew tight as hours passed and I did not move, but I ignored it. Why should my body feel any differently than the dark expanse of my mind? It was fitting that I should suffer physically when I was so mentally crippled.

I was barely aware of Grace's breathing evening out behind me; she did not try to touch me again after I'd brushed her off. I couldn't let her comfort me the way I knew she wanted to. In my state of mind, I could never accept it. I needed to be firm and resolute in my thoughts and actions, and her kindness and love would ruin that. Her comfort would just get in the way.

It had been a few hours since we'd got into bed, and she'd finally succumbed to the heavy pull of sleep. I could easily hear the change in her breathing and feel the release of the tension that had lingered in the air. A quiet sigh of relief pushed past my lips, yet still I did not move. Despite being unable to be there for Grace or allow her to be there for me,

I didn't want her to suffer, relieved she'd get a few hours of respite from the turmoil she would surely wake up to.

Again, Jonah's face flitted through my mind. The green eyes that were so eerily similar to Grace's glared at me mockingly, sneering as if proud of what had happened to Jett. The figment of my imagination goaded me, boasting silently and taunting me. My hands clenched to fists and my eyes squeezed shut, fighting off the images conjured up by my mind. All I could focus on was the countless different ways I knew to hurt him, kill him, make him suffer.

My dark thoughts were suddenly interrupted when I felt the bed shake once. Grace jerked beside me as a quiet whine slipped from her throat. Pressured breathing forced its way through her nose, and her jerky, frantic movements became more frequent as she fought off invisible tormentors. Her breathing became more erratic, and I could feel her shaking slightly from the way the mattress quivered.

'No . . .' she mumbled, voice strained and tight.

My heart sank as I recognised this from the other times it had happened. Just as before, her actions, breathing, and muttered words gave away what was going on: she was having a nightmare.

'No, no . . .!' she repeated, thrashing more violently to one side as the entire bed shook again. A quiet, frightened whimper slipped past her lips as she breathed unevenly.

I squeezed my eyes shut once and rolled over, catching sight of her for the first time since we'd lain down. Her eyes were squeezed shut and her jaw was clenched in a tense grimace, loosening only when the few words she managed to utter forced their way out. Her chest caved in and rose quickly with every shaky breath, and her limbs reached around blindly before getting tangled in the covers.

'Hayden . . .'

The sound of my name leaving her lips in such a tight and frightened tone caused my heart to clench in pain. When her head turned and she grimaced again as if trying to get away from something, a faint hint of light glinted off the thin chain still around her neck. I sucked in a breath as I realised she was wearing my mother's necklace, causing yet another rocket of pain to shoot through me.

'No, not Hayden,' she gasped sharply before she let loose another whimper.

I bit my lip into my mouth and took a deep breath as I finally was able to reach forward, grasping her lightly on the shoulder to shake her gently. She was hot to the touch and already damp with sweat that always seemed to come with the nightmares. She jerked away from my touch like she always did.

'Grace, wake up,' I murmured. My voice was raw and raspy from tears and lack of use.

Her brows lowered even more over her closed eyes and her lips parted as her teeth bared in a grimace, fighting me off subconsciously. It got more difficult to wake her with every nightmare she endured. I shook her again, careful not to hurt her.

'Grace, come on, wake up,' I continued, shaking her one last time.

She sucked in a gasp between her teeth and her eyes popped open, looking bewildered and frightened as she searched the dark frantically before finally finding me.

'Hayden,' she whispered breathlessly.

'You were having a nightmare,' I told her, unable to speak in anything other than a monotone. As soon as she'd woken, I'd retracted my touch. At least a foot of space existed between us and I made no move to lessen it.

'I know,' she murmured. She looked disappointed that

I'd let her go, and her eyes searched mine desperately in the darkness. I held her gaze for a few moments, and I felt myself being pulled to her, but I resisted. I knew if I let her so much as touch me, I'd lose my strength that I so urgently needed. Even if it hurt her, even if I was being selfish, I had to resist.

'Goodnight, Grace,' I whispered quietly before rolling back again, cutting her off from my view once more as I returned to my previous position.

'Hayden . . .'

My eyes squeezed shut as I tried to mentally block her out, ignoring the way the tone of her voice poked at my heart.

I couldn't do it.

I couldn't let her in.

'Goodnight,' I repeated flatly, hating myself more and more by the second. I could practically hear her deflate as she let out a deep breath behind me. The pain was evident in her tone as she finally spoke, voice no more than a breath of a whisper.

'Goodnight, Herc.'

Grace

Three days.

It had been three days since Jett's death, and there had been no improvement in Hayden's demeanour.

He remained cold and closed off as ever, if not more so with each passing day. Any attempt I made to talk to him about what had happened was quickly shut down, and he hadn't so much as touched me since the start of everything. I'd almost begun to forget what it felt like to have his arms around me, what it felt like to tangle my fingers with his. What it felt like to feel his lips on my own. Any former source of comfort that he'd usually provided was long gone, and I'd never felt more disconnected from him.

Despite how increasingly painful it was to be around him and remain unable to do anything to improve the circumstances, I didn't dare let him out of my sight. I was absolutely petrified he'd sneak off the moment I looked away to do what I knew he so desperately desired: seek his revenge.

It was strange to see him this way, uncomfortable and foreign in every way possible. He didn't speak unless absolutely necessary, didn't smile, didn't laugh. He didn't look at me the same way he used to and he hadn't uttered a word with even a hint of affection since he'd said goodnight to me that night Jett had died. His every thought and move revolved around what he could do to Jonah, leaving him as little time as possible to think and actually deal with what had happened.

I knew he was doing it on purpose. He was staying busy, blocking everything and everyone out, so he wouldn't feel it. He pushed down the pain that was growing more and more impossible to ignore by the day, and I could practically see him walking around like he was about to shatter. Every time someone spoke to him, I braced myself for the breakdown I thought would have happened long ago, but it never came. He internalised his emotions and pushed them down, breaking his own heart even further in the process while he made no effort to fix it.

Meanwhile, I could feel my own breaking point fast approaching. Despite my desperate desires to remain strong, my own pain, disappointment, and rejection were eating away at me until I felt the all-too-familiar numbness creeping back in. Pain from losing Jett, disappointment in my failure at killing Jonah and potentially ending everything. Perhaps the worst part was the rejection I was constantly subjected to from Hayden. As hard for me as it was to admit, I needed him.

I needed him, and he wasn't there.

I found myself feeling stirrings of anger and resentment, which only caused more internal conflict. Did I have any right to be angry with Hayden while he was dealing with such a thing? Did I have any right to resent him for shutting me out when I needed him most?

I didn't know the answers to these questions, but that didn't stop me from feeling them. Anger and resentment piled onto my already heaving pile of emotions, ripping me apart more and more by the second as I walked beside an ever-silent Hayden.

'What are we doing?' I asked, determined to keep my voice strong.

'I need weapons,' Hayden answered gruffly. He stalked forward briskly and purposefully as we headed towards the raid building. Panic flared inside me and I tried to remain calm.

'What for?'

'I'm going to Greystone. Tonight.'

Alarm bells clanged around wildly in my head as I sucked in a breath.

'Hayden, I don't think—'

'I'm going, Grace. There's nothing you can say to change that.'

'But you're not—'

'*Grace!*' he hissed, glaring at me for the first time. 'I'm going.'

Anger I'd tried to press down flared up once more.

Shutting me out and checking out mentally was one thing, but yelling at me was another.

'Don't you yell at me, Hayden. I won't allow that.'

His jaw clenched tightly and the muscle ticked beneath the skin on his cheek before he let out a tight breath. I watched as he pushed his hand roughly through his hair and cast me a stressed sideways glance.

'Sorry,' he muttered.

I didn't reply as we arrived at the raid building. We pushed our way inside and I watched grudgingly as Hayden moved to the gun case to remove his weapons. This was exactly what I'd been afraid of, and I wasn't sure if it was better or worse that he'd made no effort to hide his intentions from me. It made me even angrier that he was very obviously planning to go and kill my own brother but hadn't said a word about it to me.

This wasn't the Hayden I knew, and it was breaking me in half.

Thirty-Two: Turmoil

Grace

Hayden's back was to me as he prepared his weapons, physically blocking me out as well as mentally. I was desperately trying to think of an argument that would get through to him, but his closed-off demeanour was making it practically impossible. He'd made up his mind to go to Greystone, and it seemed he didn't care in the slightest what I thought. It was like we'd taken a hundred steps backward in our relationship, like it was the first day I'd arrived when he'd been cold and distant with me. Now, instead of being uncomfortable, it was just painful.

My emotions started to career out of my control as his harsh words and actions started to chip away at my sanity. While I knew he was suffering and I wanted to be there for him, my urge to comfort him was being contended by several other emotions when I finally replied.

'Do I have a say in this?' I asked sharply, allowing the anger to leak into my voice.

'No.'

Frustration ripped through me again.

'He's my brother,' I pointed out. 'The last member of my family.'

It wasn't a great argument considering what I'd decided and failed to do, but I was desperate to appeal to some part of him that he'd buried deep down.

'You were going to kill him, weren't you? What's the difference if I do it?' His voice was cold and flat.

'But I couldn't do it, Hayden,' I argued. My arms crossed over my chest to keep them still as I leaned tensely against a table. I glared at Hayden's back as he readied his weapons across the room from me.

'Well, now you won't have to.'

'Hayden, just stop for a second,' I requested sharply. 'You're not thinking straight and you're going to get yourself hurt if you do this now.'

'I'm not talking about this right now,' Hayden muttered stubbornly as he slammed a clip into his gun. He finally turned around to face me as he tucked it into his waistband, carrying another in his hand.

'Well, I want to talk about it now,' I replied, equally as stubborn. I had the feeling that I was dealing with a hurt, petulant child who refused to see reason simply to spite me.

'Of course you do,' he murmured bitterly as he moved past me, exiting the building. I pushed myself away from the table and forced myself to bite my lip to keep from replying just yet. I'd wait until we were back in the privacy of our hut before I spoke any further.

Hayden stomped down the path towards our hut, shoulders tight and gait stiff as he moved. My own hands were clenched to fists as I stalked after him, catching up enough to remain a few paces behind him but not moving to stand next to him. I needed space to think and organise my thoughts, because I couldn't take much more of this.

Organising my thoughts proved impossible, however, as we arrived far too quickly back at our hut. Before I knew it, Hayden had pushed his way inside and deposited his guns on the table, keeping his back to me as he fiddled with them.

I stewed silently and glared at his shoulders, daring him to say something even though I knew he wouldn't.

'Hayden, you can't go,' I restarted, refusing to drop this.

I watched as his shoulders tightened once. He rolled his head slowly from side to side and let out a deep breath as if I were causing him great stress, but I couldn't find it in me to feel bad for him after what he'd put me through. Grieving and mourning would have been okay, welcome even, but this was different. This was a refusal to feel, to let anything in. This felt personal against me.

'Why not?' he asked flatly, his voice impossibly low. Still, he did not turn around.

'Because, Hayden! You're not thinking clearly. You're driven by revenge and that's going to get you hurt, I promise you,' I said, appealing to his reasonable side that seemed to have completely disappeared lately.

'Maybe I don't care,' he muttered dismissively with an unconcerned shrug.

'Don't start with that shit again,' I snapped, unable to hold back. 'How many times do we have to go over this? *I* care, and you know it. Don't throw that in my face.'

Finally, he turned to face me. His brows were pulled low over his usually blazing green eyes, though they looked flat and dim as he watched me now.

'I have to do it, Grace,' he said. He shrugged again as if it were inevitable.

'I know you think that, but you don't have to,' I argued, shaking my head. 'At least not now without any sort of plan.'

My voice lost some of the anger as I tried to calm down, but the hurt I was feeling was clearly evident in my tone. Hayden didn't reply. The blank, void expression I'd seen so much of over the last three days returned. He was back to shutting things out after I'd managed to pull a few words out of him.

'Please don't do this,' I begged quietly, voice no more than a whisper. He held my gaze as I pleaded silently, to no effect.

'I'm sorry, Grace. I'm going.'

I had to hold back from actually stomping my foot in frustration.

'No!' I replied sharply, irritation dominating my tone. He was so stubborn. 'You *can't*, Hayden! You need to stop and think about this. You need to *feel* what happened and deal with it, not shut it out. You can only block it out for so long before it destroys you and I can already see that happening. It's *killing* me.'

'I don't need to feel it,' he said in a deadly quiet whisper.

'Yes you *do*!' I shouted angrily as tears of dread and frustration started to prick at my eyes. I absolutely hated crying, but there was not enough strength left in me to stop it. I'd finally reached my breaking point, and I was too spent to try and hold back my emotions any longer. 'You're shutting everything out and refusing to deal with it. That's not going to solve anything,' I continued tightly, shaking my head as my throat burned.

'What do you want from me, Grace?' Hayden asked with an almost sarcastic, resigned shrug and shake of his head.

An angry scoff forced its way through my lips and my head tilted back momentarily as my lower lip drew sharply between my teeth. When I looked back at him, I could see the same flat stare meeting mine.

What did I want?

I wanted him to stop pretending like it wasn't absolutely killing him to have lost Jett. I wanted him to feel the pain he was stifling so he could accept it and move on. I wanted him

373

to stop shutting me out and let me comfort him. I wanted him to hold me, be there for me, comfort me, like I so desperately wanted to do for him. I wanted him to smile and laugh and be happy again, to look at me like he used to. I wanted him to be able to move on from this without letting it tear him apart.

I wanted my Hayden back.

My Herc.

All of these thoughts swirled chaotically in my head, refusing to settle into any sort of logical order. When I spoke, it was from a place of pure emotion and frustration, and I couldn't help that from seeping into my voice.

'I want you to *feel something*! I want you to stop shutting me out and let me be there for you. I want you to deal with what happened and stop trying to just ignore it. I want you to—'

I sucked in a sudden gasp of a sob that I hadn't felt coming, taking me by surprise.

'I want you to be there for me, too,' I finished, my voice tight and thick with sentiment. 'You need me, and I know *I* need you.'

He watched me for a few long moments as a silent, angry tear streaked down my cheek. Several feet separated us as we stood across the room from each other, and neither of us made any move to close the distance. Finally, he shook his head slowly, never breaking our eye contact.

'I can't.'

His reply was like a dagger straight through my heart, and I felt my chest cave in as if it'd made physical impact to try and knock me to the ground. My eyes squeezed tightly shut as a choking sob burst out, releasing a few more tears to spill down my cheeks.

The man I loved seemed so far away, as if he were lost

from the world; worse, I felt like he was lost to me.

My heart thumped feebly in my chest as I tried to search for another angle to stop him or get through to him. His walls he'd built up were so high that I couldn't even see the top, much less break them down and close the gaping distance that had appeared between us.

Just when I thought all hope was lost, a sudden idea struck me. It was a last resort, but I was desperate to break down the invisible wall that taunted me now. If it would stop him from going on this reckless and deadly mission, I'd do it. Before I could change my mind, I went to his desk and jerked open the bottom drawer to pull out the journal. My hands moved to open it to the last few pages while my feet carried me back to stand in front of Hayden.

I could feel his gaze burning into me as I stopped and pointed down at the book. The names I'd recorded were written clearly there, ending with the most painful of them all: Jett.

'Look at this, Hayden,' I demanded sharply. His jaw opened slowly in shock as he absorbed the words. Several long moments of silence stretched between us, and a sudden tension so thick it was almost stifling settled over us.

'What did you do?' he questioned in a deadly whisper, voice laced with anger as he stared transfixed at the page.

'I wrote them down for you. I didn't want you to feel the pain of doing it yourself, but if I'd known you'd shut down like this, I wouldn't have done it. I was trying to help you and save you from that, but it only made it worse because now you're just . . . numb.'

I glanced up at him to see his jaw tick sharply, and it looked like he was shaking slightly as he stared at the page. My stomach flipped as I caught the first hint of emotion in ages: anger.

'You had . . . You had *no right* to do this,' he muttered so tightly I was surprised the words made it past his lips. My heart clenched but I held my ground.

'But I did it for you, because I love you,' I told him firmly. 'And I'm doing this now because I love you . . .'

He seethed in front of me, and I was certain he was shaking now.

'You shouldn't have done that,' he hissed, still in a scarily quiet whisper. I ignored his statement and carried on.

'Look at the names, Hayden. I know you lost so many and . . . we lost Jett, but shutting everything out won't help. I know it hurts, but you need to feel it so you can heal.'

'Lost,' Hayden repeated flatly, taking a step away from me and flicking his gaze up to meet mine now.

'Yes—'

'Did he lose his way in the woods, Grace?'

'No—'

'Did he get turned around in the city?' he continued, rage dripping from his oddly quiet tone now as he glared at me.

'Hayden, don't, I didn't mean—' I said, shaking my head in a silent plea.

'Are we playing a fucking *game* and we can't find him?' Hayden hissed, livid now as he took a menacing step towards me.

'No,' I said, forcing myself to remain calm.

'Is he just going to show up later? All happy and giddy despite being *lost*?' he continued, anger seeping out of him as he glared at me. He didn't yell, but this felt much worse.

This felt dark, heavy.

This felt like pure, unadulterated pain.

'No,' I repeated gently yet firmly. I could feel the palpable shift in the atmosphere as our gazes remained locked on each other's.

'No, he's not. Because he's not *lost*, Grace, he's fucking *dead*. He's dead and he's not coming back no matter what you want me to *feel*.'

His voice finally rose in volume as he started to crack, unable to hold back the emotion. It was like his words had been physically hurled at my chest as I felt their impact resonate through my body. I watched in surprise as he moved across the room suddenly, and my heart skipped a beat as he reached up to pull Jett's painting from the wall. He stalked back over to me and held it in front of me. His grip was so tight that his knuckles and fingertips blanched over the wood.

'This,' he spat, gesturing to the picture, 'is over. This can never happen again, because Jett is *dead*, not *lost*.'

I held my ground and managed not to flinch as he flung the painting across the room suddenly, where it collided with a loud *thud* against the wall before clattering to the floor. My breathing had grown uneven and shaky as I watched him, heartbroken and relieved all at once that this breakdown was finally coming.

'Jett—' he sucked in a gasp and shook his head angrily. 'Jett is *dead*, Grace.'

'I know, Hayden,' I whispered, nodding a few times as silent tears poured down my face. Watching him finally succumb to the agonising pain was making me feel it as well, and I knew there could only be a few moments before he finally gave in completely.

'He's dead, and I couldn't save him,' he choked out. He stared at me so intently, shaking ever so slightly as he clung to his quickly slipping control. His eyes glowed as traces of tears gathered there.

'I know,' I repeated as calmly as I could manage, keeping my voice quiet and gentle though riddled with pain.

His breathing grew shakier and shallower as his jaw tightened, fighting to hold off tears. The few seconds that ticked by seemed like an eternity as we watched each other, tension and agony and so many other emotions lingering in the air around us. His voice was broken and weak as he spoke, the last word he said before finally giving in to what he'd avoided for so long: breaking down.

'Grace.'

I saw the glint of a tear fall down his cheek before I launched myself forward, winding my arms around his neck as I hugged him desperately to me. A small flicker of relief washed through me as I felt his arms wrap tightly around my waist, clinging to me with every bit of strength he possessed. A heart-wrenching sob ripped through his chest as he broke, and I felt my own tears streak down my face while my throat burned.

Hayden's tears wet the skin on my neck where he'd buried his face, and the sounds of his sobs echoed around in my skull as we clung to each other desperately. Finally, *finally*, he was feeling every loss he'd suffered, the special one in particular. His entire body shook against me wherever we were pressed together, and each breath he drew felt like it was surely burning his lungs as he cried. My heart felt like it was shattering into a thousand pieces as he fell apart in my arms.

'It's all right, Hayden,' I murmured as steadily as I could in my fragile state.

My hands moved over wherever I could reach: his hair, his shoulders, his back. Anything I could reach, I tried to soothe. Another gasp of a sob ripped from his chest, and I tightened my grip on him even more. He seemed unable to speak as the sound of his cries filled the room. I blew out a deep breath and tried to still my tears, but the shaking of my limbs and the tight burning in my throat made it almost impossible.

I didn't know how long we stood like that. Hayden sobbed and endured the pain he'd stifled for so long, and it was as if I could physically feel it ripping through him. If emotions could exact a physical toll, he'd have been bleeding from every pore on his body. It could have been hours later when he finally spoke, but the only thing I was aware of was how his body shook, how his heart broke, and how desperately he clung to me as I tried my best to soothe him.

'I'm sorry, Grace,' he whispered, his voice cracked and weak as my neck muffled the words.

'It's okay,' I replied, shaking my head dismissively. I knew the damage that had been done would heal now that he'd finally let me back in; it would just take some time. Right now, I didn't care, because he'd finally done what I'd hoped: felt.

He surprised me by pulling back just enough to connect his gaze with mine once more. His soft cheeks were wet with tears and the harsh red that had set in around his eyes contrasted sharply with the green, bringing out hints of blue that had been difficult to see before. Pain was written so clearly across his features that I could practically feel it radiating off him.

'Do you still love me?' he asked desperately, hanging eagerly on my reply.

'Of course I do,' I answered instantly, intensity burning between us. 'I love you, Hayden. So much.'

'I love you, Grace. More than you know.'

I managed a weak smile at his reply. I felt the comforting wave of warmth wash through me as hope sparked back to life inside me. We still had a long, long way to go before things were right again, but this was a start, no matter how painful it was to endure.

Thirty-Three: Token

Hayden

The comforting warmth of Grace's body allowed some heat to creep back into my cold, stiff form as I held her to me. We'd migrated to the bed, where we lay as tangled together as could be. She faced me, and my arm that was draped around her waist had her hauled close. Her fingers trailed lightly across my back absent-mindedly while her other arm folded between us, putting light pressure over my feebly beating heart.

I could finally feel what I'd been craving but had denied myself as I focused so intently on my pain: love. She loved me more than I deserved, something she'd proved by sticking with me through my worst behaviour when I was mentally so far away from her. It still hadn't really sunk in how lucky I was to have her, but it was something I could feel with every fibre of my being. I let out a heavy sigh and ducked forward, pressing my lips lightly to her forehead. Soft breath pushed against my neck as she exhaled slowly and snuggled into me further.

'I'm sorry for being a selfish dick,' I murmured. That didn't even begin to cover it, but I had to say it.

To finally feel the full weight of the crushing agony that I'd resisted so long had been so incredibly painful, but like Grace had said, I had to *feel* it. I had to accept that Jett was truly gone, and that shutting it and everything else out wouldn't help. I'd felt like I was bleeding emotion, falling apart in every sense of things, as I launched myself into Grace's waiting arms. Every breath I'd taken had burned with tears, every beat of my heart agonisingly painful as it tried to keep me going. It was a visceral reflection of my mental pain, tearing me apart while Grace held me together.

'It's all right, Hayden,' she murmured softly. Her hand pressed lightly into my back momentarily. 'I understand why.'

'I still shouldn't have shut you out like that,' I said as guilt rushed through me.

'No, you shouldn't have, but at least you see that now,' she cajoled gently.

I was quiet for a while as I felt a myriad of negative emotions roll through me. Sadness, defeat, guilt, sorrow. So many things I didn't want to feel but knew I wouldn't be able to escape for a very long time. There was something else there, too. It was tiny and almost completely smothered by everything else, but it was there.

Gratitude.

'Thank you for everything. For staying with me and putting up with that.'

I was desperate to see her reaction.

'Of course. That's what people do when they love someone, right? I could never just give up on you,' she said honestly. Her brows lowered as if concerned I wouldn't believe her. I ducked forward again to kiss away the fine wrinkle her concern had left.

'Right,' I agreed quietly.

Another thought floated through my mind, something else I needed to both apologise and thank her for.

'And . . . I'm sorry for yelling at you about the names in

the journal. I should never have shouted. That was . . . amazing of you, and I should have thanked you, not snapped like I did.'

She sighed and pressed a light kiss into my throat. 'It's all right, Hayden. Thank you for apologising.'

'I can't believe you did that for me,' I admitted, voice laden with awe. It can't have been easy for her, either, yet she'd sacrificed that bit of herself to save me from it. 'God, I love you so much, Bear.'

I was surprised when a quiet squeak slipped past her lips before she suddenly hugged herself snugly to me by winding her arms around my neck. After quickly recovering, I tightened my arm around her waist and held her against me as we hugged some more.

'I'm so happy to hear you say that,' she whispered, words muffled by my neck.

I held her to me and closed my eyes, revelling in the moment and the comforting pressure of her body against mine. It felt so good to hold her that I couldn't begin to imagine why I'd deprived myself of it for so long.

'I love you, Herc,' she returned, voice just as soft and quiet as before.

My heart gave a warm, heavy thump in my chest. The nicknames that had started out as something silly and playful had transformed into more, carrying an emotional weight that each of us could feel with every exchange. It was one piece of us that remained solely between us, and it was something I'd never stop loving.

When Grace finally pulled back, she aimed a soft smile up at me as we resumed our previous position. Again, her fingers tickled at my back and I kept her as close as physically possible. I was reminded of the time I'd first set eyes on her, months and months ago. There was one major reason she was in my life now, and the sad fact of the matter was that that reason was no longer here.

'You know what I've been thinking?' I asked her gently.

'What have you been thinking?' she replied with a small smile.

'He's the reason I have you,' I said slowly, as I watched her absorb my words. 'Jett,' I winced as I said his name. 'Jett is the reason you're in my life at all.'

Her lips parted slightly and I saw her brow tick up in surprise as she realised what I said was true.

'If he hadn't snuck along on that raid, I never would have found you . . .' she said slowly, catching my train of thought.

'And you'd never have let me go. Then I wouldn't have owed you, and I might not have saved you to take you here . . .'

Everything that had happened with my relationship with Grace went back to Jett. Jett had got us caught, allowed us to be spared, and forced my repayment of Grace a few days later. Grace came to Blackwing as a prisoner because of that, and I'd fallen hopelessly in love with her.

All because of Jett.

My throat suddenly felt tight again as these thoughts roamed around in my skull. He'd never know how incredibly grateful I was to him for that one little mistake. His one rash action had led to the absolute best thing that could ever happen to me, and he would never know it. I could never thank him for that or tell him exactly how much I loved him.

'Wow,' Grace murmured, blinking as her eyes drifted out of focus with thought. She shook her head gently and looked up at me once more before repeating herself in slight awe. '. . .Wow.'

'He'll never know . . .' I murmured. My brows were tight

over my eyes as I watched Grace, suddenly intense. 'He's never going to know that he gave me the best thing that could have happened to me.'

Grace remained silent as she waited, sensing I had more to say. Her fingers never stopped their gentle movements along my back.

'He gave me you and I can't thank him for that. He'll never know how grateful I am for his reckless move . . . He'll never know how much I really loved him.'

Again, my throat tightened and I suddenly found it difficult to hold her gaze. My eyes squeezed shut for a moment while I blew out a deep breath. A light touch of her hand on my face made me open my eyes.

'Hayden, he knew,' she said with a small shake of her head. 'He loved you so much and he knew you loved him, too. You didn't have to say it.'

'But I should have told him—'

'He knew,' she said, cutting me off gently with a nod of her head. 'Trust me. Don't worry about that, okay?'

I let out a deep sigh and nodded, trying to believe her. I really wanted to believe that Jett knew how much I truly cared about him even if I never said it, but it was difficult. 'But what about you? I can't thank him for leading me to you.'

'I think he knew that, too,' Grace said thoughtfully. 'I mean, he did that painting of us, right? I think he was more observant than you realised. He knew that we're together.'

I couldn't seem to reply as I listened to her speak. I felt her shift and noticed her fingers trail lightly across the necklace looped around her neck.

'What if . . . this was for him, too? The little circle?' she asked gently, referencing the thin gold necklace she wore.

My heart panged painfully once, but I had to admit I liked the idea.

'That would be perfect, Grace,' I said honestly. That necklace already represented so much: my parents, their death, my love for Grace. Adding Jett's name to the list only seemed right.

'Done, then. One little circle for Jett.'

'He'd have loved that,' I mused aloud, growing thoughtful.

It was strange to talk about him in past tense. It didn't feel real, like I was waiting for him to show up and do his best at whatever it was we were going to do. Grace's mention of the painting set a rocket of guilt through me as my eyes darted across the room, where it still lay on the ground exactly where it had landed after I'd launched it into the wall.

'Hang on,' I murmured softly, pressing one last kiss to her forehead before I pulled myself reluctantly from her warm grasp.

My feet carried me across the room, eyes trained on the painting the entire time as I approached. I was relieved to see it had suffered no damage from my outburst, and I reached out to pick it up gingerly as if afraid it would shatter the moment I touched it. Both of my hands gripped each side and my thumbs ran along the smooth wood, taking in the details Jett had painted with his thin fingers.

Three figures stood together, defined by their unique characteristics, stick arms linking them together. I took a deep breath as my heart clenched painfully, unable to tear my eyes away. I trailed the tips of my fingers over the smallest figure, noting the wild hair painted on top of his head that looked nearly identical to the hair adorning my own figure.

I felt the sudden warmth of Grace's arms winding loosely around my waist from behind and the small source of comfort as she pressed her lips lightly into my shoulder blade. One of my hands moved to cover hers as it rested over my stomach, melting into her comforting touch. Neither of us spoke as I examined the painting a few moments longer before pulling myself gently from her touch to move to the wall. I forced my hands to stay steady as I hung it up once more, careful to make sure it was secure and even.

When I stepped back, Grace appeared beside me, and we studied the painting together.

'Beautiful,' she commented simply.

I sighed and nodded once slowly before lifting an arm to throw around her shoulders and haul her into my side. Again, her arms looped easily around my waist as she hugged me loosely. A few moments of silence passed before she spoke again.

'You're not going tonight, right?' she asked tentatively.

I could feel her watching my profile, but I couldn't tear my gaze from the painting. So badly did I want to avenge Jett's death, but I knew the words Grace had spoken just before my breakdown were true: I needed an actual plan to do such a thing.

'No, Grace,' I murmured. 'I'm not.'

'Thank God,' she breathed softly, voice laden with obvious relief as she sagged into me slightly.

'But we should meet with everyone. We need to form a plan. We've known for a while now that we need to kill him, it's just more . . . personal now,' I said. I could feel Grace's fingers toying with the hem of my shirt as I held her to my side while she hesitated.

'Yes, you're right,' she admitted somewhat reluctantly.

Even though she'd been the first one to suggest it, I knew it was still incredibly difficult for her to wrap her head around.

'I should have just done it when I had the chance,' she said tightly, pain evident in her voice. 'I just couldn't do it and now . . .'

'It's all right, Grace,' I said with a shake of my head, turning so I faced her. Her arms fell from around my waist as she stood before me. 'We'll figure it out.'

She nodded once and bit her lower lip into her mouth, eyes dropping to the ground in self-doubt. I hated seeing her doubt herself or regret her actions. Slowly, I reached a hand up to land along the side of her face, where my thumb gently tugged her lower lip free. The soft skin of her cheek passed beneath my thumb a few times as I cradled her face.

'We will figure it out,' I repeated with a reassuring nod. 'Together, yeah?'

She gave a quiet sniff and nodded. 'Yeah.'

The corner of my lips quirked into a sad smile, my eyes locked with hers. One more stroke of my thumb across her cheek was all it took to build up the moment enough for me to duck forward, suddenly desperate to feel her lips on mine. Slowly, gently, I pressed mine to hers, kissing her for the first time in what felt like years. She melted into me, fitting her lips in the spaces between my own while I held her close with my hand on her face.

The kiss didn't deepen or go any further, but it lingered on for several moments as the warmth flooded through my body. It felt so good to finally kiss her again, to be connected in such a physical and emotional way, that I felt like I'd never be able to stop. My heart gave a few heavy beats, healing some of the cracks I'd endured over the last few days. Finally, we parted, though my hand stayed on her face and my forehead dropped to hers. My eyes, which had closed during the kiss, opened slowly to see Grace's doing the same.

'I missed you, Hayden,' she whispered.

I hadn't gone anywhere, but I knew what she meant. I had been so far away from her mentally that it was like I wasn't even there. Guilt flashed through me again for putting her through what I had.

'I'm back now, don't you worry,' I soothed gently.

Her eyes closed momentarily as she blew out a deep, steady breath. 'Okay.'

I pulled back a few inches and studied her for a few moments, relieved when she opened her eyes and shot me a small smile. I stroked her cheek one last time before dropping my hand to grab hers. She squeezed it once in return.

'Let's go and find everyone, yeah? Do something productive for once.'

My heart fluttered when she let out a soft laugh and a genuine smile. 'Yes, let's.'

With that, I led her from our hut. We moved through camp together, stopping by various places to find those necessary for planning. Soon, we had Kit, Docc, Dax, and much to my surprise, Leutie, tagging along as we made our way to the raid building. I'd honestly completely forgotten that Leutie was even here, but she'd been in Dax's hut with him when we'd stopped by and had offered to help in whatever way she could. I tried not to feel disappointed when Grace pulled her hand from mine with a small, apologetic smile before falling into step with Leutie, trading places with Dax, who now walked beside me. Kit and Docc conversed a few feet ahead of us, completing the third of the pairs we'd formed.

'You're looking better,' Dax commented as we moved through camp.

I shot him a confused look. Had I seen him in the last three days? I couldn't seem to remember. It was like my grief had blocked everything out. I could hardly remember anything I'd done in the last three days besides stew in my desire for revenge.

'Yeah,' I agreed vaguely. 'You are, too.'

I wasn't sure if that was true, but I assumed it to be as I snuck a quick glance at him. He appeared slightly sobered compared to usual, but there was still the general lightness about him, even if it was dimmed.

'Mmhmm,' Dax murmured non-committally. I glanced over my shoulder at Grace and Leutie, who were about fifteen feet back. They were talking quietly and I noticed a soft smile on Leutie's face.

'She's been staying with you, right?' I asked as casually as I could, ticking my thumb back at Leutie in front of my chest so she wouldn't see.

'Yeah, the last few days now. Since . . . it happened,' he replied, suddenly avoiding my gaze. 'I figured you needed to be alone with Grace.'

'Hmm,' I said with a light tick of my eyebrow. For the first time in a long time, I felt a flash of amusement. 'You sure that's it?'

Dax shot me an exasperated look and rolled his eyes.

'She's nice, all right? Give me a break,' he said with a non-committal shrug.

'Pretty, too,' I commented nonchalantly, watching his reaction closely.

'Don't you have Grace?' Dax shot back playfully with a ghost of a grin.

'I do. You could have someone, too, you know,' I said sincerely, keeping my voice quiet so the girls wouldn't hear.

Given he'd always been so supportive of Grace and me, he deserved to know I'd support him and Leutie as well. I had Grace, Kit had Malin. Dax needed someone, too.

'She reminds me of Vi,' he said softly, voice dropping

390

some of the playfulness he'd just had as it grew more serious. 'Is that bad? I can't decide if it's bad or not.'

I pondered his question for a few steps. We were almost to the raid building and our conversation was about to be cut off.

'I don't think so,' I replied honestly. 'Just . . . Make sure it's her you like and not the memory of Violetta, you know?'

'Yeah, you're right,' he agreed, nodding. 'Thanks, man.'

'Sure thing,' I said easily.

Kit and Docc had already filed inside the raid building when we got there. I opened the door and held it for Dax as he disappeared within, then waited for Leutie and Grace as they closed the short distance between us. I gave Leutie a causal nod of a greeting as she passed. Her eyes flitted to me for a moment and she shot me an awkward smile before following Dax inside. Next Grace came through, who gave me another genuine smile. Automatically, my hand reached out to pinch her side lightly as she moved past me, earning a quiet giggle from her.

The small, light-hearted exchanges I'd shared with Grace and Dax, however, were almost immediately forgotten as I moved into the room. Everyone knew exactly what we were here to discuss, and the topic wasn't one to be taken lightly. It was a dark subject alone, killing another camp's leader, but even more morbid when one considered that his own sister, Grace, would not only be present, but strategising against his favour.

Dax and Leutie stood across the table from Grace and I, leaving a side each to Kit and Docc. Everyone's mood was sombre. Again, I found it difficult to pinpoint the last time I'd really seen any of them. In my selfish downward spiral, I'd very clearly cared about only one thing: avenging Jett's death.

That thought was still heavily prominent in my mind, although now some of that dark haze had cleared, allowing me to think more clearly and rationally. Again, I felt gratitude to Grace for that, even if the agony I'd finally let myself feel was still doing a number on my heart. Each heartbeat felt painful, but I had to admit it was a masochistic pain that I knew I needed to feel.

Everyone's eyes were on me, waiting for me to speak while I processed my thoughts. I glanced around the circle we'd formed, meeting each face in turn until I reached the last pair of striking green eyes right next to me. Grace gave a small, reassuring nod, though it was impossible to miss the faint hint of sadness on her features. I held her gaze for a few seconds, judging her reaction and trying to read her thoughts before I spoke.

I knew this conversation would hurt her, but it had to be done. I allowed one more second of studying her before ripping my eyes away to address the group.

'All right, everyone. Let's come up with a plan.'

'What kind of plan, son?' Docc asked smoothly, watching me attentively.

I could practically feel Grace bracing herself next to me as she waited for me to say what she'd understood a long time ago.

'We're going to end all this for good. We're going to kill Jonah.'

392

Thirty-Four: Strategy

Grace

Silence greeted Hayden's bold statement, and I could practically feel everyone's eyes shifting to land on me as they absorbed his words. I tried not to look at anyone and forced myself to keep my face blank. I knew it had to be done. I'd been the first one to suggest it, after all, but I was struggling with it more than I had anticipated. Now, as everyone waited for someone to break the silence, Jonah's face flashed through my mind. I saw his expression fall when he'd caught me aiming my gun at him. I saw the flash of hurt that had crossed his features before he'd run away.

That was what had stopped me – that tiny flash of emotion that gave way to the possibility that my brother still lurked somewhere inside his deranged mind. He'd never been nice, supportive, or any of the things a brother should be, but he hadn't always been the terrible man he was now. At one point in time, we'd had a sort of dependence, more of an alliance than a sibling relationship, but it was far removed from what we were now.

Subconsciously, my hand drifted up over my heart, where my finger trailed down the scar. My reminder imprinted by my brother himself that people change.

I shook my head, more determined than ever to carry out the task that I knew needed to be done. Jonah was responsible for possibly hundreds of lives, one more painful than all the others: Jett.

I'd failed once, but I would not fail again.

'Yes,' I finally said, breaking the silence. 'Jonah needs to die. Jonah dies, this all ends.'

'Oh, Grace . . .' Docc murmured slowly. He looked sympathetic and understanding. He nodded and let out a deep breath. He looked saddened by the news, but he did not dispute my words. Even Docc knew it was time.

'Shit,' Dax murmured, raising his brows and blinking a few times. 'That's your brother, Grace.'

'I know,' I said calmly. 'But he's not who he used to be. He's lost something in him and if he doesn't die, more people will. He's already lost so many at Greystone and caused so many deaths here . . . including—'

'Jett,' Hayden filled in, his voice tight with pain.

My eyes darted to his and I shot him a sad smile.

'Yes.'

A heavy, sad silence fell off everyone as they thought of the young boy who had lost his life too soon. It felt like something that we'd all carry forever, the others even more than I would because they'd known him all his life.

'So what's the plan?' Kit asked.

'That's what we're here to figure out,' Hayden said, his voice low and steady.

'What are you thinking? Some kind of attack on Greystone?' Dax questioned with a glance between Hayden and me.

'That's one option,' Hayden said. His eyes were unfocused as he stared at the centre of the table, clearly distracted by his thoughts.

'Hayden, have you spoken with Shaw?'

Hayden tensed up immediately and a sneer pulled at his

features, unable to stop himself. A shiver ran down my spine as I remembered the feel of Shaw's hand on my body and the way Hayden had nearly killed him with his bare hands. I hadn't seen him in a while, but I knew he was still making his recovery in the infirmary with Docc.

'No,' he spat sharply.

'It could be worthwhile,' Docc prodded gently.

'He's against Jonah, right? He was leading the resistance against him?' Dax questioned.

'So she says,' Hayden said, ticking his head towards Leutie.

'He *is*,' Leutie insisted, looking slightly offended but not brave enough to confront Hayden's passive accusation. 'He was trying to bring Jonah down before he got stuck here.'

'How do we know we can trust you, huh?' Hayden asked her with a raised brow.

'Hey, come on, man,' Dax muttered quietly. He shot a reproachful look at Hayden, which he ignored.

'We can trust her, Hayden,' I said calmly, reaching out to place a hand on his lower back.

'Fine. I'll talk to him and see what he says,' Hayden muttered belligerently.

'To the infirmary, then?' Docc questioned, raising his greying brows as he glanced around. Everyone nodded and started to move away from the table we always gathered around.

'Wait,' I said. Everyone's eyes fixed on me again. 'Before we go, I need to say something.'

No one spoke as they waited patiently for me to continue. I took a deep breath, drawing strength from every bit of fortitude that I had.

'I don't know how we're going to do this or what's going to happen but . . . I need to be the one to kill him.'

I was met with immediate protests from nearly everyone.

'Grace, no.'

'You don't have to do that.'

'That's not true.'

'Someone else can.'

Only Docc and Hayden's low voices were missing from the protests. I could feel Hayden's eyes on me. He looked almost like he was in pain as he watched me, brows furrowed over his intensely burning green eyes with a soft frown on his face. I could practically read his thoughts, and it was very clear that he'd known I was going to say that.

'It has to be me,' I insisted, shaking my head to cut them off.

'Why?' Dax asked, thoroughly confused and somewhat frustrated.

'Because . . .' I trailed off and raised a shoulder in a submissive shrug before shaking my head. 'Because I don't want to resent any of you for doing it.'

'Grace, that's silly,' Leutie said, shaking her head. She stood next to Dax, closer than seemed necessary.

'It's not,' I argued firmly. 'When he's gone, you guys will be my only family left. I don't want to have to think about what one of you did for the rest of our lives, you know? If it's me, I can accept it.'

Part of me knew that it'd be nearly impossible for me not to put some blame on whoever did it. I could blame myself and deal with it, but I didn't want to blame anyone from my new family.

Kit.

Dax.

Hayden, most of all.

'Grace . . .'

Hayden's voice ripped through me as I heard it, the tone loaded with a silently desperate plea. I locked eyes with him to see his expression the same as before. He gave one slow shake of his head but didn't speak again.

'Let someone else, then,' Kit suggested. 'Shaw, maybe.'

'Have you seen him? He's not leaving that infirmary for a long time. This needs to be done soon, before anyone else dies.'

No one could argue with that point, and again they fell silent as they searched their minds for some other argument.

'Maybe I'll get lucky and someone in Greystone will do it first, but I doubt it. If it comes down to us, it's got to be me,' I said.

Slowly, a few of them nodded, agreeing to my words.

'There's no doubt in my mind that you're one of the strongest women I've had the pleasure to meet, Grace, but even you will struggle with this. The magnitude of this situation is not to be overlooked,' Docc said slowly.

'I know,' I replied. 'But I can do it.'

I'd failed once, but I would not fail again. Things were different now, and I had to do it. For Jett. For Hayden. For everyone who had died in Jonah's insane quest to destroy Blackwing.

'I know you can,' Docc said with a small nod. I took a deep breath and nodded, forcing myself to believe his words. We were quiet a little longer when Kit muttered a few words.

'Jesus, Grace,' he said with a partly confused, partly impressed look. 'You're something.'

Hayden cleared his throat and stepped closer to me, stopping me from replying.

'So, infirmary?' he said again, redirecting everyone. They nodded and filed out, so Hayden and I were at the back.

'Really?' I questioned, a ghost of an amused grin on my face at his inability to hide his jealousy.

'What?' he shot back, feigning ignorance. I let out a small, humourless laugh.

'Nothing,' I replied. He reached out to pinch my side once as if to lead me out of the room when I stopped him. 'Hey, Hayden . . .'

He stopped and turned back to me. 'Yeah?'

'I know that you wanted to do it . . . to avenge Jett but . . . I need you to promise me that you won't.'

'Grace—'

'Please, Hayden,' I begged, staring intently into his eyes. He let out a short huff, clearly reluctant to promise me such a thing.

'*Why*, Grace?' he pressed. 'Why does it have to be you?'

'I just told you all,' I said earnestly. 'I don't want to resent anyone for doing it. *Especially* you.'

'Don't take this the wrong way,' he started, arching a brow at me.

'Okay . . .'

He hesitated, frowning at me. 'Are you going to be able to? Truly?'

'*Yes.*'

He paused again, studying me closely to try to decide if I was lying. I stared resolutely back at him.

'I don't want you to have to do it, Grace,' he said, softening his words now. 'That's going to hurt you so much, you know that right?'

'I know,' I admitted quietly.

'I don't like it when you hurt,' he continued, voice even softer now.

'Hayden, I know,' I insisted gently. 'But it has to be this way. If you do it, I don't trust myself enough not to resent you. I'm not strong enough to know that I won't, so I don't want to risk it. If I do it . . . yeah, it'll hurt . . . but it'll be all right because I have you. *You* are what matters to me. *You* are what's going to keep me going after something like that. I'd rather do it myself and have you be there for me than risk losing you because I couldn't get over resenting you for doing it.'

Hayden was quiet as he absorbed my words, his eyes never leaving mine. He stood very close to me, only a few inches away, and he felt even closer when he reached out to snake his fingers into the hair at the base of my neck.

'All right, Grace,' he murmured softly. He chewed on his lower lip once before nodding. 'All right.'

'Thank you,' I breathed, sagging slightly with relief. Hayden didn't look happy, but he did lean forward to press a light kiss into my forehead before leading me outside after the others.

When we caught up, we found them waiting outside the infirmary for us.

'Yeah, that's fine, take your sweet time,' Dax joked, tapping his wrist as one would if they were wearing a watch.

'Shut up, Dax,' Hayden muttered, failing to hide the hint of a smirk that crossed his features. 'Let's get this over with.'

With that, he pushed his way through the doors. I followed close behind, and Dax, Kit, Docc, and Leutie filed in after us. Shaw came into view almost immediately, where he sat propped up in one of the beds. A guard was next to him, gun trained on him unwaveringly. As soon as we arrived, the man left to give us some privacy. I was surprised to see that Shaw was awake and fairly alert, though he was still badly bruised and swollen pretty much everywhere I could see. We gathered around his bed while he watched us coolly.

'You going to hit me again?' he challenged Hayden. I could practically feel Hayden tense up beside me, and I didn't miss his hands clenching into fists by his side.

399

'Depends on how well you want to cooperate,' Hayden hissed, trying to control his anger. Shaw was already making things difficult and we hadn't even been there for a minute.

Shaw didn't reply and simply stared at him, waiting for him to continue. He had some nerve to put up such an attitude when Hayden was the reason he looked like he currently did, especially when considering how truly vulnerable he was.

'You led the resistance against Jonah, correct?' Hayden questioned, keeping his tone sharp.

'Yes,' Shaw admitted easily.

'You were trying to kill him?' Hayden pressed.

'Obviously,' Shaw said with a raised brow, as if annoyed by the conversation. Again, Hayden tensed beside me, clearly very irritated with him when he was already so angry with what he'd done to me in the past.

'Tell me everything,' Hayden demanded, glaring down at him.

'What's in it for me?' Shaw dared to ask. His demeanour was far too confident, and it grated on me.

'I'll let you live,' Hayden spat, voice deadly serious. I knew that this threat was one he meant. If Shaw did not cooperate, I had no doubt that Hayden would kill him.

Shaw shrugged as if considering the offer. His eyes darted to me before they dropped down my body, bringing a suggestive leer to his face.

'Good to see you, Grace,' he said smoothly. My stomach churned at his slimy tone and I was about to jump forward to actually punch him when Hayden stepped in front of me, cutting off my view.

'All right, let's get one thing straight right now,' he hissed. 'You will not talk to her. You will not touch her. You will not even fucking *look* at her, you understand?'

'Jeez, all right, all right,' Shaw said easily, raising his arms by his head as best he could in surrender. 'Can't blame a guy, can you? You assholes took our two prettiest girls. What's a guy to do, am I right?'

'I swear to fuc—'

'Hayden,' I hissed, cutting him off. I placed my hand on his back, drawing his attention away from Shaw. 'Ignore him, yeah?' I whispered quietly. We had to get as much information out of Shaw as we could, but Hayden was very quickly losing focus. He let out an angry, frustrated huff before nodding and turning back around.

'All right. Let's try to forget that you're a disgusting piece of shit for a moment,' Hayden started again, glaring down at him.

'Let's try, mate,' Shaw shot back, ticking his teeth while his eye dropped in a wink.

'For the last time, tell me what you know,' Hayden demanded sharply.

Shaw gave an exasperated sigh before speaking.

'First of all, you should know Jonah's a complete lunatic now. I mean, he was always a bit of a nutcase, right? But he's gone off the deep end now,' Shaw started. His eyes flicked to me before refocusing on Hayden. 'And people are dying. Lots of them. Greystone is about half the size it used to be, all because of Jonah. He keeps sending people on these suicide missions into the city or over to Whetland. He thinks he can control them, but you know as well as I do that the Brutes can't be controlled, and Whetland is too smart to get mixed in with any of our bullshit. They keep to themselves, as they always have.'

'Go on,' Hayden urged, looking down on Shaw with a clenched jaw. His arms were crossed tightly across his chest as he listened.

'About half the people left in Greystone are against him, but most are too scared to say anything. They think if they resist him, he'll force them into the city. You know what happens when inexperienced people go into the city,' Shaw said darkly.

I was immediately reminded of Violetta. Hayden had said she died on the first raid she ever went on, and I suddenly wished Dax wasn't here for this.

'They die,' Dax murmured, speaking for the first time. Everyone turned to look at him and he blinked in surprise, as if he hadn't realised he'd spoken out loud. An awkward silence stretched on before Docc cleared his throat and spoke.

'Please continue, Shaw.'

'Right, well, that's about it. Jonah's going nuts trying to control everything, but all he's really accomplishing is getting a shitload of people killed. I *was* going to try and take him down before I got landed here with you lot,' he finished, casting a reproachful look at all of us.

'*You* got yourself in this situation, not us,' Hayden hissed. 'If you're against him, why were you on the raid that night, huh?'

'Do you think I'd have accomplished much if he didn't trust me?' Shaw shot back sarcastically. 'Do you think he'd have let me live if he knew I was going to try and kill him? Of course not. It's all part of the game, my friend.'

'I am not your friend,' Hayden bit sharply. Shaw shrugged and shook his head in exasperation.

'How do we know you're not lying?' Kit asked, speaking for the first time. His arms were also crossed tightly over his chest in a disbelieving manner.

'Ask her,' Shaw said, ticking his head to Leutie. 'She knows.'

'He's telling the truth,' Leutie said. 'Everything he's said is true. That's even more people lost since I left . . .'

She looked truly troubled and I caught the slight quiver to her jaw as the realisation started to set in. Dax murmured something to her that I couldn't hear and let his hand run soothingly along her back.

'So how do we do it? How do we get rid of him for good?' Hayden asked.

'I don't know how you all work, but I know what I'd do,' Shaw said, glancing around at each of us in turn. My heart thumped a little harder in my chest as I waited.

'Well?' Hayden snapped impatiently.

'I'd do it in the city. He goes there with this little crew every three weeks. Tries to force the Brutes into working for him, but he never succeeds. Always loses about half the people, but he always goes back. That's how you get him — when he's distracted and not surrounded by all of his supporters in Greystone. You take him out, take out his crew, take out the rest of the crazies left in Greystone, and that's it. Problem solved.'

'That's it, is it? You're talking about killing around a hundred people,' Hayden said flatly.

'I didn't say it'd be pretty,' Shaw rebuffed casually.

'You know who's with him?' Hayden pressed. 'Who's on his side and who's against him, openly or not?'

'Yes.'

'Good.'

Hayden didn't say anything further, but I could see his train of thought. We needed to kill Jonah and maybe a few of his biggest supporters, but not everyone, as Shaw had suggested. As long as we knew who they were, we could figure something else out.

'You said he goes every three weeks. When will the next

one be?' I asked, drawing Shaw's attention. His blue-green eyes settled on me, where he scrutinised me closely.

'You really going to kill your own brother?' he asked, ignoring my question.

'Yes,' I said through gritted teeth.

Shaw's face was difficult to read as he absorbed my words. He paused for a few moments while he continued to stare at me.

'Maybe you're more like him than I thought,' he said thoughtfully. There was an undertone of malice to his voice. My stomach twisted involuntarily and my blood ran cold in my veins. That was a comparison I did not want to hear.

'What did I fucking say to you?' Hayden hissed, interrupting. 'Don't talk to her.'

'She talked to me first, mate, what am I supposed to do?' Shaw rebutted.

'I don't care, you stay the hell away from her.'

Hayden's protective words brought a bit of warmth back into my blood, but the chill remained, as Shaw's words haunted me.

'When will he go back to the city?' Kit demanded, repeating my question.

'You folks are in luck,' Shaw said with a ghost of a dark smirk on his face. 'Jonah will be in the city tomorrow night.'

Thirty-Five: Radiant

Grace

A shocked silence rang out around us as Shaw's words settled in. Tomorrow was so soon. It was already getting to be late afternoon; could we even prepare in such a short amount of time?

'That's too soon,' Dax said, finally breaking the tense silence. 'There's no way we'll be ready by then, right?'

He glanced around, but his certainty that we would all agree was waning by the second.

'I don't know. It'd be very difficult,' Hayden murmured, brows furrowed in thought. 'Grace?'

I didn't respond right away, equally as confused as Hayden.

'We have absolutely no plan,' I pointed out. Everyone waited, sensing I'd continue. 'And it'll probably be really dangerous.'

'And we don't know where he'll be,' Hayden added.

'Or who he'll have with him,' said Kit.

'Or what other things we'll have to deal with in the city,' I finished, frowning at the group.

'I thought you said this would be difficult? Sounds like a walk in the park to me,' Dax said sarcastically, shrugging and pulling the edges of his lips down in a mock frown.

No one laughed, too tense and preoccupied. Shaw, who

had remained silent while our mini debate ensued, finally spoke.

'You realise I know the answers to most of those questions, right?' he said flatly with a raised eyebrow.

'Yeah, that's if we decide we fully trust you, and, frankly, I don't,' Hayden growled, glaring at him.

'You trust me enough to consider going into the city tomorrow but not enough to take my information that could make things easier on you? Makes a whole lot of sense,' Shaw replied sarcastically.

'I think he's right, guys,' Leutie agreed. 'Jonah and some people would disappear every three weeks, and every time they came back, they'd have a few less people.'

'If we don't go tomorrow, more people will die. Not just those he brings with him but whoever he decides to send on more suicide missions when he returns . . .' I mused aloud.

I could feel myself leaning towards going tomorrow the more I thought about it. The fact of the matter was that the faster we acted, the more lives we could save. Wasn't the whole point of killing Jonah to save lives? Would more time really prepare me any more to kill my own brother?

I doubted it.

I didn't think there would ever be enough time to fully prepare for what I had to do. One night, three weeks, ten years. It was all the same, and it wouldn't change how much it was going to hurt me. Might as well get it over with as soon as possible.

Hayden seemed to reach the same conclusion just as I did, because when I glanced at him I saw the resignation written on his face. He shot me a reluctant frown.

'I think we have to go tomorrow,' he said firmly, glancing around at everyone. I waited anxiously for someone else to speak, secretly wishing for everyone to agree and disagree all at once.

'I think so, too,' Kit agreed soberly.

'Me, too,' I murmured softly.

'Well, shit,' Dax said with an exasperated huff. 'Looks like we're going tomorrow, then.'

'Make sure you have as good of a plan as possible,' Docc advised. 'You have Shaw and Leutie on your side. Use them.'

Shaw didn't react much to Docc's words, and Leutie gave each of us a brave, earnest smile. Once it was decided, no one even mentioned reconsidering. Our thoughts were focused on forming a plan and gathering as much information as we could, not on backing out or searching for other options.

The next hour or so was spent getting every bit of information possible out of Shaw and Leutie. Hayden, Kit, and Dax questioned them relentlessly while Docc wrote down little notes on a scrap of paper. Shaw quickly grew bored of their questions but answered them evenly and thoroughly. He told us where they went, what time they moved, who he brought, what weapons they'd have, what they'd be looking for. He told us places to avoid and places that could be opportune for taking action. He told us, perhaps most importantly, how to identify those that were most like Jonah and who needed to go as well, which Leutie corroborated.

After all that, we had a relatively strong plan. I felt confident that even if Shaw had lied about every single detail, we'd manage to avoid some kind of trap. Every move we'd planned had some sort of second option in case something bad were to happen. We were meticulous as we mapped out our route, careful to avoid any places that could result in some kind of dangerous situation.

For the first time in a long while, I felt like we were in control. Jonah's and Greystone's moves had dictated ours for so long that it felt reassuring to be the offensive side for once instead of constant defence. We were finally acting, and soon, hopefully, mercifully, it would all be over.

'All right, everyone,' Hayden finally said with a deep sigh. 'I think we can call it a day. Get some rest. We leave first thing in the morning.'

Everyone agreed and mumbled their assent, saying goodbye to Docc, who had already started to head towards his desk. I cast one last glance at Shaw, in his hospital bed, before turning to follow Hayden, Kit, Dax, and Leutie out of the infirmary. Hayden, I noticed, appeared to be trying very hard not to look at Shaw as we exited.

Outside, it was evening. A quiet rumbling in my stomach reminded me that I was quite hungry, and it appeared I wasn't the only one when Dax suggested we all grab something to eat. Everyone was quiet and deep in thought, and it wasn't until we walked through the door to the mess hall and I saw Maisie that my mind finally abandoned the thoughts of tomorrow's plan.

My heart sank when I took in the heartbreak and sorrow evident in the way she moved. As always, she stood behind the counter and dished out food to those who waited, but today, instead of a bright grin and warm hello, she greeted us with hardly a nod, dishing our food without a word. I shot her a sad, sympathetic smile that broke my heart even more as I accepted my plate and moved on.

The five of us settled into a table together and, again, it appeared I wasn't alone in my feelings.

'Should she really be working right now? Jett was practically her son . . .' Dax asked.

'She wants to,' Kit answered. 'I talked to her yesterday. She said staying busy helps, but she looks miserable . . .'

I understood completely. Sitting idly with nothing more

than your thoughts to distract you was the worst possible way to cope imaginable, in my opinion. Every stressful event I'd faced had been dealt with by keeping busy or taking action. Alone, your thoughts controlled you, and that control was often so tight and rigid that it crushed you to dust.

'She's very strong, I think,' Leutie commented softly. She gazed wistfully at Maisie, who continued to work without a word. Everyone nodded solemnly in agreement.

Hayden, I noticed, hadn't said a word. He appeared entirely focused on his food, though I knew he was surely hurting. I suddenly wanted nothing more than to lock ourselves away for the rest of the night; we both needed a reprieve from the stress and heaviness of things, especially considering what tomorrow would bring.

The rest of our meal was finished quickly, and before long everyone was preparing to part ways. Kit headed off for a last check around camp before retiring to his hut. Hayden and I walked along with Dax and Leutie as we headed to our huts. It seemed odd for Dax to be so serious; hardly ever did we encounter him and not receive some sort of joke or playful comment, but today he'd hardly said anything.

Everything seemed to be off.

Hayden and I entered our hut in silence, where we both kicked off our shoes before making our way inside. It was starting to get dark now, and all I wanted to do was crawl into bed with Hayden. I watched as he gripped his shirt at the nape of his neck and hauled it over his head, casting it to the floor, leaving him in just a pair of athletic shorts as he so often was. I changed quickly into a pair of comfortable shorts and a loose tank top.

Hayden sat on the edge of the bed, burying his face in his hands, his elbows on his knees.

'Hey,' I said softly. He sat up and blinked a few times, clearing his throat as he refocused on me.

'Hey,' he replied, voice low and raspy.

I stood a few feet in front of him and he didn't hesitate to reach out for me. He tugged my hand, pulling me easily into his lap like he so often did. My legs draped over the side of his and my arms looped loosely around his neck. I melted into him, relishing the warmth of his arm around my back and his fingers that tickled lightly on the outside of my thigh.

'How are you?' I asked quietly. I expected him to brush it off and answer with his typical 'fine', but he surprised me.

'Tired,' he admitted. I knew by the weight of his tone that he didn't just mean physically. He was mentally, physically, emotionally tired; exhausted, just as I was.

'Me, too,' I agreed. He was quiet and appeared deep in thought again as his fingers drifted absent-mindedly across my skin.

'I don't know what's going to happen tomorrow,' Hayden started, allowing his eyes to connect with mine for the first time since we'd entered our hut.

'Can we not do this?' I asked, speaking before I was aware of what I was going to say.

'Do what?' he frowned.

'You know ...' I started gently. 'The whole pre-dangerous-event talk.'

I shrugged, feeling stupid that I'd said anything. Hayden opened his mouth to reply, but I cut him off.

'I just mean ... I don't want to do that tonight. I know to be careful, you know to be careful. You know I love you. I know you love me. I know it'll be hard, but I know I can do it. What else is there to say, really?'

Hayden appeared surprised by my words but nodded

slowly, allowing a bit of relief to flood through me.

'I guess that covers it,' he agreed. A hint of amusement crossed his features now as he watched me.

'I just want things to go back to normal,' I said wishfully. I gave a half-hearted shrug and a slight shake of my head.

'What is normal?' he questioned gently.

'I don't know. Not this.'

Hayden was quiet for a few moments as he thought.

'I know, love,' Hayden murmured. His hand rose to cradle one side of my face gently, where his thumb stroked across my cheek.

'Will it ever go back? Will things ever be the same as they were?' I asked, desperately hoping he'd say yes.

'No,' Hayden said apologetically. My heart gave a painful thud. 'Things will never be the same. But it will get better.'

It was my turn to drop his gaze as I pulled my lips back in thought and nodded. 'I'll take that.'

Hayden gave me a soft smile and pressed a light, airy kiss on my lips. I felt a sudden determination to enjoy tonight. I wanted to get our minds off things.

'Let's talk about something else,' I said, as I perked up.

'Something else,' Hayden repeated with a hint of amusement. 'Such as?'

'I don't know, but all this stuff, this heavy we-might-die-tomorrow kind of talk is off limits.'

Much to my satisfaction, Hayden let out a light chuckle as a grin tugged at his lips.

'Yes, ma'am.'

It wasn't the first time he'd said it, and it was always in the same tone: amused, loaded with endearment, and meant to appease me more than anything. I loved it.

'I like that,' I told him with a wide grin. My fingers tangled loosely in the hair on the back of his head. I shifted in his lap so I faced him, and I felt his hands link behind me.

'Oh yeah?' he asked, cocking an eyebrow. A dimple dipped into his cheek as he grinned.

'Mmhmm,' I nodded, barely able to contain my grin.

'Got a kink, do you?'

My mouth dropped open in surprise and my brows shot upward.

'Hayden!'

He laughed again, finally allowing his smile to reach his eyes as he beamed at me. It felt so good not only to smile again, but to see him smile as well. He looked so beautiful when he smiled, and he didn't get to do it nearly enough.

'I meant your neck . . . don't know what you're on about . . .' he trailed off, raising his brows playfully as if judging me.

'No, you didn't,' I laughed.

'No, I didn't,' he admitted with a cheeky grin. My fingers continued to tangle loosely in his hair.

'You're kind of a perv sometimes,' I told him in a mock-scolding tone.

Hayden shrugged and closed his eyes for a second while he gave an exaggerated frown.

'You love it,' he said confidently.

I shook my head, unable to suppress the light-hearted grin threatening to break through. 'Nope.'

'You definitely love it,' he continued, even more confident this time as he held my gaze.

'Nope,' I denied, biting on my lower lip to hold back a laugh.

I failed, however, when his hand shifted to my side to tickle me lightly. I let out a shriek of laughter and squirmed away from him, nearly falling out of his lap in the process. I barely made it onto the bed when his arms looped around

412

me, grabbing me and flipping me onto my back. His body followed, landing on top of mine to pin me down. One of his hands gathered both of mine and held them above my head, making me helpless, as his other hand trailed lightly down my side.

'Say you love it,' he said quietly, amusement clear on his face as his fingers brushed along my stomach, threatening to tickle me again.

'Never,' I said determinedly, challenging him with a playful grin on my face.

'Say it, Grace,' Hayden whispered, causing goosebumps to rise on my skin. His fingers, which had been trailing lightly up and down my side, continued their path.

I didn't reply this time but just shook my head, suddenly breathless as I held his intense gaze. I sucked in a breath when he ducked his head to drop his lips to my neck. I felt their warmth on my skin as he trailed a few kisses down my throat and back up again, pausing to tug lightly on my ear before he whispered again, allowing his lips to tickle at my ear.

'You love it.'

My eyes drifted shut, the playfulness all but forgotten as I enjoyed the way his lips tickled over my skin. Then I felt his fingers pinch and tickle at my sides again, taking me by surprise after he'd lulled me into such a daze. I jumped and squirmed away from his touch, but his grip on my hands and the weight of his body over mine held me in place while I cackled with laughter.

The beautiful sound of his laugh filled the room as he tickled me, and when he pulled back enough, I could see the radiant grin on his face and the way the light beamed from his eyes.

'Okay, okay, I love it!' I finally admitted, cracking under the relentless tickling. My voice was breathless and punctuated with laughter, but as soon as I admitted it, he stopped tickling me and let his hand come to rest near my face.

'That's what I thought,' he said triumphantly, a cocky grin on his face as he looked down at me.

'You cheated,' I accused, unable to maintain my feigned serious expression. He looked too beautiful and happy to pretend to be mad.

'Yep,' Hayden said with an unconcerned shrug. 'One more time, what do you love?'

'That you're a perv,' I laughed. Hayden still held my hands above my head, though his grip had relaxed somewhat on my wrists.

'Mmhmm,' he hummed happily. 'What else do you love?'

'You, all right?' I admitted with a playful roll of my eyes.

'Convincing,' he laughed sarcastically.

'I love you, stupid.'

'Aren't you sweet,' Hayden continued in the same tone as before. His eyes were practically glowing with happiness as he watched me and that made me feel more content than I had in a long, long time.

'Hey, I'm not the one avoiding saying it back,' I told him accusingly, turning my head to the side as if offended.

'Is that what I'm supposed to say?' he asked in mock confusion, pointing at himself.

'That's usually how it works, yeah,' I said with a casual nod.

'Ohhhh,' Hayden said with an exaggerated grin. 'Right, thank you for clearing that up.'

'You still haven't said it,' I pointed out, blinking at him expectantly.

'Give me a minute, bloody hell. You're quite intimidating, you know? Demanding I say I love you and all . . . It's hard to think straight with such a beautiful girl beneath me.'

'You did this,' I informed him with a grin and a laugh. 'But thank you.'

Hayden shrugged again; I couldn't seem to stop smiling.

'Okay, I'm ready to say it,' he told me, keeping his voice overly serious.

'Okay, I'm waiting. Any time now.'

'This is going to knock your socks off,' he warned me.

'I'll prepare,' I said, mirroring his mock-serious tone.

He nodded and cleared his throat, closing his eyes for a few seconds as if to prepare. When he opened his eyes, I could see the light from amusement twinkling behind the stunning green of his irises.

'I love you, Grace Cook, you intimidating, demanding, majestically gorgeous creature, you.'

'That was so poetic,' I laughed jokingly.

'I know, I know,' Hayden said seriously, raising a brow at me. 'I've been practising.'

'Have you?' I laughed.

'Oh yes,' he lied with a grin. 'How are your socks?'

'Off,' I replied. 'Knocked them clean off, you did.'

'*Yes*,' he said sarcastically, clenching a fist in victory near my shoulder. This was the happiest I'd felt in a long time and I never wanted that feeling to go away. 'But I do love you,' he murmured quietly, voice sounding sincere for the first time in practically the entire conversation. 'So much.'

Warmth flooded through my body so strongly that I was sure Hayden would be able to feel it.

'I love you, Hayden,' I replied honestly.

He had lightened my entire mood so easily, and I felt like I was going to burst with love for him.

Tomorrow was going to be one of the hardest things I ever did, but if I had Hayden, I could get through absolutely anything.

Thirty-Six: Culmination

Dax

I tried not to grimace as I stretched my neck from side to side, fighting off the ache that had settled in practically everywhere. No matter how much I shifted or repositioned myself, the couch I was occupying refused to become comfortable. I let out a quiet huff of defeat as I gave up and melted into the sunken couch cushions, pulling the blanket up over me. I couldn't stop my eyes from glancing at my bed, which was unavailable because of a sleeping Leutie.

A much-more-comfortable-because-she-wasn't-stuck-on-this-horrible-couch Leutie.

The sun was starting to creep up now, so I gave up on sleep altogether. I pushed down the blanket as I sat up, cringing as my back screamed in protest. I twisted from side to side to try and work out the ache, but I got little relief. I stood up and started to move towards the front door to wait until Leutie woke up. I couldn't take lying awake much longer with the impending danger we were about to face creeping closer and closer by the minute.

The floorboards creaked beneath my bare feet and I was about to pull on a shirt when I heard the soft ruffling of blankets from behind me. The sound of my name stilled my actions, causing me to turn around.

'Dax?' Leutie's voice was groggy with sleep.

'Hey,' I greeted quietly, keeping my voice low. I always felt the need to speak quietly when it was dark, even if the sun was coming up.

'What are you doing?' she asked softly, studying me through the darkness.

'I was just going to get some fresh air,' I told her.

'Couldn't sleep?' she assessed correctly, raising a brow at me. I sighed and scratched the back of my neck absent-mindedly.

'No.'

'Come here,' she requested. She tugged down the blanket on the other side of the bed, clearing a space for me.

I took a small step forward but hesitated, unsure if I wanted to cross that bridge. Letting her stay with me and getting to know her a bit was one thing, but sharing the bed?

'I didn't ask you to marry me, just come and talk to me,' she coaxed lightly.

I grinned and shook my head, realising she was right. I crawled into the bed with her. She was still a good two feet away, separated by an expanse of mattress and the blanket in between us. She was different when she was around just me, rather than Grace and Hayden. Hayden seemed to intimidate her, making her quieter and more serious.

'So, what's up?' she asked softly. Her fingers picked at a loose thread in the sheet for a few moments before her light blue eyes flitted up to meet mine.

'Nothing,' I said with a casual shrug.

'Liar,' she accused with a playful grin.

'No, really, it's nothing,' I continued.

'Dax,' she said flatly, raising a brow expectantly at me.

I let out a deep sigh of resignation.

'Fine . . . it's just . . .' I took a deep breath and blew it out slowly. 'That couch is horrendous and you're hogging my bed, so I can't sleep.'

Leutie giggled instantly, bringing a satisfied smile to my lips. I liked hearing the sound of her laugh, and it felt good knowing I was the one who caused it.

'I *did* offer to share, you know,' she pointed out.

'What sort of gentleman would I be if I encroached on m'lady's space?'

She giggled again and this time I thought I caught a hint of a blush on her cheeks, which only widened my smile.

'Yeah, yeah. You've been a most gracious host,' she laughed.

'Oh, I know,' I said confidently, returning her smile. Her smile softened to a more serious expression. We were both quiet, the moment loaded with tension.

'Are you afraid? For today?' she asked gently.

'I'm not afraid of anything,' I boasted, puffing out my chest jokingly. She maintained her serious expression, clearly not having it. I sighed and shrugged once. 'I don't know. A little, yeah.'

'I would be afraid,' she admitted. She peered at me across the space between us.

'Have you ever been on a raid?' I asked her. Certain parts of her reminded me so strongly of Violetta, but in other ways, she was completely different. I felt the slight pang of hurt I always felt when I thought of her, but I tried to brush it off.

'Oh, no,' she said, shaking her head adamantly. 'I've never been good at that stuff. Grace was always so strong and amazing, but I . . . I just didn't have the strength or courage.'

'There are different kinds of strong,' I told her.

418

'There's only one kind that doesn't get you killed,' she joked. Her tone was light, but her face grew even more serious. 'And that's the kind I do not have.'

I frowned. She might not have been the physical force that Grace was, but she held strengths of her own.

'But you're still strong,' I told her firmly. 'In other ways.' Kindness, understanding, and selflessness were ones I'd already identified in our short time together.

Again, a slight blush crept up her cheeks at my compliment. It was almost too easy to make her blush or fluster her, but I enjoyed it every time.

'Thank you,' she said softly.

My eyes darted to her hand resting on the mattress between us and I felt the sudden urge to reach out and grab it, but I resisted.

'You're welcome.'

'It's okay to be afraid of what's coming today,' she said, surprising me. 'Just trust yourself and your friends. You and everyone else will get through this.'

I felt a sad smile tug at my lips. Violetta used to say very similar things every time I left her to go on a raid. She'd tell me she'd be waiting for me to return each and every time until the day she finally came with us on her own first ever raid. The day she didn't say the words because she was going along.

The day she died.

My heart felt sad as I remembered that day, and I had to blink a few times to refocus on Leutie in front of me, who was waiting patiently for my reply. I felt a sudden rush of appreciation for her and a strong need to keep her safe. I couldn't let what had happened to Violetta happen again.

'You're right. We will.'

Grace

It was impossible to ignore the nerves creeping up as I walked alongside Hayden to the garage. We were supposed to meet the rest of our group before heading into the city, but I couldn't help feeling desperate to return to our bed, where I'd awoken a while ago with Hayden's arms locked securely around me. I could practically still feel the residual heat of his chest at my back, his lips at my neck as he mumbled a raspy 'good morning'. It had been extremely difficult to untangle myself from him when I knew what getting up meant.

My heart felt heavy and conflicted as I walked, but my determination was stronger than ever as I caught the small, reassuring smile Hayden aimed down at me. I was surprised when I felt him loop his arm around my shoulders to haul me gently into his side. He pressed a light kiss to my temple, his arm around me while we closed the distance to the garage.

'It'll be all right, Bear,' he murmured simply.

I sighed and nodded, reaching up to grab his hand that rested lightly on my shoulder. He squeezed mine once, and again, I drew comfort from his warmth and reassurance.

'I know,' I agreed quietly.

We entered the garage to find Kit loading supplies into the jeep while Dax and Leutie looked over a few last-minute notes on some scraps of paper. Kit shot each of us a nod in greeting after depositing a rather large gun in the back seat of the vehicle.

'We're ready when you are,' Kit said to us.

'All right,' Hayden replied, nodding to him. I stayed quiet as I followed him to grab our weapons, tucking them

420

into place. I carried two guns, my usual knife, and a few extra magazines of bullets. More weapons and ammunition were already loaded into the jeep, along with water and some first-aid supplies. I hoped they wouldn't be necessary.

Finally, we were all ready to go. Hayden had been studying me closely all morning. He wanted to make sure I was okay, and that I was still determined to carry out my task.

'I'm fine, Hayden,' I told him calmly. His lips flattened in an unhappy frown, but he nodded in acceptance.

'All right, guys, ready?' he spoke, addressing the group.

'So ready,' Kit replied with a confident nod.

'You bet,' Dax agreed, glancing at us before turning to Leutie. 'We'll see you later, Leutie.'

'I've been thinking,' she said slowly, casting a fleeting glance at Dax before avoiding his gaze. 'I think I should come with you.'

My stomach twisted anxiously. The plan had been for her to stay behind because of her lack of experience. The fact was that she simply wasn't physically capable of protecting herself, and we couldn't risk her getting hurt or holding anyone back.

'No,' Dax replied immediately, beating me to it.

'But I think I could help—'

'No, no way,' Dax repeated more firmly, shaking his head adamantly.

'It's not a good idea, Leutie,' I said, siding with Dax. 'Appreciate the thought but . . . it's just too dangerous.'

'Look, I know I won't be any good at fighting, but I can help in other ways!' she pleaded to each of us in turn.

'You can't come with us,' Dax said. Finally, she turned to meet his eye contact and frowned in frustration.

'But I want to help,' she said softly, hurt leaking into her voice.

Dax shook his head slowly, pain just detectable in his features.

'No.'

'But I—'

Dax stepped forward and closed the distance between them. He took her face between both of his hands just before his lips pressed to hers, surprising her and everyone else in the room. I felt my jaw fall open and wasn't surprised to see Kit's and Hayden's do the same on either side of me.

Leutie, who had been stunned at first, relaxed as she let her hands settle to his chest as he kissed her. It only lasted a few seconds and they didn't appear to deepen the kiss, but it was enough to shut her up and stop her train of thought. When he drew back, I watched as his thumb stroked lightly across her cheek in the way Hayden so often did to me; I took a subconscious step closer to Hayden so I could feel the comforting warmth of his arm pressing into mine.

'You need to stay. Trust me,' Dax said to her quietly.

They seemed to forget we were all there as they stared at each other, separated by only a few inches. Leutie let out a small sigh and gave a reluctant nod.

'Okay, fine. I'll stay.' Her words brought a soft grin to Dax's face.

'Thank you.'

Kit cleared his throat purposefully. 'Um . . .'

Dax and Leutie blinked and looked at us, surprised to see the three of us observing them with shocked expressions on our faces.

'Excuse me, no one likes a bunch of creepy perverts intruding on their private conversations,' Dax said with a wry grin. Leutie giggled and blushed beside him as he took a small step away from her. I chuckled at the irony of his choice of words given the nature of my conversation with Hayden last night.

'All right, now that lover boy has said goodbye, can we get this show on the road?' Kit asked lightly, grinning widely.

'Yeah, yeah, none of you lot can talk,' Dax muttered as he shook his head good-naturedly.

Leutie surprised me with a hug that took me a moment to return. I felt a smile pull at my lips when I heard her whisper a few hurried words in my ear.

'*Oh my god, oh my god.*'

I suspected she and Dax had been getting on well, but it was still quite a surprise to witness what was probably their first kiss.

'See you when you're back,' she said. 'Be careful.'

'Always,' I told her with a confident grin. 'See you. Hang with Docc while we're gone, he'll take care of you.'

'I will,' she nodded.

With that, I stepped away and followed Hayden to the other side of the jeep, allowing Kit to go to his side while Dax said one more quick goodbye to Leutie. I was about to open the door and jump into the back seat when I felt Hayden's hand close around my arm, tugging gently to twist me to face him. He pinned me between his body and the side of the jeep, secluded from the rest of the group on the other side.

'Forgetting something?' he asked with a lopsided grin.

'Be careful, Hayden. I love you very much,' I told him, smiling but keeping my voice low.

'I will. You be careful and remember how strong you are, okay? You can do this, I know you can, and I'll be there for you when it's over. I love you, Grace.'

My heart fluttered at his sweet words. I felt even warmer when his hand found my face lightly and he gave me one lingering, deep kiss to complete our promise. I almost giggled when he pulled open my door, offering me his hand with a small, playful bow of his head as he helped me into the back seat before climbing into the driver's seat in front of me.

'Here we go,' he muttered, starting the engine and backing out of the garage. I caught one last look at Leutie, who looked especially flustered and red in the face, as she waved goodbye.

The car was quiet as Hayden started the short drive into the city. No one seemed sure of what to say or how to act, me most of all. It was still very early in the day, but we wanted to beat Jonah and his crew so we could get our places figured out. Hayden and I would stick together, while Kit and Dax did the same, splitting our forces between two strategic vantage points that would give us a good view of where Jonah would appear, according to Shaw.

My gut told me we could trust him, but it was nearly impossible to trust anyone these days, much less someone as despicable as Shaw. He may have been on our side in terms of the Jonah situation, but that was about all we had in common. His information, however, made it necessary not only to work with him, but to trust him, something I and everyone else was still struggling with as we drove into the dangerous city.

I noticed the crumbling and decrepit buildings rise up around us as we made our way into the former metropolitan area. Potholes the size of cars and debris so large we had to swerve around it hindered our path, but it wasn't long until we'd reached the building we'd earmarked. I was relieved to see no signs of activity anywhere nearby.

A nervous tension twisted at my stomach as Hayden drove. I caught a flash of green as his eyes met mine in the rearview mirror, but it did little to calm the quickly rising uneasiness. My leg bounced up and down and I was unable to calm the jitteriness of my body. Everyone appeared on edge as they looked out of the windows, searching for signs of enemies. We were only a few blocks away from the auto body shop that housed the entrance to the Armoury where the Brutes stayed, adding even more necessity to be careful.

Finally, Hayden pulled into a secluded alleyway and parked the jeep behind a large skip that would shield it from view. I took a few moments to close my eyes and blow out a deep, slow breath, gathering my strength. When my eyes flitted open, I saw Hayden's stare through my window just before he opened my door for me. I jumped out and felt the light brush of his hand across my lower back.

'Okay, everyone,' Hayden said as we huddled into a small circle. 'You know the plan. You two stay to the right and we'll stay to the left. Jonah should be here in an hour or two, but stay alert. There are bound to be some Brutes running around here as well. We want to avoid being seen until Grace has a chance to shoot, got it?'

'Got it,' Dax muttered, while Kit nodded stoically beside him.

We were all very aware that shooting at and hopefully killing Jonah would bring on a fight after, and we were all prepared to face that when it inevitably came. I seemed unable to speak, so I just nodded calmly and focused on keeping my breathing even.

'Everyone be safe,' Hayden concluded. Not much else needed saying; we'd gone over the plan more times than I could count in exhausting detail. Everyone was ready to get it over with.

'You got it, Bossman,' Dax said with a tip of his imaginary hat.

I couldn't even manage a smile as we headed towards the opening of the alley, surveying the area before determining it to be clear. Hayden and I darted out first, guns raised and ready as we moved towards our target to the left. Kit and Dax did the same, heading to the right instead as we'd planned. I matched Hayden step for step as we hurdled over debris and overgrown plants that had forced their way through the cracked pavement. Adrenaline pumped through my veins as we ran, overflowing into my body.

Our destination was a small clothing store with a large front window, blackened with dirt and decay. After forcing the rusty door open, Hayden and I made our way inside. It smelled musty and the thick coat of dust and stale air told me it'd been a long time since a human had occupied this space. Clothes were strewn across the floor and the stands they had once been displayed on lay cracked and broken from looting.

I was surprised to see the fine, glittering shards of glass still lying on the ground beneath the broken front window. Perhaps a rogue bullet had shattered it not too long ago, or perhaps it had simply given out with age, but the empty space would provide a perfect window for shooting through if things played out how we hoped. If Shaw was right, Jonah and his crew would gather in the building directly across the street, giving me the ideal opportunity to take him out.

'Perfect,' Hayden murmured, voicing my thoughts.

I stood and stared out of the hole, imagining myself raising my gun and firing at the last remaining member of my family. My stomach churned at the thought, but when I reminded myself of what he'd done to me and so many others, my resolve remained firm.

I jumped when a rather loud sound reached my ears but relaxed when I saw it was only Hayden dragging a small couch in front of the window. He dropped the other end and straightened up, wiping his forearm across his brow to remove the dust that had risen off the couch and settled there.

'For you, my love,' he said with a soft, self-amused grin while he gestured grandly at the couch.

'Thank you,' I replied quietly. I allowed Hayden to tug on my arm lightly and pull me to sit on the couch next to him, close enough that his thigh and shoulder pressed to mine, but far enough that we could both keep a firm, steady grip on our weapons.

Hayden didn't speak after that, as if sensing that I wasn't in the mood for talking, or that no amount of reassurance or light-hearted distraction would make me feel better. I just wanted to do what I had to and get it over with. The sooner, the better.

We were silent for about an hour, with only the heat of his body pressing to mine and the occasional tickle of his fingers over my thighs, when I heard the first sound. I leaned forward automatically, ears searching for the slightest disturbance. Hayden reflected me, doing the same as he paid close attention. Again, I heard something – the sound of something being knocked over maybe coming from outside.

'Hear that?' I breathed, searching the view of the street closely.

'Yeah,' he replied. 'Came from down the street.'

He pointed with the end of his gun in the direction I knew Kit and Dax had staked out. I felt fear immediately erupt inside me, but I held it down; they would know to stay out of sight.

'Come on,' Hayden whispered, rising slowly and silently from his seat on the couch to inch forward, ducking low to stay below the edge of the window. I followed, so we were both sitting up just enough that our eyes could see over the sill.

I didn't see anything at first; the street looked undisturbed, and there were no obvious signs of danger. No more sounds came, and I couldn't quite figure what those first ones had been. I peered anxiously outside, desperate to see someone and desperate not to all at once.

'Maybe it was just—'

The ear-splitting sound of gunfire cut me off, making me jump about three feet in the air as a window about thirty yards down shattered.

'Shit,' Hayden swore, jumping to his feet instinctually just as I did.

'Was that—'

'Kit and Dax,' Hayden muttered. I heard the small click of his gun as he turned off the safety.

Another gunshot sounded from outside, followed by a voice I recognised as Dax's as a loud curse flew through the air.

'Plan's shot, we've got to go,' Hayden hissed.

He turned and sprinted towards the door. My own body reacted before my brain did, commanding my legs to carry me after Hayden. He reached the door before I did and wasted no time in yanking it open. With only a short glance around outside, he leaped towards the source of the noise.

A silent stream of curses ran through my mind as I pushed after him, determined to figure out what was going on and get everyone out of there. Yet another gunshot rang out, though it was impossible to tell who was shooting or if any targets were being hit. I sprinted faster, pumping my arms while clutching my gun tightly, but it would be no use if I couldn't find something to aim at.

'Hayden, Grace! Get down!'

I flattened my body to the ground before my mind registered the instruction. I'd barely hit the dirt when I heard a high-pitched whistle and felt a whoosh of air rush past my head, followed almost immediately by an ear-splitting bang as whatever it was that had just missed me collided with a broken-down car behind me. Blazing-hot fire erupted as it exploded, sending a blast of air so strong that it blew the dust up around me, making me choke and cough before I managed to take a full breath.

Just as quickly as I'd hit the ground, I was back up and sprinting forward, where I was beyond relieved to find Hayden a few feet ahead. I grabbed a handful of his shirt and tugged, springing him to action again as he pushed himself off the ground, gun still in hand.

'Come on!' I urged.

I had no idea what was going on, but I knew we couldn't stay in the middle of the street. Together, we started moving, eyes constantly searching for whoever had just fired on us, but with no success. We were running blind in the dust with no identifiable goal, left out in the open like sitting ducks.

'In here!'

Dax's voice reached my ears as we passed a small doorway, causing both Hayden and I to skid to a stop before backtracking hastily. It was still difficult to see as debris and smoke rained down on us, but when a hand reached out to grab my arm and pull me into the doorway, I quickly came face to face with none other than Kit and Dax.

'Thank god,' I muttered, sagging with relief.

'You guys okay?' Kit asked, staring intently at Hayden and me. We were all huddled very closely together, and I knew that as soon as the dust cleared, we would be visible.

'Yeah, we're fine,' Hayden answered. I felt the pressure

of his hand on my back as if reluctant to let go of me. 'What the hell happened?'

'Brutes,' Dax spat angrily. 'A bunch of them wandered by where we were hiding out and noticed the door was busted open. They came in looking, but we got a few shots off and managed to get out until they brought out a freaking bazooka.'

'Where did they get a bazooka?' Hayden asked incredulously.

'I don't know, mate, but they have one, and it obviously works,' Dax said exasperatedly as he gestured roughly towards the now blazing remains of the car.

'We have to get out of here,' Hayden insisted. 'It's not happening today, not with all this shit.'

'You're right,' Kit agreed, nodding. Dax muttered his assent before spitting a mouthful of dirt out onto the ground with a disgusted look on his face.

'Agreed,' I said. As much as I wanted to do this today, I knew it was already too dangerous with the arrival of the Brutes and their apparent heavy weaponry.

'Let's go, before the dust clears,' Hayden instructed. 'Everyone stay close.'

I nodded and felt the heat of his hand as it slid into mine, leaving each of us with a free hand for our guns. Kit and Dax nodded determinedly. The four of us bolted from the doorway, moving quickly yet stealthily through the settling dust and smoke. They couldn't see us yet, but they'd be able to hear us if we made any noise.

Each step I took added to the anxiety and fear I was trying to hold off; the adrenaline that usually powered me was there, but it was clouded by my conflicting emotions. I focused on putting one foot steadily down before following it with the other, and we had made it about thirty yards when my body collided with something firm.

I bounced backward, ripping Hayden's hand from mine and jerking out of my daze as my eyes travelled up from the ground. Horror rose in every cell in my body as I saw battered boots, torn and stained jeans, a ratty, black shirt covering a muscular body, and finally, green eyes so similar to my own that were narrowed into a disgusted sneer.

He'd appeared seemingly out of nowhere, just as surprised by the current situation as we were, yet he stood before me with a look of pure, seething hatred.

He was the reason we were here.

Jonah.

'Grace,' he hissed, tone dangerously low and full of malice.

My breath caught in my throat, unprepared for this horrific hiccup in our plan. Hayden seemed to have disappeared in the dust, gone from my grip in a split second. Though I couldn't see anyone but Jonah, the sounds of people fighting around me were more than apparent. I heard dull thuds of fists and muted grunts as people were hit. I wanted to call out for Hayden, but my words seemed anchored in my throat as I stared wide-eyed at Jonah.

'Grace!'

The sound of Hayden calling my name snapped me out of my stupor, and not a moment too soon, because in the split second it took me to react, Jonah had swung his powerful fist forward, aiming straight at my head. I ducked quickly and felt the rush of air whoosh past my head as he missed by a fraction. As quickly as he swung and missed, I straightened up and raised my gun.

I barely got it level with his chest, however, when his foot swung through the air and collided with my wrists, sending the gun flying from my hands into the dirt a few yards away.

My feet moved quickly, darting towards it before I felt a pair of strong arms wrap around my waist, hauling me to the ground. Jonah landed on top of me, pinning me down.

I struggled against him, gritting my teeth, and managed to twist myself onto my back and to the side as he aimed another blow at my face, but I wasn't quick enough to avoid the second part of his assault. I felt a sharp sting across my jaw as my head snapped sideways. The warm, bitter taste of blood flooded through my mouth almost instantly, and I spat a hasty mouthful to the ground. Then I summoned all my strength and swung my leg upward, crashing my knee into his back.

He grimaced in pain and relaxed enough for me to tilt my body and throw him off me. I scrambled to my feet, wasting no time in reaching for the second gun I had stowed in my waistband, only to come up empty. My eyes darted frantically around – it must have got lost somewhere along the way.

'*Shit*,' I hissed angrily.

In less than a minute, I'd lost both my guns.

I pulled out my knife and darted towards my first gun, which was still lying in the dirt a few yards away. I was nearly there when I felt a strong, heavy body collide with mine for the second time, knocking the breath from my lungs as he sent me sprawling into the dirt. My hand managed to cling to my knife as our bodies reconnected. He glowered at me, a slightly deranged look in his eye as he held me down.

'Are you trying to kill me?' he growled. Despite the dire situation, I couldn't help but scoff in his face.

'Don't think you can talk,' I spat as my hand that clutched my knife darted forward.

I could hardly aim with the way he had me pinned down, but the wet *thunk* and sharp hiss of pain was unmistakable as

I plunged the knife into his thigh. Blood immediately started pouring from the wound as I drew out the blade, about to strike again when I felt the sharp sting of his knuckles along the side of my face again, causing white dots to burst in my vision.

'You fucking bitch,' he groaned, voice tight as he tensed in pain.

His hand pressed over the freely bleeding wound in his thigh, giving me enough time and distraction to get out from beneath him. He was still stooped on the ground when I got to my feet, and he didn't react quickly enough as I threw my knee into his face with all the force I could muster. I heard the sharp *crack* as his nose broke, adding even more blood to the slick that was already forming around him.

He groaned and hunched forward, clutching his nose and shouting curses and insults at me. I darted away, finally succeeding in grabbing my gun. Sweat poured off my body and blood seemed to be leaking from several places, but my grip was firm on the gun as I spun and raised it. I was surprised to see him standing determinedly and challengingly, a look of pure disgust and hatred on his face as he glowered at me about ten feet away.

All around me, the sounds of fighting carried on, but I still couldn't see more than blurred shadows as the fighting continued through the smoke and dust. The muffled grunts and groans of pain told me nothing about the identities of who was winning or, perhaps worse, who was losing. It seemed like an odd recreation of the first time I'd held a gun to Jonah and failed: the fighting, the atmosphere, the utter terror and emotional turmoil rolling through my body.

'You're not going to do it,' he hissed, shaking his head as he sneered at me. 'You're not strong enough. You've never been strong enough.'

I didn't reply as I stared at him, determined to keep my hands from shaking as they aimed the gun straight at his heart. My jaw was so tight, I felt like my teeth might shatter in my mouth.

'You're going to fail and I'm going to get away. Again.'

I stayed silent. My chest heaved as I drew a heavy, unstable breath after breath. But my body felt oddly inert as I watched him with such intensity that it nearly shattered me.

'Jonah, stop all of this,' I said firmly, keeping my voice strong and commanding.

He cocked a derisive eyebrow at me, looking condescending, of all things.

'Stop what? Surviving? Because you know you're too weak and you won't be able to do it?' he seethed, shaking with rage.

'Stop everything. Stop killing people for nothing, stop fighting. Just stop it all,' I urged, shaking my head as my jaw tightened even more. My gun didn't waver from his chest.

'You're pathetic,' he scoffed. 'Begging me to stop because *people are dying*. Guess what, Grace. That's how this world works. You kill or get killed.'

His tone was mocking, meant to insult and hurt me with every single word.

'It doesn't have to be that way,' I argued. Both of us were frozen in place, me with my arms locked and ready to shoot, him in his defensive stance, ready to launch himself at me at a moment's notice.

'It does,' he said, glaring down the bridge of his now crooked nose. 'And you're too weak to do anything about it.'

Again I didn't reply but swallowed harshly. My knuckles blanched from how tightly I held the gun, and my entire body felt like it was shaking so hard that I was locked into place. The fighting around us continued, but it never interrupted our moment.

'You're not going to kill me. I'm your brother. I'm all you have left,' Jonah sneered.

'You tried to kill me!' I yelled, snapping from the calm I'd somehow managed to cling to until now. 'Don't you remember?'

I dropped one hand from my gun to yank the collar of my shirt down, showing the scar he'd caused over my heart. His eyes darted to it momentarily before locking back into my own.

'I'm all you have left too, but you don't care,' I said, tone softening as I shook my head and frowned at him. This time it was Jonah's turn to remain silent.

I lifted both hands back onto my gun as I watched him, images flashing through my mind like a movie. I saw Farmer dead in the dirt, bleeding from where Jonah had stabbed him. I saw him try to kill me, the wound that had now scarred still fresh. I saw the faces of each and every person that had died because of him, gone now from the world for no sensible reason.

I saw Jett, once laughing and smiling as he danced with me during the bonfire before he transformed into the pale, lifeless face in death.

Rage, heartbreak, anger, resentment, and so many other emotions rolled through me, stinging my throat and pricking at my eyes.

'I knew you wouldn't do it,' he sneered, sensing my hesitation. 'Pathetic.'

All the emotions I was holding down boiled over, tearing their way through my insides before ripping through my skin, destroying me from the inside out as I stood locked in the moment with Jonah.

435

'Kill or be killed, right?' I asked, voice deadly calm and laced with anger.

Jonah's face fell and his jaw dropped open, body caving in as he sucked in a sudden breath. In that split second, he seemed to realise what was about to happen.

'Wait, Grace——'

But I didn't listen as I blew out a deep breath, locking eyes with him one last time before shaking my head, jaw tightened in determination. My arms tensed and my entire body tightened, the prelude to what was about to happen. With one final breath, I ticked my finger downward towards me and did the irreversible . . .

Pulled the trigger.

Bonus Chapter
YOUNG GRACE

I wiped sweat from my brow, breathing heavily as I stepped back from the centre of the crowd gathered around me. I couldn't help but smirk as I watched a boy around my age groan as he tried to pick himself up off the ground, wincing in pain with every move. Those gathered around chattered raucously, entertained by our sparring match. Much to my delight, I'd gotten the better of him.

Finally, he managed to stand and stumble out of the centre of the circle before sitting down again. He caught my eye briefly, nodding an acceptance of his defeat before flopping backward to rest in the grass. It only took a few seconds before another pair of kids my age stepped forward, starting their own training fight.

My brother, Jonah, stood nearby, watching silently. He often helped us train, and would occasionally give pointers, but during the fights he mostly stayed quiet, watching for those who excelled and could later be trained up further for raids. As much as we clashed, I couldn't help but want to impress him. Every time my turn came, my last thought was always of Jonah and his judgmental eye. I wanted to be chosen so badly, to prove myself and make my father proud.

My father, Celt, would occasionally stop by to watch our training but was mostly busy running the camp. He seldom got to watch me train, but when he did, I made sure I put forth every bit of myself. I was, most of the time, successful in beating my opponent, no matter who it was. Being the leader's daughter pushed me harder. I wanted to earn my spot on the raid team because of my abilities, not because of who my father was.

I watched the next pair fight, wincing as one of the boys took a nasty right hook to the jaw. A figure appeared beside me, drawing my attention.

'I don't know how you do this,' Leutie said, flashing her blue eyes at me. She didn't like to watch the fighting.

I shrugged. 'I don't know how you don't.'

Leutie had been my best friend for as long as I could remember. My first memory of her was when we were maybe five or six, and some boys had been picking on her for not wanting to fight. I'd stepped in and stopped them, punching one of them in the face before they ran off. We'd been best friends ever since. Not much had changed in our natures between then and now.

'Just don't have it in me, I guess,' she replied lightly. She sucked in a gasp as one of the boys was knocked out cold. The crowd around them gave a cheer and high-fived the victorious fighter. Someone splashed water on the unconscious boy's face, rousing and encouraging him before he got up and shook hands with his opponent.

'That's alright,' I told her. The crowd started to dissipate, finished with today's training.

'Do you need to talk to Jonah at all?' Leutie asked. My eyes searched the crowd before I found his face. He stood with another boy about his age, talking seriously.

'No,' I said.

'Tree?' she asked with a grin. I nodded, returning her smile.

438

We walked through camp together, making our way towards one of the few trees Greystone had. We liked to spend time beneath the branches, enjoying the shade on warm days. We arrived and I sat down, leaning against the trunk while Leutie sat cross-legged next to me. Her fingers ran over the grass as she settled in.

'Has Jonah said anything about you going on raids yet?' she asked.

I felt a wash of frustration roll through me as I shook my head.

'Nope. Nothing.'

Leutie frowned. 'He has to soon. You're too good for him not to pick you.'

'He won't because he knows I want to,' I muttered bitterly. Jonah knew exactly how much I wanted to go on raids and help our camp. I suspected he didn't choose me specifically because he knew it would make me happy.

'Maybe he's just trying to protect you,' Leutie said gently. Kindness was one of the strengths she possessed that I didn't. Leutie automatically looked for the positive in people, while I struggled with that.

'I doubt it,' I said, flatly.

'Well, either way, he can't ignore you forever. You beat almost anyone you go up against!'

'Except him,' I pointed out.

'Yeah but he's five years older than you. That's a huge difference.'

I shrugged. The few times I'd had the chance to spar with Jonah, he'd beaten me easily. It frustrated me beyond belief.

'What does Celt say?'

'Not much,' I sighed. 'He thinks I'm good, but he doesn't want me to get hurt.'

'I don't blame him,' she replied, fairly.

I didn't reply. I felt disappointed that I still hadn't been given the chance to join a raid, and the conversation wasn't helping. I let my eyes rake over the bits of Greystone in my line of vision, taking in the bleak stone buildings. They all looked the same, only differing in size and by the tiny marks on the doors that indicated what was inside. Some were people's homes, some stored supplies. I zeroed in on one that I knew Celt was probably in right now: his office. I sighed and shook my head in an attempt to distract myself.

'What's new with you?' I asked Leutie. She smiled and pushed her light brown hair behind her ear.

'They're going to start letting me train with the teachers,' she said proudly. 'Margaret's getting quite old, so they figured once she stops teaching, I can step in and help.'

I grinned. 'That's great, Leutie.'

Leutie was wonderful with children. While I felt awkward and uncertain around them, she had a way of connecting with them. We'd finished our 'school' a few months ago, meaning we had to start focusing on whatever it was that we would do to contribute to camp. For me, it meant training to go on raids and learning medical knowledge. For Leutie, it meant learning how to teach the children of Greystone basic skills like reading, writing, and how things worked in camp.

'Thanks, I'm really excited!' she said happily.

'So, does that mean you don't have to train anymore? Physically?'

Growing up, everyone was required to go through physical training. We all had to learn the basics of combat, weaponry, and surveillance. Leutie had been terrible at all three. She was far too kind to fight anyone, too fragile to handle a weapon, and too uncoordinated to be any good at surveillance.

'Yes, thankfully,' she said, grinning sheepishly. 'I can finally stop embarrassing myself.'

I laughed, shaking my head. 'You weren't *that* bad.'

'I was, you can say it,' she laughed. 'Especially compared to you.'

'What did your grandmother say?' I asked, dodging her compliment.

'She's thrilled. She was always convinced I'd somehow end up on the raid squad and get killed the first day,' she said, rolling her eyes.

Leutie had been raised by her grandmother in Greystone. She didn't remember her parents at all, and her grandfather had died long before her birth. It was so different from how I'd grown up with both of my parents and my brother. We had been one of the few families left fully intact until a few years ago when my mother died of cancer. Leutie was there for me through it all even though she didn't remember what it was like to lose a parent. I shook my head, wiping away the thoughts.

'Well now she doesn't have to worry,' I said with a soft smile.

'She worries about you, too,' she told me. 'It's a more legitimate worry, if you ask me.'

'That's just part of it, I guess,' I said, shrugging. For some reason, I wasn't afraid of going on raids. The thought excited me, and it was what drove me to train so hard.

'I'll never understand you, Grace,' Leutie said with a good-natured shake of her head.

'Back at you, Leutie,' I laughed.

Then a sudden movement caught our attention. We both turned to see Jonah approaching, his face set in his usual scowl. Leutie visibly stiffened as he grew nearer. She was afraid of him, even though she'd never admit it.

'Grace,' he said, stopping in front of us. He ignored Leutie altogether.

'Yes?'

'Celt wants to see you,' he said, curtly. We both had a habit of addressing our father by his name, though I wasn't exactly sure why. It was just something we'd always done.

'Now,' Jonah continued sharply. With that, he turned and walked away. I blinked in surprise and looked to Leutie, who shrugged in confusion.

'See you later,' I mumbled, pushing myself off the ground.

'Yeah, see you.'

I hurried after Jonah, following him toward Celt's office. He didn't say a word when I caught up to him, nor as we paused outside the door and knocked.

'Come in,' a voice called from inside.

The door creaked as it opened revealing my father seated at his desk. Usually, he had papers scattered over the surface, but today it was clear. He looked serious, and it was obvious he was waiting for our arrival.

'Have a seat, please.' He gestured to the chairs across from his desk. Uncertainty washed through me. I'd been in this position many times before, usually to be reprimanded for doing something reckless. Celt was tough, but he was also kind and fair. He wanted me to be strong and independent, but he also wanted to protect me from harm.

I sat and waited silently. Jonah remained standing as he leaned against the wall beside me, hovering like a dark cloud.

'How did your training go today?' Celt began. His green eyes, so similar to mine, watched me closely

'Good,' I answered shortly. He waited expectantly, so I cleared my throat and continued. 'I won.'

Celt smiled softly. 'I hear you've been doing that a lot lately.'

'Yes.' My heart thudded nervously.

'How about your weapons training?'

'It's going well, too,' I replied. My eyes darted briefly to Jonah before returning to meet my father's gaze.

'What have you been training with?'

'Guns and knives, mostly,' I answered. I felt like I was at some sort of job interview. 'I can hit moving targets really easily now.'

'That's great to hear,' Celt smiled. 'Jonah tells me you're the best of your age, boys and girls.'

My mouth opened in surprise as I looked at Jonah again. He nodded, though he didn't look happy about it. I was pleased, albeit shocked, that he'd spoken so highly of me.

'Now Grace,' Celt said, regaining my attention. 'You know that I've always said how important it is to be able to defend not only yourself, but your camp as well.'

'Yes,' I said, slowly.

'And that, even if I hope it's not necessary, I want you to be strong enough to do whatever it takes to survive. Even if that means killing someone else.'

I nodded, forcing myself not to fidget anxiously.

'Do you think you can do that?' He watched me intently, taking in my every reaction.

'Yes,' I answered honestly. I'd been training my entire life to be given the opportunity to go on raids, and I knew death was a very likely part of that.

Celt looked torn by my response. I detected a flicker of pride, but it was also impossible to miss the saddened look that flashed through his eyes. I waited for him to continue.

'Well, Grace,' he said slowly. 'As much as I don't like it, I think my little girl has grown enough for this. You've proven yourself to be more than capable, and I know that this is what you want . . .'

He trailed off and, again, a mixture of emotions ran across his face. My heart thudded heavily as I waited with bated breath, unable to stop the elation from creeping up through my body. I was about to hear what I had worked so hard for, what I wanted more than anything. When Celt spoke again, it was with the grim determination of a reluctant father sending his willing daughter into the fray.

'Grace, you're going on your first raid. There's no going back from here.'

After the revolution

COMES ANNIHILATION

Don't miss the final book in the *Anarchy* series

Read on for an extract now.

One: Peril

Grace

A deafening *bang* ripped through the air the moment my finger put pressure on the trigger, launching a bullet from the chamber of my gun. Everything seemed to freeze around me as I stood locked in place, somehow still standing despite being torn to shreds on the inside.

It was surely impossible, but in that moment, I could have sworn I saw the bullet as it sliced smoothly through the air. My eyes stayed fixed on it, riveted and horrified all at once, as the distance between it and the gun increased more and more. A strange buzzing sounded in my ears, blocking out everything but that odd, muffled noise that crept its way into my brain, as the bullet met an obstacle.

The sound I should have heard was the bullet making contact with a human chest. It should have sounded heavy, wet, painful. There should have been a ripping of flesh, a gush of blood, maybe a crack or two of bone.

The muffled sound only grew louder, threatening to suffocate me and press me down into the dirt.

Though my ears couldn't hear it, my eyes could see it. I stood captivated in the worst way as I watched the bullet rip through his shirt, his skin, his muscle. It hit in the most lethal place, directly over his heart, before making its way through the heart itself. A shiver ran through my body as blood immediately filled the hole, soaking his shirt and dripping to the ground as he plummeted to his knees, face paling more and more by the second.

Blank, lifeless eyes seemed to lock on to my own as his body hovered for a moment, caught between the balance of standing and falling down. My stomach churned as I watched, unable to look away even though I so desperately wanted to. That tiny fraction of time ended as his body fell forward, landing with a solid thump in the dirt. Dust rose from the ground to mix with the smoke already obscuring the air, adding an ominous haze so reminiscent of the terrible act I'd just committed.

His chest didn't move as he lay face down on the ground; the blood was pooling so quickly around him that I already knew it was too late to go back.

I knew what I'd done.

Just like that, Jonah was dead.

I sucked in a harsh breath, inhaling smoke and dirt alike, but I was still unable to move. My muscles stayed firm, locked into place. Every beat of my heart felt like it was pumping knives through my veins, then working their way through my skin, piercing wherever they could reach until I was a bloody, battered mess.

I couldn't tear my eyes away from where Jonah had landed. The deep red of the blood seemed to burn into my brain, and the stark contrast of his quickly paling body only made it seem more drastic. I couldn't see his face, but I didn't need to; the last, silently pleading look he'd given me followed by the flat, lifeless one as he fell would be cemented into my memory forever, never to be forgotten.

Another image suddenly shoved its way through my mind. It was that of decaying bodies, some dismembered and some rotten, piled in a corner like rags. It was that of hands severed from their limbs, with spikes spearing through them to pin them to the walls. It was that of threatening words scrawled on the walls in the blood of those bodies that haunted me. Before my eyes, Jonah's body morphed into one of them, my mind tormenting me and playing tricks as payment for what I'd done.

I'd killed my own brother.

Still, I was unable to move, though I felt a prominent shake set into my body. My hands quivered in front of me, unable to lower the gun or even move my arms. Still, I could hear nothing, though I knew the world around me must have been filled with chaotic noise. I could see nothing but the oppressive haze and the blood surrounding Jonah's lifeless body, not that I could rip my eyes away. I felt bile creeping up my throat as my body rebelled against me, but I couldn't even manage to lean over and expel it.

I could feel my mind shutting down, desperate to spare me from realising what I'd done. My hands were shaking so badly now I thought I might actually drop my gun, and my legs felt like they might collapse at any moment. Air ripped so harshly through my lungs that it was painful, and my heart was either beating wildly or not at all.

I couldn't even tell.

Just when I was about to lose all hope and give in to the crushing agony threatening to overtake me, I saw a figure appear out of the cloud of dust and smoke. A familiar hand, adorned by a tiny cross just above his thumb, closed around mine as he took my gun from me. His long fingers intertwined with mine as he tugged on my arm, wasting no time in taking me away from the evidence of what I'd done.

The heat of his touch seemed to snap me out of everything, and the sound came crashing down so quickly it was like someone had lifted a vacuum from around me. My feet stayed rooted in place as all my senses started to function once again, and his grip on my arm jerked my body sideways. His voice reached me as I watched his lips move in complete shock.

Hayden.

'We have to go, Grace.'

His voice was laced with urgency and resolve, and it was clear he was trying to remain as calm as possible for my sake, but his desperation to get us out of there was more than apparent.

'Grace, come on, move,' he urged, tugging on my arm when I continued to stare at him. I couldn't seem to process anything, and my mind felt hazy with either too many thoughts or too few.

Again, I couldn't move even though I could now hear the relentless noise. Gunfire, shouting, fighting, burning, and other noises bombarded me from all directions, their volume magnified times a hundred in comparison to the odd buzzing silence I'd heard moments ago.

'Jesus Christ,' Hayden muttered lowly.

I watched blankly as he stashed our guns behind his back before stooping quickly in front of me. I didn't have time to realise what he was doing before I felt his arms wrap around me, lifting me off my feet. He draped my legs over one of his arms while he threw my arms around his neck, holding me firmly against his chest as he started to run.

He moved quickly, and it was obvious we were still in great danger from the urgency of his actions, but still I couldn't react. Each step he took felt like a jarring blow to my body as the emotional pain manifested into physical. Even though I wasn't hurt, it felt like it as Hayden carried me away.

'Hang on, Grace,' he instructed as calmly as he could.

I managed to tighten my arms slightly, but it wasn't enough to keep my weight from shifting around as he ran as fast as possible. When a high-pitched whistle whizzed just inches above our heads, I realised how real the danger actually was. I sucked in a harsh breath and blinked furiously, clearing my head for the first time since I'd pulled the trigger.

'Put me down,' I gasped.

Hayden let out a sigh of relief that I suspected had nothing to do with carrying me and everything to do with me finally snapping out of my trance. He set me down as quickly and gently as possible. Then, he grabbed my hand and tugged once more, taking off at a sprint as I finally managed to make my limbs cooperate. He whipped a gun from behind his back and handed it to me before taking the other for himself.

Another whizzing bullet narrowly missed us as we tore along the street, which was strewn with more debris and obstacles than before. Horror twisted at my stomach as I realised Hayden and I were fleeing alone.

'Where are—'

'Duck!' Hayden shouted, cutting me off as his hand yanked me to the ground.

He barely managed to throw his body over mine, pressing his chest to my back, as yet another familiar high-pitched whistling sounded above us. Just as before, it was followed almost immediately by a deafening boom as something crashed into the pile of rubble in front of us, springing fire and debris into the air from the explosion.

Apparently the Brutes had more ammunition for their bazooka.

I coughed and sputtered a few times, pawing at my eyes to get the dirt out of them. Hayden recovered more quickly, wasting no time in hauling me back to my feet.

'Come on!' he urged, shooting a fleeting glance over his shoulder.

Again, we started sprinting. The air was even thicker than before, thanks to the fresh disturbance, making it even more difficult to see and breathe. I tugged my shirt up around my nose to filter the air, but my tank top offered little protection. Hayden's grip was tighter than ever on my hand as he led me through the fray, dodging debris and heavy fire with every step. Gunshots echoed around the space and bullets whizzed past us, but the new smoke and dust gave us cover we had desperately needed.

We ran, desperate to know where Kit and Dax had gone but not brave enough to ask and find out. We seemed to run forever. The sounds never went away and the blanketing dust was relentless. I was about to suggest we figure out a new plan when I heard a screeching of tyres on pavement not too far ahead of us.

'There,' Hayden muttered quickly, picking up the pace.

I could hear muffled shouting from behind us as the Brutes and whoever was left of Jonah's crew pursued, but the familiar rumble of an engine was closer, calling me to it through the haze. Finally, I could make out the vague outline of the jeep, though it was impossible to tell who was inside.

'Is it them?' I asked, coughing yet again as I squinted towards the vehicle.

'I don't know,' Hayden admitted gruffly.

Together, we ran and closed the remaining distance between us and the car. I felt like my heart was about to pound out of my chest in anticipation as I tried desperately to identify the driver. For a moment, it had occurred to me that whoever it was might not have been our friends but enemies waiting to kill us.

My fears were placated, however, when I saw Kit behind

the wheel. A huge breath of relief pushed from my lungs as I saw him waiting, urging us on with waves of his hand. But I couldn't see Dax anywhere in the car.

Hayden and I skidded to a halt right outside the door, sending dirt flying beneath our feet. He whipped open the door and practically threw me in before following, leaning forward urgently between the seats to shout instructions at Kit.

'Go, go!' he shouted. 'We have to find Dax!'

'I don't know where he is,' Kit said quickly, stress radiating from his tone.

My stomach dropped like a rock, terrified. Dax couldn't be dead, right? He'd survived this long; it didn't seem possible that he wouldn't make it out now.

'He's got to be out there still,' I said, shaking my head firmly. 'We'll find him.'

Hayden shot me an anxious look over his shoulder and placed his hand on my thigh, squeezing tightly as if clinging to the hope I was right.

'Let's go, we have to look,' Hayden instructed. 'Drive!'

Kit obeyed immediately and slammed his foot down on the pedal, bringing smoke from the tyres as the jeep shot forward. Hayden's shoulder collided roughly with mine before he managed to right himself as Kit whipped the vehicle around.

'You two better be ready to shoot,' Kit muttered darkly, squinting tightly to try and view the road ahead.

I nodded sharply even though he wouldn't see and released the magazine on my gun to check my ammo. I knew only one bullet would be missing. I'd fired once, and that bullet was now firmly buried in Jonah's chest.

Almost immediately, the loud bangs of gunfire sounded around us, and the familiar crunch of metal echoed out as the bullets missed us but ripped through the jeep.

'Dax!' Hayden called, leaning out of the window before firing a shot into the smoke.

Kit honked the horn and called out Dax's name as well. All the noise would only draw more attention to us, but everyone knew it was necessary to try to find our friend.

'Dax!'

Again and again, we called his name. Kit manoeuvred the jeep as quickly as he could around the area, narrowly missing buildings, debris, and missing chunks of road. Again and again, Hayden and I fired into basically nothing. Our targets were hidden from us, just as we were from them, except the people we were firing at weren't driving around in a raucous jeep while shouting.

'*Dax!*'

My voice was laced with fear and frustration, squinting and listening carefully for any sort of reply, but it was almost impossible to hear over the chaos consuming everything around us.

I could feel the fear that we wouldn't find him creeping up, but I forced it down as I reloaded my gun and fired once more. Hayden seemed to be growing increasingly anxious beside me as well, and I noticed him firing his gun more and more often as his fear countered his usual reluctance to kill.

'Where the hell are you?' Hayden muttered impatiently. His knee jumped up and down beside me as his leg bounced nervously. '*Dax, Jesus Christ!*' Hayden roared. He sounded angry with frustration and desperation.

'I don't see him anywhere,' Kit admitted tightly, face contorted in deep concern. He whipped the jeep around for what felt like the hundredth time as yet more bullets whizzed by us.

'We can't leave him,' Hayden snapped angrily.

'I didn't say that—'

'You were about to—'

'No, I—' Kit was cut off by a different voice this time, which sent a wave of careful hope rushing through me.

'Over here!'

'Dax?!' Hayden shouted, rigidly alert as he heard what I did.

'I'm here!'

This time it was more than obvious that we'd all heard him. I sagged with relief immediately as I identified the voice.

Dax.

'I see him!' I shouted, leaning forward suddenly and pointing straight ahead.

He was no more than a shadowy figure, but I could see him standing about twenty feet away, waving his arms while coughing in the smoke and dust. Kit accelerated even more before slamming on the brakes, sending Hayden and I crashing into the seat backs before snapping backward.

'Try not to kill us,' Hayden snapped again, clearly still on edge.

I hardly had time to absorb his words. I watched as Dax moved as quickly as possible, hindered by a heavy limp and a shockingly large amount of blood pouring from somewhere unidentified. He reached the side of the door and fumbled with the handle before Hayden leaned over the seat and threw it open. Dax winced as he climbed inside, pulling the door shut, not even a second before Kit hit the accelerator and whipped away again.

I could feel no relief as I saw Dax's shockingly pale face. There was no hint of his usual smile or lightness; only extreme pain and obvious injury registered there.

'What happened?' Hayden demanded, leaning forward to study him.

I followed the trail of blood with my eyes, raking down his left arm, noting the bloody bandage at the end concealing whatever lay beneath.

Dax didn't reply as he leaned his head back against the headrest and blew out a deep breath, eyes closed tightly. His breath was shaky and uneven, but at least he was breathing. Kit cast a worried glance across the console as he drove, and I was relieved to hear the sounds of gunfire and shouting getting softer and softer as we finally managed to pull away from the chaos.

'Dax!' Hayden hissed, frustrated with his lack of response. Fear and anxiety were clearly written across his face as I glanced at him quickly before refocusing on Dax.

'Bloody Brutes, mate,' Dax muttered, grimacing in pain as the jeep hit a divot in the road.

My eyes returned to the bandage at the end of his arm, and my mind was instantly flooded with the same horrific images from before.

Decaying hands nailed to the wall.

Severed limbs ending in ragged stumps.

Thieves.

Thieves.

Thieves.

I suddenly squeezed my eyes shut as I sucked in a terrified breath. My nightmares and reality were starting to mix before my eyes, and there was nothing I could do to stop it.

'Grace.'

My eyes snapped open at the sound of Hayden's voice. I blinked a few times to find him studying me closely, and I felt the heat of his hand on my leg once more. His thumb rolled over my thigh before he squeezed once, concern written across his face as he watched me beneath lowered brows.

'It's okay,' he mouthed, giving me a slow, reassuring nod. I gave a shaky nod in return and tried to hold it together.

Again, I forced myself to look at Dax and focus on my medical training.

'Dax, what happened?' I asked as calmly as I could.

Again, he didn't reply, but he finally opened his eyes and lifted his head from the seat. With a slightly unsteady hand, he reached to unwind the makeshift bandage from his left arm. I watched, transfixed and horrified, as bloody layer after bloody layer was removed. I was all but convinced I was going to see a rotten stump of an arm by the time he finally removed it.

But instead of the shocking stump I'd been expecting, I saw a battered, bloody hand. His pinkie and ring finger were gone, severed by an obviously sharp weapon, and the middle finger was bleeding badly, but the rest of it was there.

'Jesus Christ . . .' Hayden muttered as he stared, lips parting in shock.

'You're telling me,' Dax muttered bitterly. He paused for a few moments before continuing. 'At least it wasn't my good hand.'

I let out an oddly relieved gasp of a laugh. Dax had lost two fingers and gained a limp, but I could see no other obvious signs of injury or bleeding. If he could already make a joke, I dared hope that it meant he'd be okay.

'You don't need two full hands anyway, mate,' Kit said lightly from the driver's seat, also obviously relieved.

'Just good old Righty,' Dax said, waving it weakly by his side. I groaned as I realised what he meant.

'Dear God, Dax, it's been minutes and you're already making jokes,' I said.

I was surprised by that flicker of amusement, but it didn't

last long as the cold, heavy truth of everything we'd just been through crashed back down on me. I collapsed back into the seat and let out the deepest sigh yet, closing my eyes now that I knew Dax probably wasn't going to die.

We might have all survived, but one person had not.

Jonah.

It was only a few seconds before I felt Hayden shift beside me. He looped his arm around my shoulders and hauled me onto his lap. There, in the back of the jeep, I curled into a ball on his lap, hiding my face in his chest as his strong arms held me as closely as he could manage. I felt the warm heat of his lips at my ear and heard the soft whisper of his voice.

'I love you, Bear.'

I could feel my body starting to shake as reality set in all over again. My throat burned and my eyes felt hot, but no tears came. Instinctively, I wrapped my arms around Hayden's chest, hugging him as tightly as I could manage while he held me securely.

'It's okay, you're okay,' he murmured, continuing even though I couldn't manage to respond.

His fingers drifted over my skin wherever he could reach, comforting me and soothing me when I so desperately needed it. Even when Kit hit a bump in the road, Hayden held me still, protecting me in every way he could. My fingers twisted into the now ragged fabric of his shirt, desperate to haul him even closer and revel in the comforting warmth he provided.

'I'm so proud of you, Grace.'

I bit my lower lip as I drew a shuddering breath. I felt tears pricking at my eyes now. His words were hushed and just loud enough for me and only me to hear. He murmured things over and over, never stopping even though I didn't reply. The entire ride back to Blackwing, Hayden held me and whispered, doing his very best to comfort me after what he knew I'd done.

'You're so strong, Bear.'

Every word he spoke wrenched the tears closer and closer to the surface. A single choking sob escaped from my lips before I succumbed to them – they were oddly silent, yet no less painful as they burned me from the inside out. Hayden's grip tightened on me even more when he realised I'd finally given in, and still his gentle words continued.

'I love you so much.'

It was finally over and done with.

I'd been strong enough to finally do it, but in that moment, I had never felt weaker.

Thirty million readers worldwide.

Don't miss out – *Annihilation* is available to order now.